Order
■ of ■
Battle

Also by Ib Melchior

QUEST: SEARCHING FOR GERMANY'S NAZI PAST
(with Frank Brandenburg)

Order
· of ·
Battle

Hitler's Werewolves

Ib Melchior

LYFORD
B O O K S

*With love to my wife, whose constant
encouragement and understanding when she
found me staring into space made it
possible for me to finish this book.*

Copyright © 1972 by Ib Melchior
Copyright © 1991 by Ib Melchior
This edition printed in 1991.

LYFORD Books
Published by Presidio Press
31 Pamaron Way, Novato CA 94949

Library of Congress Cataloging-in-Publication Data

Melchior, Ib
    Order of battle : Hitler's werewolves : a novel / Ib Melchior.
      p.   cm.
    ISBN 0-89141-430-4
    1. World War, 1939-1945—Fiction. I. Title.
[PS3563.E435074 1991]
813'.54—dc20
                                                91-13771
                                                CIP

Printed in the United States of America

"ORDER OF BATTLE" intelligence consists of carefully sifted and evaluated information received from a great variety of sources on the organization, strength and disposition of enemy forces. This information, if complete and accurate, not only facilitates the planning of military operations but helps commanders in the field to judge the enemy's local capabilities and to make their decisions accordingly.

ORDER OF BATTLE
OF THE
GERMAN ARMY
1943

MILITARY INTELLIGENCE SERVICES
Washington, D.C.

Restricted

Prologue

As I write this prologue, bands of terrorists, unleashed by the desperate and defiant Saddam Hussein in the weeks before his defeat, spread foreboding and fear throughout the world:

• In Manila, the Philippines, Iraqi terrorists attack a U.S. establishment, the Thomas Jefferson Library, resulting in the death of one terrorist and the wounding of another. The first secretary of the Iraqi Embassy is expelled for his complicity.
• In Cairo, Egypt, the speaker of the parliament is gunned down by an Iraqi terrorist, who kills not only the diplomat, but also his driver and bodyguard in a hail of machine-gun fire.
• In the Turkish cities of Iznir and Istanbul, Ankara and Adana, U.S. installations and the French consulate are bombed and a U.S. civilian is struck down on the street.
• On the Pakistan-India border a bomb placed in a passenger car kills five people and injures twenty-seven.
• In Athens, Greece, government troops are employed to reinforce the police in an attempt to stem a wave of bombings and rocket attacks on British and American facilities by terrorists supporting Iraqi president Saddam Hussein.

The list of such senseless atrocities is growing daily.

Nearly half a century before, another ruthless dictator let loose *his* gangs of savage terrorists—Hitler's Werewolves. As a crumbling Nazi Germany faced her *Götterdämmerung*, in November 1944, on orders from the Führer, Adolf Hitler, Reichsleiter Martin Bormann decreed the immediate formation of a guerilla/terrorist organization to be known as "Werewolf." Its members were to be recruited from fanatic Hitler Youths and BDMs (*Bund Deutscher Mädchen*, the equivalent female group), from the SS and the Wehrmacht, the German Army, and even from the ranks of civilians.

Bormann placed an officer from his own staff, *Gruppenführer*, (SS Major General) Hans Prützmann, in overall charge of *Unternehmen Werwolf*—Operation Werewolf. Prützmann was to orchestrate and supervise the recruiting, training, and logistics of the organization, but there is relatively little evidence or knowledge of his contribution. Caught by the British at war's end, he committed suicide by swallowing a hidden cyanide capsule before he could be interrogated, taking his knowledge with him, in contrast to other high ranking Nazis such as Baldur von Schirach, the Hitler Youth Leader; Hans Fritzsche, Head of Radio Broadcasting in Goebbel's Propaganda Ministry; and Albert Speer, Hitler's Armament Minister, whose testimonies regarding *Unternehmen Werwolf* can be found in the records of the Nürnberg War Crimes Trials: "International Military Tribune—Trial of the Major War Criminals," Volumes XIV, XVI and XVII. In my own correspondence with Albert Speer, which took place after his release from Spandau Prison in Berlin, he wrote to me regarding the Werewolves in a letter dated 3 April 1972:

The biggest and strongest German transmitter, as a matter of fact, broadcast daily Werewolf messages. In addition Dr. Ley [Dr. Robert Ley, Leader of the German Labor Front, IJM] and several other hot-headed gentlemen concentrated on building up a sabotage operation behind the American and English lines which in general was named the Werewolves. Already conferences to that effect with the Army and other agencies had taken place, regarding making supplies of weapons, ammunitions, etc. available.

The name was aptly chosen. According to encyclopedic sources the term *werewolf* comes from the old English words *wer*, meaning man, and *wulf*—man-wolf: a person, according to medieval lore, who was transformed into, or was capable at will of assuming the form of, a ferocious man-eating wolf at night, returning to human form by day. Thus the Nazi Werewolves would appear to be normal citizens by day, but at night would venture out to "deal death and destruction" to their enemies.

From the beginning Hitler's Werewolf organization had its own radio program aimed at both Allied personnel and Germans who might be tempted to surrender to, or even cooperate with, the enemy, a program that began with a bloodcurdling wolf howl, followed by a sepulchral voice intoning: Beware Americans! Nightly the program would boast of new acts of terror inflicted on the enemy by the Werewolf.

A feature article in the Army paper, *Stars and Stripes*, dated April 21, 1945, quotes a Werewolf broadcast of April 1st, which in their own words describes the aims and purpose of the organization's members:

A free German movement called the "Werewolf" has been formed in the enemy-occupied areas. Every Bolshevik, every Briton and every American standing on German soil is free booty for our movement. Wherever an opportunity presents itself to extinguish his life we shall take it with joy without regard for our own life. The German, whatever his class or profession, who places himself at the disposal of the enemy and collaborates with him will come to feel our avenging hand.

The Werewolf is an organization born in the spirit of Naziism. It does not know the restrictions in battle which are imposed upon regular troops. Every means is legitimate in order to inflict injury upon the enemy. Be as brave as lions and as poisonous as snakes. Work in the dark. Make night your ally. Fall upon the enemy whenever a favorable opportunity offers itself. Do not hesitate at the thought of taking his life since he wants to destroy the

life of our people. It is up to you to exact vengeance upon
every foreign soldier now standing on German soil. There
is only one watchword now: Conquer or die!

Leaflets and proclamations such as the one below, adorned
with strangely twisted swastikas, began to appear throughout
Germany:

"The Werewolf"   To all Townships: 25.4.45
Upper Bavaria

W A R N I N G

to all Traitors and Collaborators with the Enemy

The Upper Bavaria Werewolf warn all those who would lend
support to the enemy, threaten or harass Germans and their
allies, or withhold their allegiance to the Führer. We warn you!
Traitors and criminals against the people will pay with their
lives, they and all the members of their families.

Townships that offend against the lives of our own, or show
the white flag of surrender sooner or later will suffer an an-
nihilating disaster.

Our vengeance is deadly!

"The Werewolf"
Upper Bavaria

It was not long before the Werewolves made their deadly
presence known. The *Stars and Stripes* reported many murders and attacks on Army troops and installations in the rear,
and other killings that spread fear among the German population. Decapitation wires were found strung across country
roads—thin, taut wires stretched across the roadway at neck
height to catch unwary drivers riding in open jeeps or on motorcycles; incautious GIs were waylaid and killed; mines would

be placed on thoroughfares frequented by military traffic. And there were other murders, some gruesome in the extreme:

In the town of Giessen just thirty miles north of Frankfurt, Werewolves led by a Belgian SS officer penetrated the American lines and executed a doctor who had been accused of collaborating with the *Amis*—the German derogatory slang word for Americans. Further south, near Ulm in Bavaria, a GI was found shot to death, a Werewolf leaflet pinned to his chest, his penis cut off and stuffed in his mouth.

In Bavaria, a 4th Armored Division gasoline dump went up in flames, one of several. Also in Bavaria, in April, eight GIs were killed and three wounded when members of a bomb disposal squad lifted a box of TNT from a pile of four crates of enemy explosives which previously had been inspected and found free of booby-traps. Witnesses recalled that three innocent-looking young boys had been lurking in the vicinity that afternoon. One of these youngsters was subsequently caught and confessed to being a Werewolf, trained for just such action.

Near Lübeck to the north, on 3/4 May, British troops shot and killed a Werewolf in civilian clothes who had been sniping at them; but in another Werewolf ambush/sniping confrontation, Field Marshall Bernard Montgomery's favorite liaison officer, a young officer of the 11th Hussars named John Poston was killed by a group of teenage Werewolves when they ambushed his jeep on a country road.

There were numerous such acts of terrorism by the Werewolves, but perhaps the most notorious, code-named Operation Carnival, took place in March of 1945 in the German town of Aachen in North Rhine–Westphalia, hard on the Dutch-Belgian border. A group of Werewolves was parachuted into the vicinity of the town from a Flying Fortress captured by the Nazis. There were seven of them, including a sixteen-year-old Hitler Youth and a girl—a former member of the BDM, as well as SS personnel. Their prey was a classic Werewolf target, a "traitor" who had to be eliminated, the mayor of Aachen, Franz Oppenhoff, an official who had been installed in office by the Americans.

On March 25 they invaded his home and gunned him down. The Werewolf radio bragged about the action for weeks and used it as a warning to all those who would collaborate with the enemy.

At SHAEF (Supreme Headquarters, Allied Expeditionary Force) most of the staff officers were concerned about the Werewolves— an "unknown factor" in the scheme of things. Even as the Russians encircled Berlin, and the end of the war was mere days away, Gen. Omar Bradley was still worried that the Werewolves would rendezvous in the National Redoubt in the Bavarian Alps, the *Alpenfestung*—the Alpine Fortress, as it was called by the Nazis— there to dig in for a last ditch, long lasting fight. Allied strategies and battle plans were influenced by apprehension about the Werewolves.

Gen. Dwight D. Eisenhower in his *Crusade in Europe* writes:

> Equally important was the desirability of penetrating and destroying the so-called "National Redoubt." For many weeks we had been receiving reports that the Nazis' intention, in extremity, was to withdraw the cream of the SS, Gestapo, and other organizations fanatically devoted to Hitler, into the mountains of southern Bavaria, western Austria, and northern Italy. There they expected to block the tortuous mountain passes and to hold out indefinitely against the Allies.

Eisenhower goes on to describe one of the fanatical organizations he feared would be part of that Alpine resistance:

> The purpose of the Werewolf organization, which was to be composed of loyal followers of Hitler, was murder and terrorism. Boys and girls as well as adults were to be absorbed into the secret organization with the hope of so terrifying the countryside and making so difficult the problem of occupation that the conquering forces would presumably be glad to get out.

Many historians of international renown have in their writings corroborated the above information about the Werewolf organization. Prominent among them are such chroniclers of history as H. R. Trevor-Roper and Glenn B. Infield; Gerhard Boldt and Simon Wiesenthal; Cornelius Ryan and Charles Whiting, who in his book *Hitler's Werewolves* details Operation Carnival, the murder of the mayor of Aachen.

Order of Battle is closely based on fact, told in the form of a novel for dramatic reasons, particularly the desire to be able to present both the American and the German sides. It was my own case, while working as counter-intelligence agent with CIC Detachment 212 of XII Corps, as a member of MII Team 425-G. A note on one detail: Because of the nature of a CIC agent's work, which depended upon being able to obtain the instant assistance and cooperation of any troops available at any given moment, the rank of a CIC agent was confidential; he wore no rank insignia of any kind except the Officer U.S. emblem on his collar, be he an enlisted man or officer. Should anyone up to and including a full colonel ask for the agent's rank, the standard reply was: "My rank is confidential, but at this moment I am not outranked." Only general officers were entitled to a full answer.

Order of Battle is the complete and accurate account of the ferreting out and destruction of the vaunted Werewolf headquarters, *Sonderkampfgruppe Paul*. The action begins on 28 April 1945, eleven days before the war would be over. It is the eleventh hour. The Werewolves are deployed and ready to go into action in earnest. Like the venemous snake Reichsführer SS Heinrich Himmler had extorted them to become, they are ready to strike.

It is at this time the story of *Order of Battle* begins.

Ib Melchior
February 1991

Part I

12-17 Apr 1945

■

12 Apr 1945

Neustadt

0917 hrs

His knuckles stung.

He glared at the German lying sprawled against the wall. He'd struck him as hard as he could across the face—a backhand blow brought up from the hip.

The German stared back at him. He looked shocked; his eyes were wide open in a mixture of surprise, doubt—and fear.

Erik Larsen recognized that look of fear. Good! He stepped up to the man, looming over him. He was suddenly awkwardly aware of his right hand. He had the strange notion that he could still feel the bristly stubble on the German's face imprinted on the skin. He resisted an urge to rub it. He might have to hit the man again. . . .

The German seemed to shrink into the dirty wall of the Bavarian *Bauernstube*. He stared at Erik incredulously. For a long moment the two men faced each other.

Erik felt a constriction in his throat. With a conscious effort he forced himself to look grim. Ruthless. He could not afford to let the German suspect his doubts. He felt a compelling need to reassure himself, to confirm that he'd been right. And for a split second he felt resentful, frustrated. That was the problem with these screening cases. You had to rely on your instincts too damned much. There wasn't time for a real interrogation. The cases had a tendency to run together in their tedious sameness, to bog down in a morass of routine questions and evasive answers, permeated with the stink of fear.

This bastard on the floor. Erik *knew* there was something wrong about him. He was certain of it. But how in hell do you prove it in a few minutes? And that was all the time he could spend on any screening job. Already German war refugess were spilling through the lines from the east by the hundreds in a frantic effort to get away from the advancing Red Army. Who were they? *What* were they? A lot of them had good reasons for not wanting to face the Russians. It was up to CIC to screen those people before allowing them to continue into Germany, behind the American lines. . . .

Anton Gerhardt was one of them. He came rolling into the little Bavarian village of Neustadt in a small Citroën loaded to the roof with household goods, boxes and suitcases. Calmly he let himself be stopped and ordered from his vehicle to join the line of refugees waiting to be screened. While his car was driven off the road and the MPs began to search through his mountainous belongings, Gerhardt was taken to Erik for screening.

After the first few routine questions Erik knew.

Gerhardt was in his early fifties. His only papers consisted of an expired *Kennkarte*—a German identification card—which listed him as a minor post office employee from Budweis in the Sudeten area of Czechoslovakia. That was standard. Had his papers been more complete he'd have been one in a thousand, and cause for real suspicion. There was something else about the man. He seemed too cocksure, almost condescending, rather than displaying the usual servile apprehension.

Erik felt the hunch strongly, that hunch which every interrogator developed after questioning hundreds of suspects. The kind of hunch which was difficult to explain—but which was seldom wrong.

Gerhardt was no petty official.

There were plenty of those in Nazi Germany. Arrogant and haughty enough in their dealings with the public, but when confronted with authority, cringing and servile; the little German *Beamte*—the civil servant—a breed all his own. Erik knew them well from his travels in prewar Germany, and the stamp didn't fit Anton Gerhardt.

But Erik got nowhere with his questioning. Gerhardt stuck to his story. Things were bad in Budweis. Chaotic. The threat of Russian occupation created panic among the Germans. Orderly and regular functions had come to a standstill in the postal services, and he— Gerhardt—thought it best to return to Germany. The man seemed confident, and Erik had no proof that he was not, in fact, telling the truth.

Except for a damned insolent little smile that never left the man's face. And the hunch.

Erik studied him. "I don't believe your story," he said flatly. His German was faultless.

Gerhardt shrugged. "It is the truth."

"I'm not buying it."

The German remained silent. Erik regarded him dispassionately. He spoke matter-of-factly:

"You realize, of course, that if you don't tell *me* the truth, someone else, with more time, will have to get it out of you."

The German smiled thinly. "You are making a threat? Physical violence?" There was faint mockery in his tone. "Forgive me, but now it is I who cannot believe you. I know American officers are too civilized to resort to that kind of—of Russian barbarism. And I *am* telling the truth."

That was when Erik knew what he had to do.

He got up and walked over to the man standing before his desk. Slowly, deliberately he walked around him.

"So you believe we won't lay a hand on you?" he asked casually.

"Of course," Gerhardt answered. "I am an educated man. I never believed the propaganda ravings of Dr. Goebbels. They were designed for the more gullible."

"And you are not gullible."

"I am not."

"You're too clever to be fooled, is that it?"

"I am."

"But you still belonged to the Nazi party, didn't you? Supported it?"

Gerhardt didn't answer. This was getting nowhere, he thought.

He had been right; the Americans were fools. He felt gratified. It was as he had known it would be. That boy would never get anything out of him with his stupid questions. They had no idea of how to conduct an interrogation properly. How different, if the situation had been reversed!

"And being so clever, you've figured out that we won't rough you up a bit to get the truth." Erik interrupted his thoughts.

Gerhardt shrugged. "But you have the truth. Also, you go by the Geneva Conventions."

Erik nodded. "No rough stuff."

"Yes. No physical violence against prisoners."

Erik studied the German thoughtfully.

"Do you know where you are now?" he asked.

"No, I do not know. But I can guess. The American *Sicherheits-dienst?*"

"Close enough. I'm a special agent in the U.S. Army Counter Intelligence Corps. And it's my job to get you to talk. Right now!"

Gerhardt looked curiously at the young man facing him. He wondered what his rank was. The American wore no insignia of any kind—no rank, no branch, no unit—only two yellow-brass U.S. officers' emblems on the collar tabs of his olive drab wool U.S. Army shirt. Tall, well built. A good, strong Aryan face—and so young. Twenty-five? No more. A boy sent to do a man's job, he thought.

"I have already talked," he said patiently. "And you have my identification papers."

"Papers can be false."

"They can also be real. Mine are." He shrugged his shoulders in a gesture of resignation. "I *have* told you the truth."

"Not quite." Erik made his voice suddenly cold. "But you will!"

Gerhardt's thin-lipped smile drew down at the corners of his mouth. "But you will not—rough me up, as you put it, to make me say what you want to hear."

"What makes you so sure?"

"I have studied about America. I know what the Americans are like. You are fair. You do not consider a man guilty before his guilt is proved." He smiled. "You are trying to frighten me. To intimidate me. You think if I know something I will tell you, because I am afraid." Again he shrugged. "But you see, I know nothing. I have told you the truth about me."

Erik watched the German. He appeared to be entirely at ease. He believed what he was saying. No one was going to hurt him. Not the Americans. Not the soft, decadent democrats. He stepped in front of the man. He looked squarely at him.

"I'll tell you what," he said pleasantly. "You and I are going to play a little game."

Gerhardt looked at the CIC agent as if he were looking at a backward child who was being particularly exasperating. Erik continued:

"Here are the rules. Very simple. You will stand at attention, and I will ask you questions. Every time you tell a lie, I'll knock you across the room!"

The faint smirk never left Gerhardt's face. He drew himself to attention. He was humoring the childish American. Erik stood directly in front of him.

"Do you come from Budweis?" he asked.

"I do."

"Is the car you're driving yours?"

"It is."

"Were you a member of the Nazi party?"

Gerhardt hesitated. Then he shrugged his shoulders.

"Of course."

"Good. As a civil servant you'd have to be." He stepped a little closer to the German.

"Were you a post office employee?"

"Yes."

And Erik hit the German as hard as he could. The blow knocked the man off his feet and slammed him sprawling against the wall. Incredulously Gerhardt brought his hand to his face; there was a touch of bright red at the corner of his mouth. He was unaware of it as he stared up at the CIC agent looming above him.

Erik's voice was harsh.

"On your feet!"

Gerhardt stayed on the floor. His smirk was gone.

"*Los!* We've just started our little game! *Aufstehen!* Get up!"

Gerhardt stared at him. The American had hit him. He had been proved wrong. Where else was he wrong? What else might happen to him? Were the Americans just like the Russians after all? Or like—like his own? The world of logical certainties he had built so carefully and shored up with wishful thinking was collapsing. . . .

"Well?"

Gerhardt seemed to sag.

"Were you a post office employee?"

Gerhardt slowly stood up. A little of his dignity returned, but his arrogant condescension was gone.

Had he been like that from the start, Erik thought, I would have believed him. He said:

"Let's have it!"

Gerhardt felt naked, unprotected. His rational convictions crumpled in a card house collapse, he had nowhere to seek asylum. He drew himself up with pathetic pride.

"I am Standartenführer Gerhardt Wilke," he said.

"Your position?" Erik snapped.

"Chief of Gestapo in Budweis."

Erik returned to his desk. He didn't have to look in the book. The man was a mandatory arrestee. He called:

"Murphy!"

Sergeant Jim Murphy entered the room. Erik nodded toward the German. He suddenly felt tired.

"We've got ourselves a Gestapo colonel, Jim," he said wearily.

Murphy shot a curious glance at Gerhardt.

"Give him something to write with. He's going to put down his entire Nazi career for us." He looked at the Gestapo officer.

"*Verstanden?*"

The man nodded. "*Jawohl.*"

"When he's through put him in the enclosure. We'll want to talk to him again."

"Okay, sir." Murphy turned to the Nazi. "Come on. Let's go."

For a moment Erik sat at his desk. He'd caught another one. He should feel good about it, but his thoughts were bleak.

It was the first time he'd used physical force in the literally hundreds of cases, and the thousands of subjects, he'd investigated since splashing ashore at Omaha Beach more than ten months before. He'd always felt that to do so would put him on a par with the Nazis.

He suddenly recalled, word for word, the bitter argument he'd had with a line officer who'd beaten up a PW.

"Your lily-livered methods won't get you anywhere," the man had told him contemptuously. "There's only one way to deal with those bastards. Beat the shit out of them! *Make* them talk! Be as ornery— as unscrupulous—as they are."

"And what does that do?" he'd countered. "Make *them* right? Or *us* wrong?"

"What's the matter with you? You afraid to sacrifice one of your precious principles?"

"One? And then maybe another? And one more? Where do we stop?"

"Oh, for Christ's sake! All you have to do is *show* them. . . ."

"And if that's *not* enough? . . ."

"Dammit, man! What's more important? The creature comforts of a bunch of fucking Krauts, or a few hundred GIs ending up wearing mattress covers?"

Erik sighed. He had not been able to agree.

And now?

He'd just struck a man, a suspect, with all the force he could muster. And at that single moment he'd *wanted* to strike him. Was he then becoming like—them? After all this time? All the pressure?

He quickly derailed his train of thought. Hell of a time to get morbid, he thought. What I need is some bunk fatigue. Pretty damned soon!

Okay. So he'd knocked the Kraut down. But, dammit, it had been the right thing to do!

This time.

Would it have been right if the man actually had been telling the truth? . . .

It had been a textbook case. Just as he'd been taught at Camp Ritchie in Maryland by the IPWs: Do the unexpected. Break the prisoner as quickly as possible. Once he'd discovered the cornerstone of the man's defenses, he'd had no choice but to knock it out.

He sighed. He felt bone tired. Well, he'd asked for it. And in writing!

He remembered the letter he'd written to the War Department, dated December 8, 1941. . . .

He had graduated from the University of Minneapolis, after majoring in journalism, only a few months before and had returned to his native Rochester. He had been born and raised in that Minnesota town, and he felt closely tied to it. His father, Christian Larsen, had come to Rochester in 1913 from the Finsen Light Institute in Copenhagen to work as a radiation expert at the Mayo Clinic and was still there, as head of the department. Four years after he arrived he'd married a young, second-generation Danish-American girl, Karen Borg, and Erik had been born in September 1918.

Erik spent the eighteen months following his high school graduation with his father's sister, Aunt Birte, in Copenhagen. He studied languages and psychology at the university and spent his vacations bicycling through Europe and skiing in Norway in the winter. It was because of his intimate knowledge of Denmark, and France and Germany and their languages, that he felt he could be of special use in some military intelligence capacity, and that was what he suggested in his letter to the War Department, volunteering his services.

Less than a week after he'd written, he received a note acknowledging his letter. It said: "This will acknowledge receipt of your recent application for Military Intelligence work." It was on impressive stationery, headed "WAR DEPARTMENT GENERAL STAFF, Military Intelligence Division, G-2." It was signed by a captain in MIS.

A few days later he got another letter of acknowledgment saying substantially the same thing, but signed by a lieutenant commander, USNR. And the next day a third letter, this time signed by a civilian. He was by now totally perplexed, and his confusion was not diminished when, during the next couple of months, he got strange looks from his friends and acquaintances—including his barber— and even an occasional concerned postcard from people in places he'd visited. Finally, the direct query: "Hey! What've you been up to? The FBI was around asking questions about you!" made him realize he was being investigated thoroughly.

One day he got a phone call from a young woman. She referred to his letter to the War Department and asked him to meet with two officers, a colonel and a captain, for a personal interview. Strangely, she set up the meeting at an obscure little hotel in downtown Rochester. Erik went, of course. The two men, both in civilian clothes, were friendly and relaxed. They offered him a good stiff drink before getting down to their talk—and Erik remembered very little after that. There was one thing he recalled quite clearly. A question. Perhaps the nature of it had startled him enough to make an impression. The colonel had casually asked, "Tell me, Larsen, how would you feel about sticking a knife in a man's back?" But try as he would, he wasn't able to remember what he'd replied. He vaguely remembered mentioning a local hardware store owned by a good friend and feeling very loyal to that store, insisting that his friend supply the knife! He returned to the hotel the next day to apologize for his peculiar performance, but the two men were not there. In fact, the hotel management protested they'd never heard of them. And Erik never heard from them either.

But after three months he received another letter, this time signed by a Navy lieutenant. It contained a questionnaire the length of the *Encyclopaedia Britannica* for him to fill out, and the letter asked when, at his earliest convenience, he could put his personal affairs in order and report for duty. It didn't say what duty. He wrote back: "You name the place and the time, and I'll be there," and he received a wire, stamped with the little red wartime star of officialdom, asking him to call a certain executive number in

Washington, D.C. He did. He had a very nice conversation with a sexy-voiced girl, who instructed him to report a week later to Temporary Building Q. "Be prepared to remain out of communication with anyone for at least three months," she said sweetly, "and bring nothing but your toothbrush!"

When he reported to Temporary Building Q in Washington on the specified date he was shown to the office of the Navy lieutenant who had written to him earlier, Lieutenant Martin Harris. Harris occupied a long, narrow office. He was a stern-faced man with a great mane of prematurely gray hair. He looked up when Erik entered. "Come in, Larsen," he said. "And close the door behind you."

Erik did. Lieutenant Harris studied him searchingly. "When you stepped across that threshold," he said dramatically, "you lost your identity!" Erik almost turned around to look, but he caught himself in time. Harris pulled a piece of paper from his desk drawer and held it out to Erik. "Did you write this?" he asked. Erik looked at the paper. Indeed he'd written it. It was his own letter to the War Department. "Fine," said Harris. He shoved another paper toward Erik. "Sign this."

It was a simple document, brief and to the point: "I hereby volunteer for hazardous duty, no questions asked," and there was a space for his signature and that of a witness. Harris, presumably.

Startled, Erik wondered exactly what he was getting himself into. Harris glared at him, and he was thoroughly intimidated. He didn't have the nerve to refuse. He signed.

Harris witnessed his signature. He looked up at Erik. "About your identity," he said. "From now on you will be known as Lars G-8. That and *nothing* else! Your true identity must not become known to anyone through you. Is that clear?"

Erik understood what Harris was saying—but clear? He nodded. Harris told him that for the next three months he would be in special training, incommunicado. "The others will try to find out who you are," he cautioned. "Don't let them. *You* try to find out who *they* are instead."

The whole rigmarole made not the slightest sense to Erik, but he dutifully nodded his head.

"Have you got your toothbrush?" Harris asked. Erik showed him.

"Good. Take off your clothes."

Erik stared at the officer.

"All of them," Harris ordered. He got up and took out a large paper bag from a closet. He gave it to Erik. "Put everything in there," he said. And presently Erik stood facing the Navy officer as naked as a navy bean, clutching his toothbrush.

"That's all!" Harris dismissed him. He indicated a door. "Go through there. You'll be told what to do."

Erik had very little choice. He did exactly as he was ordered— and walked into a large room filled with about three hundred people, or so it seemed.

He stopped short. He held on to his toothbrush as the only link to sanity, and surveyed the situation.

There were actually about thirty men in the room. All of them stark naked. All of them more or less nonchalantly grasping a toothbrush. All of them politely bent on carrying on a stream of small talk.

Erik quickly entered into the spirit of things and was soon enagaged in an animated discussion about the life expectancy of a "temporary building" like Building Q with a young man possessed of an extremely hairy chest, and another, impressively hung young man with a prominent appendix scar. Everyone was pointedly steering away from anything remotely personal—a not inconsequential feat under the circumstances.

Nothing was settled, the fate of Building Q remained undecided, when finally everyone was issued GI fatigues and loaded onto two large trucks. The trucks were closed up—hermetically, it seemed— and during the trip, which lasted a good part of the night, no one could make out where they were going.

It wasn't until four weeks later that Erik found out he'd ended up with the Office of Strategic Services—the OSS!

By that time he was already well into the basic training program and settled down in OSS training camp B-5, hidden away in remote, wooded hill country. His class numbered thirty-six. The morning after they arrived at the camp they'd all been herded out at 6 A.M. They were taken to an isolated spot outside camp and found themselves in a small cemetery. There were several graves marked simply with a code-name and a number. And one open pit. Ready. Here they were introduced to their class instructor. Porter was his name. He told them that they were facing a tough course. Too tough for some. Not everyone made it, for one reason or another. And he casually indicated the graves. Then he took an Army .45 automatic from his belt holster and showed it to the group of sleepy recruits. He realized that some of them had little, if any, military training, he said. Patiently he demonstrated that one end of the gun was called the butt and the other the muzzle. "There is a big d:fference," he explained, "at what end you find yourself. Like this!" And he suddenly fired the gun, emptying the clip at the group of badly startled men facing him, the bullets whizzing closely by to slam into a dirt mound behind them. Some of the men flinched but stood their ground; others hit the dirt, and a few took off. Erik was too petrified to move. The whole crazy performance was witnessed by two silent, grim-looking men, who took notes in small black books. The next day the class was down to twenty-eight.

That was the beginning of the fantastic training course given the potential OSS agents. It was designed to tear a man down and reduce him to his basic survival strength, and then build him up again to be able to face anything with confidence. It succeeded— at least temporarily. After the first month Erik got up in the morning and thought, This is the last day I'll see alive—if I get through the whole day. After the second month he got up and thought, Okay. Bring 'em on! I can lick Germany and Japan, single-handed! The course was compact and thorough. Nothing was omitted. From communications to cryptography; from terrain orientation to silent killing, and "dirty" hand-to-hand combat taught by the fabulous, fiery Major Fairburns, late of the Hong Kong police force. The budding agents learned to fire every possible weapon, Allied and

Axis, and to drive every type of vehicle. They learned breaking and entering from experts—whoever *they* were—and the handling of high explosives. And constantly the grim men with their little black books were silent observers. If a man showed reluctance to crimp a highly unstable detonator cap onto a fuse with his teeth, he was apt not to be seen in class again.

And finally there was the parachute jumping. They trained two whole days for that. And then they made their five qualifying jumps in one afternoon. They rode to Quantico Marine Base in Virginia in a truck and took off from there in a C-47 to make their jumps over a small clearing in a forest nearby. The truck would pick them up, take them back to the base for the next jump, and the procedure was repeated until all the jumps had been made. Erik remembered with amusement the guard at the gate, who checked them onto the base each time—but never out. His eyes had bugged bigger and bigger each time around.

The parachute jumps had been like a graduation exercise. Basic training was over. Of the class of thirty-six, six were left. "Lars G-8" was one of them.

Soon after, Erik was given his first mission to be carried out in enemy-held territory. He joined a group of eleven Norwegian commandos to be dropped in Norway to blow up a heavy water plant operated by the Nazis. Erik was the only non-Norwegian on the team and was selected only because the approach route to the plant followed a ski trail with which he was very familiar. With the Norwegians he went through the intense mission briefing, and a fiercely close relationship sprang up among the men. With them he flew to Westover AFB in Massachusetts to board the plane that would take the team to Iceland and on to the drop in Norway. And here he was literally taken off the plane and returned to Washington. No one would tell him why. No one would give him any explanation at all. For a week he was kept in strict seclusion. He was worried sick. And then, finally, the situation was explained to him. They'd found out the mission had been compromised. Someone had infiltrated the organization and given the show away. But the mission was too vital to cancel. The raid had to be carried out at the time planned, or it would be too late. In the last minute the approach route had been changed. Erik no longer would have been useful; in fact, as the only non-Norwegian he would have been a liability in a tight situation. He had consequently been taken off the team and kept incommunicado until the operation was completed. The infiltrator had been ferreted out, and the mission had been successful. But all eleven commandos had been caught trying to make good their escape after the raid. And all eleven had been executed.

Erik was shocked. His first reaction was Thank God I didn't have to go! and then he experienced an overwhelming sense of guilt for not having been with his comrades. The organization gave him two weeks in Washington to work it out with himself. He used the time writing scripts for overseas shortwave broadcasts for the Office of War Information.

When he reported back for assignment he found that things had changed. The big powers had carved up the European Theater of Operations among themselves, and each had a separate territory in which to operate along OSS lines. The Scandinavian countries were in the British area of operations, and Erik—who had been trained for missions in those countries—was given the choice of being transferred to British authority or remaining with the U.S. Forces. He chose the latter.

Because of his knowledge of languages—particularly French and German—he was commissioned into the Counter Intelligence Corps, perhaps on the theory that "it takes a thief to catch a thief," and he completed an exhaustive course in investigation and interrogation. He always felt grateful for the OSS training he'd received. It had stood him in good stead on many occasions. . . .

It hadn't all been duck soup. He'd done his share of griping. And with justification. But he knew that if he had it to do again, he'd write the damned letter once more.

He got up. He went to one of the files standing along one wall. He pulled it open and started to look for the blacklist. If Colonel

Gerhardt Wilke was listed, he could be crossed off.

Murphy stuck his head in the door.

"Ready for another one? We've got 'em stacked up out here like shit on shingles!"

Erik grinned. "Okay," he said. "Next!"

Next. Another one. And another one. And . . .

The war was in its final weeks. Had to be. The German fronts were collapsing all over. Berlin itself was threatened. But the CIC work was really just beginning. And a lot could happen in a few weeks. A hell of a lot. Especially in a few weeks of war . . .

He rubbed his hand. That damned stubble *had* made his skin itch.

It was 0928 hrs—almost nine-thirty in the morning. In Dachau, 183 miles to the south, two Waffen SS officers were just being checked through the main gate of the concentration camp. . . .

Dachau

1634 hrs

Untersturmführer Wilhelm Richter squinted up at the smoke that belched from the tall brick chimneys. It was oily gray as it billowed into the clean blue Bavarian sky. The ovens of Dachau were roaring around the clock. There was only a little time left in which to carry out the final solution to the Jewish problem.

The young Waffen SS lieutenant leaned against the squat building hiding the infernal roots of the towering smokestacks. The bricks were warm, and discolored with greasy soot, and Willi had carefully sought out a clean spot. A dozen inmates of the concentration camp were loading a military truck parked nearby. Willi was watching them.

The men had a cadaverous look. Their threadbare striped *KL* uniforms hung loosely on their emaciated bodies. Across the back of each man's pajamalike jacket a large S had been painted—S for Sonderkommando, the special details of camp inmates who'd volunteered to do the most loathsome of the crematorium jobs in return for a few weeks of life.

Just a few weeks, Willi thought. And what kind of life? Anyway, sooner or later they all end up the same way. Up in smoke!

He started to whistle softly as he watched the men work.

> *Du kleine Fliege,*
> *Wenn ich dich kriege—*

It was an old German nursery rhyme he remembered from his childhood, though he was not aware of that.

The prisoners labored wearily. The wooden boxes they were man-handling were heavy and the men were weak. It took four of them to lift each box and struggle it into place on the truck. They toiled in dull, leaden silence, and the half dozen black-uniformed SS Totenkopfverband guards ringing the pitiful work party, lazily cradling Schmeisser machine pistols in their arms, hardly seemed necessary. But Sturmbannführer Kratzer had insisted.

Kratzer himself, standing at the rear of the truck, followed the loading intently.

A small man, wearing steel-rimmed glasses, with closely cropped hair and an imitation Hitler mustache, the SS major was not an imposing figure.

But there was something intense, something compelling about him, which gave even Willi an uneasy feeling.

The last box was placed on the truck. The Sonderkommando inmates were herded together in a small group. With the unerring perception of the hopeless, they knew that they had done their final job. Their sallow, sunken eyes stared at the ground; only a few of the still defiant dared lift their eyes and watch their future billowing darkly from the chimneys.

Sturmbannführer Kratzer beckoned to the Totenkopfverband noncom in charge of the guards. Almost absentmindedly he nodded toward the group of inmates.

"You know what to do," he said flatly, in the same tone of voice he might have used giving instructions to a file clerk.

The noncom nodded. *"Jawohl*, Herr Sturmbannführer."
Kratzer turned toward Willi.
"Richter!" he called. "Let's go!"
While two SS guards jumped into the rear of the truck, Willi
walked to the cab. He kept his eyes averted from the waiting camp
inmates. There was suddenly an unpleasant stench in the air. He'd
be glad to get out of the place. He stepped up into the driver's seat
and took the wheel, as Kratzer joined him in the cab.

The truck swayed ponderously as it bounced down the dirt road.
The load lay heavy on the floorboards in the back. Willi drove care-
fully. This wasn't the time to break a spring, or an axle.
He whistled softly to himself: *"Du kleine Fliege—"*
He remembered it now. Mutti used to sing it to him—so long,
long ago.

> *Du kleine Fliege,*
> *Wenn ich dich kriege,*
> *Dann reiss ich dir dein kleines Beinchen aus.*
> *Dann musst du hinken*
> *Auf deinen Schinken—*
> *Dann kommst du nie mehr wieder nach deinem Haus*

Funny he should think of it now. And of his mother . . .

Willi was a war child. His father, Walter, was killed on the
western front in 1916, the very day he returned from home leave.
Willi was born nine months later. He was brought up by his mother.
He remembered her well from his early childhood. Mutti would
sing to him the old German nursery songs and she would read
stories from *Der Struwwelpeter*: about Konrad, who sucked his
thumbs, and had them cut off by the tailor; about the crybaby,
whose eyeballs dropped from their sockets; about Cruel Paul and
Slovenly Peter, and little Fritz, who was eaten alive by a wolf;
about Hans, who was sliced in two sliding down a banister; and
the little girl who burned herself to a pile of ashes. . . .

He still remembered the book cover vividly: Konrad, with his bleeding thumb stumps. It said: "Merry Stories and Funny Pictures for Children 3 to 6 Years of Age." He hadn't liked the picture of Konrad at first; it made him afraid to suck his own thumb. Then he stopped that, and he was proud of it. He always secretly felt that it served Konrad right, having his thumbs cut off—because he didn't stop. And he got used to the pictures.

Later he was less and less close to Mutti, especially during the four years up to his nineteenth birthday, when he was in the Hitler Youth. And then, of course, he joined the Waffen SS. . . .

Kratzer brought Willi out of his reveries.

"Up there," he ordered. "Turn left. Into the forest."

In a small clearing just inside the woods, hidden from view from the road, another truck was waiting. It was not a Wehrmacht vehicle, but a run-down civilian truck which had been converted from gasoline- to wood-burning in the wartime effort to conserve vital resources. The big cylindrical furnace tank and the wood storage bin were mounted clumsily behind the cab. A man in civilian clothes, leather jacket and cap stood puffing on a pipe nearby. He carefully extinguished it with a work-hardened thumb and put it in his pocket as Willi brought his truck to a halt next to the other vehicle.

The men jumped from the truck.

"*Los!*" Kratzer commanded. "*Die Kisten umladen!* All the boxes into the other truck! Get going!" He made an impatient gesture with his submachine gun.

The two SS guards put away their weapons. At once they and the civilian began the transfer of the heavy boxes from the Wehrmacht truck to the wood burner. Willi looked curiously at the battered vehicle. Kratzer joined him. He grinned.

"We don't want to attract too much attention," he said. "The enemy has air patrols in the area we have to go through. But they won't waste ammunition on a decrepit old wood-burning truck like that!"

"Will we make it?" Willi asked dubiously. "Into the mountains?"

"Of course. It's four hundred and twenty kilometers to Rattendorf from here. We'll be there tomorrow. Early."

Willi hoped the major was right. It wouldn't be easy to negotiate the Alpine roads in a shitty, worn-out wood burner.

The men had almost finished reloading the boxes. The three of them were swinging the last heavy box to heave it up onto the pile on the truck. Suddenly one of them lost his grip. The two others, unable to hold the box, let go. The box crashed to the ground, splintering open.

The three men stared at the shattered box. Mingled with the broken wood were a number of crude gold bars! As one the men looked toward Kratzer. And froze!

The SS major was contemplating them regretfully. His Schmeisser machine pistol was aimed directly at them.

"I'm sorry, gentlemen," he said softly.

Two brief staccato bursts from the submachine gun raked in short arcs across the men.

The bullets cut them in half. One of the SS men stared in disbelief at the bloody entrails spilling out of his torn abdomen into his hands, before he collapsed across his comrades.

A flock of black crows in a nearby tree took wing in alarm—and flapped away with raucous cries of protest across the bleak fields.

Willi felt the bitter taste of bile in his mouth. His knees were suddenly weak. He forced himself to swallow. He stared at the SS major.

Holy Mother of God, he thought, they were Germans! They weren't just Jews—they were Germans!

Kratzer's face was without emotion as he looked intently at the three bodies. For a split second Willi had the illusion that the man's eyes were mere jet-black hollow pits. Against his will his own eyes were drawn toward the lifeless bodies. Again he felt the bile rise in his throat. He seemed to have difficulty getting enough air.

Kratzer was unaware of him. He stared raptly at the bodies. He walked up to them, taking small, mincing steps. He prided himself on the fact that he was an expert in detecting fakers. But he was also very efficient. There was no need for any *Genickschuss*. The three men were all dead.

Kratzer suddenly became aware of Willi. He seemed to read the young man's thoughts.

"Willi! Come here," he ordered quietly.

Willi joined him. He was still shaken.

"They knew where we are going," he said. "We can't afford to have rumors spread around that twenty million Reichsmarks in gold can be found in Rattendorf."

He is right, of course, Willi thought. He was getting hold of himself again. He felt a little ashamed. He'd almost gone to pieces.

Kratzer kicked the gold bars with his boot.

"Teeth!" He grinned. "A hell of a lot of teeth!"

He laughed coldly.

"The Jews are not all bad," he said. "There's a kernel of gold in most of them."

He laughed again. A chilling sound.

"And enough good little Jewish kernels will help the Third Reich survive. We'll see to that."

He turned to Willi.

"Come on. Let's get the rest of it on the truck. The sooner we get to Rattendorf, the sooner we can return to Thürenberg. . . ."

The old wood burner made good time rumbling down the dirt road. Willi was driving. It was a beautiful afternoon. There were only a few gray clouds in the sky. Or was it smoke from the crematorium? . . .

Kratzer was dozing beside him. Willi again began to whistle softly his old favorite nursery tune that Mutti used to sing: *"Du kleine Fliege—"*

> You little fly,
> When I catch you,
> Then I'll tear out your little legs.

Then you must hobble
On your hams—
Then you'll never again get to your home.

He gave it up.
For some reason his mouth was dry.

Berlin

2337 hrs

The Berlin *Stadtmitte*—the city center—was in flames. An RAF bombing raid had just rained down destruction upon the German capital. Many buildings had. been severely damaged by the high explosives; some, like the big, fashionable Adlon Hotel at the corner of Unter Den Linden and Wilhelmstrasse, were ablaze. But the Propaganda Ministry down the street was relatively undamaged.

The mortally wounded city was fighting for its existence. Fire trucks, ambulances and military vehicles roared through the rubble-strewn streets, where soldiers, civilians and firemen were trying desperately to swamp the raging holocaust, and Red Cross workers, wielding their heavy utility daggers, were tearing and hacking and digging at the smoking debris in their efforts to reach the dying and the dead trapped below.

The flames from the remains of the Chancellery licked toward the now empty night sky and were mirrored in the darkened windows of the Ministry of Propaganda, transforming the building into a looming monster of many eyes that winked with red malevolence.

Down the street of chaos, from the direction of the blazing Adlon, a small motorcade approached the ministry. A large black limousine, with two SS motorcyclists in front and two behind, made its way through the maze of masonry rubble as speedily as the rescue and fire-fighting activities would permit. They drew up to the front steps of the ministry and came to a halt.

An orderly jumped from the limousine and opened the door. Quickly the lone passenger got out. He was a small man. He wore a Nazi uniform cap and a long leather overcoat with broad lapels and a wide belt. He walked toward the steps of the ministry with a pronounced limp. At the steps he turned to look at the destruction around him.

Dr. Joseph Goebbels, Minister of Propaganda for the Third Reich, was appalled. His strangely simian features were grim. It wasn't going to be easy, he thought. He was well aware that a growing number of Berliners no longer shared his unshakable belief in the Führer. They were misled, of course. They were wrong. But it wasn't going to be easy to ensure their continued support in the face of daily and nightly air raids like this.

He started up the broad steps. A small group suddenly came hurrying from the building. Obviously agitated and excited, they met him halfway up. Urgently, with unconcealed exhilaration, a ministry secretary spoke to "the *Doktor*."

The flames from the burning buildings were reflected in a flickering *danse macabre* on Goebbels' lowering face. The secretary was trying to make himself understood above the din from the streets. And suddenly Goebbels grabbed the man's arm. His face lit up with triumphant elation, and followed by the others he hurried into the building.

The minister made straight for his office. As he hastened down the corridor, eager and willing hands helped him out of his great leather coat. Everyone seemed to be in a high-spirited mood.

Goebbels went directly to the massive desk that dominated his richly and solidly furnished office. He sat down and faced the excited people gathered expectantly before him.

He rubbed his hands, a grin of satisfaction on his face.

"Now!" he said. "Bring out our best champagne. And get me the Führer on the phone."

Someone hurried away to carry out the minister's order. The secretary at once began to establish contact with the Führer Bunker, where Hitler was sitting out the air raid. Dr. Goebbels' eyes were bright as he looked around him. He noticed the large desk calendar before him. It showed Thursday, April 12, 1945. He glanced at his watch, and reached over to tear off the page. A new day had begun.

The secretary handed him the phone. For a moment Goebbels waited in silence. The others watched him intently. There was not a sound to be heard in the big room. Then Goebbels spoke:

"My Führer," he said emotionally. "I congratulate you! It is written in the stars: 'The last half of April will be the turning point for us!' This is Friday, April the thirteenth! My Führer—this *is* the turning point. I have just been informed, *President Roosevelt is dead!*"

13 Apr 1945

Berlin

0249 hrs

The domed lights studding the ceiling at regular intervals gave a yellowish, unnatural light to the concrete walls of the long corridor connecting the Staff Quarters Bunker with the Führer Bunker deep in the ground under the Chancellery.

Oberst Hans Heinrich Stauffer, adjutant to Generalfeldmarschall Wilhelm Keitel, Chief of the High Command of the Armed Forces, buttoned the last button on his uniform tunic as he hurried along the corridor. A summons to report to the Führer Bunker meant *now* —even at three in the morning. There were more people about in the bunker complex than usual at that hour, and Stauffer wondered what was up. Perhaps the Allies have at last surrendered! he thought with sardonic gallows humor.

Stauffer made his way through the various bulkheads, through the mess hall, where a few SS guards were drinking hot black ersatz coffee, and down the stairs to the lower level of the Führer Bunker, fifty feet below the street surface. He hurried through the empty lounge and into the conference room.

A handful of officers were in the room, among them the Führer's Adjutant, General Wilhelm Bergdorf, and his personal aide and bodyguard, SS Colonel Otto Günsche. Everyone turned to look at Stauffer when he entered, but no one said anything. They all looked tense and expectant.

Stauffer glanced around for the field marshal, but he didn't see him. He concluded that the chief of staff was with the Führer. He looked questioningly at Günsche, who nodded.

With the others Stauffer waited. He'd been in this bunker conference room countless times before, yet he never got used to it. It was comfortably though haphazardly furnished with odd chairs and tables brought down from the Chancellery offices above. The walls were hung with paintings of German landscapes, and with two large maps, one of Greater Germany and the other of the Berlin area. Both of them were dotted with military signs and symbols. The areas east of Berlin were so thick with red markers that they looked blood-spattered. A long table held stacks of additional maps. For the hundredth time Stauffer wondered about the luxurious Persian rug that incongruously covered the cement floor. From which Chancellery office did it originally come? The edges had had to be folded under to make it fit. He noticed that the folds were already getting worn. They would always show.

The other officers were talking among themselves in low voices. Colonel Stauffer settled down to wait. He was used to waiting. He'd spent hours doing it. He was a career soldier. . . .

0327 hrs

The metal door to Hitler's study suddenly opened. At once the waiting officers fell silent. Generalfeldmarschall Wilhelm Keitel stood in the open door. Stauffer could see past him into the study. It was quite small and simply furnished; a sofa, a desk, a few chairs, a table heaped with a mountain of maps. There were only a few personal touches of Adolf Hitler: an ornate clock and, hanging over the desk, an oval portrait of Frederick the Great, the Prussian warrior king, whom Hitler revered. Hitler stood staring at the painting, his back to the door, his hands clasped behind him.

Keitel was about to close the door behind him, when the Führer spoke:

"*Sie! Herr Feldmarschall!*" he said. He did not turn around. "*Ich verlasse mich auf Sie!*"

There was surprising strength in Hitler's voice, Stauffer realized with interest. It was almost like the old days. It was unusual. Hitler was already a broken man physically. He was stooped and hunched. His injured left hand and arm trembled badly, and he walked dragging his left foot. Yet his eyes could still be bright, burning with strange mesmeric powers.

"My Führer," Keitel said. "I shall do my utmost."

He gave the *Heil Hitler* salute and closed the door. For a moment he surveyed the officers before him. . . .

Generalfeldmarschall Wilhelm Bodewin Johann Gustav Keitel looked like the personification of a Prussian Junker. Tall, erect, with close-cropped graying hair and a small, well-groomed mustache; cold, pale eyes, a sometime monocle screwed into the left one; immaculate field-gray uniform and high boots polished to a black gloss, he presented the perfect image of a haughty Prussian aristocrat. Yet he was neither Prussian nor an aristocrat.

Keitel was actually a farmer at heart, who came from an intensely anti-Prussian, Hanoverian family. He loved nothing better than to busy himself with the bucolic duties of running his farming estate, Helmsherode, in Braunschweig, and holding *Treibjagd* to shoot deer, wild boar and pheasant. That's what he would do whenever he could break away for a few days from carrying out his Führer's orders and signing his name to documents that would cost millions of lives. . . .

Keitel was worried. It had been some time now since he had seen his beloved estate. The Americans had overrun it only two days before. There had been no word since. And now this. He was far from enthusiastic about this latest idea of Hitler's—but he had been given his orders; orders from the Führer. He couldn't change them. Wouldn't. But there *was* something he could do.

"*Meine Herren,*" he said solemnly. "What I am about to say here, now—this night—must never go beyond this room!"

He searched the faces before him. The men were watching him raptly. He walked to the two big wall maps.

"Gentlemen," he continued. "The fortunes of war are about to change. The Führer has instructed me to inform you—President Roosevelt is dead!"

He waited patiently for the excited reaction that raced through the group of officers to die down.

Stauffer, too, felt his pulse quicken at the announcement. It was the kind of news that could trigger—well, anything, or nothing. He watched his chief closely. He grew puzzled.

This is only the curtain raiser, he thought.

Stauffer felt uneasy. He'd worked with Keitel for a long time. He knew most of the man's idiosyncrasies. Whatever Keitel had to say was still to come. And it was important. The field marshal always managed to sound stiff and stilted when he had to speak to any group. The more concerned he was with what he had to say, the stiffer he appeared, the more stilted he sounded. Stauffer decided his superior was very concerned. Keitel continued.

"In the words of the Führer: Destiny will not be denied!"

He turned to the map of Berlin behind him.

"The Russians shall yet meet their bloodiest defeat at the gates of Berlin!"

He turned to the map of Germany and swept his hand across it in a decisive gesture. "We shall roll the Allies back into the sea!"

He faced the officers, fixing them with his pale, cold eyes, framed by the map of a defeated Germany behind him.

"The Führer has said: 'The victor of the last battle is the victor of the war.' That last battle, *meine Herren*, shall be ours!"

Stauffer cringed inwardly. *My God!* he thought. Another invincible secret weapon! The other officers listened and watched the chief of staff with reactions ranging from fascination to pure incredulity. Stauffer was worried. Keitel was outdoing himself. Stauffer had no great respect for his superior officer. Privately he considered him a spineless brown noser, who was ruled by blind obedience to his god, Adolf Hitler. . . .

Keitel had been *Chef des OKW* (*Oberkommando der Wehrmacht*)—Chief of the High Command of the Armed Forces—since

February 4, 1938. He was a perfect choice for Hitler's purposes. His loyalty was unquestionable—and unquestioning. His dossier was above reproach. He'd taken part in the Nazi conspiracy to build up the German armed forces in the early thirties in direct violation of the Versailles Treaty, and he had done so with complete dedication, giving orders and issuing instructions verbally, whenever possible, on the principle that "matters communicated by mouth cannot be proved—they can be denied." Ever since then he'd shown himself completely subordinate to all Hitler's orders and demands, never questioning his Führer's motives or morality—and permitting no one else to do so. The field marshal was a pedantic, uninspired man without humor but with a great capacity for detail and the routine of administrative work. Wilhelm Keitel, the farmer, was exactly the kind of staff officer Adolf Hitler needed to carry out his wishes without questions, without opposition. Keitel stayed close to the Führer, wherever he was. It was on his arm Hitler had walked from the bomb-shattered building at Rastenburg, injured, burned and bruised, his hair singed, his face blackened, after the abortive assassination attempt by Colonel Stauffenberg. Keitel himself had been shaken, but uninjured. . . .

Keitel walked to the map table. The officers gathered around him. He selected a map, and Stauffer spread it out on the table. It was a map of the Alpine areas of Bavaria, Austria and northern Italy. Keitel's voice and delivery, as he went on, was familiar to them all from previous briefings. Yet this was to be something more than just another briefing. This was to be something extraordinary. They all felt it. The air itself was electric with their curiosity.

"The time is now," Keitel stated. "At the earliest opportunity we shall regroup—consolidate our forces as planned—here."

He placed his whole hand over the map. "The Bavarian Alpine Fortress—*Die Alpenfestung*. From here the war shall be won! I have recommended to the Führer that Field Marshal Kesselring be given the Southern Command."

Keitel looked from officer to officer.

"The Americans have sustained a great blow in losing their war-intoxicated President at this crucial time. They are confused, demoralized. The German people—our troops—need a focusing point. Now. A bold, a dauntless stroke to rekindle them, to make the *Alpenfestung* truly invincible! We shall give it to them!"

Stauffer watched the field marshal, spellbound. Did the man really believe what he was saying?

Keitel went on.

"The Americans have been struck to their knees by fate. *We* must act now. *We* must bring them all the way down! They have lost their political head. *We* shall cut off their military head as well! *Meine Herren . . .*"

He paused dramatically.

"*Meine Herren,* the Führer has ordered General Eisenhower killed. *Now!*"

15 Apr 1945

Feldstein

2047 hrs

Riding on rubberless metal rims, the battered bicycle made
a grating, crunching sound on the gravel at the roadside. A group of
six men and a woman came walking along the dark country road.
They carried bundles and knapsacks. One man had two old suitcases
hanging from a rope across his shoulders, and the bicycle, pushed
by another of the men, was loaded with bundled-up gear. All seven
looked tired and bedraggled—a typical little group of aimless
civilian refugees left in the wake of war. The night was dark; the
sky was overcast, and there was a hint of a cold drizzle in the air.

Three and a half miles west of Feldstein in the Frankfurt am Main
area, the road wound through a sparsely wooded region. Here a
large area had been enclosed in accordion-rolled barbed wire. Scattered among the trees mountainous stacks of jerry cans and drums
could be made out dimly. At the guarded gate in the barbed wire
a well-lit sign showed the area to be a U.S. Army Supply Dump,
Class III Supplies. Gasoline and Oil.

The group of weary refugees trudged past the gate on the opposite side of the road and disappeared around a bend.

T5 Henry Williams watched them go. He was in his fourth hour
of guard duty and he was itching to be relieved. He wondered
briefly if he should call the sergeant of the guard and report the
refugees. He decided against it. He wasn't really sure what the hell
the curfew hours were out here, and he wasn't that eager to get
his ass chewed out if he guessed wrong. Those Krauts could be

perfectly okay—and anyway, they were gone. So why rock the boat?

Around the bend in the road the barbed wire enclosure came to an end and the wire ran into the woods at a ninety-degree angle. The band of refugees shuffled across the roadbed toward the corner of the compound. They left the main road and started down a dirt path along the wire running through the darkened woods. And a striking metamorphosis took place.

Almost instantly the weary group of wayworn refugees was transformed into a deadly efficient commando team. Two of the men at once picked up the old bicycle and carried it along, as they hurried silently down the path. There was not a sound to be heard. Then, as if on an unspoken command, they all sank to the ground next to the wire.

For several moments they listened intently. Then they looked toward one man. He nodded. Not a word was spoken. A pair of wire clippers, a Schmeisser submachine gun and a couple of Luger pistols quickly appeared from the bundles, while four of the men loaded up with the knapsacks.

Expertly, noiselessly two men cut the wire, strand by strand, until an opening was made, large enough to let them through one by one. The woman stayed behind with one of the men, armed with the submachine gun. The other five quickly melted away into the shadows among the stacks of cans and drums.

Pfc David Rosenfeld was disgusted. Utterly disgusted. He'd been sitting in that Godforsaken Repl Depl back in Normandy for weeks, waiting for assignment. He was nineteen and raring to go. And what happened? Two days ago he finally got his orders.

This is it! he had thought. I'm finally going to see some action. Tie down Germany, fellers, here I come!

Rosenfeld kicked a stone in resentment. Some action! Guarding a fucking pile of tin cans. Walking peripheral post, yet. What a crock of shit!

Rosenfeld looked toward a small group of huts located a short distance inside the area. A few jeeps, a staff car and an olive drab Cadillac sedan were parked outside. A couple of GI drivers lounged around the vehicles. Something was up at the Dump HQ. A lot of high brass had arrived not long ago. Probably another supply route snafu, Rosenfeld thought.

He sighed. Sourly he contemplated the jerry cans, piled high in row upon row; the towering heaps of oil drums. Some action!

He didn't see the furtive shadow that darted between two stacks of jerry cans. He was too busy griping to himself. . . .

The first blast obliterated Pfc Rosenfeld.

It slammed a fist of roaring, boiling sound into the night sky. A split second later another explosion rocked the depot, and another. In an instant the dump was transformed into a blazing holocaust. Flaming gasoline, hurled into the air by the thunderous blasts, showered down on the HQ huts. The explosions shook the buildings violently.

One of the drivers, drenched in gasoline, burst into flame. Like a flailing, fiery scarecrow he ran stumbling into a stack of jerry cans. Tumbling, the cans cascaded around him. Instantly the man was engulfed in a blinding eruption of fire.

From the huts several men came running, silhouetted against the leaping flames. Desperately they tried to protect themselves from the flying incandescent debris. Some of them leaped into the two cars. The staff car was the first to race away. The sedan followed almost at once. Gathering speed, it careened down a path between huge piles of oil drums. Suddenly a tremendous explosion immediately next to the lurching car lifted it into the air and slammed it to the ground in a tortured mass of twisted metal showered with blazing oil. The car shuddered in its death throes, as the gas tank exploded into flame.

Three bodies could be made out trapped in the funeral pyre. They were charred and mangled beyond recognition. But a rectangular piece of metal fastened to the front bumper could still be recognized, and on it the star of a U.S. general!

Within seconds the entire dump area was alive with frantic action.

Pfc Rosenfeld missed it all.

16 Apr 1945

Kronach

1019 hrs

The Liaison Room adjoining the top secret War Room on the second floor of the Corps CP building was relatively calm when Erik and his teammate, Special Agent Donald Lee Johnson, walked in. Major Lund, who ran the place, and who'd managed to make himself indispensable doing it, was briefing a brigadier general and two bird colonels gathered around a map spread out on a table. He acknowledged the arrival of the two CIC agents with a friendly nod, and without missing a comma in his situation briefing.

Erik and Don had themselves taken Gestapo chief Standartenführer Gerhardt Wilke to Corps HQ for strategic interrogation. The man had turned out to be a veritable encyclopedia on the Gestapo setup in Sudetenland. The Czechs would be very interested.

They had arrived in the picturesque little town of Kronach, where the forward echelons of XII Corps were headquartered, the day before, in time to attend the memorial services for President Roosevelt, held in the gardens behind the Corps HQ buildings. The moving commemorative address had been given by the Corps CG, Major General "Matt" Eddy.

The sudden death of the Commander in Chief had been deeply felt by everyone. Erik, though he'd never even seen him, felt a sharp personal loss. FDR had been President ever since he was old enough to remember. It was as if part of the United States was gone.

Erik perched himself on the corner of a desk and began to riffle through a stack of mimeoed intelligence reports. Don sauntered over to the window. He looked out.

From a rocky hilltop on the opposite bank of the river the great medieval fortress Feste Rosenberg looked down majestically on both the old and the new sections of the town of Kronach—seemingly without paying any special attention to the complex of two- and three-story brick buildings with gray tile roofs that housed the Corps CP.

Don had an excellent view of the old castle. He enjoyed it. In fact, he'd enjoyed seeing—and being in—a lot of places. In England, in France, in Luxembourg—and Germany. To his own great surprise he found that his interest in actually seeing places linked with history could go hand in hand with the grim business of wartime counter intelligence work. A little guiltily he sometimes thought of himself as a tourist in GI boots—although he'd never admit it, least of all to Erik, who'd tramped all over Europe and spoke five or six languages fluently. Just as well. It sure was an advantage to someone born and raised in Amarillo, Texas, who had trouble even with English!

Don contemplated the massive stone castle on the hill. Proud. Forbidding, he thought, even under enemy occupation. Well, it wasn't the first time. History did have a way of repeating itself—even if it occasionally took a little time. Some three centuries before, the Swedish king Gustavus Adolphus had made his headquarters in Feste Rosenberg when he had invaded Germany, bent on liberating his German Lutheran brothers. This century it's the Jews' turn, Don thought wryly.

He wondered idly where that bit of useless information came from. Part of that ninety percent of his college education he was supposed to forget? Only hadn't?

Don joined Erik. Major Lund was finishing up. He walked the general and the two colonels to a large map on the wall next to the area situation map. The map bore the legend:

Unconfirmed Installations in
REPORTED REDOUBT AREA

It showed the Alpine regions of Bavaria, Austria and Italy, with the city of Munich to the north. A large area in the center had been marked off with a heavy broken line and was studded with military symbols. Lund indicated the map.

"There it is," he said. "Up to date."

"And unconfirmed," the general commented dryly.

"Yes. But indications show that the Nazis *are* preparing for a bitter fight from there."

"Sort of a last stand, you mean." The general sounded vaguely patronizing. Brigadier General Millard P. McGraw was a combat officer. He didn't think too much of desk officers and tabletop campaigns.

"Exactly." Major Lund turned to the map, continuing the briefing he'd given hundreds of times before. "As you can see, sir, the actual area of the National Redoubt—the so-called Alpine Fortress —takes in parts of the Bavarian Alps, western Austria and northern Italy—some twenty thousand square miles of virtually impregnable mountain terrain."

"Quite a piece of real estate!" said one of the colonels, impressed.

"You bet! Hitler's own stronghold—Berchtesgaden—lies right in the center." He pointed it out. "Right—there."

The general studied the map. He looked skeptical. He turned to Lund.

"What about the supposed fortifications? The military installations?"

"We've had literally hundreds of reports, sir."

"From what kind of sources? *Any* of them reliable?"

Major Lund looked up. Pretty damned snide way of putting it, he thought.

"Yes, sir," he said. "From our own intelligence sources. From the British. The OSS. And from neutral sources through Switzerland. Even from anti-Nazi factions inside Germany."

The general grunted. Major Lund pointed to the symbols on the map. He spoke with a conscious effort to keep from sounding testy.

"As you can see, General, they indicate food, gasoline, ammunition, chemical warfare dumps—most of Germany's supply of poison gas is there—pillboxes, concrete bunkers, power stations. Troop concentration points, lines of heavily fortified positions—some of them reported to be connected for miles by underground railroads . . . We've even had reports about underground bombproof factories."

General McGraw looked at him.

"It's a helluva scary picture you're painting, Major—even if it's only half true." There was a ring of sarcasm to his voice. It wasn't lost on Major Lund. The G-2 officer felt the warmth of hot blood rising on his neck. That one-star SOB, he thought. It isn't up to me to go out and verify the reports that come in. But I'd better damned well post them—for bastards like him to make snide remarks about! Lund knew, of course, what he himself thought about the Alpine Fortress bit. A lot of it was propaganda. Goebbels talk. A lot of the reports were exaggerated. A lot unreliable. But there was enough left to make him worried. Good and damned worried. He glanced at the general. He was again studying the map.

"Munitions?" he asked curtly.

If it's a picture you want, you bastard, Lund thought, I'll paint you one! Aloud he said:

"Yes, sir. *All* kinds . . ."

The general looked at him with a slightly raised eyebrow. Lund went on:

". . . including V-2 missiles capable of carrying heavier explosive loads than the ones they used on London."

He looked directly at the general, speaking with studied candor:

"In fact, sir, the intelligence chief of the Seventh Army reports that several supply trains have been arriving in the Redoubt Area every week since February, and some of them have been reported to be carrying a new type of gun. The report even mentioned an underground factory that's set up to produce Messerschmitts!"

Despite himself the general looked impressed.

"Patch's G-2 boys said that?" he asked incredulously.

"Yes, sir. Lieutenant General Alexander Patch's intelligence chief, sir."

"I'll be damned!"

"Yes, sir."

The general shot Lund a quick glance. Was that little prick putting him on? Lund quickly continued:

"I mean, sir—both General Marshall and General Bradley are extremely concerned, sir."

The general grunted. It was true enough. The wires to his CP had been burning up with messages. He looked at the map again. I'll be double-damned, he thought. If the Nazis did get a real foothold in that bitch of a place, they *could* hold out for years.

"What's the estimated capacity of the Redoubt area?" he asked.

"About three hundred thousand troops, sir. At this time."

For a moment the general was silent. Then he looked at Major Lund.

"Thank you for your briefing, Major. It was most—helpful."

He turned on his heel and, followed by his two colonels, left the room.

Don grinned at Major Lund.

"Who's your friend?" he asked.

Lund was cooling off. "Some division CO too big for his britches, and not big enough for his star," he said.

"So you had your fun with the poor bastard." Don nodded toward the Redoubt map. "What about that stuff? Anything to it?"

Lund grinned.

"I only paint pictures, boys." He didn't quite manage to keep a little bitterness from showing.

One of the intelligence noncoms, who worked in the room, brought him a cup of coffee. It was just what he needed. He gave the soldier a grateful nod.

"We're going back up. Anything special?" Don asked.

Lund was sipping his coffee. It was hot.

"SOP," he said. "You can take the local poop off the Enemy Situation."

Erik had picked up one of the mimeoed intelligence reports from the desk. He held it up.

"Is that the full report on the Redoubt?" he asked.

Lund, sipping his coffee, nodded.

"Never had a chance to read it."

Erik scanned the report. He became interested. Suddenly he looked up.

"Listen, Don," he said. "Listen to this! Here's a real picture of doom. It's from the March 11 SHAEF Intelligence Summary." He began to read:

". . . defended by nature and by the most efficient secret weapons yet invented, the powers that have hitherto guided Germany will survive to reorganize her resurrection. . . . A specially selected corps of young men will be trained in guerrilla warfare, so that a whole underground army can be fitted and directed to liberate Germany from the occupying forces."

Don shook his head slowly.

"Sounds more like a page from a Nazi mythology than an intelligence report!"

Major Lund put down his empty cup.

"Bradley and SHAEF don't agree with you."

"Could happen!"

"There's been a little change since you were here last. Our main effort now is to split Germany in two by driving through the center —prevent their forces from consolidating in the Redoubt. And to pull it off, orders have just come down from SHAEF diverting more than half our forces."

"Looks like we're going to have quite a race," Erik observed. "Can we cut them in half before they can get set in their Alpine Fortress?"

Don brightened. "Hey!" he said. "I'd like to place a small bet on that race, sir! Where's the two dollar window?"

Major Lund grinned. Then he grew sober.

"Save your money, Don," he said. "It's still anybody's race."

He turned and walked slowly to the big wall map of the Reported Redoubt Area.

"But I'll tell you this. A hulluva lot of men on both sides will be dead or wounded by the time you'd be ready to collect your bet. The whole damned campaign has been changed. Our prime target has been changed. We're going for the Alpine Fortress—*not* Berlin!"

Berlin

2207 hrs

All around the outskirts of Berlin the night sky was tinged with a blood-red glow, and the distant, deep-throated booming of heavy artillery washed in waves over the battered city.

At exactly 0400 hrs that morning the eastern front at the approaches to the capital had exploded into an earth-trembling roar as, in the same instant, Marshal Georgi Zhukov's twenty thousand guns fired their high explosive shells into the Nazi defenses.

The battle of Berlin had begun. The final guns were thundering the *Götterdämmerung*. . . .

Potsdamerstrasse, leading to Potsdamer Platz and on to the Chancellery, had been heavily damaged in the American and British air raids. The buildings lining the street had been gutted. Walls enclosing emptiness stood like beat-up sets on some gigantic studio back lot. The street itself was littered with rubble. On the corner of the square the ruins had been cordoned off and skull-and-crossbones signs proclaimed: ACHTUNG! MINEN! There were many unexploded bombs cuddling their unleashed death in the wreckage. Water from broken mains gurgled in muddy bomb craters and ran sluggishly through the littered gutters. Fire still smoldered and smoked among the ruins, wherever anything remained that could still burn.

A path had been cleared down the middle of the street, but Stabsgefreiter Werner still had trouble guiding his motorcycle between the blocks of shattered masonry and torn pavement. His left shoulder hurt. It never had healed quite the way it should. He was doing all right, though. It was only a few blocks to the Chancellery and the Führer Bunker.

Stabsgefreiter Stefan Werner had been a Wehrmacht motorcycle courier in Berlin for over a year now. He used to consider himself lucky. He was. He still remembered vividly how it had been. He had been wounded at Stalingrad on January 19 two years before. He still had cold-sweat nightmares about it. . . .

He, and two of his comrades, had manned a machine gun. Their position was set up in the wreckage of a devastated building. A Russian artillery shell had landed in the ruins and a wall had collapsed on their position. His two comrades were killed. Werner was half buried and knocked unconscious. When he came to, Russian soldiers were picking their way through the rubble. He buried his face in the brick chips. He lay dead still. He knew the Russians were taking no prisoners at Stalingrad. He felt the soldier come up to him. He felt him stop and look down at him. He could smell him. He tried not to breathe. Fear crawled like an icy spider along his spine. And then he felt the searing hot lance of pain, as the Russian jabbed his bayonet into his back. He nearly bit his lip in two, trying to keep from moving or crying out. Then once again he lost consciousness.

He was lucky. His heavy overcoat and his shoulder blade deflected the bayonet just enough. His blood froze over the open wound, keeping him from bleeding to death. And when he regained consciousness, he was on a *lazarett* train, going home. . . .

The street looked blocked ahead, and Werner cut across the Potsdamer Square and over to Wilhelmstrasse. Ahead he could see the ravaged, fire-blackened Chancellery buildings.

Suddenly two shots rang out in front of him. A lone man came running down the dark street, his long, field-gray army coat flapping around his ankles. Behind him two uniformed figures pressed in pursuit, their metal breast shields clanging as they ran. Military police.

Again a shot rang out, as the fleeing man ducked behind the burned-out bulk of a Wehrmacht truck. One of the MPs shouted after him.

"Halt!"

Werner pulled up to get out of the line of fire. Deserter, he thought. Or looter. He felt sorry for the running man. He knew what would happen to him if he was caught alive.

Another shot. It clanged off the metal truck body. The man suddenly leaped from his hiding place and raced down the street. Quickly one of the MPs brought up a submachine gun and fired a burst of bullets after the fleeing man. He fell to the ground, screaming. At the same time Werner felt a sharp blow on his left arm. Surprised, he looked down. It was dark and he could see nothing. His arm felt numb. He removed his heavy leather glove and touched the spot. His fingers came away sticky with blood.

Damn! he thought savagely. Ricochet! Of all the goddamned, stinking luck!

The wound suddenly began to burn with pain. He flexed his fingers and gingerly moved the arm. It was only a flesh wound, but it hurt like hell.

Out on the street the MPs had reached the man lying in the gutter. They tried to stand him up. He screamed. Both his ankles had been broken by the submachine gun bullets. The MPs took hold of his arms and dragged him toward a lamppost standing starkly alone in the desolation. . . .

Werner dismounted. He checked his courier pouch and started on foot for the Chancellery.

The two SS men standing guard in the shelter of the shrapnel-scarred Chancellery archway barred the way. Werner stopped. He was holding his left arm to keep the pain at a minimum when he moved.

"*Papiere herzeigen!*" one of the guards demanded curtly.

"Urgent dispatch. Generalfeldmarschall Keitel," Werner said, as he handed the SS man his orders.

The guard examined the papers by the light of a flashlight. Werner's arm dripped a few drops of blood at his feet.

The SS man returned the papers. He motioned Werner into the darkened passage.

"*In Ordnung.*"

Werner hurried on. He knew the way. He'd brought other dispatches to the Führer Bunker before. He knew the harsh, rigid security followed by the SS.

He emerged from the Chancellery ruins into the gardens and made straight for the massive windowless blockhouse with the single heavy steel door leading to the Führer Bunker deep underground. From above, black, empty holes in soot-stained walls, where the windows used to be, stared down at him and the desolate gardens below, like huge, gaping sockets robbed of their eyes. The once beautiful grounds around him were ruthlessly destroyed; bomb craters, chunks of concrete, broken columns and smashed statuary lay scattered among uprooted trees. An abandoned cement mixer squatted next to the concrete blockhouse, its bowels crusted, its usefulness long since past.

Werner's orders were checked again at the blockhouse bunker entrance, and he started down the long, narrow flights of stairs as the steel door clanged shut behind him. His arm throbbed and ached. He supported it as best he could.

In the brightly lit concrete-walled corridor at the bottom of the steps two grim-looking SS men, armed with Schmeisser machine pistols, gruffly halted him.

It's crazy, he thought. I guess they don't trust anybody after that assassination business. Automatically he said:

"Urgent dispatch. Generalfeldmarschall Keitel."

"Stay where you are," one of the SS guards ordered curtly. He stepped up to the courier.

"Your dispatch pouch!"

Werner handed it over.

While the other guard covered him, the SS man examined the case. Werner stood patiently, holding his wounded arm. The pain was getting worse. He tried his best not to drip any blood on the floor.

The SS man turned to him. He motioned with his gun.

"Get them up!"

Werner stared at him. He started to speak in protest.

"Move!" snapped the guard.

Werner raised his right arm. The two SS guards glared at him dispassionately. What the hell, he thought angrily. Do they think I've come to blow up the place? Do they think the damned hole in my arm hides a gun? The devil take them! Biting down the pain, he managed to lift his injured left arm. He could feel the warm blood run down his armpit inside his clothing. He looked straight ahead. He'd be damned if he'd give those SS bastards the satisfaction of seeing him suffer.

The guards searched him—roughly, thoroughly.

From the bunker area beyond, an SS captain entered the reception corridor. With a glance he took in the scene. The SS men came to attention. Werner didn't move. The officer turned to one of the guards.

"What is it?"

"Courier with a dispatch for Generalfeldmarschall Keitel, Herr Hauptsturmführer," the guard answered at once.

The SS officer glanced at Werner. Then he looked questioningly at the SS men.

"All in order, Herr Hauptsturmführer."

The officer motioned to Werner.

"Come with me."

Werner took his hands down. His left arm felt like a balloon swollen with agony. The SS man threw the pouch to him and he hurried after the officer.

Colonel Hans Heinrich Stauffer had a throbbing headache. It had been a long day. An impossible day. And it wasn't over yet. He looked up from the papers on his desk, as the SS captain, followed by Stabsgefreiter Stefan Werner, entered the office. He felt a twinge of distaste when he saw the SS officer. The SS were getting more officious, more impossible every day. The man had simply barged right in!

The SS captain raised his arm in the Nazi salute.

"Heil Hitler!"

Stauffer deliberately turned back to his papers. He did not return the salute. Without looking up, he said acidly:

"Come in, Captain. I did not hear you knock. What is it?"

The SS officer's face grew tight. His voice grated as he said:

"Courier with an urgent dispatch for Generalfeldmarschall Keitel, Herr Oberst!"

Stauffer looked up. He held out his hand. Werner quickly took a large sealed envelope from his pouch; he stepped up to Stauffer and handed the document to him. He let his left arm hang at his side. The blood was again running down his wrist. He cupped his hand, trying to catch it, before it dripped on the carpeted floor.

Stauffer took the dispatch. He noticed Werner's bleeding arm. He felt a shock of annoyance. He fixed the SS captain with a cold stare. The man must have seen it before. He must have known. And he'd done exactly nothing. Stauffer felt a surge of disgust. Brutish beasts, all of them! His voice was icy when he spoke.

"This man is wounded. He is bleeding. I presume you have noticed? I want him taken care of. At once! I'll expect your personal report on his condition within the hour!"

Tight-lipped, the SS officer gave a curt nod.

"As the colonel wishes."

Stauffer looked at the dispatch in his hand.

"That's all."

Again the SS captain gave the Nazi salute—pointedly:

"Heil Hitler!"

Stauffer ignored him. The officer turned on his heel and stalked from the office. Werner followed him quickly. He tried to be as inconspicuous as possible. He didn't at all relish being in the middle. But his arm did hurt like hell. . . .

Stauffer tore open the envelope. Quickly he read the message. His face clouded.

Damn! he thought bitterly. They bungled it. His headache was suddenly much worse. *He'll be furious.* . . .

Field Marshal Keitel marched stiffly up and down his office. He slapped the dispatch angrily into the open palm of his hand. His face was pinched with frustration and acrimony.

"Imbeciles! Incompetents!"

Stauffer longed for a headache powder. He tried to think where he could find one. He said:

"Herr Feldmarschall. It's a very efficient, very reliable group. . . ."

Keitel whirled on him.

"Reliable! They're lucky if the Führer doesn't have them shot!"

"It was the same group that was responsible for the time bombs at Saint Avold, Herr Feldmarschall, last December. . . ."

Keitel held up a hand in dismissal. Stauffer pretended not to see it. He went on:

"There were sixty-nine casualties. Many high-ranking American officers. Even more important, it forced the enemy to change his occupation procedures entirely. A whole new security system had to be worked out before they dared take over any building. It caused a great deal of confusion. The Führer ordered the group leader decorated."

Keitel was silent. Stauffer added quietly:

"There was very little time to prepare this mission."

"That's no excuse!"

"It was a matter of last-minute change of plans. On the Americans' part. Eisenhower didn't go to Feldstein himself. He sent someone else. They could not possibly have known. . . ."

"So all they got were a few cans of gasoline and some obscure officers," Keitel said caustically. "The Führer will be delighted at the way his orders were carried out!"

Stauffer said nothing.

Keitel went to the situation map on the wall. He stared at it without actually seeing it. He was deeply troubled. He had never doubted his Führer, but with profound shock he realized that he found it impossible to share his belief that the tide could be turned at this late hour and the war won from Berlin. He felt it imperative that Hitler abandon the capital and go south to the Alpine stronghold, to Obersalzberg above the village of Berchtesgaden. The fight could continue from the mountain positions there. From there defeat might be turned into victory.

He scowled in an earnest attempt to find a proper perspective. Sometimes events happened too fast for him. And without order. Above all without order. It was impossible to make anything work smoothly without order. He felt irritated. He hated to have plans changed, once they were decided upon. And everything had been arranged.

Already a week ago the Führer had sent his personal household servants to Berghof to prepare the mountain retreat for his arrival. The Führer planned to follow on the twentieth of April. On his fifty-sixth birthday. But now there were more and more indications that he might stay in Berlin and lead the defense of the city himself.

The situation was developing rapidly. Keitel frowned. He only hoped not too rapidly. Hitler's presence in the *Alpenfestung* was imperative. His personal leadership was essential. If only the Führer would not wait too long. Everything was ready to be activated. Everything.

Keitel's frown deepened. How could he tell the Führer of the failure? The first attempt to carry out his orders! The whole thing made him uneasy. He had a nagging suspicion that the Führer placed too great an importance on nonmilitary matters. On the advice of mystics and astrologers. On special missions like the assassination scheme. On promises of new superweapons, like those abortive experiments with nuclear chain reaction the scientists were conducting at Haigerloch. They'd actually told the Führer they could make a bomb the size of a pineapple that could wipe out an entire city! Bah! Puttering around in their caves in the Black Forest. More like black magic! And just as unmilitary and implausible. It was a disturbing suspicion to Keitel, and he did not allow it to grow beyond just that.

He felt resentful, however, at finding himself involved in the assassination plot. Not for any moral reasons. And the idea did have a certain merit.

The Führer had been obsessed with the assassination of enemy leaders, both political and military, ever since the failure of "Operation Long Jump," that abortive assassination attempt at the Big Three meeting in Teheran in the winter of '43. This time he felt certain failure would not be tolerated. It had become too personal a matter for the Führer. After all, he had been a target himself! At Rastenburg.

But Keitel anticipated a lot of difficulties. A lot of negative reports would have to be given Hitler. And he didn't like that. He had enough to contend with. Anyway, it was not the kind of responsibility *he* should have to shoulder. It was the kind of thing that should be supervised by someone else.

Someone else? Of course!

He had the answer. And it could be made part of the greater plan. That was the beauty of it! He turned to Stauffer.

"Where's Krueger?" he asked. "What is his status now?"

"At Thürenberg." Stauffer joined Keitel at the map. Good for you, Willi! he thought with cynical amusement. I knew you'd find a way to dodge the blame!

Keitel continued. Once more he sounded like his old stiff self.

"Krueger is the one to carry out the Führer's orders. It is to be *his* responsibility. Part of *his* overall mission. I want orders prepared at once."

"Yes, sir."

Keitel was pleased with the solution. Simple. Logical.

"What's he doing now?"

"He's already received his orders to close down Thürenberg. Go operational. Orders from Reichsführer Himmler."

"When?"

"Two days ago. His positions are being prepared now."

"Where?"

Stauffer indicated the locations on the map, all in southern Bavaria.

"Here . . . here . . . here . . . Headquarters near Schönsee—here— close to his ultimate position in the *Alpenfestung*."

"*Prima!* His new orders will have top priority. He is to carry out his mission without delay. The Führer wants results!"

"*Jawohl*, Herr Feldmarschall," Stauffer said. The old man was back in form again.

The field marshal contemplated the situation map.

"The Russians are battering the gates of Berlin. The Americans are still pressing on." Almost to himself he added, "We *must* carry on the fight—from the Alpine Fortress. . . ,"

Stauffer turned to leave.

"Wait!"

He stopped. He looked expectantly at Keitel.

"Krueger is only a colonel, is he not?"

"Yes."

"Promote him. Make him a general. Generalmajor. In the name of the Führer!"

He paused for a moment.

"One more thing. Reichsamtsleiter von Eckdorf. He is still in Berlin?"

"I believe so, Herr Feldmarschall."

"He has family in the area around Schönsee. Farmers, if I remember correctly." He sighed. "Send him to Thürenberg. Make the orders effective immediately. I want him to report directly to me. He will be responsible only to me—and to the Führer personally!"

"Yes, sir."

Stauffer left. Keitel looked after him. He felt somehow delivered of a depressing burden. With the Führer's plan carried out, and the Americans badly shaken; with Krueger and his backbone organization in position; with the *Alpenfestung* ready to become operational under Hitler's personal leadership, the German phoenix might still rise from the ashes of temporary defeat. . . .

17 Apr 1945

Thürenberg

1322 hrs

Werewolves! he thought disdainfully. For the fiftieth time he shifted his weight on the back seat of the gray 1939 sedan.

Reichsamtsleiter Manfred von Eckdorf was extremely uncomfortable. And extremely disgruntled. It was close to three hundred kilometers from Berlin to the Czechoslovakian village of Thürenberg and the old Germanic castle of the same name. Three hundred kilometers. Three hundred thousand meters—and a hole in the road every damned meter of the way!

Von Eckdorf was in a sour mood. He'd been on the road more than seven hours. They'd awakened him in the early morning hours and taken him to the Führer Bunker. Here an insufferable Wehrmacht colonel had handed him top priority orders sending him off to a Godforsaken place in Czechoslovakia with less than two hours' warning.

The briefing by the colonel had been short and to the point, but von Eckdorf had a disquieting feeling of veiled mockery in the officer's attitude. And the whole thing wasn't at all what he'd expected. He'd come up to Berlin from Munich to report to the Führer on the financial state of Bavaria. In a gesture that was simply meant to show his loyalty, he'd offered his services to Adolf Hitler, in any capacity. But he certainly hadn't counted on this! Riding herd on a flock of Werewolves!

The car hit another bump in the road and von Eckdorf was thrown forward. Angrily he caught himself.

Before his briefing earlier he had known only a little about the

Werewolves. He'd always mistrusted the word. He was under the impression it was something thought up by that little "poison dwarf," Goebbels. He had been genuinely surprised to learn that the Werewolves, complete with mission and name, had been created by the Reichsführer SS, Heinrich Himmler, himself, quite some time ago, and with Hitler's full approval. Of course, the Führer had always had a penchant for that word, "wolf." In the early days of the National Socialist movement he'd used "wolf" as a cover name. And it seemed that ever since he'd seized every opportunity to use this savage symbol. His headquarters at Rastenburg in East Prussia had been named *Wolfsschanze*—Wolf's Lair. Somewhere else, he'd forgotten where, it had been *Wolfsschlucht*—Wolf's Throat; at Vinnitsa in the Ukraine, *Werwolf*. And now these Werewolves. They were supposed to be highly trained, specially equipped guerrilla fighters, operating under top secret orders. They were supposed to form the backbone of the resistance forces in the *Alpenfestung*.

His briefing had really been quite inadequate, he thought resentfully. He knew little more now than he had before. He was supposed to inspect the organization headquarters, under the command of some newly promoted Generalmajor Krueger, and make sure the Werewolves were ready to start operations as soon as possible. As a high-ranking civilian party member he was supposed to observe the subsequent Werewolf activities and report on them. The Werewolves had some vital, top secret mission to carry out within the next few days. Then they would take up their position in the *Alpenfestung*, and von Eckdorf's responsibilities would end.

It was all ridiculously mysterious. But von Eckdorf was an economics expert. Everything with which he concerned himself had ultimately to add up. Everything had to be mathematically precise and correct.

This would be no different.

The driver turned off the road. In the hills ahead loomed the old Thürenberg Castle.

Spring had already begun to splash the mountain slopes with

fresh pale greens. The groves of darker-colored evergreens contrasted sedately with the light exuberance of new growth. Built long ago with massive blocks of weathered stone native to the mountains themselves, the unpretentious castle, rising with solid grace from the rock, seemed to be part of the countryside. It was a scene of peace and beauty.

The approach to the castle led under a heavy stone archway between two square guard towers. In the portal a barricade had been placed across the road.

The car was flagged to a halt. Two armed Waffen SS soldiers examined von Eckdorf's orders under the watchful observation of other armed guards at the barricade. The boom was raised and the car was waved on.

The courtyard of Burg Thürenberg was surprisingly large and entirely surrounded by the castle buildings and a high stone wall. Opposite the portal a broad, imposing flight of stairs led to the main entrance to the castle itself. The place had a decidedly medieval atmosphere—much in keeping with the werewolf tradition, von Eckdorf thought wryly. The car slowly made its way across the courtyard toward the massive stairs. Von Eckdorf leaned forward and in astonishment looked out the window. He had expected nothing like the spectacle before him.

The sprawling, cobblestoned courtyard was the scene of brisk, organized confusion. A large number of horse-drawn wagons and carts of all descriptions were pulled up in several rows. Von Eckdorf made a quick calculation. At least sixty. A small fleet of motor vehicles, both military and civilian, were parked along one wall, including an old truck converted into a wood burner. Two men— one a civilian clad in short Bavarian lederhosen and wearing a gray wool jacket embroidered with a green oak leaf design, the other a Waffen SS Rottenführer—were loading wood logs into the truck's storage bin.

Nearby four men were struggling a heavy mortar onto a cart. A wagon next to it was being loaded with cooking pans, with pots, kettles, boxes of utensils. Several Wehrmacht soldiers were stowing machine guns on a truck; others were piling up ammunition boxes. Throughout the courtyard, around the wagons, carts and motor vehicles, men were swarming, fully half of them in their teens. Stacks of supplies and equipment of all kinds were scattered among the rolling stock. Crated small arms, mortars, MGs; ration boxes and barrels of provisions; cans of gasoline; hampers filled with clothing; furniture and crated office equipment. One wagon was already piled high with batteries; another held tools, rolls of wire, cut lumber.

The men beside a truck set off from the rest showed extra care in loading a stack of crates. Each one bore a warning in large red letters. HIGH EXPLOSIVES.

Von Eckdorf took it all in. In his amazement his mind turned for comfort to a cliché. Like ants, he thought. Like scurrying ants in a suddenly exposed anthill. Only they weren't like ants at all. There was no uniformity. There were Wehrmacht soldiers, Waffen SS, Hitler Jugend, civilians, indiscriminately mixed together, even men wearing only parts of uniforms.

A disgraceful conglomeration, von Eckdorf thought. His orderly mind was offended at the complete lack of military conformity and the obviously haphazard discipline.

The sedan came to a halt before the stairs. Waffen SS Lieutenant Willi Richter hurried down the steps and opened the car door for Reichsamtsleiter Manfred von Eckdorf.

The Nazi party official was a smallish, wiry man of about fifty-five. He wore conservative civilian clothes. Smartly Willi raised his right arm.

"Heil Hitler!"

Von Eckdorf returned the young officer's salute. His face had a pinched, arrogant look.

"Welcome to Thürenberg, Herr Reichsamtsleiter," Willi said.

Von Eckdorf didn't answer. He turned and with deliberate displeasure surveyed the kaleidoscope of activity in the courtyard before him.

"Colonel Krueger is expecting you, sir."

Abruptly von Eckdorf started up the steps, immediately followed by Willi. At the big solid double doors they had to stand aside for two men carrying a Wehrmacht field communications console. With a last petulantly disapproving look down into the bustling courtyard, von Eckdorf entered Burg Thürenberg.

The massive, ornately carved desk was fully eight feet long. It obviously belonged in the big room with the inlaid wood panels, beamed ceiling and lead-paned windows set in the four-foot-thick stone walls. Not so the purely functional steel filing cabinets which lined one wall—most of them with their drawers protruding, slack-jawed and empty. Several men were busily emptying the rest, selecting and transferring papers and documents to various boxes; others closed and sealed the boxes and carried them away.

At the big desk, sorting through stacks of papers, stood an officer in the uniform of a Wehrmacht colonel. It was Colonel Karl Krueger. He looked up as Willi and von Eckdorf entered.

"Reichsamtsleiter von Eckdorf, Herr Oberst," Willi announced formally.

Von Eckdorf gave the Nazi salute:

"Heil Hitler!"

Krueger walked around the desk to his visitor. He was a slender man, graying already at the age of fifty-one. He carried himself erect, but without the Prussian ramrod stiffness. His long face, dominated by penetrating, intelligent eyes under bushy eyebrows, was etched with deep nose lines and with determined furrows at the corners of a thin-lipped mouth. There was no warmth in his expression as he regarded von Eckdorf, rather a deliberate politeness prompted by necessity.

"Heil Hitler!" he said without demonstrative enthusiasm. "Or, as we shall soon be saying, *Grüss Gott!*"

Von Eckdorf inspected the officer. His petulant mouth set in distaste. No wonder, he thought primly. No wonder there's no order around here. An *officer*, greeting you with a Bavarian peasant greeting!

"Generalfeldmarschall Keitel sends you his regards," he said. His voice was unpleasantly high-pitched.

Krueger nodded. "Thank you. You must excuse the appearance of our quarters. We aren't prepared to receive guests."

Von Eckdorf drew himself up. "I'm not a *guest*, Colonel Krueger," he said testily. "I am an emissary from Feldmarschall Keitel. I have brought you your orders. The Feldmarschall is most eager that you start operations as soon as possible." The little man bristled with indignation.

Touchy little twerp, Krueger thought.

"Of course," he said.

Von Eckdorf glanced pointedly at the men working at the files. "I am a little—taken aback"—he tasted the words delicately—"at the state of affairs around here, Colonel. I should have thought you'd have been ready—actually moved before now."

Krueger shot him a quick glance. So that's the game we're going to play, he thought. The big shot, come to throw his weight around. Not in my command!

"It would have been inadvisable, Herr Reichsamtsleiter," he said. He did not elaborate. Let the little bastard ask, he thought.

Von Eckdorf fixed him with an imperiously inquiring look.

"Well?" he asked irritably.

"Our prepared position would not have been ready for us," he said simply. "I'm sure you are aware of that."

Willi was watching the two men. He was fascinated. He recognized the juggling for superiority that was going on. A superiority claimed by von Eckdorf by virtue of having it bestowed upon him, but in reality belonging to Colonel Krueger simply because he already had it.

Von Eckdorf's face looked pinched. His voice was becoming even sharper.

"You have been informed, I believe, that I am to act as the Führer's personal representative?"

"I have."

"Good. I shall be staying in a village quite close to your headquarters area."

"I see."

"I shall, of course, expect to be fully informed of all your activities, once you go operational."

"Of course."

"And when will that be, Colonel?" Von Eckdorf's voice carried more than a hint of sarcasm. He felt on top of the situation again. "Things still seem to be—well, in quite a state of disarray."

Krueger regarded the little man. That's all I need, he thought with annoyance. To be saddled with an insufferable, self-important little prig like that! He gave him a look of studied astonishment.

"On the exact date planned, of course, Herr von Eckdorf," he said deliberately. "I presume you know it?"

Von Eckdorf colored. He hadn't asked to be sent here. But he certainly wasn't going to put up with any impertinence!

He was about to give a sharp retort, when Krueger turned from him and motioned to an orderly, who had just entered the room. The man hurried over.

He was about thirty-five, with a ruddy complexion and large, guileless, water-blue eyes. He carried an armful of clothing—a pair of gray forester's knee britches, heavy woolen socks, a coarse green shirt and a gray Bavarian jacket with carved bone buttons. Krueger inspected the clothing idly as he continued to talk to von Eckdorf. There was an undisguised suggestion of dismissal in his voice.

"The first units leave tonight. The rest, including myself and my staff, tomorrow."

Von Eckdorf searched frantically for something significant to say. He felt his importance, his authority slipping away from him.

"We shall be in position the day after, Herr Reichsamtsleiter—as planned," Kreuger finished.

"Good," von Eckdorf said curtly. "I should like, however, to inspect the state of your readiness myself." It was the best he could do.

Krueger looked at him with a small, slightly mocking smile.

"Of course," he said with condescending amiability. "Untersturmführer Richter is at your disposal."

He took the Bavarian jacket from the arms of the orderly.

"You will excuse me." It was a statement, not a request. "I'm about to change into my new—uniform."

He turned to the orderly.

"*Schon gut*, Plewig." he said. "Let's get on with it."

Von Eckdorf glared at him. Then he turned on his heel and stalked off, followed by Willi. Suddenly he stopped. He removed an envelope from his inside coat pocket. He turned back to Krueger and handed it to him.

"Yes. One more thing," he said coldly. "The Führer sends you his congratulations, Generalmajor Krueger!"

Without waiting for comment, he turned and walked from the room.

Krueger looked after the little man. He was faintly amused. Small man in a big job, he thought. Inevitable result—officiousness! He looked at the envelope in his hand. It bore the official Nazi emblem embossed on it—the proud eagle holding a swastika in a wreath of oak leaves. He threw the envelope on the big desk without opening it. He sighed. Thoughtfully he fingered the coarse, heavy fabric of the gray Bavarian peasant jacket. . . .

Von Eckdorf was still smarting from Krueger's insolence. He was scowling, tight-lipped, as he marched down the broad corridor. Soldiers and civilians were streaming back and forth in an unceasing flow of activity. The Werewolf school was closing down, preparing to go underground. Von Eckdorf slowly relaxed. That's why he was here, after all. To observe. To calculate and evaluate. And to report. And that's exactly what he would do. Accurately. Systematically. And with orderly precision. He felt better. He was on familiar ground.

The two men passed a doorway. Both the heavy carved oak doors stood wide open. Von Eckdorf glanced inside. It was the great hall of arms. An expanse of carved oak paneling; long, narrow, deep-set windows; two rows of old, colorful banners heavy with dust hanging under the opulently painted ceiling; a huge rectangular area of a lighter color on one stone wall, where once a priceless tapestry must have hung. The hall was empty, except for two men burning papers and documents at a blazing fire in a huge walk-in fireplace at the far end.

Von Eckdorf strode into the hall and walked to the fireplace. Willi followed. He said nothing. He'd decided to keep quiet until the Reichsamtsleiter spoke to him. Then play it by ear.

One of the men at the fireplace took a large sheet of cardboard from a pile on the floor. He bent it in half and threw it on the fire. He reached for another. Von Eckdorf held out his hand.

"Let me see it," he ordered.

The man glanced quickly at Willi. Willi nodded. The man handed the cardboard to Von Eckdorf.

"Bitte."

Von Eckdorf turned it over. There were words printed on it:

RISE	ROSE	RISEN
RUN	RAN	RUN
SAY	SAID	SAID
SEE	SAW	SEEN
SEEK	SOUGHT	SOUGHT
SELL	SOLD	SOLD
SEND	SENT	SENT
SET	SET	SET
SHAKE	SHOOK	SHAKEN
SHALL	SHOULD	SHOULD
SHED	SHED	SHED
SHINE	SHONE	SHONE
SHOOT	SHOT	SHOT
SHOW	SHOWED	SHOWN
SHRINK	SHRANK	SHRUNK
SHUT	SHUT	SHUT
SING	SANG	SUNG
SINK	SANK	SUNK
SIT	SAT	SAT
SLAY	SLEW	SLAIN

He looked questioningly at Willi.

"What is this?" he asked.

"It's from our classes in English, Herr Reichsamtsleiter," Willi explained. "A lesson in grammar. The members of our intelligence group speak excellent English."

"So."

Von Eckdorf threw the chart aside. With his foot he spread apart the others in the pile on the floor. He cocked his head to study a particularly colorful one. It showed the insignia of U.S. Army noncoms and officers with the corresponding ranks written in English and German. He was pleased. He approved of the charts. Orderly. He marched from the hall.

The two men reentered the corridor. A group of young girls walked past. Every one was pretty, with the natural, healthy, shiningly clean look of the German girl. They were all dressed in attractive dirndl dresses with provocative necklines, and they all carried a small piece of civilian luggage. Von Eckdorf and Willi watched them go by. Despite their charm and femininity they moved with precise military bearing.

Von Eckdorf looked inquiringly at Willi.

"They're trained office workers, Herr von Eckdorf—in English. We expect they will work in American military government offices." Willi grinned. "And they'll make good girl friends for the Amis!"

"I see.'"

Von Eckdorf frowned. He did not entirely agree with that sort of thing. Sacrifices had to be made, of course, but was it quite necessary to—to defile German womanhood in that way?

Willi pointed to a bulletin board on the wall.

"There's a list of the courses in English office work, Herr Reichsamtsleiter," he said. "It might give you an idea of what we've been doing along those lines."

Von Eckdorf turned to the bulletin board. The courses seemed well planned. Complete. He studied the list.

Willi stared after the girls disappearing down the crowded corridor. Even from behind they made an appealing sight. Especially the little blonde, who always looked at him with such brazen appraisal.

Gerti, he thought. Gerti Meissner. That's who she looks like. The

same round little ass moving so deliciously under the skirt. What
was it? Two years ago? Almost. He'd still be in officers' school.

He wondered about Gerti. And his son. He was sure it was a son.
He didn't often think back to Bodenheim. He never had made
up his mind about it—whether to be proud of it or regret it. He let
his thoughts drift back. . . .

Willi was uneasy when his commanding officer at the officers'
training school summoned him to his office. He stood stiffly at attention. The CO had his service records on the desk before him. He
was pleased with them, he said. Willi Richter was just the sort of
young German the Third Reich wanted. Man to man he confided
in Willi. They'd investigated his personal background thoroughly;
his ancestry—all the way back to the eighteenth century, he told
him; his entire medical history. They'd made certain he was of
healthy, pure Aryan stock. And then he put the question to him.
Would he like to volunteer to spend two weeks at Bodenheim?

It was quite a shock to Willi. Actually to be asked! He was excited.
He knew about places like Bodenheim. They used to kid about
them in the barracks. Stud farms, some of the men called them.
There were several of them scattered through Germany, usually
hidden away in the most secluded and beautiful surroundings.
Bodenheim in the Schwäbische Alb near Stuttgart was such a place.
A *Lebensborn* establishment—"Source of Life."

Willi's CO gave him the whole story. The Third Reich had long
realized the vital necessity of keeping the German race pure. If
you mated a brood mare of pure stock with a pure-blooded stallion
the issue would be thoroughbred. It had something to do with
chromosomes and things like that, which carried the hereditary
traits, he explained. Germany needed such "thoroughbreds." Perfect German children produced by two racially pure human beings
of unmixed Aryan blood. A new race—the first generation of pure
Aryans, pure Nazis—created in the womb for the Fatherland! In
the *Lebensborn* the Führer made it possible. Here young German
girls selected for their perfect Nordic traits were made available for

young men of equally pure Aryan stock. There were no responsibilities. No obligations. The resulting offspring belonged to the
Third Reich!

Willi felt vaguely disturbed by the clinical explanations and
analogies, but his discomfort was easily swamped by his pride in
having been selected. And the excitement. It was like a dream
come true. Two weeks of bed calisthenics! he thought with enthusiastic anticipation. And at the state's expense!

By the time Willi reached Bodenheim some of his high excitement
had turned to apprehension. He wondered what he'd let himself in
for.

Bodenheim was nestled in a wooded valley in the mountains. It
was apparently a small village that had been taken over entirely
by the *Lebensborn*. There was much new construction among the
old houses. The headquarters of the establishment was in the
former guest lodge, the only large building.

Willi felt the cold, impersonal atmosphere of the place. It clamped
a further damper on his waning enthusiasm. A sharp-faced, indifferent woman in the uniform of a BDM noncom took his orders and
filled out his card. Apparently the place was run by the Bund
Deutscher Mädel—the female counterpart of the Hitler Youth.
Probably most of the girls were BDM. He looked around curiously.
He hadn't seen any of his future bedmates yet.

He was assigned to a room in a little house close to the lodge.
He'd stay there two weeks. It would be the scene of all his activities.

And then once more the inevitable medical examination.

When the doctor, an SS Stabsarzt, was finished with him, he was
turned over to a hospital orderly, a coarse, disagreeable fellow with
an unpleasant, perpetual smirk. Maybe he's jealous because he's
not getting any, Willi thought with amusement. It would be a hell
of a thing in a place of plenty like this! The man took a blood
sample and a urine specimen from him for analysis.

Blood and urine, Willi thought. Blood and urine—the measures
of a man!

Then the orderly handed him a little beaker already labeled with his name.

"Here," he said "Give me a specimen of your semen."

Semen? Willi looked at the man, perplexed. Suddenly understanding flooded him. He felt the blood rising on his neck. Semen! But how? How would he get it? Uncertainly he looked at the orderly.

"Well, you can't piss it out," the man snapped impatiently. "Jerk off!"

Willi stood rooted to the spot. The orderly nodded toward a door.

"In there. It's all yours." He leered at Willi. "There's a couple of girlie magazines in there. Might help!"

Willi walked into the little examination chamber. He closed the door behind him. There was no lock. He sat down. He knew he couldn't do it. Not on command. The whole thing was impossible. He couldn't even get a hard on.

He squirmed on the chair. I've got to try, at least, he thought. He fumbled his pants open. Christ, he thought. No good. All he could think about was that obnoxious orderly right outside.

He saw the magazines lying on a glass-top table. Well, anyway, they've thought of everything, he mused. He picked up a magazine. He started to thumb through it. The pictures were fantastic. Not merely suggestive. Graphic. The women were delectable. Sexy as hell! Willi looked closer. He became interested. To his surprise he suddenly felt the familiar swelling in his groin. He looked down. I'll be damned, he thought.

Tentatively he put his hand down. Gently he stroked. He chose a picture of a voluptuous blonde in a transparent negligee lying invitingly on a sofa, and concentrated on her. After a short while he was actually enjoying himself.

It took him much less time than he'd thought, before he had the specimen in his beaker for the orderly. He looked at it curiously. He held it up to the light. He'd never really examined the stuff before. Millions of perfect little Aryans, he thought wryly. Half of them anyway.

He buttoned himself up. Now that it was all over he felt vaguely ashamed, degraded. It was a hell of a thing to have to do for one's country!

He saw the girl in the social hall at the lodge the next evening. She was standing by herself at the little juice bar sipping a lemonade. She looked very young—and somehow vulnerable. He thought she was lovely. His tests had all been positive—or was it negative? Anyway, he had been instructed to mingle and get acquainted. The quicker and the more intimately the better.

He started over to the bar, making his way through the couples dancing to the gramophone music. There were at least twenty couples on the dance floor; others were sitting around in the comfortable room, talking. The young men were all in uniform. Most of them were SS, but there were uniforms from every branch of the armed forces. The girls wore a variety of attractive dresses.

As Willi neared the bar, a young man in a Luftwaffe uniform stopped and spoke to the girl.

Willi felt a pang of anxiety. Would she go with him? He was surprised at the intensity of his feeling. He hadn't even met the girl yet. But she shook her head, and the Luftwaffe soldier walked away.

Her name was Gerti Meissner. She came from Nürnberg. She was just eighteen.

They were attracted to one another right away. Months of getting acquainted, of dating, of discovering each other seemed to be telescoped into a few hours. Of necessity, of course. But they chose to ignore that.

It was late. Many of the couples had left the hall. Willi and Gerti were dancing. He held the girl close. She was soft and yielding in his arms. It had happened so fast, he thought, but he knew she was the one he wanted. He thought how it would be with her. He dwelt on it. He felt his excitement grow. He held her tightly. He couldn't help himself. His fantasies, the soft girl body pressed against him, controlled him. He felt the swelling, the rising hardness. Suddenly he was frightened. They were so close. She would feel it against her. He pulled away a little, but Gerti moved to him. She held on to him, desperately. He could feel her soft thigh between his legs. He knew she must be aware of his erection. And he strained against her.

She looked up at him. Her eyes were big.

"Willi," she said softly. "You will be the first. Ever."

Hand in hand they walked from the hall. They were crossing the reception foyer, when a strident voice called to them·

"You there! Just a minute!"

It was the sharp-faced BDM noncom. She came up to them. She glared at Willi.

"Are you booking her?" she asked.

Willi felt himself go cold. "Yes."

"Let me see your card," the woman ordered. "Yours, too, girl."

Dumbly they handed her their cards.

"Haven't you read the instructions?" the woman asked irritably. "You can't just walk out of here and hop into bed without going through the proper procedure!" She turned and marched toward her desk. "Come here!"

Automatically Willi and Gerti followed her.

"Your cards have to be stamped." With a flourish she banged an official-looking rubber stamp on each of their cards. Then she quickly wrote in a large brown ledger. "The union has to be recorded." She looked at Gerti. "*She* has to be checked out of the dormitory."

She fixed Willi with a baleful eye.

"You understand, don't you, there's no second choice? Once you book her, she stays with you until you leave."

She shrugged.

"After that—we see. If it took, fine! If not, she goes back to the dormitory."

Gerti was deathly silent. Her hand in Willi's was like ice. He could feel her nails biting into his palm.

The woman handed them their cards, properly stamped.

"*In Ordnung,*" she said.

Willi's entire body felt clammy. *In Ordnung,* he thought. Regulations of Lebensborn Bodenheim complied with!

He suddenly had a quick vision of that funny framed photograph on the mantel in his boyhood home. Mutti in her long white dress; his father with his imposing mustache. Both stiff, and formal, and proud. Mutti's and Vati's absurd wedding picture.

Gerti was tense. With pathetic defiance she made straight for Willi's bed and sat down on it. Wary. Stiff.

"Your card has been stamped," she said tonelessly. "Mine, too." She looked steadily at him. Her eyes were unnaturally bright.

Willi understood. In a rare moment of real insight he understood. He knew the emotional turmoil that must be surging inside the girl. He knew because he felt it, too. Feelings that were never meant to be coupled. Tenderness and shame; desire and disgust; need and debasement.

He said nothing. Quietly he sat down beside her and felt her grow rigid. He didn't touch her.

"I feel sorry for her," he said softly.

Gerti looked up at him in surprise.

"I really do feel sorry for that woman," he continued. "She'll never know."

Gerti regarded him curiously, her attention steered away from herself, from her own humiliation.

"She'll never have what you and I can have together." He stood up. "She'll never know what it can be like." He walked away from the bed. He went to the window and held the curtain aside.

"It's beautiful," he said. "The way the moonlight shines through the evergreens like that. Come look."

For a moment there was silence. Then he heard the girl get up. She came to him. Together they watched the still night forest outside. He put his arm around her waist, and she leaned her head against his shoulder.

Suddenly she was in his arms. She clung to him in fierce desperation. Great rending sobs shook her slender body.

He held her tenderly. He buried his face in her golden hair. He didn't move, didn't talk. And presently the girl grew quiet.

He took her face between his hands. He kissed her dry, bright eyes, that could produce no tears. He kissed her smooth throat and felt the hot blood beating wildly inside her. He found her mouth, parted, eager—waiting for him.

Slowly he led her back to the bed. With tender clumsiness he began to undress her. Impatiently she helped. And soon they were gazing at each other's young, naked bodies with excitement and delight.

He caressed her cool, silken skin. He kissed the small, thrusting breasts and felt the nipples grow jewel hard. He stroked her loins and felt himself close to bursting with desire.

And they were together. Nothing existed except the two of them. He felt the obstruction that guarded her and thrust against it, her nails raking his back. And he felt it break in a surge of motion. And they were no longer two. Gerti moaned. Her musky scent intoxicated him. And suddenly the girl screamed. It was a clarion sound to him. He felt himself explode in a burst of sensual agony inside her. He felt his life force spurt and flood from him.

They belonged to one another in that moment. Completely.

After that they were insatiable. The night darkness was already graying when they finally fell asleep in each other's arms. Gerti was still asleep when he woke up. A fine ray of sunlight squeezed through the drawn curtains and sent a line of gold across her hair. Gently he disentangled himself from her arms. He stood up and looked at himself. With wonder he saw that his thigh had a spot of dried blood on it. He looked closer. There was more dried blood on his pubic hair. He looked at the sleeping girl. He suddenly felt an overwhelming tenderness toward her. He thought, I won't wash it off. There was something almost sacred about it. This was the way his child had been conceived. With the blood of innocence.

Outside a motorcycle backfired. Lebensborn Bodenheim was waking up.

Willi went to the showers. . . .

It had been a long time ago. He knew now that he'd simply been a "stud" in a National Socialist breeding station. Like others. He knew his child—his son?—was a "Hitler baby." He knew the boy belonged to the Third Reich, and he knew he'd never see him. He had only his memories. And he didn't know whether to be proud of them or to regret them.

Von Eckdorf turned from the bulletin board. He started down the crowded corridor and Willi followed. Coming toward them was a small, stocky man in dirty civilian clothes. He carried an oily rag. Von Eckdorf regarded him with repugnance. When the man came abreast of him, he stopped him. He held out his hand.

"Your papers!"

The man looked startled. He shot a quick glance at Willi. Willi said nothing. The man turned back to von Eckdorf. He shook his head. He looked confused, frightened. Haltingly he jabbered something unintelligible. Von Eckdorf was taken aback.

"Your identification papers, you idiot," he snapped.

The man flinched. He looked petrified. But he did not respond.

"Well?"

The man cringed before von Eckdorf. He shook his head violently. *"Nein—verstehen,"* he stammered.

Von Eckdorf stared at the man in astonishment. The whole place is a lunatic asylum, he thought. With a little smile, Willi said:

"The man has orders to speak only Russian, Herr Reichsamtsleiter."

"Russian?" Von Eckdorf was startled. "But—he is a German?"

"Of course, sir. But to the Americans he will be a—a foreign laborer. A Ukrainian. He has been instructed to speak only Russian, even here, to get him used to it—to condition him." He turned to the cowering man. "You may answer, Kunze," he said.

At once the man's attitude changed. He snapped to attention.

"Jawohl, Herr Untersturmführer."

Quickly he brought out his identification papers and handed them to von Eckdorf. The Reichsamtsleiter examined them curiously.

"They are completely authentic," Willi said with obvious pride. "Every stamp. Every signature. Everything. Nothing is forged." He grinned. "Except, of course, the information they contain!"

Von Eckdorf fingered the papers. "What is the purpose?" he asked.

"Kunze will be an outside agent. A collector of intelligence for us," Willi explained. "His foreign laborer identity is simply his cover. We know the Americans often use these foreigners—Displaced Persons, they call them, or DPs—for various jobs. For example, as waiters or cleaning personnel in their service clubs. In their motor pools." He smiled. "The Americans don't like to do the dirty work themselves if they can get someone else to do it. We'll be glad to help them out!"

"I see. A Werewolf spy among the Americans. Of course. It might prove valuable," von Eckdorf said with grudging approval. He turned to Kunze. "Do you carry a gun?"

"No, sir."

"Not even a knife, Herr Reichsamtsleiter," Willi interjected. "Obvious weapons would betray him. But he *is* armed."

Von Eckdorf looked nonplussed. Willi was beginning to see the course of action to take. He felt he was capturing the Reichsamtsleiter's interest despite the man's prejudiced antagonism. Willi knew it was important not to make an enemy of a high-ranking party official like von Eckdorf, even if he was a self-important bastard. He knew better than most that everything done in Germany today had political overtones, and he realized it had to be like that. It was the only way the Fatherland could survive. Krueger, on the other hand, was strictly a soldier. The best! Willi would follow him anywhere. The colonel—general now—was an expert in guerrilla warfare. For over a year he had fought Tito's partisans in the Balkans, and he had learned much from them. But he had little use for politicians, sticking their ignorant, meddlesome noses in military matters. If Willi could help by mellowing Reichsamtsleiter von Eckdorf, he'd damned well break his back to do it! He reached over and took a pencil from the breast pocket of Kunze's threadbare jacket. He handed it to von Eckdorf.

"He does carry a weapon," he said. "This!"

Von Eckdorf turned the pencil over. He examined it. He scratched it with his nail. He tested the point. Then he turned to Willi.

"It's just an ordinary pencil," he said.

"Yes, sir," Willi confirmed. "It *is* just a plain pencil. But—" He looked at von Eckdorf like a kid showing off a new toy. "If I may show the Herr Reichsamtsleiter."

He turned to survey the stream of people flowing through the broad corridor. I hope I'm not overdoing it, he thought with sardonic self-appraisal. He motioned to a passing soldier carrying a rifle. The man came over. Willi took the soldier and Kunze aside and gave them some brief instructions. He retrieved the pencil from von Eckdorf and returned it to Kunze, who put it back in his breast pocket in plain sight. Von Eckdorf was watching the proceedings with an impatient frown. Willi joined him.

"Please, Herr Reichsamtsleiter," he said eagerly. "The men will demonstrate for you." He nodded to the two men. The soldier slung his rifle over his shoulder, and took up position as if he were a guard.

"Please imagine," Willi commented in a conspiratorial *sotto voce*, "that the soldier is a sentry who must be eliminated. Silently. Efficiently. Please watch. . . ."

Kunze and the recruited soldier entered into their roles with proper enthusiasm. They'd done it many times before. In training.

Kunze walked up to the soldier. The man brought his gun to port arms and challenged him. With a big, disarming grin Kunze held up his empty hands in a gesture of harmless submission. He spoke a few words in Russian.

"Speak German, you clod," the soldier barked. "What do you want?"

Kunze shrugged ingratiatingly. His grin grew wider. "No—speak," he said. He launched into a stream of Russian. The soldier obviously understood nothing. Kunze kept his distance. Clearly he presented no threat to the sentry, as he gestured and babbled on.

God, what a ham, Willi thought with amusement. He's putting on quite a show. But it'll take more than that to get a positive reaction out of a critic as sour as that pompous little ass! He chanced a glance at von Eckdorf. The Reichsamtsleiter was watching with wary interest.

Kunze was getting nowhere. He stopped talking. He cocked his head in cogitation. He suddenly seemed to get an idea.

"Tovarich!" He beamed. "I—show . . ."

From his breast pocket he carefully fished out an old scrap of paper. And the pencil. He studiously wetted the point on his tongue and began laboriously to scrawl something on the paper. He seemed completely engrossed in his task. In his concentration he edged closer to the soldier, who was watching him.

Even though he knew what was going to happen, Willi felt himself growing tense with suspense. He was aware of von Eckdorf beside him. The little man was absorbed in the scene, sensing the climax was near. He was clutching Kunze's papers in his hand, forgotten. Now, Willi thought. *Now!*

Suddenly, with lightning speed, Kunze made a vicious stabbing sweep at the soldier's stomach with the pencil. With instinctive reflex action the man pulled his stomach back. For a split second he was leaning slightly forward, his head thrust out, his neck exposed. The sweep to the stomach had only been a feint. Without hesitation, in continuous motion, Kunze stabbed the sharply pointed pencil upward straight for the soldier's exposed jugular vein! In the last possible moment he veered it away. With the same motion he brought the pencil up high, and drove it down hard—this time with the metal-capped blunt end first, so he didn't have to reposition the pencil in his hand—directly toward the soldier's eye, stopping only short of piercing it! The soldier collapsed. His rifle clattered to the floor. He would have been a dead man.

The "kill" had taken less than two seconds.

Von Eckdorf stared at the man on the floor. Willi spoke matter-of-factly.

"The pencil point will pierce the jugular vein, Herr Reichsamtsleiter. Death is instantaneous. Should he miss, he can ram it down through the man's eye into his brain. The bone is quite thin there."

Von Eckdorf said nothing. Despite himself he had been excited by the scene he had witnessed. But this was not the place, not the time to show it.

Willi dismissed the soldier. "It's a very effective maneuver," he said. He glanced at von Eckdorf. The Reichsamtsleiter was still clutching Kunze's papers in his hand. The little bastard is impressed, Willi thought. He's just too damned mulish to admit it! No matter. We've just begun, little man!

Von Eckdorf made a point of sounding uninterested. "So I imagine," he said. He suddenly became aware of Kunze's papers in his hand. He gave them back to the man at once. They were wrinkled and crushed. He nodded curtly.

"You may go," he said.

Kunze clicked his heels and left. Willi looked after him. He was pleased.

"We have many of these—DPs," he said with satisfaction. "They'll get us information—reliable information—about a lot of important targets. It is a very effective program. General Krueger's idea, of course."

Von Eckdorf said nothing.

There were fourteen Lilliputs left in the box. Hauptmann Ludwig Schmidt made a quick head count of the men gathered around the table. It would be enough. There would be at least half a dozen extras. He'd instruct Steiner to load them with the HQ supplies.

Out of the corner of his eye he saw Willi Richter approaching, accompanied by a small, imperious-looking civilian. That would be the man from Berlin Krueger had said would be arriving. He walked over to meet them.

Willi turned to von Eckdorf.

"Herr Reichsamtsleiter," he said. "May I present Hauptmann Schmidt. Our executive officer."

Schmidt saluted. "Heil Hitler!"

Von Eckdorf returned the salute. He inspected Schmidt with curiosity and consternation. The Wehrmacht captain was in uniform, but his right leg and right arm were encased in prominent steel and leather braces.

"You are—a cripple, Hauptmann Schmidt?"

"So are many of us, Herr Reichsamtsleiter," Schmidt said with a cold smile. He indicated the group of men gathered around the table. Several of them were in some way crippled. One of them, a man in his late thirties, turned from the table and walked away from the group. He was clad in civilian clothes. His left arm was missing, the empty jacket sleeve pinned up to his shoulder. He wore a patch over his left eye and walked with a limp.

"Heinz lost his arm and his eye in the Afrika Korps, El Alamein," Schmidt said. He slapped his leather-encased right arm against his steel brace. "I got mine at Salerno." He looked steadily at von Eckdorf.

"We're crippled. But it makes us no less loyal to our Führer." A thin smile narrowed his lips. "And who considers a poor cripple dangerous?" he added.

Von Eckdorf looked at the officer with approval. Here is a real German officer at last, he thought. "Excellent," he said.

The three men walked over to the table. A noncom, Steiner, was distributing handguns to the men and recording serial numbers in a ledger. Schmidt took one of the guns from the box and handed it to von Eckdorf. The Reichsamtsleiter inspected it gingerly. It was exceedingly small and compact.

"It is the Lilliput, Herr Reichsamtsleiter," Schmidt explained. "German made. Four point two five millimeters. Magazine load. Easily concealed. It's the smallest effective automatic made."

Von Eckdorf weighed the little gun in his hand. He could cover it completely with his palm. He was impressed. You can't beat German know-how, he thought pridefully. He returned the tiny gun to Schmidt.

"Very good," he said. He still managed to sound patronizing. It pleased him.

"It's standard equipment, Herr von Eckdorf," Willi said. "Have I the Herr Reichsamtsleiter's permission to show him something— special?"

"You have."

Willi turned to Steiner.

"Steiner," he said. "Show us!"

Steiner grinned. "*Jawohl*, Herr Untersturmführer!"

He walked a few steps away from the table. The men gave way. He was a big, muscular man clad in a brown shirt with the sleeves rolled up and a pair of gray Wehrmacht uniform pants held up by the standard broad leather belt, the solid metal belt buckle embossed with the Nazi eagle. Steiner stopped. Everyone was watching him.

Suddenly he whirled toward a big, ornate mirror leaning against the wall. At the same moment his right hand slapped his belt buckle. Instantly it sprang open and with the same movement four short-snouted gun barrels leaped into position. At once Steiner fingered the side of the buckle—and four shots rang out in rapid succession, shattering the mirror, and sending Steiner's image cascading to the floor in myriad pieces.

Von Eckdorf started with shock. He caught himself, aware that all the men were watching him and conscious of their carefully concealed amusement. They were expecting me to jump, the louts! he thought angrily. They set me up. Steiner came over.

"You just aim with your belly." He grinned. "You can't miss!"

"It was developed especially for us," Willi said. He held out his hand and Steiner took off his belt and handed it to him. Willi was careful not to betray how much he'd enjoyed seeing von Eckdorf jump. He'd been watching for it. Might take him down from his pedestal a notch or two. He showed the belt to von Eckdorf.

"The device is built into the belt buckle," he explained. "It fires four .32 ACP cartridges. You press a lever on the side of the buckle. The four barrels are released and instantly lock into position. Each barrel can be fired singly by squeezing an individual trigger—or as you saw Steiner do it."

Von Eckdorf hardly heard him. He pretended to examine the device minutely. He needed the time to compose himself, to control his mortification. He *had* been badly startled. Jumped like a rabbit. And everyone had seen it. He was impressed with the device, but he was much more acutely conscious of having been made to look undignified in front of the men. It was, of course, intolerable.

He returned the belt to Willi. Then he turned deliberately to Steiner. He regarded him coldly.

"That mirror," he said. "No doubt it was the property of the Reich!"

Steiner frowned with puzzlement. "Yes, sir," he said soberly.

"You will account for it then. Personally," von Eckdorf said with icy calm. He turned on his heel and stalked off.

Willi quickly followed.

They had been through everything. Von Eckdorf was a very thorough man. But despite Willi's efforts, the Reichsamtsleiter had remained overbearing and aloof throughout.

They were approaching the main entrance. From a door marked with a red cross a man entered the corridor. He was naked from the waist up. A fresh bandage encircled his upper left arm. Willi stopped him.

"How many more to go, Pitterman?" he asked.

"Only two or three, Herr Untersturmführer," the man answered. Willi nodded. The man walked off. Von Eckdorf looked after him.

"It will heal within the week," Willi said. "There will be no scar. In another week it cannot be detected at all."

He glanced at von Eckdorf. There was no reaction. What the hell do you make of a son of a bitch like that? he thought, frustrated.

"We have thought of everything," he added.

Von Eckdorf turned to him.

"Thank you for your time," he said coolly. "You need not accompany me to my car. I am certain you have much to do. Convey my—congratulations to the general. If you fail in your mission, it will not be because your Führer and your Fatherland neglected to prepare you."

"We do not think in terms of failure, Herr Reichsamtsleiter!"

"You are wise. Heil Hitler!"

Von Eckdorf turned on his heel and marched off, leaving Willi staring after him. He didn't think he'd done much good. He couldn't understand why. He'd given the little man the impressive, triple grade A tour of the whole damned place. He'd explained programs, tactics, procedures to him. He'd staged demonstrations for him. He'd shown him everything. The works! And the bastard had been about as enthusiastic as a flower vendor in a fish market! What the hell was wrong with him?

Willi watched von Eckdorf disappear through the huge double doors. Above them the big framed Werewolf motto still hung: ES GIBT KEINE KAMERADEN . . .

> THERE IS NO SUCH THING AS
> A FRIEND! IF YOUR MISSION
> IS AT STAKE, ATTACK HIM—
> IF NEED BE, KILL HIM!
> Heinrich Himmler

Wonder if we'll leave it here or take it along, Willi thought irrelevantly. He put von Eckdorf from his mind. The devil take him, he thought. But he was right in one thing. There's still a lot to do!

Willi turned away from the doors and walked quickly down the corridor. He whistled softly to himself:

> *Du kleine Fliege,*
> *Wenn ich dich kriege—*

2309 hrs

The great, massive desk stood in a pool of yellow light in the middle of the dark, empty room. The heavy draperies drawn across the big windows kept the light from the lone desk lamp from seeping outside. Even here in the Bohemian Mountains blackout regulations were strictly enforced.

General Krueger was alone in his office. He sat behind the big desk. Spread out in front of him were the orders and reports brought by von Eckdorf. Every page, every photograph, every overlay was stamped GEHEIMSACHE—"Top Secret." He had gone over all the material carefully. Evaluated it. There was not much time left. The Americans were less than a hundred kilometers from his Schönsee positions.

Krueger had cut through all the stilted, formal military language of the final orders from the *Führerhauptquartier* and broken every-thing down to two principal missions, separate yet interdependent. First—eliminate the Supreme Allied Commander, General Dwight D. Eisenhower.

The mission did not disconcert him. He did not regard it as an assassination. It was a military operation different from others only in its ramifications. Eisenhower, in his capacity of Supreme Commander, was a legitimate military target. He could see the reasoning behind the order. Eisenhower's elimination would directly affect many phases of the war vital to the plans of the Third Reich. It was bound to create a certain amount of confusion and attendant delay in the conduct of the Allied campaign, even if they were only temporary. This would give the German forces much needed time and perhaps a short respite in which to consolidate and occupy the *Alpenfestung*. At the moment, the situation was deteriorating much faster than anyone had anticipated. He had no illusions that Eisenhower's elimination would alter the course of the war. The Supreme Allied Commander was not indispensable. Others would carry on. However, if the elimination was carried out in such a manner that it was irrefutably an act of the Werewolves, the Americans would be forced to divert many troops and expend much effort on future protection against Werewolf activities. Again the result would be a much needed measure of relief for the German armed forces. In addition there was, of course, the undeniable propaganda value of the affair, the lift to the spirit of German resistance, both civilian and military. The plan would work, if executed correctly. He would concentrate on it as soon as the move to Schönsee had been carried out. The mission would be accomplished.

Secondly—and still of primary importance to Krueger—was the long-range mission: To serve as the hard-core, backbone force of the *Alpenfestung*. To battle the enemy through centrally controlled, efficiently organized guerrilla warfare. To wear him out with a barrage of hit-and-run strikes and buy the time necessary for the culmination of the Master Plan.

Alone in the dark, disemboweled room, he smiled to himself. It was ironic. The Werewolf concept had been Himmler's, but he, Generalmajor Karl Krueger, was entirely responsible for putting it into operation. He had been Himmler's personal choice to carry out the Reichsführer's concept. And with excellent reason. He knew better than any other German officer what guerrilla warfare could accomplish. For almost two years he had fought the Yugoslav partisans all over the Dinaric Alps. For two years he had been continuously and ignominiously defeated doing it! But he had learned.

His schooling had begun in the early fall of 1941, when he was still a lieutenant colonel. In occupied Yugoslavia the Tito partisans were rapidly growing into the most effective, most dangerous guerrilla organization ever to fight an invader. Time and time again throughout the following months full-scale offensives had been mounted against the partisans, maximum efforts of up to ten divisions with heavy artillery and air support. He had commanded elements of these offensives. Time and time again the guerrillas had evaded all attempts to destroy them and escaped to keep fighting their hit-and-run war.

Krueger smiled ruefully. He had been beaten. Badly beaten. By a Croat metalworker! In a way he supposed he should be grateful to him. Josip Brozovitch Tito. Two years ago he had cursed him and his partisans. Today he was preparing to imitate them, to use everything he'd learned from them about underground fighting! He had the greatest respect for the effectiveness of such unorthodox operations. Guerrillas by themselves may never have won a war, but they *have* prevented one or the other side from winning, he thought. Strike suddenly. Attack the enemy where he presents the richest target. Hit him where he is weakest. Above all, strike where he least expects it. And after the strike do not hang around. Fade away at once. Melt into the countryside. These were the partisans' tactics. They would be the tactics of the Werewolves.

He was confident. It had been proved conclusively these last years that a well-organized guerrilla force constituted a military

factor of first-rate importance, against which a modern army of occupation was in many respects powerless.

The Werewolves would be such a force. With wry amusement
Krueger recalled the words of Dr. Goebbels a few weeks before,
when the decision had been made to publicize the existence of the
Werewolves on the state radio. He'd thought them rather egregious.
"The Werewolves will be the Siegfried's Sword that will slay the
Dragons seeking to devour our Fatherland," the little *Doktor* had
declared. And he'd added, "On *them* will depend the success of the
Master Plan!"

So be it.

Krueger idly pulled the thick mimeographed report to him.

GEHEIMSACHE
ZUSTAND DER ALPENFESTUNG
Führerhauptquartier den 15.4.45

There was a set of map overlays and a stack of aerial photographs
as addenda to the report. He picked up one of the pictures and
looked at it thoughtfully. It was an aerial view showing a peaceful
valley between two majestic Alpine ranges; a string of mountain
meadows ringed with evergreen woods and dotted with a few barns
and shacks. He turned it over. On the reverse was a long list of
specifications headed: LwUFH-7. He inspected the photograph
again. The camouflage was remarkable. It was impossible to detect
the slightest indication that this was indeed a Luftwaffe underground airfield. The runway access—like the entrance to a giant
beehive, he thought—was completely hidden in the woods. The
shacks and barns on the meadows effectively concealed the necessary ventilation intakes and exhausts for the field below. He tossed
the photograph back and picked up a map overlay. He read the
legend. Each symbol on the overlay marked the location of a very
special kind of cache. Money. Valuables. Gold. Some of them he
already knew. The gold coin hoard from Kremsmünster Monastery
hidden in the Tyrol near Salzburg. He remembered with distaste the
little SS major, Helmuth von Hummel, one of Bormann's aides,

who had been in charge of setting up the cache. That one alone must be worth not less than 25 million RM. The foreign currency collection at Berchtesgaden. Who knew *how* much? The gold cache near Rattendorf. At least another 20 million. And others. He wondered how much actually was available to finance the stand at the *Alpenfestung*. He gave up. At any rate, there'd be more than could possibly be needed.

He gathered the documents together. It was an impressive report. More than that. It was a record of the staggering, overwhelming potential of the *Alpenfestung*.

He stretched and looked at his watch. It was late. There was a knock on the door.

"*Herein,*" he called.

Schmidt and Willi entered. They stopped just inside the door.

"The last units have left, Herr General," Schmidt reported.

"Thank you."

"Everything is ready for our departure tomorrow."

"Very good."

The two junior officers came briefly to attention. They turned to leave.

"Wait!" Krueger stood up. He stretched again. He walked around the big desk. "I think tonight calls for a little celebration schnapps," he said. "What do you think?" He was relaxed, informal. The men took their cues from the general.

"Of course, sir. Thank you," Schmidt said. He smiled. "And congratulations—General!"

"Congratulations, sir," Willi echoed.

"Thank you, gentlemen." Krueger opened the door to the hall. "Plewig!" he called. "Plewig!"

He turned to Willi and gestured around the empty room. "Not much left," he said. He pointed to the steel file cabinets. "Pull up a file. Sit down!"

Willi grinned. "Yes, sir!"

Plewig came hurrying around the corner. He was in stocking feet, holding up his pants with one hand. He skidded to a halt.

"The general called," he panted.

"The general did," Krueger said. "I want you to fetch a bottle of brandy from the cellar. The last of the Armagnac. And three glasses."

"Yes, sir."

"And, Plewig. Take a bottle of schnapps for yourself and the others."

"Yes, sir! Thank you, sir!" The little man was off. Krueger returned to the room.

Willi and Schmidt had upended an empty file cabinet and pulled it up to the desk. The general sat down in his chair. He indicated the file cabinet.

"Have a seat, gentlemen. It may not be the most comfortable seat in the world, but you might as well get used to roughing it."

The men grinned. They sat down on the overturned file. The metal protested with a hollow groan. Krueger put his hand on the documents on his desk.

"We've already gone over the orders," he said. "We know what we have to do." He studied the two younger men briefly. "Off the record. What are your opinions?"

Willi and Schmidt glanced at each other. Schmidt said:

"There's not much time, General, if a substantial number of troops are to reach the *Alpenfestung*."

Krueger nodded. "I agree. We're being badly squeezed." He looked at his officers. "But Himmler has given me his personal promise to keep the approaches to the area open as long as possible."

"Munich?" Willi asked.

Krueger nodded. "The SS troops have been ordered to force resistance to the utmost."

There was a knock on the door, and Plewig entered with a bottle of Armagnac and three brandy snifters. He had put on his boots and a jacket. Krueger motioned him over to the desk.

"Ah," he said enthusiastically. "Best brandy in the world. It rivals the finest cognac, gentlemen. Same quality, but a somewhat different style. More finesse." He looked reverently at the bottle.

"Thirty years old. From Grand Bas-Armagnac. The very best brandies come from that district. You are in for a treat!"

Plewig poured an inch of the brandy into each glass. He put the bottle on the desk and left. Krueger picked up his glass.

"*Prost!*" he said pleasantly.

The two men held out their glasses to him. "*Prost!*"

They drank. Willi felt the deliciously burning sensation of the strong, smooth Armagnac gliding through his mouth and down his throat. He exhaled slowly through his nose, enjoying the rich flavor of the brandy to the fullest. This is the life, he thought. Boozing it up with the general!

"You are right, Schmidt," Krueger said. "Time *is* of vital importance. It's up to us to make as much of it available for our purposes as possible."

Willi looked at the general. Why not? he thought. Why not take a chance? It's only a question, after all. He cleared his throat.

"Sir," he said. "When we do reach our positions in the *Alpenfestung*. The others, too." He swallowed. "What *are* our chances? Really."

Krueger regarded the young man for a moment.

"Willi," he said. There was an almost fatherly affection in his voice. "I think you should know." He paused. Seriously he contemplated his brandy snifter, slowly turning it in his hand. Then he looked at the two officers.

"At this moment," he said soberly. "At this moment our Fatherland stands defeated. The war is lost."

Willi stared at the general. It wasn't that he had not considered the same possibility himself. He had. But it was a shock to hear it said so unequivocally. By the general. Krueger continued.

"But we can still turn today's defeat into tomorrow's victory. There is one way of doing it, and only one way. Reichsführer SS Himmler's Master Plan!"

He settled back in his chair. Willi and Schmidt watched him intently. He took a lingering sip of his brandy.

"We can no longer win the war by ourselves," he said. "We lost that chance in June last year, when the Allies established their beachhead in Normandy. Only a miracle could have given us victory after that. And no miracle came to pass. No, gentlemen—we need help. We need the help of either Russia—or America."

Willi started. Krueger didn't seem to notice. He went on.

"Already Himmler has been successful in sowing mistrust in the minds of the Russians. Persuading them, for instance, that despite the Americans' protestations, they intend to drive for Berlin, leaving the *Alpenfestung* as a thorn in Stalin's side. There is no love lost between the eastern and western allies. They are already on the brink of open hostilities. It'll be up to us to push a little. To send them over that brink! There are many ways it can be done. Diplomatically, of course, through planting false 'leaks' of 'confidential' material. In neutral countries. Sweden. Switzerland. On *our* part, through special missions. Staged provocations. Our men in Russian uniforms attacking an American unit. Americans killing Russians! Little incidents of no importance by themselves. But—the retaliations will be real. In the armed conflict between East and West that will result, it will soon become apparent who is the stronger. And to the winning side Himmler—in the name of the Führer—will be able to offer the deciding strength of the Third Reich, sustained in the *Alpenfestung*. On our terms! The Master Plan will turn defeat into ultimate victory."

He took a sip of his Armagnac.

"But we must act quickly now. Decisively. At best we have to the end of this month."

He looked straight at the two officers. There was a grim glint in his penetrating eyes.

"The elimination of Eisenhower will give us a few more days. Perhaps. We make our move to the *Alpenfestung* immediately after that mission is accomplished," he said.

He sipped his drink. Twelve years, he thought. Twelve long, hard years—half of them spent at war—the National Socialist Third Reich had fought to attain her rightful place as the leading power of the world. And now two weeks would decide her ultimate fate! He felt awed at the realization. He looked at the two young men before him. Did they know the roles they were about to play in shaping history?

"Two weeks, gentlemen," he said soberly. "Two weeks before the Americans seal off the Alpine area. Unless we can prevent it."

He stood up. The two junior officers quickly followed suit. Krueger raised his glass.

"To the Master Plan," he said. "*Sieg Heil!*"

"*Seig Heil!*"

They drank. Krueger looked at his glass. He looked at the Bavarian civilian clothes he was wearing, the forester's knee breeches, the coarse green shirt, the gray jacket with the carved bone buttons. Again he raised his glass. It was nearly empty. He drew himself erect. Quietly he said:

"*Hoch! Hoch*—the Werewolves!"

Part II

28 Apr 1945

■

Weiden

0957 hrs

    The white sheets of surrender hung from the windows, limp and dejected, speckling the old, colorful buildings of the little Bavarian town of Weiden with their signals of submission. They had greeted the American troops when they rolled into town a week earlier. They were still there, calculated insurance against the violence of war.

    Erik and Don dismounted from their jeep and made their way toward the town jail. One of the few larger and newer buildings in town, it served as quarters for the Counter Intelligence Corps.

    Erik glanced down the street. It never ceased to amaze him how quickly the people of the small German towns seemed to accept the upheaval of their world. Already the Weiden townspeople walked the streets on purposeful errands of their own, pointedly ignoring the raw scars of battle that marred most of the buildings. Many of the old houses wore the shrapnel-chipped signs of more imperious times crudely painted on their walls—like rueful dowagers wearing the faded finery of better, bygone days: the ever-present swastikas, the Nazi propaganda slogans. SIEG ODER SIBIRIEN —"Victory or Siberia"; EIN VOLK EIN REICH EIN FÜHRER—"One people, One Country, One Leader"; HITLER BRINGT BROT, STALIN DEN TOD—"Hitler Brings Bread, Stalin Death." And other, less arrogant, more sober messages: WIR SIND IM KELLER—"We Are in the Basement"—lettered on the only standing wall of a bombed-out house, with a large white arrow pointing down. Or a terse ABGEREIST—"Gone"—on the shell of a gutted shop.

The jail itself, a substantial stone structure, was almost undamaged. Only the doorframe of the main entrance and part of the wall around the door had been badly cracked by shrapnel from a shell that landed in the street. An elderly German civilian wearing a soiled leather cap was in the process of repairing the damage, carefully removing a hand-lettered sign fixed to the wall to cover part of the hole. ROOMS WITH ADJOINING TOWELS, it proclaimed.

The German doffed his cap as Erik and Don walked past him into the building. They did not acknowledge his greeting, nor did they notice the glint of hate that flitted across the man's eyes as he glared after them.

The corridor was crowded with people. Civilians and German soldiers; men and women; young and old. All sorts of people—but all with one thing in common, the tension of fear. At the far end of the corridor a bored MP stood guard at a door. The blue and orange windmill insignia with the letters CIC was tacked on the wall next to the door. Beneath it was written: SCREENING & INTERROGATION. Erik and Don pushed open the door and entered.

". . . and your entire unit was disbanded more than a week ago?"

The question was sharp, incredulous, as it was shot at a German soldier standing at attention before a large desk littered with papers and books. The two CIC agents seated behind the desk glared at the soldier. He looked pinched and gray with apprehension.

"*Ja!* Y-yes, sir!" he stammered.

The interrogator fixed him with a baleful eye.

"Then *how* do you account for the fact that *no one else* from your outfit has come through here? Only you!"

"Why *you?*" the other man snapped.

"What's so special about *you?*"

"What are *you* after?"

The German was shaken, flustered. He looked pleadingly from one to the other of his interrogators.

"I—I don't know. I don't understand. There should have been
—others. Please, Herr Hauptmann. It's true! I'm telling the truth!"

Erik stood just inside the door with Don. He knew the routine.
It was one of Agent Hacker's favorite ploys. The soldier was probably okay. Just exactly what he said he was. Discharged. Probably
a lot of his comrades had already been screened by Hacker and his
teammate, Pierce, and been sent on their way. The man's confusion
at being told he was the only one was genuine. And believable.
Had he come up with a clever, logical explanation—that would
have been reason for suspicion, and a more searching interrogation.

Erik looked around the room. He thought wearily of the many
hours he'd already spent here, the many hours still to come.

The room was a bleak-looking affair, cold and unfriendly.
Through a broken windowpane ran the wires to two field telephones
on the desk. A large area map was tacked up on the wall behind
the desk. It had no markings of any kind. A small potbellied stove
squatted in a corner, its black pipe disappearing through a sooty
hole in the wall. There was no fire in it. On the dirty wall was a
large rectangular spot, cleaner and lighter in color. Erik was certain it had only recently been occupied by a portrait of the Führer.

Agent Hacker handed the German a slip of paper.

"Take this to the military government office. The sergeant outside will show you where. They'll give you a travel pass."

The soldier clicked his heels smartly.

"*Jawohl*, Herr Hauptmann! Thank you! Thank you very much!"
He saluted.

"You may go," Hacker said.

The German left. Don sauntered over to the desk.

"Okay, fellers," he said pleasantly. "You're sprung. We'll take it
from here."

"And you can have it," Pierce grumbled with feeling.

"What's the matter?" Don asked with mock astonishmennt. "I
thought you *liked* screening duty."

Pierce looked sour.

"Don't make me laugh. It strains my stitches."

Erik was riffling through a bunch of papers in a basket on the desk.

"Anything interesting turn up?" he asked.

Hacker shrugged.

"Not much. Couple of SS officers and a concentration camp guard. Member of the Deathheads."

"Big deal," Don commented.

"And one character we sent back to Army Interrogation Center." Hacker ignored Don. "Just had a hunch he'd have something to tell."

The door opened, and Sergeant Jim Murphy stuck his head into the room.

"Sir, you ready for another one?" He grinned broadly. "Think this one'll interest you."

"Okay, Jim. Just one more. Send him in."

Murphy disappeared. Hacker turned to Erik and Don.

"After this one, they're all yours."

Don drifted over to the filing cabinets.

"I can hardly wait." he mumbled.

Erik followed him. He was conscious of the sudden almost tangible change of atmosphere in the room. From friendly informality —to cold efficiency. He looked at Hacker and Pierce. They're putting on their ruthless bastard faces like shrugging into field jackets, he thought. I suppose we all do it. He looked toward the door as it opened.

The girl ushered into the interrogation room by Murphy was what the young sergeant would have reverently described as "a knockout." Tall, beautiful and blond, she was the kind of girl who looks wonderful without any makeup at all, and she wore none. She was dressed in a gay dirndl skirt, tight at her slender waist, and a low-cut, short-sleeved Bavarian blouse adorned with fine embroidery across her jauntily thrusting breasts.

Talk about straining stitches! Erik thought, glancing at Pierce. Even *his* dour face softened as he stared at the girl—but only for an instant.

"Here you are, sir!" Murphy had trouble keeping the merriment in his eyes from contaminating his otherwise carefully set expression of stern efficiency.

He ducked out.

Hacker looked at the girl dispassionately.

"*Kennkarte, bitte!*"

The girl rummaged around in a little handbag and came up with the small gray identification card. She handed it to Hacker. She looked frightened and enormously appealing. Nervously she glanced at each one of the men in turn. Hacker was examining the ID card.

"Anneliese Leubuscher. Correct?"

"Yes." She answered in a small, soft voice.

"Age?"

"Twenty-two."

With deliberation Hacker made a note on a piece of paper. He showed it to Pierce. Both men looked searchingly at the girl, then Pierce grimly began to leaf through a large mimeographed volume. Anneliese's apprehension increased. She was trembling.

"Why are you in a combat zone?" Hacker's voice was cold and harsh.

"I was in Pilsen. In Czechoslovakia." She bit her lip. "I—I wanted to go home before the Russians . . ."

Her words trailed off. She bowed her head. Her silence was eloquent. Hacker studied her for a moment.

"Where do you want to go?"

"To Regensburg. I think my parents are still there."

Pierce closed the volume he'd been looking through. He shook his head almost imperceptibly at Hacker.

"What did you do in Pilsen?"

"I worked in an office. Stenotypist."

"What office?" Pierce demanded curtly.

Anneliese looked startled. "The NSKK." Her voice was low.

"I see." Pierce sounded ominous. "The Nazi Motor Tranport Corps. Why did the NSKK have an office in Pilsen?"

"I don't know." Anneliese frowned. "Perhaps because there was so much heavy trucking from there. The beer, you know."

Don suddenly had a slight attack of coughing. Hacker quickly broke in.

"Party member?"

Anneliese started. "What?"

"Were you a party member?"

"I was—I was in the BDM."

"Who wasn't?" Hacker was insistent. "Did you join the Nazi party?"

Anneliese looked trapped. She lowered her eyes. She whispered: "Yes."

"When?"

"Two years ago. In Regensburg."

"Why?"

"I *had* to. If I wanted to work."

Suddenly Pierce stood up. He walked to the girl. She seemed to want to shrink from him, but she stood her ground. Pierce glared at her.

"Raise your left arm!" The command was brusque. Anneliese looked startled. She obeyed.

Carefully Pierce looked at the inside of her upper arm. Then, without a word, he returned to his seat.

Hacker looked up at the girl. She was standing motionless, her arm still in the air.

"You may take your arm down now," he said.

With an awkward yet appealing motion, Anneliese complied. She looked humiliated, vulnerable—like a fawn caught in the sight of a hunter's gun. Her huge eyes stole around the room. They met Erik's —and held for just a brief moment.

He looked away.

"If we let you go, will you go straight to Regensburg?" Hacker's voice had lost some of its harshness.

"Yes! Oh, yes, sir!"

Hacker scribbled on a slip of paper and held it out to the girl.

"Here. Take this. The sergeant will tell you what to do."

Anneliese took the paper.

"Thank you," she said. "Oh, thank you so much!" She looked as if she were going to embrace him.

"That's all. You may go."

A quick curtsy, and the girl was gone from the room. Hacker got up. He stretched.

"Well, that's that. It's all yours." He turned to Pierce. "Coming?"

"Okay."

"See you later." Hacker started for the door followed by Pierce. Don called after them.

"Hey! Hacker!"

"Yeah?"

"Watch your fraternizing!"

Hacker turned to Don. He spoke with mock concern.

"You know, I haven't had a girl for so long, I wouldn't know what to do."

"Don't you worry," Don assured him gravely. "It's like riding a bicycle. It comes back to you once you get on."

Sergeant Murphy stuck his head in the door.

"We're really stacking them up out here," he stated reproachfully. Don turned to him.

"Okay, Jim. Send the next one in. And see if you can do as well for *us*."

"Got you."

Don joined Erik at the table. He let himself plop into the chair.

"Well, here we go again." He sighed. "This screening routine kills me. About as exciting as knitting cockwarmers for the Red Cross."

"Didn't know they used them," Erik commented dryly.

Murphy appeared. Deadpan, he showed a woman into the interrogation room; a middle-aged hausfrau type running to fat, with a stony, hostile face. She glared at the two CIC agents.

"That's the closest I could come, sir," Murphy said innocently.

"Thank you, Sergeant. *Thank you*—very much," Don answered. As Murphy left, he turned to the woman.

"*Kennkarte, bitte.*"

And time oozed on. An endless sameness of screening questions put to subject after subject; an endless sameness of answers—as if every man and every woman in Germany had studied the same implausible script . . .

"No. I was not a Nazi. Never belonged to the party, or anything. . . ."

"Well, we heard *rumors* about those camps. But we didn't believe them. . . ."

"All of us non-native Germans were placed in the Waffen SS automatically. We had no choice. I only followed orders. . . ."

The soldier was ushered into the room by Murphy. He was number thirteen that morning. He stood quietly at attention just inside the door.

Erik studied him. He was not remarkable in any way—like hundreds, thousands of others. He was about thirty-five, with a ruddy complexion and large, guileless, water-blue eyes. He met Erik's steady gaze with friendly confidence. Erik held out his hand.

"*Soldbuch, bitte.*"

The man handed him his soldier's paybook. Erik began to look through it.

"Where do *you* want to go?" Don asked.

"To the Rhine, Herr Hauptmann." The answer was quick and straightforward. "I have a vineyard there, right on the river. I have not been home for a long time."

Erik looked up from the paybook.

"Your unit was disbanded a week ago?"

"That's correct, Herr Hauptmann. Rather than surrender to the Russians."

"And you were simply told to go home?"

"Yes, sir." He brought out a folded paper. "I have here my discharge papers." He handed the papers to Erik with a click of his heels.

"Your name is Plewig?"

"*Jawohl*, Herr Hauptmann. Plewig. Josef Plewig."

Don got up from his chair. He walked over to the German.

"Take off your jacket," he ordered, "and your shirt."

Plewig at once began to undress. He was not in the least worried. He knew exactly what the American was looking for. Let him look! he thought. He felt completely confident. He'd known he would be screened by the American Gestapo. Everything was going exactly as he'd been told it would at Thürenberg. He knew what to do. He'd gone through the exact same situation time and time again in training. He had all the answers. . . .

"Raise your left arm."

Plewig at once obeyed. Don glanced at his upper arm.

"You know what I'm looking for?"

"Yes, sir. To see if I have my blood type tattooed on my arm. Only the SS have it. But you see I don't."

He grinned disarmingly at Don. Erik handed the soldier's papers back to him.

"Your papers seem to be in order," he said. He sounded vaguely reluctant. "Take your clothes and go over there and put them on." He indicated the opposite side of the room.

"*Jawohl,* Herr Hauptmann."

Plewig retired. Don joined Erik at the table.

"You, too?" His voice was low.

"Yeah." Erik looked thoughtful. "Nothing to put your finger on, but . . ."

"Just that old feeling."

"Too pat. Too confident, unconcerned. I don't know. I just don't trust him." He looked toward the German. What *was* it? he thought. An attitude? The man's papers were all right—not perfect, nobody's were—just right enough. His answers made sense. His name was not on any list—and yet . . . He glanced at Don. He, too, was contemplating the soldier. Don feels it, too, Erik thought. He stretched. "I could do with a cup of coffee about now. What do you say we put Joe here through the wringer?"

"I'm for it."

Erik beckoned to the German. The man had finished dressing.

He walked over to the table and stood at attention. Erik looked directly at him.

"Just one more thing, Plewig," he said slowly. "We want you to write down your entire military career. As much as you can remember. Units—campaigns—dates—commanding officers. The works. Is that clear?"

Plewig felt a quick pang of alarm. What was *that* all about? He controlled any show of anxiety. There's nothing to worry about, he reassured himself. There could be a hundred reasons why the Americans wanted such detailed information from him. His unit. The fact that he was recently fighting the Russians. Anything. They probably just wanted to get as much intelligence for their records as possible. Anyway, he was fully prepared. His confidence returned.

Erik pointed to a small table.

"You'll find paper and pencil over there."

Plewig clicked his heels. He went to the table, sat down, selected a sheet of paper, licked the point of the pencil, and with deep concentration began to write. . . .

Don was at the door.

"Sergeant Murphy!"

"Sir?"

Don nodded toward Plewig, engrossed in his writing.

"Keep an eye on him. He's writing the story of his life. Let us know when he's through. We'll be in the rec room."

Betty Grable, coy and cuddly, smiled over her shoulder. Glamorous Lucille Ball looked radiant, and Ann Miller dazzled with her smile and that *wow* figure in a sexy bathing suit. Under the array of *Yank* pinups tacked to one wall some comedian had penciled in large letters: MEMORY AIDS.

The recreation room held a conglomeration of comfortable furniture obviously gleaned from diverse households. A battered radio stood on a table, and the inevitable potbellied stove had a cheery fire in it and was crowned with a large, softly steaming kettle.

Don made straight for the radio.

"Should be about time for our girl friend. A little music from home."

He fiddled with the dials. Erik poured black coffee into a couple of canteen cups. He brought one to Don. Out of the jumble of noise and static, a dulcet-toned female voice could be made out. Don carefully tuned it in.

". . . and remember, all you lonesome GIs, they miss you as much as you miss them, even though they may be brave and not show you how much in their letters. That is, of course, if they haven't found someone else! And now a little sweet music from home for my American boys."

Don settled down in one of the easy chairs. "That's it, Sally baby, now you're talking."

The strains of a melodious ballad flowed softly from the beat-up radio.

"Harry James," Don murmured. He closed his eyes and just listened. . . .

A girl was singing, " 'You made me love you. I didn't want to do it—I didn't want to do it. . . .' "

Erik cradled the warm canteen cup in his hands. He needed to relax. He thought of each of his muscles in turn, starting with his legs, consciously willing them to lose their tenseness. In less than a minute he felt completely relaxed. It was a trick he'd learned from Aunt Birte, when he lived with her. He remembered how startled he'd been when he came home one day to find her stretched out on the floor. "Relaxing," she'd explained. "Each separate muscle in turn. A few minutes of it is like a couple of hours' nap." And it worked. He didn't even have to lie flat on the floor anymore.

His thoughts strayed to the girl. She'd looked so—so appealing, lovely, standing with one bare arm raised. Awkward and graceful at the same time. Anneliese, was it? Of course it was. He knew it perfectly well. Did he have to pretend to himself that he'd forgotten? Anneliese . . .

No! No—he did *not* want to think of her. He felt himself go tense again. It was no damned good. No goddamned good! He forced himself to think of other things. How difficult it was to stand in a corner and *not* think of a white rhinoceros. . . .

He was suddenly and violently torn from his reveries. A blood-curdling shriek sliced through to his awareness. It wailed through the room like the baleful scream of some monster in excruciating pain.

It came from the radio.

Both Erik and Don stared at the instrument.

"Beware! Beware! This is the Werewolf Station! Death to all Americans!"

The grating masculine voice with its heavy, guttural accent gave way to the measured tones of the "Horst Wessel Lied." Don and Erik relaxed. Involuntarily both had snapped taut at the sudden scream. Don laughed.

"Boy, are they corny! But they make me jump every damned time." He settled back in his chair again. "Let's listen. They always put on a good show."

The door was suddenly flung open, and Hacker and Pierce came hurrying into the room. Hacker looked around quickly.

"What the hell's going on? Oh. The Werewolf program. What're they trying to do? Scare the shit out of us?"

"Seems to be the general idea," Don commented. "Have some java."

Hacker and Pierce helped themselves. The music on the radio came to an end.

"This is the Werewolf Station. Beware, Americans! You will never be safe on our holy German soil. Death will be your constant companion!"

Hacker flopped in one of the chairs.

"Hell," he said. "Anything's better than Pierce, here."

"Ve-ry funny." Pierce looked as sour as ever.

"Like the dreaded werewolves of the Middle Ages that came out of the night to spread terror and disaster, so shall we, the immortal defenders of Adolf Hitler, spring from the dark to deal destruction and death!"

Hacker shook his head. "Oh, brother!"

"Erich von Stroheim in one of his most villainous roles, right?" Don suggested.

"Von Stroheim was at least a ham," Erik said. "That guy's just corny."

"Beware, Americans! For it is you who shall feel the death grip of our fangs! *Sieg Heil! Sieg Heil!* . . . Beware the Werewolves!"

Again the marrow-freezing scream rent the air. Don switched the radio off.

"Who do they think they're kidding?" he asked. "Who'd fall for that melodramatic horseshit?"

Erik sipped his coffee. "Probably trying to bolster their own morale."

Hacker nodded. "Whistling in the dark."

"Could there be anything to it?" Pierce asked soberly of no one in particular.

"Could be," Erik answered. "Some fanatic diehards. But I doubt it."

"Anyone ever run into one of these Werewolves?"

"Not that I know of."

Sergeant Murphy stuck his head in the door. He looked at Erik. "You got visitors, sir."

Erik frowned. "Don't tell me . . ."

"Yep! The Rover Boys."

"Shit!" Erik looked disgruntled. He got up. "Well, I guess I'd better go see them." He turned to Murphy. "And, Jim. Get me the latest *OB* book, will you?"

Murphy looked dubious. "Well, I . . ."

"Even if you have to liberate it from the IPWs!"

Murphy grinned.

"Okay. I'll get it."

He left. ·

"What's up?" Hacker wanted to know.

"Just a hunch. We got this guy from the Rhineland. Wants to go home. His papers are in order; discharge and everything. But—"

·"He doesn't ring true—that it?"

"Yeah. We want to check his version of his military career with the facts in the *Order of Battle* book."

"That ought to do it."

Erik left the room. Hacker turned to Don.

"Didn't take Erik long to line up informants, did it?" He sounded impressed.

"The Rover Boys?" Don grimaced. "You can have them!"

One of the thick, greasy lenses of his spectacles was badly cracked, but the squat little man seemed quite unaware of it. Solemnly, silently he stood with his companion, a man of indeterminable age, tall, cadaverous, almost hairless and toothless. The two of them made a sight both grotesque and pathetic as they stood facing Erik in the Interrogation Room, clad in their threadbare striped clothing. *KZ'ler*, liberated concentration camp inmates. Deadly earnest, they were intent upon him, their eyes burning disturbingly, deep in dark sockets.

Erik contemplated the papers in his hand. Just like those they'd brought every day for the last week. Two sheets covered with a tiny handwritten scrawl. And in that all but impossible to read Gothic script. He looked at the two men in front of him.

"Thank you for your report." His voice was kind. "We're always glad to get them."

The little man bowed gravely; the tall one kept regarding Erik steadily.

"Please have something to eat with us. Sergeant Murphy will show you. . . ."

Again the little man bowed.

Erik nodded. *"Auf wiedersehen!"*

The two *KZ'ler* started to follow Murphy from the room. Erik looked at the papers disconsolately. He sighed. It would take him hours to wade through it all. He flipped a page and glanced at it. Suddenly he tensed. He looked up quickly. The two *KZ'ler* were just about to go through the door after Murphy.

"Just a minute!" Erik called. Excitement made his voice sound sharp. The two stopped in their tracks, their shoulders tensely hunched. All at once they looked trapped and terrified.

Erik walked up to them. They stood motionless. They did not look at him. He held the papers out to them.

"What does this mean?" He pointed to some words. " 'Hitler's Right Hand'?"

The two men stared at the floor—frightened, rigid. They made no answer.

"You wrote it, didn't you?" Erik was beginning to sound exasperated. He tapped the papers. "Here: 'In Katzbach, on the last farm on the Regensburg road, hides Hitler's Right Hand.'" He looked directly at the two men. "What do you mean by this? Who is 'Hitler's Right Hand'?"

He made a move toward the men. Without moving they seemed to shrink from him. They trembled. They made no sound.

Oh, Christ, Erik thought bleakly. Now I've done it. I should have known. Those poor bastards. After living so long in those hell holes, they clam up at any note of authority. They retreat into themselves and just take it. What can you expect, when a command, a rough voice, could mean death—or worse? He spoke to them in a low, calm voice.

"Don't be afraid. I just want to know what you mean. *Who* is hiding? Who told you about him?"

There was no answer. Erik turned to the short man. His voice was patient, soothing.

"Please tell me. How do you know?"

He looked away, suddenly realizing that his inquisitive gaze might be frightening to the little man, intimidating him. Like a dog used to beatings, growing apprehensive at a steady gaze, he thought. Quietly he said:

"You don't *have* to tell me, of course. Nothing will happen to you if you don't. But I'd be very grateful if you'd help me. Who is Hitler's Right Hand? Who told you about him?"

The little man stared at the ground. He looked clammy with fear. He blinked his eyes rapidly behind his thick-lensed glasses, struggling with himself to find courage somewhere in his tortured, shattered spirit. Finally he whispered:

"People . . ."

"What people? Who?"

The little man flinched, then stood silent, withdrawn into himself, appalled at his own boldness.

"There's no need to be frightened," Erik assured him. "No one will hurt you. Please believe me. Just answer me. . . ."

But there was no answer. Both men stood mute, cowed—and unreachable.

Erik watched them with a mixture of compassion and frustration, but he realized there was nothing he could do. He sighed and turned to Murphy.

"Get them something to eat," he said wearily. "Then meet me out front with the jeep."

"Okay." Murphy beckoned to the two *KZ'ler*. "Come along, fellers!"

His young voice held a surprising amount of understanding.

He saw her as soon as he stepped outside the door. She was standing in the street at a small wooden cart heaped with boards and tools, in earnest conversation with the German repairman. His first reaction was to walk by her as quickly as possible. But when the two of them looked up and noticed him, the workman touched his dirty leather cap, picked up a tool and turned back to his work repairing the bomb-damaged building. Anneliese watched Erik come toward her. She smiled.

"*Grüss Gott!*"

Erik stopped. He looked at the girl. He forced himself not to think. She was just a girl. Any girl. He felt cold. The gun in his shoulder holster suddenly weighed a ton.

"Well," he asked. "Are you all set?" His voice sounded strained to his ears.

"Yes. Thank you." She had a lovely, childlike smile. Then she frowned prettily. "I must come back to the military government." She looked up at him. "Tomorrow morning."

"Tomorrow." Erik felt trapped. He felt hot anger rise in him. Anger against himself. Dammit, he thought savagely. Isn't it about time I got over this crap? She's just someone in trouble. It doesn't mean a thing. He looked at her with professional concern.

"What about tonight," he asked. "Do you have anywhere to stay?"

The girl shook her head solemnly.

"I have been trying to find room." She glanced toward the workman. "Herr Krauss says it will be most difficult. So many refugees are here." She looked at Erik with her large eyes. "I will find somewhere."

But it was obvious she didn't think she would.

Erik avoided her eyes.

"Well," he said slowly, "perhaps—"

He looked up as a jeep with Murphy at the wheel came driving up, stopping short. Murphy grinned.

"Sorry it took so long!"

Erik quickly climbed in. He turned to Anneliese.

"I'm sure you'll find someplace. If not, I'll see what I can do when I get back."

"Thank you."

Erik turned to Murphy.

"Let's go."

Anneliese stood quietly, alone, watching the jeep disappear down the street. There was a little smile on her lips. She glanced toward the workman, Krauss.

She grew sober.

The jeep careened out of Weiden on the Regensburg road toward Katzbach. Erik sat silently, Murphy's carbine across his knees.

Murphy glanced at Erik.

"Those two guys," he commented. "They've been trading you reports for a good meal every day. What's in them, anyway?"

"Everything—nothing." Erik looked thoughtful. "Rumors. Their own observations. Fantasies. Gossip. But they're not just looking for a handout. They're really trying to help."

"But not much use, huh?"

"We've got to check on anything that sounds interesting."

"So what're we looking for now?"

"Hitler's Right Hand."

Murphy looked startled. Erik grinned.

"Or whatever other pieces of his anatomy we might find."

"Some Nazi big shot, huh?"

"Could be." Erik shrugged. "Could be anyone, from a farmer who once chased them away, to Martin Bormann himself!"

The last farm on the Regensburg road was just another typical Bavarian farm. A main house directly connected to the stables and a barn. A few sheds, and a big dunghill oozing liquid over the cobblestones of the yard.

As the jeep with Erik and Murphy came driving into the farmyard, a young girl sitting on a wooden bench at the front door of the house jumped to her feet in alarm, spilling the contents of a sewing basket in her lap out onto the ground. Quickly she ran into the house.

Murphy brought the jeep to a halt before the house and the two men dismounted. They were walking to the door, when it was suddenly flung open. Erik walked up to the door. Murphy, his carbine at port arms, stayed back a little, unobtrusively covering him.

The woman standing in the open doorway with the young girl was heavy-set, obviously used to hard work. She glared in silent hostility at Erik. The girl, perhaps seventeen or eighteen, was suntanned, blue-eyed and full-blown, with long blond pigtails wound around her head. She, too, regarded the two men with ill-concealed antagonism.

Erik stopped in front of the women.

"*Grüss Gott!*" he greeted them pleasantly.

There was no answer.

Erik turned to the older woman. He spoke in a firm, no-nonsense tone of voice.

"What is your name?"

The woman glared at him. Her voice was sullen.

"Hoffmann. Anna Hoffmann."

"Who owns this farm?"

"My husband."

"Where is he?"

The woman shrugged. "In Russia."

Erik nodded toward the young girl without looking at her.

"The girl?"

"My daughter. Lise."

"Who else lives here?"

"Just us." The woman hesitated slightly. Her eyes briefly flickered away from Erik's gaze. "And my brother."

"Where is he?" Erik was not unaware of the woman's reaction. She nodded toward the woods beyond the farm.

"Out there. In the woods. He's a forester."

"I see."

Erik walked over to Murphy. He spoke in a low voice.

"Jim. I'll take a look through the house. The woman comes with me. You keep the girl here."

"You bet!" Murphy grinned. "Best piece of ass I've seen all week! I'd sure like to be her drill instructor in a little bed calisthenics!"

Erik whirled on him.

"Shut up, damn you," he snarled. The command was spat out with sudden, unexpected savagery. "Keep your goddamned mind on your job!" His voice was harsh, his eyes haunted. He turned on his heel and quickly walked to the woman. Together they disappeared into the house.

Murphy stared after Erik. He was startled. What the hell got into him? he wondered. Must be going out of his fucking mind. He dismissed the incident and looked at the girl.

She ignored him. She was picking up the sewing things she had dropped when she ran into the house, and placing them in the basket. She was squatting, her back to Murphy. Her dress was pulled tight across her softly rounded buttocks.

Murphy stared. Yes, sir! A real fine piece of ass, he thought admiringly. He felt a pleasurable tension in his groin. He let his fantasies fly free. He visualized the girl in the sack—and he did a good job.

The girl turned and saw him watching her. She straightened up and sat down on the bench. She picked up a brightly colored kerchief and tied it around her hair.

Murphy was enjoying himself immensely. He was pleased to note that he'd gotten himself a hard on. Getting those old juices flowing, he thought with satisfaction. Makes a man out of you!

She's a damned pretty little thing. She reminds me of someone, he thought idly. That's it. The kerchief—

Suddenly the flash flood of memory inundated his mind. The swelling in his groin shriveled up. He felt chilled, clammy—and he was all of a sudden acutely aware of the surging sound of his blood pumping through his tense body. *Holy Mother of God!* he whispered in his mind. *Not again! . . .*

He was back seven months. In Baraville. A little French village just across the Moselle River. The scene was vivid in his mind.

The girl had come to the CIC office. She was a Ukrainian. A DP. A slave worker. Pretty, young, her big eyes filled with pain—and a kerchief tied around her blond braids. She walked into the Interrogation Room. She waddled like a duck, her feet wide apart.

She seemed in shock. She muttered softly, a moan in Ukrainian and broken German:

"Please—help me. . . . The SS . . . SS . . . Please—help me . . ."

She stopped. Still mumbling her pathetic pleas, she slowly lifted up her gaily colored skirt. Carefully she pulled away a large bandage from between her legs—a bandage soaked with clotted blood and pus.

And Jim saw.

Sweet Jesus! he thought in shock. *They cut it out!*

He stared for a seeming eternity at the angry, gaping wound, opened as if in a scream from hell. Putrid blood slowly oozed down the girl's white thighs. He gagged on the bilious taste of his own vomit—and suddenly he was conscious of a warm, wet feeling between his legs. With detached astonishment he realized he'd lost control of his bladder.

I've pissed in my pants, he marveled. He tore his eyes from the ghastly sight. He looked at Erik.

Erik was white, drawn. He grabbed the phone and ordered Doc Sokol to the office—on the double!

Jim had always liked his girls. In and out of bed. Since he left the States he'd never had any trouble finding a willing miss or mademoiselle—or even fräulein. But for months after seeing the young Ukrainian girl he lost interest whenever the opportunity for a lay presented itself. He kept visualizing that raw, angry cut.

He wasn't used to that. A pressure built up in his balls that at times became almost unbearable, and not even a wet dream gave him relief. It frightened him. He talked it over with a buddy, who told him he *had* to get rid of the stuff. If he couldn't do it with a girl, he'd have to do it himself.

He tried. He felt as if he were back in school in Beloit, Wisconsin. But as soon as he managed to get an erection, the sight of the bloody, mutilated genitals of the Ukrainian girl would again flood his mind, and he'd go limp. He couldn't do it. And the pressure kept getting worse.

Finally he had a sexual nightmare that still made him shudder when he thought of it—and after that, release.

But it had taken several months before he could look at a girl again and get a hard on without seeing that ravaged girl in his mind. . . .

And now it's happening again, he thought bleakly. Or is it just because of that damned kerchief reminding me? He had a sudden thought. Did Erik remember, too? Was that it?

Frantically he began to think of women he'd laid. He dwelt on moments of sexual pleasure, conjured up exciting intimacies, trying to shield himself against the crippling memory.

To his enormous relief, it worked.

He looked back at the young girl on the bench. But there was no real pleasure in it anymore.

In the *Bauernstube,* the large combination kitchen-dining-living
room of the main house with the ever-present wood-burning stove,
Erik stood before the older woman seated stiffly on a bench at a
massive table.

"Your brother," he asked. "Where is he?"

"I told you." Anna Hoffmann barely concealed her animosity. "In
the forest."

"Where?"

She shrugged.

"When will he be back?"

Again an indifferent shrug.

"How long has he lived here?"

"Always."

"What branch of the armed forces did he serve in?"

"He didn't." There was contempt in Anna Hoffmann's voice. "He
was too old. He is fifty-three—no, fifty-four years old."

"And what does he do?"

The woman sighed with resentful exasperation.

"I told you. Farming. Work in the forest."

"And he has been here all during the war?"

"Yes." But again Erik noticed the slight hesitation, the flicker in
the eyes.

"He was never gone?"

"No." Erik stared at her. His face was hard. He didn't say a word.
The woman looked away. She licked her lips. "Only—"

"Yes?"

"He—he was away. A couple of months. In the Volkssturm. Near
Cham." She suddenly flared in defiance. "He *had* to go!"

"When did he get back?"

"About—about a week ago."

"All right. Stay here!"

Erik went to the door and called Murphy over.

"Keep an eye on her, Jim," he said, nodding toward the woman.
"Nothing in the house," he continued. "Her brother has a room back
there. He's out. Working." He glanced toward Lise. "I'll have a talk
with the girl."

He steeled himself. He did it quite consciously. She was a lovely girl. Young. Appealing. Like—Tania. She's just another subject to be interrogated, he told himself firmly. There's something funny going on here, who knows what? He sighed. Who knows? Someone always knows. It's my problem to find out who. And maybe she's the one. If she is, what does she know?

For a moment he looked at the girl. I'll find out, he thought. There really are no secrets. No safe secrets. Just things some people know—and others don't. And there's always some way of finding out. . . .

He went up to her. She sat stiffly on the bench, studiously ignoring him as he approached. She seemed quite unconcerned, but he knew she was tense and apprehensive. She kept digging the toes of her naked, sun-browned feet into the dirt. Erik stopped before her. He tried to make himself sound friendly and relaxed.

"How old are you, Lise?"

"Seventeen." Her voice was flat.

"Your father is away?"

"Yes."

"How long has he been gone?"

"Three years almost."

"You must miss him."

The girl made no answer. Erik continued.

"But it must be nice to have your uncle come around now and again."

Lise eyed him coldly. "He *lives* here," she said. "*All* the time." There was scorn and barely concealed triumph in her young voice. She wasn't that easily tricked!

"Didn't he ever go away?" Erik asked.

"Yes." The girl dismissed him with contempt. "To the Volkssturm. For two months. I'm sure my mother told you that."

With deliberate impudence she turned to the task of bringing order to the chaos in her sewing basket.

Erik watched her. He suddenly looked interested. He reached over and picked out a small white box with black printing on the lid. It looked quite new. He shook it. It rattled. He turned to the girl, who was watching him with a little puzzled frown. He scowled.

"Is there a gun in the house?" he asked abruptly. He suddenly sounded disturbingly ominous. The girl gave a disdainful smile.

"No!" she said quickly. Too quickly?

Erik frowned. "What's in this?" He rattled the box again.

"Buttons."

"I see." Erik seemed deflated. "Where'd you get it?"

"My uncle gave it to me."

He looked at her. She stared back at him defiantly. He opened the box. It contained a collection of buttons. Different sizes, different colors. He couldn't quite keep his disappointment from showing. Buttons and bullets, after all, rattle alike. His friendliness disappeared. He became coldly aloof. Lise watched him with a derisive smile. The round was hers!

He intended her to think just that.

Erik strode to the door. He called Murphy and the woman out into the farmyard. He gave the little box back to Lise and addressed himself to Anna Hoffmann. He was impersonal, correct.

"We'd like to talk to your brother, Frau Hoffmann. Tell him to report to the Counter Intelligence office in Weiden tomorrow morning."

"To the American Gestapo." Anna Hoffmann's voice was acid.

"Yes. I shall tell him."

Erik nodded to the two women.

"*Grüss Gott*," he said. He turned and, followed by Murphy, mounted the jeep.

The women stared after the vehicle until it disappeared through the farm gate.

Murphy was concerned. He was frowning as he hunched over the wheel, driving back toward Weiden. He glanced at Erik.

"You know, sir," he said tentatively, "I thought there was something—something fishy about that place. You sure we shouldn't stick around?"

Erik regarded him quizzically. He looked secretly pleased with himself.

"Why?" he asked pointedly. "The girl?"

Murphy gave him a quick glance. That's a switch, he thought. And what the hell makes him so cheerful? The whole thing was a bust! Aloud he said, "No. No, sir."

He grinned.

"And 'no' is a terrible wrong word to be using about a dish like that." He grew sober. "No, I just had a feeling. That guy being away and all. Everything wasn't—uh—kosher."

"Kosher!" Erik laughed. "I thought you were Irish."

"And so I am. But the Irish don't have a monopoly on a well-turned phrase."

"That's quite an admission, Jim. Anyway, you're learning."

"Learning? Learning what? If I'm learning something, you'd better tell me what it is. How am I supposed to see the light if you keep me in the dark?"

Erik turned and looked back. He seemed satisfied. Up ahead a narrow dirt trail led off the road into the woods.

"We're out of sight by now. Turn in there." He pointed to the trail.

Murphy turned the jeep onto the dirt road. It was a sandy lane with deep ruts. He engaged the four-wheel drive. Soon they were well into the woods and nearing the ridge of a slope.

They stopped the jeep and dismounted. From the back Erik picked up a pair of binoculars, and the two men quickly made their way among the trees to the top of the ridge. Here the forest ended. On the far slope plowed earth and grassland stretched down to the Hoffmann farm below. Erik and Murphy took cover under some bushes at the edge of the forest and Erik began to scan the farm through his glasses. It was a perfect vantage point. The farm below lay deserted in the sun.

"It shouldn't be long now," Erik observed in a low voice. He felt that tingle of excitement that always coursed through him when something was about to happen.

"Okay, okay," Murphy complained. He glared at Erik with mock exasperation. "So don't tell me nothing!"

Erik only smiled. He was watching the farm. Suddenly he whispered, "There they are!"

From the farmhouse below Anna Hoffmann and her daughter came hurrying out. They stopped outside the door for a moment, looking around and listening intently. Then Lise ran to one of the sheds and disappeared inside. She quickly emerged with a bicycle, and at once she pedaled through the farm gate and on down the road toward the distant woods. Anna stood for a brief moment staring after her, then she hurried into the house.

Erik lowered the binoculars. He looked at Murphy. He nodded.

"Right on schedule."

"Sure!" Murphy gazed toward the disappearing figure of Lise. "What now, Mr. Holmes?"

"Now we wait."

"You sure like to play it dramatic, don't you? How did you know she'd take off like that?"

"I didn't." Erik grew serious. "Just a hunch they'd do something. Too many questions without answers."

"What answers? You didn't *ask* any questions."

"Didn't have to."

Murphy looked questioningly at him.

"That little box I had," Erik went on. "You saw it?"

"Sure. Little white box. What about it?"

"I picked it up from Lise's sewing basket. Her uncle gave it to her. For buttons." He looked soberly at Murphy. "It was a box from a haberdasher in Berlin. A box for a white dress tie!"

"I'll be damned!"

"You probably will," Erik agreed dryly. "But I wouldn't brag about it."

He surveyed the road through the binoculars. Lise was no longer to be seen.

"Now, that little box was quite new." He looked thoughtful. "*When* was her uncle in Berlin? *Why*? And what was a poor farmer doing with a white dress tie?"

Once more he inspected the area through the binoculars.

"Or did he get it from someone else? If so, from whom?"

"Some questions, all right." Murphy was impressed. "How do you figure the answers?"

"I'm hoping they'll be coming down that road pretty soon," Erik answered.

"And I thought you'd given up on those two dames!"

Erik grinned.

"So did they, I hope. That's what I wanted them to think."

The two men settled down to wait, huddled as comfortably as possible under the shrubbery. The earth smelled sweet and moist. The air was filled with a steady soft hum of a host of busy insects, occasionally accented by the insistent whine of a curious fly.

Suddenly Erik tensed. He watched through the binoculars. Instinctively he spoke in a whisper.

"Here they come!"

Below on the road Lise came bicycling toward the farm. She was accompanied by a middle-aged man clad in Bavarian forester's clothes: long woolen socks, knee breeches and a gray wool jacket. The two cyclists quickly turned into the farmyard and made straight for the shed.

Erik lowered the binoculars. He looked at his watch.

"Twenty-three minutes. He wasn't far away."

He turned to Murphy, suddenly all business.

"Okay, Jim. We'll give them fifteen minutes."

Murphy glanced at his watch. Erik continued:

"You get around in back of the house. I'll go in from the front. If you hear anything that sounds remotely like trouble, come running!"

The yard of the Hoffmann farm was drowsy and peaceful in the sun. Even the scraggy hens scratched and pecked only lazily among the cobblestones. But they flapped frantically out of the way in loud, squawking protest as Erik's jeep came barreling into the yard, skidding to a dirt-spraying halt at the door to the house. Erik leaped from the jeep and burst through the door.

Only Lise was present in the *Bauernstube*. She was standing at the table, frozen in shock, her eyes huge with fear. On the table sat a large, half-filled rucksack, and the girl clutched a loaf of coarse bread and a sausage in her hands, partly wrapped in newspaper.

"Where's your uncle?" Erik's voice was sharp, commanding.

The girl stared at him. She didn't move. She didn't answer. Suddenly the door to the rear of the house was flung open. Erik whirled toward it. His gun was in his hand, locked firmly against his abdomen, pointing directly at whatever he'd be facing. In the doorway stood Anna. Her face was hard, her eyes blazed with malevolence.

"Your brother," Erik demanded curtly. "I want to see him. Now." He nodded toward the rucksack. "Before he takes off."

Anna filled the doorway. She seemed totally unaware of the gun pointed at her.

"He is not here," she stated tonelessly.

Without a word, Erik pushed past her into the hallway beyond. A narrow staircase led to an attic door. Two doors led to rooms off the hall, a third, in the rear, to the outside.

Erik went directly to one of the doors and kicked it open. The small room beyond was empty. On the unmade bed several items of a man's clothing were scattered about. An old, half-packed suitcase sprawled open on the table.

Erik turned to the two women cowering in the hallway, watching him.

"*Where is he?*"

"He is not here!" Anna glared at Erik, her face white and strained.

Erik took a step toward the women. Lise stared at him, ashen-faced. His eyes bored relentlessly into hers. He saw her gaze involuntarily flit away from him for a split scond, to his right, and up. . . .

The attic door.

At once Erik followed her glance. The door stood ajar, but there was no movement, no sound.

Suddenly Lise cried out:

"He's got a gun!"

Almost at once there was a shot from the attic door. And another! The bullets whizzed by Erik, who was already diving for the cover of the staircase railing, and buried themselves in the wall behind him. The two women screamed.

Erik fired a couple of shots at the door. They tore into wood as the door slammed shut.

In almost the same instant, Murphy came crashing into the hallway through the back door, his carbine hip-ready. Erik shot a glance at him.

"Cover me!" he snapped.

Murphy at once aimed his gun at the attic door, as Erik cautiously started up the steps. He was nearly to the top. . . .

Suddenly there was the sound of a muffled shot from the attic.

Erik bounded up the last few steps and kicked open the door. He threw himself back, flat against the wall. Nothing happened. Not a sound. Not a movement.

Warily he peered into the attic. He turned, motioned to Murphy and stepped through the door.

The body sprawled on the dusty floor looked grotesquely out of place among the old pieces of broken furniture and wooden chests that ringed the attic.

Anna Hoffmann's brother was dead.

Slowly Erik walked over to him and looked down. The dead man's staring, unseeing eyes looked back at him from a blood-spattered face. Crazily pushed-out teeth forced his torn lips apart. From one corner of his mouth the blood flowed steadily, unhurriedly, to form a pool on the floor, pushing the dust before it.

Erik felt drained. Death had come so swiftly; the taking of life so easy. . . .

Almost too easy, he thought angrily. I hadn't planned to kill him. Somehow he felt outraged at the face of death. It seemed obscene. Life should not be that quickly erased. That easy to take away. It ought to be more—defiant.

Murphy joined him. He stared at the body.

"Holy shit," he whispered. It sounded almost like a prayer. "He —he stuck his gun in his mouth and pulled the trigger." He was shaken.

Erik knelt down beside the dead man. He wrested the gun from his fingers. Then he suddenly turned over the dead hand.

"No wonder he couldn't let himself be seen by us," he said. He touched the palm of the dead man's hand. It was soft. It was full of blisters, some of them newly broken.

"Yeah. Some farmer!" Murphy concurred. "His hands must have been as soft as a baby's ass!"

Erik frowned. He knew he'd made a discovery, and he struggled to capture its full meaning. It eluded him. He examined the gun. He whistled in astonishment.

"What do you know," he said, impressed. "*Ehrenwaffe*."

"*Ehren—waffe?*" Murphy cocked an inquiring eye.

"Means 'honor weapon,'" Erik explained. He straightened up and gave the gun to Murphy. "It's a Walther 7.65 millimeter. Look at the ornamentation on the steel. All hand carved. It is given by Hitler personally to special friends, high-ranking Nazis."

Murphy was inspecting the gun.

"Yeah. His name's on it." He pointed to a small plaque on the butt of the gun. "What's it say?" He showed it to Erik.

"It says: 'To Reichsamtsleiter Manfred von Eckdorf. Faithfully, Adolf Hitler.'"

Murphy looked down at the dead Nazi.

"A very useful gift," he commented thoughtfully. He looked back at Erik.

"But I don't get it. Why kill himself? And what was he doing here? That's no brother of that Hoffmann dame, that's for sure. Just a big shot Nazi hiding out? Afraid to face the music? Or what?"

Erik shook his head soberly. He'd wanted answers to his questions. And all he got was a whole list of new questions more puzzling than ever. He sighed. He had his work cut out for him. It would be a cold day in hell before that woman, Anna Hoffmann, and her daughter would come up with any answers.

"Beats me," he said.

He stared at the dead man. Hitler's right hand? he thought. Well, maybe not quite . . .

He felt disturbed, uneasy. As if he were missing something.

2042 hrs

It was dark when Erik and Murphy finally drove up to the Weiden jail. The street was deserted. The half-finished repair job of Herr Krauss, the workman, looked like an open wound on the building, waiting to heal.

Erik had taken care of loose ends. The Hoffmann women were in custody; the body of Reichsamtsleiter Manfred von Eckdorf had been sent to AIC for positive identification. Erik and Murphy had searched the Hoffmann farm thoroughly—and found nothing. Anna Hoffmann had finally admitted that the dead man was a stranger to her and to her daughter. He'd shown up at the farm about a week before, asking to be allowed to hide there as a member of the family. He'd threatened them with dire consequences if they gave him away, they maintained. Erik did not believe them.

But whatever von Eckdorf's reasons were for being at the Hoffmann farm, he no longer could do anything about them, one way or another.

Erik dismounted from the jeep slowly. He was bone tired.

"See you in the morning," Murphy called. He grated the jeep gears and took off for the motor pool. For a moment Erik stood in silent thought, then he started for the front door of the jail. The single naked bulb suspended over it cast only a limited pool of dim light directly in front of the entrance.

He almost missed it—the faintest scraping sound coming from the black shadows to his right.

He whirled toward it and stood balanced in a crouch, gun locked at his abdomen.

"Come out of there," he ordered. "Easy—real easy."

A figure dimly made out, huddled at the base of the wall, stirred and stood up.

"Into the light! Move!"

The figure walked toward the pool of pale light. Erik slowly pivoted with the move, his gun trained straight at the shadowy form. Suddenly he could make out who it was.

"Anneliese!" he exclaimed. "What are you doing here?"

The girl stood quietly in the light. She clutched an old piece of hand luggage wrapped with a leather strap in front of her. Her cheeks were streaked with dried tears. In her rumpled dirndl skirt and blouse she looked both vulnerable and appealing. Erik put his gun away. He stepped up to her.

"What are you doing here?" he repeated.

"I was waiting." Her voice was small. "For you."

He felt his insides tense up. "What is it?"

"I—I can find no place to go. There is no room for me anywhere."

She was fighting valiantly to blink away the tears brimming in her eyes. She looked down. A single tear broke loose and rolled down her cheek.

Erik stared at her. He felt drawn to her. Strongly. Needfully. And he felt the chill of guilt. He ached with the conflict that raged within him. He was fully aware of the harrowing memories the girl brought back to him, memories that threatened to devour him. But for once he refused to bury them and he repelled the impulse to run away and retreat into his shell. He forced himself to look straight at the girl. She was so much like—her.

Baraville, France. Seven months ago, that's when it happened. She, too, had had tears in her eyes, but they'd been tears of joy.

Erik and his CIC team had entered the little French village on the heels of the assault troops that took the town.

Tania was just twenty. She was Ukrainian, brought from her native land to labor for her conquerors in a strange, faraway place when she was only seventeen. Her happiness at being freed was boundless. Years of pent-up misery, humiliation and despair miraculously and instantaneously changed into a wellspring of joy, and delight—and love.

Erik was entranced with the girl and her inexhaustible exuberance. It had been a long time, and Tania was eager to give of her overwhelming gratitude and her love.

They were together. Their hunger for one another had the fervor of desperation and profound need. His, to cling to sanity through tender closeness, an abandonment in passion. Hers, to give of herself without limit, with no thought of time or place.

And throughout that one night Erik loved her. Loved her with his every embrace, his every thought. Tania.

The next day the Germans counterattacked.

It was a seesaw battle, and the Germans drove the Americans from Baraville. They held the village for less than twenty-four hours. The front rolled inexorably toward the Rhine, and Baraville once again fell to the American troops.

Erik returned.

It was a hectic time. He had little opportunity to give any thought to his Ukrainian girl.

And then she walked into his office.

Tania.

Horribly mutilated. Punished by the vengeful SS troops when they learned she'd given herself to the enemy. With malignant brutality they had reduced her to a nonwoman, making certain she'd never love or be loved again. Because of him.

Because of him! Because of him . . .

Since then he had felt that he'd never be able to hold a woman in his arms again. Rationally he could argue that he was not to blame. That's what his conscious mind understood and accepted. But not his so much more exacting, so much more punitive subconscious. He was not allowed to forget Tania. . . .

Erik looked steadily at the young girl standing before him. Anneliese. Somehow he felt calmer. He was suddenly aware of her despondency.

"Don't worry, Anneliese," he said. His voice had lost its tenseness. He smiled at her. "There's got to be someone who can put you up. We'll see."

"I am not from here," she said quietly. "They do not want me.

I have nowhere to go." She looked up at him with her huge, tear-bright eyes. "Unless—" She stopped.

Erik made up his mind.

"You can't stay out here," he said resolutely. He started toward the door. "I hope you don't mind spending the night in jail."

Anneliese gave him a little smile.

"It is where you stay, yes? I do not mind. . . ."

A makeshift blackout curtain had been hung over the window in the Interrogation Room. A cheery fire in the potbellied stove cast a warm, flickering glow across the wooden floorboards.

"You can put your things here," Erik said. He did not turn on the light. "We'll find a place for you to sleep." He looked at her. "Perhaps one of the cells . . ."

Anneliese held on to her battered suitcase. She returned Erik's look.

"Thank you," she said softly. "But I do not think I should like to sleep in—in a cell."

Erik felt confused, unsure of himself. He felt intensely attracted to the girl. He wanted her. The realization astounded him. His nightmare memories seemed to have faded. They were still there, but he could look at them, face them without being obsessed. He wanted to take the girl in his arms, crush her to him, lose himself in her warmth, her softness, her woman scent. He wanted to love, and forget everything else. But could he forget? Could he? . . .

He took a step closer to her. Her face shone with promise, as the soft, shimmering light from the fire played light and shadow across her expectant features. She looked infinitely lovely and desirable. Erik felt a heaviness pressing in his chest.

"Anneliese," he said hoarsely. "There's no place else for you to sleep, unless . . ."

Suddenly the door flew open and Don came barging in. He flipped on the single glaring light bulb and took in the situation at a quick glance.

"It's about time," he growled. "What the hell kept you?"

Erik stepped away from the girl.

"I ran into a little trouble."

"So I see." Don glanced at Anneliese.

"Took time to straighten out."

"She part of it?"

"No." Erik felt vaguely resentful. "She's got no place to go. She'll sleep here tonight."

Don brightened.

"And I've got just the place for her," he announced cheerfully. "Your bunk!"

Erik glanced quickly at Anneliese. She was looking at the floor. He turned to Don angrily. Don held up a hand in mock defense.

"You won't be needing it, my friend. Not tonight." He slapped the bunch of papers he held in his hand. "We've got a little trouble right here."

"So what's new?"

"Joe!"

"Joe?"

"Yeah. I've got him on ice. That Kraut we had write out his life story. Josef Plewig." He grew sober. "Erik—the guy is lying in his teeth!"

Erik was at once attentive. He took the papers from Don and frowned over them. Anneliese was watching the two men. Her face was grave. She didn't move. She stood quiet, as if unwilling to call attention to herself.

Murphy appeared in the open door.

"Anything else?" he asked. "Me, I'm ready for some serious bunk fatigue." He spotted Anneliese. His face lit up happily. "*Gu-te a-bend, Fräu-lein,*" he pronounced in laborious and atrociously accented German.

Anneliese acknowledged his greeting with a little awkward smile. Erik looked up from the papers.

"We'll have to check this whole fairy tale with the *OB* book."

"But good!" Don nodded agreement.

Erik turned to Anneliese.

"You can stay here tonight, Anneliese. In my room." He felt a strange mixture of regret and relief.

"Thank you."

Erik turned to Murphy.

"Show her where it is, will you, Jim?"

"With pleasure!" Murphy reached for the girl's suitcase. Reluctantly she gave it to him. "Come on, honey." They started to leave. Don stopped them.

"And, Jim." He looked at the young sergeant with mock concern. "You *do* look as if you could use that bunk fatigue you mentioned. Better get it." He grinned a sardonic grin. "Pleasant dreams!"

Murphy snapped to attention. He clicked his heels a couple of times in exaggerated Teutonic fashion and saluted elaborately.

"Yes, *sir!* At your orders, *sir!*"

With great dignity he ushered the girl from the room.

Erik walked to the table. He picked up a heavy volume. The *Order of Battle* book.

"Come on, Don. Let's catch us a spy!"

Werewolf Headquarters

2309 hrs

Waffen SS Lieutenant Willi Richter was out of uniform. He felt vaguely uncomfortable. His civilian jacket and open shirt disturbed him.

Ill-tempered, he pushed a crate marked STIELHANDGRANATEN 24 closer to the wall. The positions prepared for General Krueger's headquarters were far less roomy than had been specified. Typical army incompetence, he thought with disgust. Boxes and crates were stacked along the wooden walls, weapons and equipment lay everywhere. It was difficult to move around in the cramped quarters. And they'd had a lot of trouble with the motorcycles. He wondered if the operations units had the same problem. It was not efficient.

He entered the small radio room. A man in civilian clothes was seated before a shortwave set. He was wearing earphones and writing on a pad. Glancing at Willi, he held up a hand for silence.

Willi leaned against the wall, watching the operator. The man was listening attentively. After a while he sent a short acknowledgment. He tore off the message he'd written and gave it to Willi.

"Munich," he said laconically.

Willi glanced at the message. Then he read it through with mounting excitement. At last! he thought. *Jetzt geht's los!* It begins! He hurried off.

General Krueger's personal quarters occupied the largest room of the installation. Here, too, equipment and weapons, boxes and crates were stored against the walls. The general himself was sitting at a large table spread with maps when Willi entered. He was wearing his Bavarian clothes. Willi still wasn't quite used to seeing his commanding officer in civvies. Some of the officer's military authority seemed to be gone. He looked rather like a nice, quite ineffectual old man, Willi thought. He had to keep reminding himself that he knew better. He handed the message to the general.

"A message, Herr General!" He had trouble keeping the excitement out of his voice. "From Hans-32, over Munich."

Krueger took the message. He read it. It was short and to the point:

AMERICAN OFFICER COURIER LEAVING FOR U.S. ARMY
HEADQUARTERS AT SCHWARTZENFELD 29.4—06 HOURS.
MAY BE CARRYING IMPORTANT PRIME TARGET INFORMATION.
HANS-32.

Krueger scribbled a note on the message. He handed it to Willi. "Have this sent at once," he ordered. "Unit B. They'll take action."

Willi came to attention.

"Herr General!"

Krueger looked up at him.

"Yes, Richter?"

"Herr General. I should wish to have the honor to lead this first action of the Werewolves!"

Krueger studied him.

"Unit B is capable of carrying out the mission, don't you think?"

"Of course, Herr General." Willi thought fast. He *had* to be part of this. His whole body was tense with the need for action. "May I submit the following, Herr General?" he said quickly. "The area of the action is between here and the location of Unit B. I would need two men from there. We could rendezvous near the place selected for the ambush. The risk of discovery prior to action would be dispersed, and minimized, sir." He looked straight at Krueger. "My English is fluent, and I would be able to bring the general a firsthand report on our initial mission."

Krueger contemplated the earnest young man standing before him. The kind of officer he'd need. The kind of officer Germany would need to be victorious. Perhaps to survive. Young. Eager. Dedicated. Perhaps this kind of zeal ought to be rewarded, he thought. He smiled to himself. So like the way I used to be.

"*Einverstanden*, Leutnant Richter," he said. "Very well—the mission is yours."

Willi clicked his heels. He felt a surge of excitement.

"Make your own plan of action. And report back as soon as the mission is carried out."

"*Jawohl*, Herr General!"

Once again he clicked his heels. He hurried off. He looked at the paper in his hand with awe. He felt elated. It was the first, the very first order for action given by Sonderkampfgruppe Karl—General Krueger's Werewolf Headquarters—and he would lead the mission!

It was the beginning.

Tomorrow the enemy would learn that the Werewolves were more than a scream over the air.

Tomorrow!

Part III

29 Apr 1945

■

The Road to Schwartzenfeld

Emmy Lou was tooling along the road to Schwartzenfeld at a steady 50. Emmy Lou was the young wife of T5 Elbert Graham from Florida City, Florida, and her name was painted boldly—although somewhat unevenly—in white letters on the olive drab front of the jeep just below the windshield. The Emmy Lou back home was a mighty pretty girl, and T5 Graham, working in the corps motor pool, took pride in keeping her namesake in top condition. He'd painted the name himself. He felt real proud of "his" jeep; he felt almost affection for it. Emmy Lou. He felt kind of good every time he got in behind the wheel. The smart-ass motor pool sergeant kidded him he'd made the jeep into a sex symbol. What a crock of shit! He just liked driving a neat and sound vehicle. The damned jalopy he'd been driving back home was so old, he pretty near had to apply for upper and lower plates for her. Sex symbol, my ass!

The road was deserted. It looked drowsy and peaceful in the early morning light. The war had come—and gone on. It was quiet. T5 Graham was making good time.

Like the eye of a hurricane back here, he thought. The storm is raging around us.

He glanced at the officer sitting next to him. A captain. What the hell was his name again? Lorrimer? Lattimer? Lattimer—that was it. An officer courier. A dispatch case was slung over his shoulder, and he cradled a Thompson submachine gun across his knees. He was staring straight ahead.

T5 Graham took a quick squint at the signpost on a side road as he barreled past. The arm pointing down the main road read: SCHWARTZENFELD 60 Km. Good! He'd be there in time for a second breakfast.

Ahead, a small wooded area crept down a hillside on the right and straddled the road. T5 Graham didn't slow down. He was aware that the officer next to him repositioned his submachine gun for quick action.

They entered the little forest.

Rounding the first bend, T5 Graham hit the brakes.

A crude tree-branch barrier had been thrown across the road, blocking it except for a narrow passage on the side. An MP jeep was parked nearby, and two MPs were standing at the barrier. One of them flagged Emmy Lou to a halt.

The two MPs approached the jeep, one on each side.

"Sorry to stop you, sir," one of them addressed the officer courier.

"What is it?"

"The engineers, sir," the man answered. "They're clearing the stretch ahead of Teller mines. The road was lousy with the damned things."

Impatiently the officer glanced at his watch.

"How long a delay?"

"Oh, you can go ahead now, sir. One side has been cleared. Just keep well to the left."

"Thank you." The captain turned to T5 Graham. "Let's go, Corporal. You heard what he said?"

"Sure did! I'll keep two wheels in the left ditch all the way, sir!"

Emmy Lou had gone about a quarter of a mile, carefully hugging the left road shoulder.

Suddenly the forest quiet was shattered by a tremendous explosion. Automatically T5 Graham stomped the brake pedal to the floorboards. Emmy Lou skidded to an instant halt. The two men ducked, as the shock wave slammed an almost visible fist into the jeep.

For a moment neither man moved. Then the captain straightened up. He looked around. He motioned for T5 Graham to drive on, and Emmy Lou cautiously crept toward the next bend in the road.

Beyond was a sizable clearing. Several GIs were crouched at the roadside. Near the bend a sergeant and a corporal were kneeling by a detonator. At the sound of the slowly approaching jeep the sergeant looked up. He waved for them to stop, and turned back to the clearing.

"Fire in the hole!" he shouted. "Fire in the hole!"

The GIs hugged the ground. The sergeant gave a quick twist of the detonator handle, and out in the clearing an instantaneous geyser of dirt and smoke shot into the air. A fraction of a second later the deafening sound of the explosion crashed across the men's ears.

The sergeant came over to the jeep.

"Okay, sir, you can go ahead now," he said. He nodded toward the clearing. "Just getting rid of a pile of Kraut mines. The road's clear from here on."

"Good. Thank you."

The captain nodded to T5 Graham.

"Let's go."

Emmy Lou started off again, down the road to Schwartzenfeld. Sure, T5 Graham thought sourly. Let's go! . . . We've lost a goddamned fifteen minutes as it is. Probably miss that second breakfast now. Dammit!

Weiden

0659 hrs

A door banged. Someone padded down the corridor. Don looked at his watch. It was later than he thought. He stretched. He was getting hungry.

He pushed his wooden chair back from the desk and stood up. His bladder all at once felt uncomfortably heavy and bloated.

He was surprised. He hadn't been conscious of any pressing need to relieve himself as long as he was sitting down. He walked across the Interrogation Room to the window. The makeshift blackout curtain was still drawn, but newborn daylight seeped into the room around the edges.

Don threw the curtain aside. He walked to the door and turned off the strong electric bulb hanging overhead. He shook the grill in the potbellied stove. The fire was long dead. It had been one hell of a long night. . . .

He looked at the desk, strewn with papers and books. Erik was still poring over the *OB* book and Plewig's military biography.

Don stretched again.

"It's damned well done"—he yawned—"but the little things trip him up."

"Here's another one." Erik nodded. "Look at this."

Don walked to the desk and leaned over Erik's shoulder.

" 'Served with 173rd Engineer Battalion attached to General Bünau's 73rd Infantry Division,' " Erik read from Plewig's carefully penciled biography. " 'Participated in the Balkan campaigns. Also South Russian front. My Commanding Officer was Major Horst von Wetterling.' "

He looked up at Don. "Right?"

He stabbed an accusing finger at a page in the *OB* book.

"*Here* it says: '73rd Infantry Division. Commander: Lt. Gen. Rudolf von Bünau (56). Home Station: Würzburg—Bavarian personnel. Composition.' Let's see. . . ."

His eyes skated across the printed words.

"Infantry. Artillery. Reconnaissance. Signal. *Engineer*. Okay, now . . ."

He pointed at the words:

"Commanding Officers: 1. Maj. Horst von Wetterling. Campaigns: Poland, Saar, France. Killed in France."

He looked up at Don.

"The man was *dead* when our little SOB here claims he served under him!"

Don flipped Plewig's biographical notes with his hand.

"Sure looks memorized to me."

"You can say that again, old buddy."

"Wonder what the guy *really* did, what he is."

"I think we're about ready to trot him out again. Okay?"

"Okay." Don nodded. "You want to use the 'good guy, bad guy' routine?"

"Don't think so." Erik stroked his nose in thought. "It's pretty damned obvious the guy's a phony. He's probably wise to that kind of fun and games. We wouldn't accomplish anything except wasting time."

"Okay. We'll give it to him with both barrels!"

Don straightened up. Again he was painfully conscious of the full pressure in his bladder.

"How about a shower and some chow before we light into him?" he said.

Erik stood up. "I'm for that."

They walked from the room. Don began to hurry. Now that relief was in sight, he could hardly wait. One good thing about always picking the biggest and best building in town to set up shop, he thought with all the gratification of a hedonist. Indoor plumbing!

"Be with you in a minute," he called over his shoulder. "And get a ration, will you? Pierce used the last of the soap."

0733 hrs

"Two to one he's SS."

"No tattoo." Erik pointed to his upper left arm.

"So he hasn't got the SS tattoo. Could be many reasons for that," Don countered.

"My guess is he's Gestapo," Erik said. "From some little town about to be overrun by the Russians."

"Could be," Don agreed. "Prefers us 'decadent democrats' to the 'savage Slavs,' no doubt!"

Erik grinned. The two CIC agents were once again seated behind the big desk in the Interrogation Room. But the desktop was now clean—with the conspicuous exception of Plewig's biography and the big *OB* book. The men looked fresh and somehow eager with anticipation, ready to "engage the enemy" in their own way. . . . Erik felt quite certain of the outcome. A good interrogation—like a good lay—could come to only one predictable end.

The door opened and Sergeant Murphy ushered Plewig into the room.

"Josef Plewig, sir," he announced crisply.

Plewig snapped to attention.

Erik looked up from the papers in front of him.

"That's all, Sergeant."

Murphy saluted formally and left the room.

Erik looked at Plewig for a moment.

"Stand at ease, Plewig," he said. His manner seemed friendly and informal. He returned his attention to the papers on the desk. Don lit a cigarette.

Plewig stood at ease. Outwardly he seemed not the least apprehensive but he did not allow himself to relax. He studied the two Americans unobtrusively. He saw his biographical notes on the desk. He felt a quick twinge of alarm. Had he made any mistakes? No. No, he hadn't. At least nothing the Americans could possibly know. He wondered what the big book lying open on the desk had to do with it, and he correctly guessed it was some sort of summary of information. The smoke from the cigarette wafted toward him, tantalizing him. He suddenly felt completely confident. Let them enjoy their cigarettes and read in their fat book, he thought. I'm ready for them.

Erik looked up at him.

"Now then," he said pleasantly. "That biography of yours. It seems to be quite complete."

"*Jawohl*, Herr Hauptmann."

"However . . ." He suddenly frowned. "However, there are a few questions we'd like to ask you. You don't mind answering, do you?"

"Not at all, Herr Hauptmann."

"Good. It shouldn't take long. . . ."

The Road to Schwartzenfeld

0741 hrs

Emmy Lou was purring along.

T5 Graham enjoyed himself. It really pleasured him to let Emmy Lou run wide open down the empty country road. He was quite literally seduced by the feel of speed, the roar of the air whistling around the windshield of the open jeep.

Shouldn't be long now, he thought. Another fifteen or twenty kilometers. Might just squeeze in that second breakfast after all. . . . He glanced at the officer next to him. As long as he don't come up with the wait-in-the-jeep-I-won't-be-long bit. . . .

He looked ahead. He squinted. The sun was still low and straight in front of them. A small stone bridge over a stream with trees and shrubs seemed to hurtle toward them. As they came closer they could see three men walking on the road shoulder in the same direction they were driving. Hearing the jeep approach, the three men stopped and turned. One of them waved an arm.

The captain motioned for T5 Graham to stop, and he brought Emmy Lou to a halt some twenty feet in front of the waiting men.

T5 Graham stared at them with curiosity. What the hell kind of a snafu detail is that? he thought.

The three men were a strange sight. Two of them were German Waffen SS soldiers. Sterling specimens of the Master Race. One had his hands clasped behind his neck, the other had his right hand on top of his helmet, his left arm in a bloody makeshift sling. The third man was a GI. He was covering the two Germans with a carbine. His right pants leg was ripped open and a slipshod bandage had been tied around the calf of his leg. It, too, was bloody and wet.

The captain carefully got out of the jeep. He covered the little group with his tommy gun. The GI took a couple of steps toward the jeep. He limped badly.

"Boy, am I glad to see you, sir!" he said fervently. "I thought sure I was going to end up wearing a mattress cover."

"What's going on, soldier?" The captain nodded toward the two Germans. "Who are these men?"

"They're a couple of SS, sir." The GI shifted his feet, favoring his good leg. "We flushed them out of a cellar this morning. At a farm back a ways. There were three of them. Me and my buddy were told to take them to a PW camp up the road."

"Where are the others?"

The GI looked grim.

"The lousy bastards jumped us." He glared malevolently at the two Germans. "They got my buddy straight off—and one of the Krauts bought it, too." He nodded toward the man with the arm sling. "That guy got a busted hand—and I got myself a knife in the leg."

He looked toward Emmy Lou, then back at the officer, hopefully.

"Maybe the captain could give me a hand getting those jokers back?"

He grinned ingratiatingly at the officer. "Sure would be appreciated, sir."

The officer called to T5 Graham without turning.

T5 Graham got out of Emmy Lou and walked up to the two Germans.

Shit! he thought with annoyance. There goes that second breakfast for sure.

He started to frisk the first prisoner. These fucking Krauts. If they don't get at you one way, it'll sure be another! He turned toward the captain.

"This one's clean, sir."

He stepped in front of the soldier with his arm in the sling. The man smiled at him. He made a small motion with his injured hand at his belt buckle. . . . .

Instantly four shots rang out in rapid succession.

T5 Graham screamed.

He grabbed his stomach with both hands. He was startled at the warmth of the oily fluid that oozed between his fingers. His eyes slid across the face of the German before him, as he pitched to the ground. The man was still smiling. He hit the dirt at a crazy angle. His sight grew blurred. The last thing he saw was Emmy Lou seeming to spin and spin and spin. . . .

The captain at once brought up his tommy gun, but in the instant the shots were fired, the GI jammed his carbine in the officer's side.

"Don't!" he said sharply. His voice was utterly without emotion. "Drop it!"

The tommy gun clattered to the ground.

Waffen SS Lieutenant Willi Richter glanced at the dead man on the ground before him. Mission accomplished. He felt nothing. He had a fleeting vision of the butchered SS guards sprawled across the Jew gold. He almost heard the protesting cries of the outraged crows. He felt strangely let down, now that it was done. But at least, this time, the bodies were not German.

Willi turned to the "injured" German soldier. He nodded toward the courier. "He's all yours, Steiner," he said.

Steiner lifted his hand from the sling and carefully closed his belt buckle. He smiled coldly to himself, remembering the last time he'd fired the gun. Back at Thürenberg. To impress that pompous little jackass from Berlin. This time there'd be no property of the Reich to account for!

He stepped over T5 Graham and walked up to the officer courier. He smiled.

"Your dispatches, please!"

He held out his hand.

Weiden

0749 hrs

So far so good, Erik thought. He was holding the Plewig biographical notes before him, apparently studying them. So far only routine questions—and routine answers. But good ones. Plausible. The man was good—or he really was what he maintained he was, an ordinary discharged Wehrmacht soldier trying to get home. Erik frowned at the papers. Could it be that he just had a bad memory? Made mistakes? The beginning of a nagging doubt brushed the edges of Erik's mind. He dismissed it. Time to drop the pleasantries, he thought grimly. Time for that elusive moment of truth. He was conscious of the familiar keyed-up feeling. Like a hound before the hunt . . .

"Now, you say here you were a member of the 3rd Platoon, 2nd Company of the 173rd Engineer Battalion. Is that correct?"

Plewig clicked his heels.

"Correct, Herr Hauptmann."

He felt confident. He'd answered all the American officer's questions. Without hesitation. Straightforward. He *must* have made a good impression.

Erik put down the papers with deliberation. He looked directly at Plewig.

"I see," he said. He seemed to think for a moment. "That's a— a partly motorized company whose main function is mine laying. Was that your chief duty?"

Plewig suddenly tensed. He thought fast. That damned American knows more than he ought to know. Is he right? Yes. Yes, that is the TO. Suppose he wants to know where? No problem. I can always give him some location he can't check out. Plewig's guileless blue eyes narrowed imperceptibly, as he met Erik's searching gaze. There was new respect in them. New wariness. That American could be dangerous after all, he thought. Better watch what I say. Don't volunteer anything. Aloud he said:

"Yes, sir."

Erik didn't take his eyes off him.

"When the company was disbanded a week ago, was it up to full strength?"

Dammit! He had to decide. Quick. Plewig's thoughts raced. It's the end of the fighting. Wouldn't be logical to expect any unit to be full strength. Half? The hesitation was only momentary. He wasn't going to be that easy to catch!

"About half strength, Herr Hauptmann."

Erik looked away.

"I see." He made a note on the paper. "Around—uh—one hundred eighty men, would you say?"

"That's correct, sir."

He felt a little relieved. It's easier when he answers his own damned questions, he thought. He does seem to know quite a bit about the organization of our army. Showing off?

Erik looked at him again.

"And did the company have its full complement of twelve light machine guns and two antitank guns?" he asked.

Plewig felt his confidence return. He'd outfox them. Of course. He could give them any plausible answer. They could never prove him wrong.

"One of the AT guns was destroyed," he answered. "We lost five or six of the MGs."

"And you belonged to this company until a week ago?"

"Yes, sir."

Suddenly Erik's matter-of-fact attitude changed. His face grew hard. His eyes blazed coldly at the German. His voice snapped like a whip.

"Then how do you explain that you don't know that one hundred eighty men is *full* company strength, *not half?*"

Plewig suddenly grew rigid. Chilled. He stared at the American —suddenly the real face of the enemy. He felt the blood drain from his face, powerless to stop it. Desperately he cast about in his swirling mind for a way out. A believable explanation. Anything . . .

"I—I—"

But the chase had begun. There would be no letup until the quarry had been run to ground.

Erik snapped at him:

"The company machine gun complement is *nine*—not *twelve.*"

Don suddenly joined the charge. Startled, Plewig's eyes darted toward this new source of attack.

"The 73rd Division's personnel is *Bavarian. You* are a Rhinelander. How come?"

"Major von Wetterling was killed in France. Long before you said you served under him. Explain!"

The questions came like quick hammer blows.

"How could he have been your CO on the Russian front when he was dead?"

"You say so right here!"

Erik slammed his hand down on the Plewig notes. Plewig looked frantically from one to the other. Automatically he'd snapped to attention—an instinctive effort to seek strength in the comforting familiarity of discipline. He tried to wet bloodless lips with a suddenly dry tongue. Little beads of sweat began to form on his forehead, and a tiny artery in his temple started to beat and beat and beat. . . .

The two CIC agents hammered relentlessly at him.

"Who was *really* the battalion CO?"

"You don't know, do you?"

"Your company has only *one* AT gun. Why did you say *two*?"

"Because you never *were* an engineer!"

"Because you lie!"

Plewig was terrified. He could feel the two pursuers snap at his mind. His world was crumbling. He did not know where to run. He had to face his tormentors. He had to make a stand. . . .

"No!" he cried. "*No!*"

Erik stood up with explosive abruptness. He thrust the papers at Plewig.

"*This is the truth?*" It was a terrifying shout.

Plewig stood rigid.

"No . . . yes! . . . That is . . . I . . ." His words trailed off.

There was sudden and complete silence in the room. Plewig was acutely aware of the rapid, rhythmic surge in his ears. Erik threw the papers on the desk. Quietly he sat down. His voice was tired, disinterested, and he didn't look at Plewig when he finally spoke.

"It's no use, Plewig. We know you're lying."

Don waved a hand at the scattered papers.

"Too many little errors in your phony military history, my friend."

Erik looked up at Plewig.

"It's impossible to memorize every little detail, isn't it?"

He sounded almost kind, a little regretful. He raised his voice.

"Sergeant Murphy!"

Murphy at once appeared at the door.

"Yes, sir?"

"You may remove the prisoner, Sergeant. Section 97, Article 4."

Murphy drew his .45. He looked alert, ready for trouble. Plewig started. He looked toward the two CIC agents at the desk. They had apparently lost all interest in him. They were looking over some papers. He cleared his throat. He suddenly felt he had to get their attention at any cost. Murphy motioned with his gun.

"Let's go," he ordered curtly.

Plewig took a step toward the door. He stopped. With a visible effort he brought himself under control. He turned toward Erik.

"Excuse me, Herr Hauptmann."

Erik looked up impatiently.

"Well?"

"What—what happens to me now?"

Erik looked slightly surprised.

"What happens? I'm sure you know the International Articles of War, Plewig. And we *are* at war." He contemplated the German for a moment, then he shrugged.

"You are obviously not what you pretend to be, so you must be a saboteur. Or a spy. In a combat area. Since you're not in uniform, you can't be considered a prisoner of war under the Geneva Conventions."

It was a dismissal. Erik returned to his papers. Plewig ran a nervous tongue over his lips. The silence hung like an oppressive fog in the room. Motion had died. Time swam endless in his mind. . . .

At last he said:

"Then I . . . ?"

Erik looked up briefly.

"You will be shot."

It was a completely prosaic statement.

Don said, "That's all. Take him away."

Again Murphy gun-gestured.

"Come on!"

Plewig's eyes opened wide.

"No! Wait! Please . . ."

With a show of irritation Erik threw the papers on the desk.

"What now?" he snapped.

Plewig looked from one to the other. He was obviously deeply torn. His drawn face showed the strain on his mind. Then suddenly the words rushed out:

"If I talk, Herr Hauptmann? If I talk?"

Erik's expression did not change. But he felt the quick surge of excitement. *It worked again!* Calmly he studied the German before him.

"What have you got to say?" he asked.

"If I tell you what I . . . if . . . I talk. Will you let me go?"

Erik frowned.

"We make no bargains. But I'll see what I can do."

He had been run to ground. Suddenly the enormity of it all hit him. He, Plewig? He stood mute.

"*Well?*"

"There's no such thing as a friend!" The motto was suddenly sharp in Plewig's mind. "If your mission is at stake, attack him. If need be kill him!" His thoughts were a black whirlpool. The Himmler motto. It didn't say anything about your *own* life, did it? No. If he did talk, he could save his life. If he did talk, all right, some of his comrades might be caught. Killed. He'd tell the Americans only what he *had* to tell them to save his life. As little as possible. To save himself. His own mission. Well, wasn't that what they said? Your comrades are expendable? Wasn't it?

He looked steadily at Erik.

"*I am a Werewolf,*" he said.

The effect on the three Americans was instantaneous. If Plewig had not been filled with anxiety about himself he might have caught it. Murphy's mouth dropped open. Don suddenly coughed on his cigarette smoke. Erik looked startled. It was the first time any interrogation subject had said: "I am a Werewolf!" He had a flash urge to laugh. It sounded so ludicrous, coming from a frightened little blue-eyed clod-kicker like Plewig. He quickly regained his composure. He managed to look bored.

"So you're one of them," he observed, unimpressed. "Just another Werewolf. You won't have much to tell us we don't already know."

Plewig was taken aback. Confused. He suddenly noticed his palms were sweaty. Funny. He never had sweaty hands. He stared at Erik. He didn't know what to say. Erik deliberately got up from the desk and walked over to him.

"Did you think you're something special because you call yourself a Werewolf?" There was scorn in his voice. And disgust. "You're nothing but a garden-variety terrorist. A saboteur. A spy. Take your pick. It all adds up the same."

Plewig felt betrayed. His plan wasn't going to work. They weren't even interested in the Werewolves. Didn't they *know*, for God's sake? Quickly he said:

"Perhaps I *can* tell you things you don't know."

Erik regarded him coldly, skeptically. He said nothing.

"I was with them from the start," Plewig went on. "When Heinrich Himmler himself ordered the first school for guerrillas and Werewolves set up. In Poland. In 1943 . . ."

Don half rose in his chair.

"Nineteen forty-three! We weren't even on the continent!" He sounded incredulous. Erik quickly broke in:

"What were *your* duties?"

"At first I was the general's personal driver," Plewig answered quickly. Perhaps he could still get them interested enough to save his neck. Without giving too much away.

"General Krueger," he continued eagerly. "Karl Krueger. He was only a colonel then."

He stopped. He'd play it by ear. Pick out unimportant items of information. Easy . . . easy . . .

"Go on!"

"He was the commandant of the school, Herr Hauptmann. And he's in command of all the Werewolves now. Under SS Obergruppenführer Prützmann himself. And he works very closely with Axman, the Hitler Youth leader. I was his personal orderly. He likes to live well, the general does. He likes the very best French Armagnac. And flowers. I took care of his flowers for him, too. He likes roses very much. . . ."

Erik interrupted him sharply. He knew that game too well. Talk a lot and say nothing.

"Stick to your military duties," he ordered. He went back to sit on the edge of the desk. He didn't look at Don. He wondered if Don felt the same excitement inside as he did. He was sure of it. But they couldn't let on that they were learning anything new. Or important.

Plewig had regained some of his confidence. It was really only a matter of *how* much he had to tell. He decided to go as far as necessary.

It really couldn't do much damage. It was too late. The Werewolves couldn't be stopped now. He clicked his heels smartly.

"*Jawohl*, Herr Hauptmann," he said. "When the school was moved from Poland to Thürenberg in Czechoslovakia in September 1944, I was put in the training cadre. To train Werewolves. It was called *Unternehmung Werwolf*—Operation Werewolf."

"Where are these Werewolves now?"

"All the ones that were graduated and left the school—about seventeen hundred, I think—I don't know where they are."

"So far you've told us exactly nothing, Plewig!" Erik sounded angry. "What *do* you know?"

Plewig tensed. Careful! He couldn't afford to antagonize the American. Not now.

"I know that the general received orders to move from Thürenberg into Germany and set up his HQ camp. In April. Early this month."

"Purpose?"

"They're supposed to start operations after being overrun by the Americans."

"*After* they're behind our lines? Undetected?"

"Yes, sir."

"What sort of operations?"

Plewig hesitated. Here it was. He hadn't wanted to reveal everything. At least nothing important. But he couldn't stop now. Not without the Americans knowing he was concealing something. He couldn't risk that. He was vaguely aware that his conduct by now was geared only to save himself. He didn't know how it had happened. He pushed it out of his mind.

"Assassinations," he said slowly, "of high-ranking Allied officers. Blowing up ammunition dumps, and equipment and gasoline depots. Especially gas and oil depots. Bombings of barracks. Murders. Things like that."

Erik and Don glanced at one another briefly. Their faces were grim. Plewig continued. He was eager now to show them that he was really cooperating. They know everything anyway, he thought.

"They have agents out. All over. They speak English. Some of them are war wounded. They're lining up targets for them."

"Like you?"

Plewig nodded solemnly.

"I was supposed to be an outside agent. But I didn't want to. Believe me, Herr Hauptmann. I'd much rather just have taken care of the general." He was pleading now. He was convinced he was fighting for his life.

"'The war is lost,' I said to myself, 'and I don't want to be a Werewolf. Even if Goebbels says it's the duty of every man and every woman.' I do not want to kill Americans, Herr Hauptmann. Believe me. . . ."

Erik looked at the man in silence. There was a time to let them talk. Just talk. It made it easier for them to talk about the really important things later. And sometimes useful information did spill out.

"I listened to them, Herr Hauptmann. I had to. Like that important man from Berlin. He came to Thürenberg. He made a speech to us. I remember what he said."

He started to quote, concentrating hard. Pompous, stilted words.

" 'It is the victor of the last battle who is the victor of the war,' he said to us. 'We are losing a battle now,' he said. 'Enemy troops are overrunning our sacred, Aryan fatherland.' "

Plewig hurried on. He had found something he could talk about safely.

"And he told us that two years ago, after North Africa and Stalingrad, the Führer already knew that the first battle would be lost. And he planned the next one. The decisive one. The one that would give us final victory. And he told us that the Werewolves were going to win that victory. . . . Please, Herr Hauptmann. I've told you a lot about them. They're important, the Werewolves! They wouldn't have sent someone important all the way from the Führer's headquarters in Berlin, if they weren't. . . ."

Some little insignificant synapse in Erik's brain was suddenly stimulated. *Important man from Berlin.* He tensed with anticipation.

"Who was it?" he asked quickly.

Plewig looked at him with his candid blue eyes.

"Who, Herr Hauptmann?"

"That important man from Berlin."

"Oh, him. He was a Reichsamtsleiter, Herr Hauptmann. Very important."

"His name?"

Plewig thought for a moment.

"Von Eckdorf. Reichsamtsleiter Manfred von Eckdorf. I remember. He was very important!"

Erik felt a quickening of his pulse. He was aware that Murphy was staring at Plewig. *Von Eckdorf!*

"Why was he at Thürenberg?"

Plewig suddenly looked stricken.

"I don't know, Herr Hauptmann."

"What did he have to do with the Werewolves?"

"Please believe me, I don't know. He talked with the general.

And he looked everything over. He was a very important official!"

Erik looked searchingly at Plewig. The man was telling the truth. His fright at displeasing his interrogator was not faked. He had been drawn in too deep now. He'd spill everything. Erik believed him. And he was suddenly convinced that the whole Werewolf story was true as well! However fantastic. However corny and unbelievable. Von Eckdorf had been tied to the Werewolves in some way. And von Eckdorf had died by his own hand in a farmhouse only twenty miles away. Rather than be forced to talk!

Plewig was telling the truth!

The German was alarmed. He didn't know how to interpret his interrogator's intense scowl.

"Please, Herr Hauptmann," he implored, "believe me! I was *not* going back to them. I was going home. I really was! To the Rhineland. I've told you all I know! I—"

Erik interrupted.

"When were you last in contact with the Werewolves?"

"Five days ago. On the twenty-fourth."

"And they're supposed to become active *after* we have overrun their positions?"

"Yes."

"What is their first target?"

"I don't know but—"

The "but" flew out without thought. Plewig stopped suddenly. He looked trapped. Scared. Erik stood up. He faced the German squarely.

"Well? Out with it!"

Plewig swallowed. It seemed difficult. He said:

"I do not know their first target, Herr Hauptmann."

Erik glared at him.

"*But* . . ." he said significantly.

He had no choice. He cursed himself. He'd let his own damned mouth run away with him. So easy. And now he *had* to give them the last piece of important information he knew.

"But the *Führungsstab*—General Krueger's command group"—

he spoke slowly—"Sonderkampfgruppe Karl—has standing orders. One priority mission . . ."

He hesitated.

"Come on! What's this 'priority mission'?" Erik's voice was harsh. Plewig wet his lips.

"To . . . to kill . . . An assassination . . ."

"*Who?*"

"Your—Supreme Commander."

"*Eisenhower*," Don exclaimed. Somehow it became a whisper.

For a moment there was stunned silence in the room; then Erik resolutely strode to the big wall map behind the desk. Briskly he turned to Plewig.

"Plewig! Over here! Show me the position of Krueger's camp."

Plewig went to the map. He studied it. The symbols and markings were unfamiliar, but he oriented himself easily. He turned to Erik apologetically.

"I do not know their exact location, Herr Hauptmann, but it is somewhere in this little forest—here."

He planted a blunt finger on the map.

Erik looked. At the desk Don exclaimed:

"Holy shit! It's—"

He stopped short. Erik turned to him. He looked grave.

"I think we'd better take a ride. Right now!"

0832 hrs

They hustled Plewig from the building. They'd decided to take their informant along to Corps Forward CP—as a sort of ace in the hole, just in case they had trouble convincing the brass that his story was true; and there'd be time to get more information out of him on the way. They realized that the case was too big for them to handle by themselves. They had to have tactical aid. A lot of tactical aid!

Murphy had brought the jeep to the front, and they hurried Plewig through the little crowd of people already gathering at the jail.

Krauss, the workman repairing the bomb damage to the building, was mixing cement on a scarred and gritty board on the sidewalk. He doffed his leather cap when he saw the two CIC agents come from the door. He started to put it back on, when he saw Plewig. For a split second he froze; then he turned his face away, a face that suddenly had gone dark and ugly.

Don took the wheel and Plewig sat next to him, his right hand locked to the handle on the jeep's side with a pair of handcuffs. Erik sat directly behind him.

As the jeep took off down the street, Krauss stared after it. Slowly he replaced his soiled leather cap on his head. He kicked the cement mixing board into the gutter—and walked rapidly away.

Reims, France
Supreme Headquarters Allied Expeditionary Forces

0835 hrs

The French city of Reims was far more than just another checkpoint on the "Red Ball Express." It was the site of SHAEF. Headquarters of General Dwight D. Eisenhower.

On a back street near the railway station stood a plain three-story building, the *Collège Moderne et Technique*, solidly built of red brick, its four sides surrounding an inner courtyard. A former technical school, with 1,500 boys pursuing an education, it used to teem with activity. It still did. But the constant hectic activity in the building, known to the staff officers as "the little red schoolhouse," was of a far more urgent and far-reaching nature and of far greater consequence than the wildest dreams of the wildest boys ever imagined.

The time was eight thirty-five on the morning of April 29, 1945. Vital policy conclusions were being reached, critical decisions were being made which would drastically affect the direction of the war effort.

The door to a former classroom on the second floor opened. A major appeared, a sheet of paper in his hand. He was just about to close the door, when a second officer stopped him. In low voices they discussed the paper. In the room behind them a briefing session was in progress. The voice of an officer came drifting through the half-open door:

". . . all intelligence reports still point to it, sir. Last-stand German resistance is planned for the *Alpenfestung*—the National Redoubt area—here. If the Germans are allowed to consolidate their forces around some kind of Nazi nucleus, some rallying force, they could hold out for as long as two years! With a heavy toll of American lives. I would like to point out, sir, that it is this kind of overwhelming mountain terrain that has kept little Switzerland a mighty fortress through the centuries, free from attack, so that now she can remain neutral. . . . Munich may well be the key to the Redoubt. I strongly recommend we drive for that city as fast and in as great a strength as possible!"

Paramount issues. Command decisions. The war was in its eleventh hour.

But the final battle was yet to be fought.

On the pockmarked road to Iceberg Forward, three hundred miles to the east as the crow flies, across two war-ravaged nations, a U.S. Army jeep was speeding along.

Manacled to it was a minute cog in the Nazi war machine.

The Road to Iceberg Forward

0917 hrs

The village had been fire-bombed. Every house, every building gutted. Yawning, scorched shells casting their long, empty-eyed shadows over the uneven cobblestone street. Dead livestock sprawling grotesquely near still smoldering barns. The blackened crater of a disintegrated WH ammo dump . . .

A military convoy was passing through, the grinding noise of the heavy trucks echoing among the hollow brick carcasses.

Don thread-needled his jeep through the traffic. He stopped before an MP directing the flow of vehicles.

"Hey, buddy," he shouted. "Iceberg Forward still in Schwartzenfeld?"

"Moved to Viechtach—0500," the MP shouted back. He pointed. "Straight ahead. Couple of miles outa town you cross a bridge, then turn left. You can't miss it."

"Thanks!" Don turned to Erik. "Dammit! That's another fifty miles!"

It was a small stone bridge over a stream lined with trees and brush. It was blocked by an MP weapons carrier and an ambulance. Don brought the jeep to a halt. An MP came over.

"Sorry, sir," he said. "It'll be just a few minutes."

"What's up?" Don asked.

"Couple of guys." He nodded back toward the stream. "In the river."

Erik jumped out of the jeep.

"I'll take a look," he said.

A small group of silent GIs stood on the bank of the river. Erik joined them. Two MPs had waded into the stream. They were carrying the half-submerged body of a man toward the bank. One shoulder bobbed up out of the water. The sun glinted briefly on a pair of silver bars.

The MPs dragged the body onto the bank. An MP sergeant bent to examine it. The man's throat had been cut. The raw wound in the pale, bloodless flesh gaped angrily. Erik walked over to the sergeant. The noncom looked up at him. His eyes were savage.

"Throat slit," he said bitterly. "Clean as a stuck pig!"

He nodded toward a form on the ground covered with a blanket. "The other one. Shot. In the belly."

Erik looked away. The face of death is not to be stared at. The MP sergeant stood up. Erik turned to him. He fished out his ID.

"Sergeant, We've got to get to Iceberg Forward. Fast!"

"Yes, sir!" The sergeant shouted to an MP on the bridge.

"Hey, Wilson! Move the three-quarter-ton! Let that jeep through!"

Erik climbed back into the jeep. He averted his eyes from Plewig. He couldn't look at him. Not now.

"GIs?" Don asked.

"Two of them." Erik's voice was grim. "Butchered!"

He forced himself to look at Plewig. The German sat stiffly. Ashen-faced, he stared straight ahead.

He knows, Erik thought savagely. The little bastard knows it's the handiwork of his goddamned playmates!

"Let's get out of here," he snapped. His voice was harsh.

Don slammed the jeep into gear. The little vehicle leaped forward and careened across the cleared bridge. . . .

Viechtach

1029 hrs

The organized chaos surrounding the two plain three-story buildings on the outskirts of the little Bavarian town of Viechtach was most certainly a source of secret contempt for the few watching German civilians, used to the order and regimentation of the Third Reich. XII Corps Forward CP—Iceberg Forward—was in the final stages of moving in and setting up shop. The empty lot between the two buildings was crammed with trucks in the process of being unloaded, the grass churned up by the massive tires. Signs were going up identifying units; communication wires were being strung; GIs were milling everywhere. Incredibly, everything was accomplished in record time, and without losing a beat in the momentum of advance.

Don drove the jeep past a large sign being erected a short distance from one of the buildings. Above the XII Corps windmill insignia were the words DISMOUNT POINT; below it, FWD ECH. He stopped the jeep near the closer of the two buildings. Erik jumped out. He started for the entrance. An MP met him halfway.

"Sir. You can't stop—"

Erik interrupted him.

"AC of S, G-2 in this building?"

"Yes, sir. But—"

"Good. We've got a PW in the jeep. He's important." He turned to the jeep and called, "Okay, Don!" He turned back to the MP. "See that nothing happens to him, will you?"

"But—"

"And have someone move our jeep to the dismount area."

Don joined them with Plewig.

"What'll we do with Joe, here?" he asked.

"Put him in the guardroom," Erik answered. To the MP he said. "You'll take care of that?"

The MP didn't look happy.

"Sir," he said. "May I see your ID?"

"Sure!"

Both Erik and Don pulled out their cards. Erik said:

"CIC Detachment 212. We've got to get to the G-2 as quickly as possible."

The lobby of the building teemed with officers and enlisted men. At a desk with the sign INFORMATION sat a harassed-looking corporal and a pfc. Behind them, on the wall, a large poster had been tacked up. Its theme: Nonfraternization. It showed a sexy-looking girl in a dirndl skirt and low-cut blouse being ogled by a wolf in GI uniform. "You've Won One War. Don't Lay the Ground-work for Another!" it proclaimed with an obvious double entendre.

"AC of S, G-2, Colonel Streeter?" Erik asked the corporal.

"I think he's on the second floor, sir," the corporal answered apologetically. "We're just getting set up."

The pfc was running a finger down a mimeographed list of names. He stopped and showed it to the corporal.

"Yes, sir. Second floor. To the right. You can't miss it."

Colonel Richard H. Streeter had the reputation of being a sen-sible man. He'd never been afraid to make decisions and take responsibilities. He expected the same from his officers. His in-telligence staff worked around the clock. Rumor had it that Streeter himself never slept. It was only a slight exaggeration. The truth was that he'd mastered the art of catnapping. Anywhere, anytime, under any conditions he could close his eyes, relax completely and sleep for a short while. He did it as often as he could. Because of that he was always available any hour of the day or night when needed. His staff of officers and noncoms had learned the trick from him. In the G-2 office, dominated by a huge situation map covering an entire wall and being constantly kept up to date by an intelligence noncom, two men were fast asleep in a corner, rolled up in their sleeping bags, totally undisturbed by the activity around them.

Streeter and one of his staff officers, Major Henry Roberts, stood facing the situation map with Erik and Don. Erik was pointing to a small wooded area on the map.

"Right here, sir," he said. "Just north of Schönsee. P 4812. Close to the Czech border."

Streeter frowned skeptically.

"Four miles inside our lines?" He turned to Major Roberts. "We've had no reports of any German units in that area, have we, Henry?"

"No. We haven't."

Streeter looked speculatively at Erik.

"It sounds a little fantastic, don't you think? That the Nazis should have started to prepare for the day they'd *lose* the war already in '43, long before D Day, at the peak of their glory!"

He looked at the map.

"How many—ah—Werewolves are there supposed to be in there?" He looked faintly amused. His tone of voice clearly said, "Convince me."

"The HQ unit under the command of General Krueger numbers between forty and sixty men, including the general's staff. It's called Kampfgruppe Karl, after Krueger's given name. That's the unit located here, at Schönsee."

"And the rest of them?"

"Our informant knows of three other units in the Bavarian area. Operational units. Each numbering one hundred fifty men. They're placed in a triangle around Kreuger's HQ unit. All behind our lines now. We don't know where."

"Just who are these people?"

"They form the hard core of the Werewolf organization, sir." Erik was acutely aware of the importance of saying just the right thing, of giving Streeter just the right information. Enough—not too much. The whole story could so easily sound like a crackpot scheme. That was a real danger. But Erik was convinced it was deadly fact. He *had* to convince Streeter as well.

"They consist of the training cadre and the last class from General Krueger's school at Thürenberg," he said carefully, trying to sound as earnest and rational as possible. "Early this month they received orders from the German High Command to close the school, move to prepared positions at Schönsee and become operational."

"What exactly *is* their mission—besides that hysterical howling on the radio?"

"To stay behind, evade capture and then destroy U.S. personnel and supplies, with special emphasis on gas and oil." Erik looked straight at Colonel Streeter. "Sir. They could do a great deal of damage."

Streeter contemplated the earnest young CIC agent before him. He no longer looked amused. He nodded thoughtfully.

"If they're there," he said.

A noncom at a switchboard called:

"Colonel Streeter, sir! General Canine. On seven."

Streeter at once walked to a field telephone on his desk. Major Roberts turned to Erik.

"What's this about wanting to assassinate Eisenhower?"

"That's their standing mission. Probably something like Skorzeny's 'jeep parties' during the Bulge."

"When our guys were running around singing 'Mairzy Doats' on command to prove they were home-grown USA and not Krauts in GI uniforms," Don added.

Roberts considered it. He nodded.

"With everything lost, I suppose at this stage of the game they might well try to get Ike. . . . . The headless serpent . . ."

"Sir?" Erik looked puzzled. Roberts looked slightly embarrassed. He grinned.

"From an old book I once read. In college. *The Ethos of Political*

Assassination. It's a phrase that stuck in my mind. 'A country without a leader is akin to a serpent with its head severed. It may thrash about a lot, but it accomplishes nothing.' " He looked sober. "Only it won't work. The military serpent has too many heads."

"I wouldn't sell the idea short," Erik said. "The Werewolves are supposed to be the backbone, the nucleus of the last-stand resistance in the National Redoubt—"

"And Goebbels is always running off at the mouth about the Alpine Fortress," Don interjected.

"If they actually *did* get Ike, it might just be the shot in the arm the Germans need, if supported by a heavy Nazi propaganda barrage. They're pretty fanatic."

Roberts nodded reflectively.

"Of course, Eisenhower does consider the Redoubt more of a military target than even Berlin."

Colonel Streeter joined them. He looked serious, hurried.

"I've got to get over to the chief of staff. Let's get this thing settled." He turned to Erik. "How are these Werewolves equipped?"

Erik answered. Quickly. To the point.

"Small arms. Machine guns, submachine guns and mortars. They've also got explosives, ammunition and food supplies to last them for at least six months of operations."

Streeter thought for a brief moment.

"Must have taken quite a few vehicles to transport all that stuff. What happened to them?" he asked.

"They didn't use much motor transportation, sir. They loaded everything on wagons. Used some hundred and twenty horses and gave the whole lot to the farmers in the area."

Streeter nodded, impressed.

Not bad, he was thinking. "It's quite a yarn," he said. "What do you want to do about it?"

"I want to get them before they can hurt us more than they already have."

"You really believe this Werewolf informant of yours?"

"I do!"

Erik looked directly at Streeter. It was time to play his trump card.

"Sir," he said. "I believe I have information that strongly points to his story being true. I have established a definite link between the Werewolves and a high-ranking Nazi official, a Reichsamtsleiter von Eckdorf. The man shot himself rather than fall into our hands. At a farm. Less than ten miles from Schönsee!"

Streeter looked at Major Roberts.

"Henry?"

Roberts nodded.

"All right," Streeter said. "You got it! Stick with it." He turned to the map. "Let's see. That's in the area of the 97th. What do you want in the way of tactical aid?"

"Two companies, sir."

Streeter frowned. "I guess you need that. They'll have to be taken off the line."

He turned toward the switchboard operator. "Get me the 97th Division CP!" He turned back to Erik. "You'll get your two companies." To Roberts he said, "Send Evans down with them." And to Erik: "Major Evans will be with you strictly as an observer. It's *your* ball game. But *I* want to know the score."

"Yes, sir." Now that he had what he wanted Erik felt drained. Streeter looked at him and Don speculatively.

"I hope you do find your Werewolves," he said quietly. "You're sticking your necks way out!"

He started to leave, then looked back.

"I hope he's not giving you the runaround, that informant of yours, what's his name?"

"Plewig," Erik said. "Josef Plewig."

Weiden

1316 hrs

"Plewig!" he said. "Josef Plewig!" His voice was cold with contempt.

It was Krauss. He stood leaning casually against a four-foot-high brick wall topped by a wooden trellis woven through with thick, withered vines. With his work pants spattered with fresh-dried cement flecks, his soiled leather cap pulled down over his forehead, he almost melted into the drabness of the little suburban side street. It was deserted. It usually was.

Krauss fished a battered old metal tobacco box from a pocket in his threadbare jacket. He seemed preoccupied with his task, yet he was acutely aware of the other man, unseen behind the wall. He knew it was Heinz. He could picture him; the patch over his eye, the pinned-up empty sleeve of his stripped Wehrmacht uniform jacket. An object of pity. Krauss ignored his presence. It was, of course, important that they not be seen together.

Heinz's voice came softly through the concealing vines. It throbbed with subdued vehemence.

"Verdammt nochmal! When?"

Krauss opened up his little metal box. Carefully he selected one of a half dozen partially smoked cigarette butts.

"Four hours ago," he said, intent upon his box.

"Direction?"

"The road to Viechtach."

"Their command headquarters! Why didn't you make contact before?"

Krauss deliberately placed the selected butt behind one ear under the leather cap while he put the metal box away and brought out a box of wooden matches.

"One must be cautious," he said slowly, "or one is dead." He took the butt from behind his ear and lit it.

"Has he talked?"

Krauss puffed on his butt. He contemplated the smoke thoughtfully.

"They would not have taken him to their headquarters had he not," he commented to the spiraling cigarette smoke.

"We will take care of him," Heinz said. The statement was cold, emotionless—and therefore deadly. "And the two Americans. We don't know how much they have found out. We can not afford to let them live."

"'And Krueger?'" Krauss cupped the butt in his hand. It was getting almost too small to hold.

"He will be warned."

"It is risky."

"He must know. He will want to take steps. We will use the Munich relay. Ask instructions."

"The Munich station has not yet been overrun?"

"Not yet. Munich will be held as long as possible. The SS is making certain the people resist. There will be no sheets of surrender on the road to Munich. The Americans will have to fight and die for every foot! Go now. There is not much time. We must move today."

There was a small rustling sound behind the wall. Krauss thought he could hear the limping footsteps of Heinz die away. Perhaps not. His butt was only a smoldering ember. He squashed it out between two work-hardened fingers and brushed the ashes off on his pants.

For the first time he glanced quickly at the vine-covered wall. Then he walked off.

The Road to Munich

1608 hrs

What the hell am I supposed to do? he thought with the bitter anguish of indecision. What what what? . . .

It wasn't the first time he'd been in a tight situation, dammit. Captain Robert Slater, tank commander, had seen plenty of action. He'd run into his share of bitchy situations. But not like this. Nothing like this . . .

He had a mental flash of how the Seventh Army G-2 periodic would report it. Under "Enemy Operations During Period." "Heavy enemy resistance encountered," it would say, "vic Heidendorf (Q8714)." Nothing about the blood, the torn limbs, the death. Nothing about the stinking sweat of fear. Nothing about the agony

of decision—when *any* decision would be wrong. He swallowed the
bile that kept rising in his throat, burning and sour. He felt cold.
He could feel the wetness trickle down from his armpits.

He stood tall in the open turret. His Sherman tank was positioned
off a narrow forest road, concealed by the natural growth of trees
and shrubs. Desperately searching for an answer he knew was not
there, he reviewed his situation once again. . . .

The little evergreen forest bracketed the road less than a quarter
of a mile from the village. Heidendorf. On the road to Munich. At
the ruins of a farm on the edge of the woods the road made a bend
and then continued straight through open fields to the village. The
other tanks of his command were in concealment in the woods. And
near the bombed-out farm, huddled among the trees, were the men
of the supporting infantry unit.

He lifted his binoculars. Bleakly he surveyed the terrain before
him.

The fields on either side of the narrow road, the only access to
the village, were studded with crazily tilted signs, skulls and cross-
bones on a black field with the words ACTHUNG MINEN! The soft
shoulders of the road had been churned to a muddy mess by heavy
traffic. Close to the village several strategically placed tank traps,
dug in the soft, wet earth, could be made out. The skeleton of a
broken, cannibalized German Wehrmacht truck stood in the field
not far from the village itself. The little town, like so many Bavarian
villages, had a fortresslike appearance. The houses and barns facing
the surrounding fields were massive stone structures with small
windows. They were connected by tall, thick stone walls, presenting
an uninterrupted stone front toward the open fields. A heavy barricade had been thrown across the road where it entered the village.

Halfway there, just off the road, sat a Sherman tank. Gutted, still
smoldering.

It had been his lead tank.

Less than an hour before it had been lumbering toward the village
of Heidendorf. There had been a sudden shattering explosion. A
shell from a German panzer, a Tiger tank, hidden in the village. The

shell had landed directly in front of the Sherman, shooting a geyser of dirt into the air. With a grinding roar of gears, the tank had veered crazily off the road, clattering into the muddy field—and almost at once a second round from the Tiger hit it broadside. The Sherman shuddered to a halt and began to burn. Two men had squeezed from the turret hatch. They'd tumbled to the ground, and in a crouched, broken run, shielded by the blazing tank, they'd made for the woods. They'd covered almost a hundred yards when they hit the antipersonnel mines. Their twisted bodies were lying in the mud where they'd been thrown by the blasts. Bob Slater had been watching it all in his field glasses. He'd been brought so close to the men, he'd seen the brief shock of disbelief on their faces before they died. . . .

A soldier came running up to the command tank. Slater looked down at him. It was Sergeant Barker.

"It's no good," Barker said. "We'll never get through."

Slater again looked through his binoculars. Not because he thought he'd find a solution, but because he desperately needed to do something.

"What the hell am I supposed to do?" he said. His voice was low and dead. He wasn't speaking to anyone.

From the village came the staccato burst of a submachine gun.

Slater was suddenly aware of the rumbling, grating sound of laboring motors on the road behind him. He turned. A convoy of vehicles was grinding down the narrow road. Several GIs were flagging them down. The road was piling up with halted trucks.

A jeep cut out from the stalled convoy and careened along the road shoulder toward Slater's command tank. It bore a plate with a single star. Even as it came to a gravel-spurting stop at the tank, an officer, a brigadier general, leaped from the jeep and came striding up to the tank.

"What the hell's going on here?" he demanded sharply. "What's the holdup?"

He stopped at the tank and glared up at Slater.

"This area should have been cleared long ago," he barked angrily.

"I've got a whole damned HQ unit back there. I've got to get through!"

Slater looked drawn.

"Sir," he said. "We're encountering heavy resistance." He had a sudden, discordant impulse to laugh. There he was, speaking "periodic reportese"! "The village up ahead is held by SS troops," he continued.

"Well, get them the hell out!"

"They have armor, sir. They—"

"Tanks?"

"Yes, sir, they—"

"Have you requested artillery? Air strike?"

Slater looked haunted.

"No, sir. I—"

"Why not, dammit?"

Slater swallowed. His voice became tinged with resentment.

"Sir," he said. "There's a Tiger tank—"

"How many?"

"One."

"*One!*" The general exploded. "Goddammit, man, you're letting your entire unit be held up by *one tank*! Knock it out!"

"Sir—"

"You *can* reach it from here, can't you?"

"Yes, sir. But—"

"But, my ass! *Blast it!*"

Slater stared at the general. His teeth were clamped so tight the muscles corded in his jaws. Stiffly he held out his field glasses.

"Sir," he said with grim defiance. "Maybe you'd better take a look."

Glaring at the young officer, the general climbed up on the tank. He grabbed the offered field glasses, angrily raising them to his eyes. For a brief moment he scanned the area. Then he stopped. He stiffened.

"Good Lord!" he said. His voice was hoarse with shock.

Slater knew what he was seeing. . . . The break in the massive wall; the ugly long snout of the Tiger tank poking through it, slowly traversing the area. And the people. The old men, the women, the children—so many children—huddled in terror against the base of the walls and the buildings; hundreds of them. All deliberately herded out there and exposed to any enemy fire. A living human shield protecting the SS defenders behind the wall; the scattered bodies sprawled in the dirt . . .

"The Tiger is behind the wall, sir," he said quietly. "At the break. You can just make it out." He looked at the general, still staring at the chilling sight through the binoculars. Let him look, he thought, good and hard. He wants to throw his weight around? Fine! Let him pull rank. Let *him* make the decision! Aloud he said:

"The whole damned population of the village must be out there. If any of them try to break away, the SS shoots them." He couldn't help sounding outraged. "Their own people!"

The general lowered the field glasses. He was obviously shaken. He frowned.

"We can't bypass the place, sir," Slater said. "And we've got to use the road. The fields are full of tank traps. And mined."

The general nodded. He looked toward the village, frowning in concentration.

"It's a helluva situation, sir. We either sit here"—he nodded toward the village—"or we massacre *them!*"

The general gave the field glasses back to Slater. He looked closely at the young officer. Quietly he said:

"What's your name, son?"

Slater was startled.

"Slater, sir," he answered. "Robert Slater."

The general sighed.

"Well, Bob," he said. "When you're confronted with an either-or situation, look for the third way. . . ."

"Sir?"

"The third way out, Bob. There's always a third way out." He was suddenly brisk again. "Do you speak German, Captain?"

Slater shook his head.

"No, sir." He was puzzled. What's he getting at? he wondered.

"Any of your men?"

"Afraid not, sir."

"Figures," the general observed with resignation. "Well, I do." He looked toward the village. "I'm going up there."

Slater gave him a quick, startled look.

"You can't!" he exclaimed. "Not you, sir." He hesitated. "I'll go, sir. If you'll tell me what you want me to do . . ."

The general shook his head.

"Won't do, Bob. Heroes are a waste. Always use the best man for the job. I'm it." He was giving an order. "I want two men. To give me fire cover." He gestured toward the field. "From that tank out there. Close enough for accuracy. Get them!"

Slater at once called to Sergeant Barker.

"Sergeant! I want two men. With tommy guns. On the double!"

"Okay, sir." Barker turned to a group of GIs sitting on the ground nearby.

"Kowalski!" he barked. "Davis! On your feet!"

The two men looked at him.

"Aw, Sarge," they chorused.

"Move it!"

They got up. The general turned to Slater. He studied him closely.

"Keep your eye on that Tiger, Bob," he said. "I don't know what's going to happen. I'll have to play this one by ear. But you'll know when you get your chance. Grab it!"

"Yes, sir. I'll try."

"Dammit, soldier! You'll do better than that!"

He looked toward the village and grinned ruefully.

"They tell me my job's supposed to be getting things *moved*." He glanced at Slater. "I'll see what I can do for you."

He jumped from the tank. He beckoned to Kowalski and Davis.

"Stick to the road. Use the ditch. Any cover you can find. Move fast. Don't get your asses blown off in the fields. When you get to the tank, open up. Give me all the fire cover you can. Make them pull their heads down. Got it?"

The men nodded.

"Got it, sir."

They started off. Slater used his intertank radio.

"Armadillo Three. This is Armadillo One. . . . Joe, you've got a shot at that Tiger, haven't you?"

The radio crackled.

"Sure do, but—"

Slater interrupted.

"No buts. Stay with it. When *I* fire, *you* fire. Don't hesitate for a second. Out."

"Got you. Out."

There was a sudden burst of automatic fire from the field. Slater started. He grabbed the field glasses and looked.

The general and the two GIs had reached the smoking tank. The men were firing at the top of the village walls and at the windows in the buildings over the heads of the cowering civilians, giving cover to the general, who was making for the wrecked German truck. They were placing the fire well. Slater could see the puffs of shattered masonry where they hit.

Sergeant Barker walked up to the general's jeep. He stared toward the village. He turned to the driver.

"Who the hell's *he*?" He nodded toward the village. "He ain't no combat officer." His voice held a grudging.respect. The driver looked self-important.

"That's General Thurston. Howard Thurston. Quartermaster Corps." He paused for effect. "That's 'Third Way' Thurston himself."

"Who?" Barker looked blank.

"'Third Way' Thurston. That's what they call him. If they get *him* stymied—man, he's always got a third way out!"

The fire from the guns of Kowalski and Davis was suddenly joined by other firing. Both men looked toward the sound.

"Some damned funny third way out he's picked himself this time," Barker commented dryly.

Slater was watching intently through his binoculars. General Thurston had reached the shelter of the German truck. Suddenly he broke cover and hurled himself into the defiladed area of a tank trap. The German gunfire probed insistently for him.

"Armadillo Three!" Slater ordered, his voice tense. "Hold your fire! Mike! Give them one round—over their heads! Make the bastards duck!"

Almost at once a tank gun fired—and immediately an answering round came screaming from the Tiger tank, searching for the hidden Sherman, crashing into the trees a short distance away. Slater stayed glued to the field glasses.

"Sit tight!" he ordered grimly.

Thurston had used the exchange of fire. He was at the wall, pressed with the others against the base, out of the line of fire from the SS troops. Kowalski and Davis kept up their fire cover. Slater kept his binoculars trained on the general. He could see him gesticulating animatedly with an elderly man and several other civilians.

Suddenly there was a thunderous explosion on the road behind. Barker at once hit the ground.

"Mortars!" he shouted. "Hit the dirt!"

Slater whirled toward the blast. One of the last trucks in the piled-up convoy had been hit. It was blazing fiercely, vomiting black smoke. The GIs were scurrying for cover even as two more mortar shells carrumped into the ground on either side of the road. He heard the deep-throated sound of one of his tanks starting up. Three more mortar rounds fell—this time in front of him. Slater felt a hot surge of dread. They're bracketing us! he thought wildly. They've got the road already zeroed in! They'll blow us to pieces!

Another tank started up. Slater shouted into his mike.

"Stay put, dammit! Keep your eyes on that Tiger! Joe! Hold your position!"

He squinted through his binoculars. Come on, General, he thought fiercely. Whatever the hell you think you're going to do—do it!

Sergeant Barker came running up to the tank.

"We've gotta get outa here," he shouted. "They're putting them down the chimney!"

The radio crackled. "Bob! Shall we give it to them?"

"Hold it!" he snapped.

Two more mortar shells crashed into the ruined farmhouse. Cries of "Medic! . . . Medic!" came from the rubble. More rounds exploded toward the rear. Barker cried:

"That convoy back there's a bunch of sitting ducks! The road's blocked behind them!"

Slater strained to look back. The road was dense with smoke. One truck, hit by the mortar fire, burning and belching smoke, was across the road; another, attempting to turn on the narrow road, was stuck in the ditch. The road was effectively blocked.

Slater felt stricken. Betrayed. Fuck the sense of relief he'd felt when General Thurston arrived and took over. Now the ultimate decision was still his, only more impossible, more desperate than ever. He raged against the injustice of it all. Dimly he was aware of Barker shouting.

"We gotta break out! Now!"

There was only one course of action. He had to knock out that Tiger tank, or he wouldn't have a chance of reaching the village to stop the mortar fire. The whole convoy would be wiped out. He *had* to open fire. Kill the civilians. The women. The kids. And now—the general . . .

Ashen-faced, he stared toward the little village that had become his personal hell. The strain was a chilling mask pulled tight over his face. More shells exploded. He felt a sudden icy shiver knife through his body. He knew what he had to do. Kill. He knew that his decision would kill him as well. The wound he would inflict upon himself would not bleed, but neither would it heal. . . . He looked at the target through his field glasses. The deadly Tiger snout poked obscenely through the break in the wall. Directly below the villagers huddled in terror, the general in their midst.

Slater's knuckles were bloodless as he gripped his binoculars.

"Stand by to fire!" he ordered. To his own ears it sounded like a croak.

The scene at the distant wall was inexorably etched on the cold lenses of his field glasses. He fought an overpowering urge to hurl them away and with them the hellish sight he knew was about to erupt. He opened his mouth to give his command.

Suddenly he saw the general jump to his feet. He stood tall among the cowering Germans. Rapidly he pumped his arm, fist clenched, up and down above his head. At once the villagers scrambled to their feet, all as one. Splitting into two groups directly under the Tiger tank, still hugging the protection of the wall, they raced away in opposite directions, leaving the area around the Tiger clear and empty, stripped of its human shield.

"He did it!" Slater shouted, his voice shrill with exultation. "He *moved* them! Fire! Fire! Get the bastards!"

His last words were drowned by the roar of the firing Sherman tanks. Round after round of armor-piercing shells tore into the Tiger tank, robbed of its terrible protection. Only a split second, and the Tiger exploded in a ball of fire. . . .

The Shermans broke from the cover of the woods. Clanging, clattering, rumbling and triumphant, they made straight for the barricaded village. The GIs followed close behind. Shells from the tanks ripped into the exposed stretches of wall and buildings, crumbling them.

The German civilians were huddled at both ends, unharmed.

Heidendorf

1712 hrs

The black-and-white barber-pole-striped signpost on the road out of Heidendorf read: MÜCNHEN 37 KM.

The battle for the village was over. The SS troops had resisted fiercely and tenaciously but had been routed by the tanks and the GIs.

Slater's tank unit was regrouping just off the road on the far side of the village. In a field on the other side of the road Barker's men were sprawled on the ground, resting. The road to Munich was clogged with advancing U.S. troops and vehicles streaming toward the Bavarian capital.

Already the villagers had begun the clean-up after the fighting. Some of the farmers were busy taking care of their livestock in the fields, some were even attending to urgent farm chores interrupted by the battle. The war had touched their lives, quickly, frighteningly, and moved on, but their livelihoods still needed tending.

A small group of elderly men, gingerly picking their way along the road shoulder, approached Slater's command tank. They had an air of dignified authority about them. They stopped at the tank and looked up at Slater, standing in the turret. One of them, hat in hand, took a step forward.

"*Ich bin Ortsbauernführer Tiemann, Herr Offizier,*" he said, his voice shaking with emotion. His eyes, deep-set in a weathered, wrinkled face, were bright with tears. "*Ich—ich möchte—*"

On the road General Thurston's jeep drove by. The general called to Slater:

"Well done, Bob! And remember—look for that third way out!"

Slater threw a salute at the general, who returned it.

"Yes, sir," he called, a huge grin on his young face.

The jeep drove off. Slater turned to the Germans. The old man went on:

"*Wir danken Ihnen, Herr Offizier. Sie haben uns das Leben gerettet! Bitte, wir—*"

Slater shook his head.

"No *sprechen sie* German," he said. "I don't know what you want." He motioned toward the village. "Go back. Go back to your homes!"

The old German bowed. The others bowed.

"*Vielen Dank, Herr Offizier! Sehr vielen Dank!*"

With great dignity the men turned and started toward the village. Slater called across the road.

"Barker! We move out in fifteen minutes!"

Sergeant Barker acknowledged. He surveyed his men. They were in good shape. He looked around. In the field behind him an odd-looking wagon, drawn by a team of plodding horses, was slowly moving across the soil. It was a manure wagon; a large wooden tank, like a huge long beer barrel on sturdy wheels. A lone elderly farmer sat on the driver's seat. Lazily he swatted the ancient horses with a long whip, as the beasts dragged the heavy wagon along, leaving a thin spray of fertilizer on the freshly plowed ground.

Unemotionally the farmer looked at the military activity on the road. It was of no importance to him, his attitude seemed to convey. Preparing the soil, that was important. And they had interrupted him. First the SS. Then the Americans fighting them. Now he could continue what was important. There was still an hour of daylight left. He would not be kept from using it. Not even by a war.

Barker eyed the wagon. He was faintly annoyed at the utter lack of interest the farmer took in him and his men. Hadn't they just beat the shit out of his "supermen"? He turned to two of his men lying flat on their backs on the side of the ditch.

"Hey! Kowalski! Davis!" he called. "Go check on that rig out there."

The men looked outraged.

"Aw, come on, Sarge!" they complained in unison.

"Get a move on, dammit!" Barker snapped. He was in no mood to argue. The men got to their feet. Kowalski looked at the sergeant. His expression was one of utter disgust. Barker glared at him.

"And wipe that opinion off your face, or I'll do it for you. Now move!"

"Okay, okay," Kowalski grumbled. "Don't get your balls in an uproar."

The men started toward the wagon.

Barker watched them. He took a swig from his canteen. The men were sidling up to the wagon, which had stopped.

Barker kept an eye on the men. Just in case. They seemed to be concentrating on staying upwind from the rig. Kowalski circled the wagon, while Davis looked the driver over. Then they beat a hasty retreat.

When they came back to Barker they plopped down on the ground beside him.

"I wisht I hadn't thrown away my gas mask," Kowalski complained. "That damned thing's full of shit!"

"That ain't what it is, you dumb jerk," Davis corrected him. "They call it 'natural fertilizer.'"

"Yeah? Well, I don't give a damn what they call it—it still stinks! Like a whole company couldn't keep a tight asshole under fire!"

Barker looked at the men sourly.

"Okay," he said. "You look it over good?"

"Sure. Nothing." Kowalski eyed the sergeant. "What'd you expect us to find? Hitler's secret weapon?" He looked toward the wagon. "Peeee-hew!" he said with feeling. "I knew them Krauts were full of shit, but I didn't know they were spreading it around."

Barker was about to snap at him, when Slater called from the road:

"Move them out, Sergeant!"

Barker got to his feet.

"Okay, you guys. Let's go!"

The driver of the manure wagon dispassionately watched the GI's move out. He scratched his left arm. He'd wanted to do it ever since the two Americans came over and he had suddenly begun to itch. The longer he waited, the more insistently he itched, but he'd deliberately kept himself from scratching as long as the soldiers were watching him.

He wondered why. He knew it would not have mattered. He knew they'd done a perfect job back at Thürenberg. There was no scar, no sign of the tattoo. Nothing to worry about.

He checked the time, squinting at a big vest-pocket watch.

Verflucht! he thought with annoyance. They'd put him behind schedule.

He swatted the horses a couple of times with his long whip. "*Kür! Kür!*" he called to the beasts as they leaned into their harnesses, jerked the wheels of the heavy wagon from their ruts and slowly moved along. The farmer carefully fished a small object from his vest pocket. He held it in his cupped hand. He glanced at it.

It was a compass.

He pulled on the reins, altering his course slightly. He checked the compass again before putting it back in his pocket, and stopped the wagon.

With great care he placed his whip firmly in two metal clamps on the side of the driver's seat.

He climbed down, walked to the rear of the wagon and turned off the spray of liquid manure. From a rack he hauled down a couple of sackcloth feedbags and walked with them toward the horses, which were watching him expectantly.

As he walked past the barrel body of the manure wagon he gave a couple of sharp raps on the wood with his knuckles.

Pitterman heard the raps.

He felt relief flooding him like a physical release. He hadn't realized how tense his body had grown. When the warning raps had come a few minutes earlier he'd at once doused the light. . . .

He sat in utter darkness, utterly silent. He knew something was wrong, something was going on outside, and he strained to hear. But the only sound he could make out was the quick, rhythmic surge of his own blood, pounding in his ears.

He sat waiting. Tense. Taut. Alone.

The stench in his cramped cubicle suddenly became stifling to him. He was nauseated. He felt an overpowering urge to get out. Had they been discovered? Would a burst of submachine gun fire suddenly riddle the tank? What a way to die—huddled inside a stinking shit wagon!

He was suddenly angry. It was a great idea to put a compact mobile radio transmitter/receiver in one half of a working manure wagon. Who'd ever think to look there? A *prima* idea—if *you* were not the one cooped up inside for hours at a time. Waiting . . .

What the hell was going on out there? He strained to hear. Nothing . . .

The wagon slowly began to move. He could hear the liquid manure sloshing in the rear half of the tank. He gagged. Then he concentrated on figuring out what was going on outside.

The wagon was moving. Was it being lined up for directional transmission? Or was it being driven off someplace for examination?

It stopped. He heard the whip being placed in the holding clamps. He knew the metal core of the long whip was part of the directional antenna, which ran down each side of the tank, strung along the inside walls on insulator tabs. He knew the clamps completed the contact. The system was ready. But was the driver actually preparing for transmission? Or was he following orders from some enemy captor?

He heard the driver climb down and turn off the manure spray, and then came the raps—"Clear to transmit."

Pitterman turned on the single light bulb. It glared off the sheet metal insulating his unorthodox radio shack.

He looked at his watch. They were two minutes' late; in another minute contact could no longer be established. Quickly he went over his checklist. Batteries connected, compass azimuth heading correct; time/location table; frequency; recognition signal. He put on his earphones, checked the panel and began to send his call letters. Almost immediately his earphones started to emit the faint beeps of a message coming through.

Pitterman listened intently. For a while he wrote on a pad in the light of the single bulb. Then he signed off, and at once began to relay the transmission. . . .

Weiden

1739 hrs

A crisp dusk was already settling over the little town of Weiden when Erik and Don returned from Corps HQ.

They entered the jail and walked quickly toward the Interrogation Room. Erik felt keyed up. He and Don had laid their plans at Corps and started the ball rolling from there. Things had gone well. There'd been less than the usual snafu. At the door he turned to Don.

"Better pick up a couple of K rations, too. No telling how long we'll be on the go."

"Right."

He pushed open the door. . . .

The girl had been crying. It was the first thing he noticed. He felt a quick surge of pity for her. She looked so damned vulnerable. He glanced away from her, acutely aware of doing so. Sergeant Murphy was sitting behind the desk. Erik glared at him.

Murphy was leaning back in his chair nonchalantly, smoking a cigarette, toying with a pencil and looking studiously self-important. He jumped to his feet.

"Oh! Hello, sir!" His surprised look changed to an embarrassed grin. "I—uh—I . . ."

He was fishing around for a face saver. He found it. He gestured toward Anneliese.

"You've got a visitor," he announced brightly. "I'm sure you remember her, sir. But there's some kind of trouble," he finished lamely.

Erik remained silent. He scowled at the scene before him. Murphy began edging toward the door.

"Well—uh—if you don't need me anymore, sir, I'll—uh . . ."

He looked from one of the officers to the other.

"I thought maybe I could—help." He was at the door.

"Thank you, Sergeant Murphy," Don said pointedly. And Murphy was gone.

Don looked after him with a grin. Erik walked over to Anneliese. He was all right now. He looked at her.

"Now, what's this all about?" he asked quietly. "I thought you'd be on your way by now."

The girl looked up at him, her big eyes moist with misery.

"Yes, but—it's only that I—I can't . . ." Her voice broke. She lowered her head and began to cry softly. From the door Don called:

"Erik!"

Erik joined him. Don nodded toward the girl.

"Don't get involved in anything now. We haven't got much time."

"I know!" Erik sounded sharper than he'd intended. It confused him. "We're due at the farm in"—he glanced at his wristwatch—"in two hours. We'll make it."

"Not if you start playing Sir Galahad, we won't. She could spell trouble."

Erik felt a sudden flash of anger.

"Oh, for Christ's sake!" he flared. "Do you have to find a witch on every broom?"

Don looked at him in surprise. He shrugged.

"Okay, old buddy," he said pleasantly. "It's your bonfire."

He turned to leave. Erik stopped him.

"Look, Don," he started. He glanced toward the girl. She had stopped crying and was drying her tears. What the hell's the matter with me? he thought fiercely. It's my problem. No good taking it out on Don. My damned problem, and I can't keep walking away from it. "The kid's in trouble."

"Who isn't?"

"She's scared. Maybe I can straighten things out in a few minutes."

"Oh, sure!"

"Why don't you start getting the gear together? I'll join you right away."

"Sure you will!" Don looked at Erik. He shook his head in mock exasperation. "Okay. Go rescue your damsel in distress. But don't fuck up the mission!"

He walked from the room. Erik went over to Anneliese. He looked at her.

"All right, Anneliese," he said. "Now tell me what's the trouble."

"They will not give me a pass at your military government," the girl blurted out. "To travel. To go home to Regensburg!" Her troubles came spilling out. "They say the road is closed for civilians. For many days closed. But I cannot stay here. I do not know anybody. And the other officer, he *said* I could go home. You *heard* him say I could go home! And you said—"

Erik interrupted her.

"Take it easy," he said. "Don't worry. We'll get it straightened out."

She looked up at him hopefully. He started toward the door.

"Come on. I'll take you over to the military government myself. We'll find out what's up."

He felt oddly satisfied.

Only a few civilians were in the street outside the jail, hurrying to get home before darkness and curfew.

Erik did see the small flare of the match being struck diagonally across the street. It stabbed a pinpoint of light upon his peripheral vision, but it did not reach his conscious mind, which was struggling with the presence of Anneliese. Much less did he connect it with himself.

The man, standing in the deeper shadows of a boarded-up doorway to an empty house, lit a cigarette butt. The striking of the match and the lighting of the butt were done in a fluid motion, although the man had only one arm. For a brief moment the flame illuminated his face. One eye was covered by a patch. It was Heinz.

On the side street around the corner of the jail, another man was kneeling in front of a time-scarred bicycle, fixing its chain. The bicycle, leaning against the wall of the building, was loaded with bundled-up house gear and string-wrapped cardboard boxes. A torn knapsack was latched to the rusty handlebars.

When the match flared across the street, the man stood up. He tugged at his dirty leather cap and pulled the bicycle from the wall. Pushing it alongside, he rounded the corner of the building and trudged on down the street a short distance behind Erik and Anneliese. The old bicycle had no tires. The naked wheel rims clanked metallically on the cement-slab sidewalk. The man plodded on. He never took his eyes from the two people in front of him. It was Krauss.

A few houses down the street from the jail, a building had received a direct hit. Rubble and broken masonry had spilled from the ruins out across the sidewalk into the street. Two men had been clearing a narrow path through the debris. They were in the process of loading their tools and a few pieces of salvageable lumber on a wooden cart as Erik and Anneliese approached. The clattering bicycle behind them was loud in the quiet. The two workers looked up.

Erik let the girl go through the passage first, then he started after her. He was halfway through. . . .

Suddenly the man loading the cart appeared to slip on a loose brick. He fell, and slammed against Erik's legs in a low tackle.

Erik went down.

He hit the ground at the feet of the second man. He looked up.

For a fraction of a second time stood still for him, his eyes locked on the German towering directly over him. The man's face was distorted with fanatic hate; a pickax, gripped by two white-knuckled fists, was raised high above his head.

The man brought the pickax down in a vicious stroke. Straight for Erik's upturned face. It seemed to obliterate the world above him.

He wrenched his head aside. For an instant he knew he hadn't made it. Then the pickax crashed into the rubble inches away, showering his face with stinging chips of mortar and brick.

He twisted away, reaching for the gun in his shoulder holster.

He was sharply aware of his two assailants. The man who had fallen against him was scrambling to get up; the man with the pickax was struggling to regain his balance.

Erik's fingers found the reassuring cool solidity of his gun.

Suddenly, Anneliese cried out:

"*Pass auf!*"

Instantly Erik twisted around. He lost his grip on the gun. Immediately behind him stood Krauss. He was aiming a savage kick at Erik's temple with his hobnailed boot.

The girl's warning had come just in time. Erik's hands shot up and caught Krauss's foot as it came hurtling toward his head. He didn't have the strength or leverage to stop the force of the kick, but he managed to deflect the heavy boot. The steel-reinforced toe of the boot hit him on the neck with jarring impact. He didn't feel it. He hung onto the boot with all his strength, and Krauss toppled heavily among the rubble.

He had an unreal sensation of being two people at once. One was strictly an observer. It's ridiculous, he thought. It can't be happening. Not to me! The other was acutely aware, with hair-trigger reflexes.

He rolled toward the street and came up on one knee, gun in hand.

One of his assailants was ducking into the street, shielding himself behind the few people who had begun to gather. The other man was also on his feet; he lunged toward Anneliese and gave her a violent shove, which sent her sprawling in the rubble, and kept running. Erik's gun instinctively shifted to cover him, but the girl was in his line of fire as she got up from the broken masonry.

Erik whirled toward Krauss. The man was just disappearing behind the remains of a collapsed wall. He squeezed off a shot knowing it would go wild.

He was suddenly aware that he was alone with the girl. The bystanders were slipping away, melting quickly into the dusk, as a couple of GIs came running toward the scene.

Anneliese stood motionless among the debris. She was watching Erik with frightened eyes. She was shivering, unaware of it.

Erik replaced his gun in his shoulder holster. He walked up to the girl. He put his hands on her trembling shoulders and looked into her face searchingly.

"Thank you," he said. His voice was low. "Thank you—Anneliese."

The girl met his eyes for a long moment. Then she closed her own big eyes tightly. She sagged into his arms and put her head on his shoulder. The little sob that escaped her was a mixture of spent fear and relief. . . .

Erik put his arms around the trembling girl. He held her. His arms tightened around her. He was intensely conscious of her softness. Her warmth. His world was filled with the fresh scent of her hair, mingled with the acrid-sweet smell of her fear. It was overwhelmingly exciting. And he thought of nothing but her. . . .

Nothing . . .

The attack had taken exactly twenty-three seconds.

A lifetime.

Don and Murphy came running. Murphy carried a carbine, ready for trouble.

"What's going on?" Don demanded. "What the hell's the shooting?"

Erik let the girl go.

"It's all over now," he said quietly. He was speaking to both of them.

"What happened?"

"Some blasted idiot tried to put a pickax through my head." Now that it *was* all over Erik felt a sudden anger. "God damn his hide!"

Don looked from Anneliese to Erik. He was relieved that nothing had happened to his partner, but he was deeply irritated with him for letting himself get into a situation where he could be jumped.

"Wouldn't have been easy," he said caustically, "with that thick skull of yours."

Erik glanced at him. Don had spoken with unwonted tenseness. He went on:

"You should have known better. Going out alone at this time of day with a goddamned Fräulein in tow! Where the hell do you think you are? Brooklyn?"

He felt better. He'd had his say.

Murphy came up to them.

"Anything I can do?" he asked.

Erik looked at him. Outwardly he was calm. But inside he felt a strong tide of emotion throb through him. Anneliese stood quietly away to one side, but he could still feel her in his arms. He could still smell the scent of her.

"Yes, Jim," he said. "Take care of the girl."

He turned to her.

"Don't worry," he said gently. "We'll get you to Regensburg."

"If you please," she said in a small voice. Erik turned back to Murphy.

"Tell Lieutenant Howard to let her ride the supply truck to Regensburg. Tomorrow morning. Understand? I'll take the responsibility."

"Okay, sir."

Murphy walked over to the girl, a big smile on his face.

"You see, baby," he said confidentially, "I told you I'd fix every-thing for you."

Erik was watching them.

"I hate to break this up," Don said, *"but . . ."*

Erik started.

"Yes. We'd better get going."

They headed toward the jail. Murphy and the girl followed. For a moment the two men walked in silence. Don inspected Erik out of the corner of his eye. Something's eating him, he thought. Has been for some time. He was concerned. He'd better work it out. Soon. Aloud he said:

"Erik, old cock, you'll get yourself in real trouble one of these days."

Erik frowned.

"I don't get it," he said. "Why should they suddenly jump me? Are we missing something?" He looked at Don. "Do you think—"

"It's not hard to figure out, lover boy. The Krauts don't like to see an 'Ami' promenading one of their good-looking Fräuleins. Es-pecially not one of the 'American Gestapo.' You just got their goat is all."

"Maybe you're right." Erik dismissed the incident. There were more important matters to take care of. "Did you get everything?" he asked.

"Yeah. But I've got to stay here. Wait for Division clearance. They haven't gotten off their collective ass yet."

"Okay. I'll take off for the farm now. Start the ball rolling."

"Good. Jim and I'll finish up here." He glanced at Erik. "Including fixing your girl friend's TS slip!"

They were almost at the jail. The street was empty of civilians except for one lone man, hurrying along the sidewalk toward them. It was almost curfew time. The man limped. One sleeve of a stripped Wehrmacht uniform jacket was pinned up, empty. One eye was covered by a crude patch.

He stepped into the gutter to let the Americans and the girl pass. . . .

Schönsee

The Zollner Farm

1913 hrs

Erik and Don had selected the Zollner farm to serve as command post for the operation for a couple of very good reasons. Located just north of Schönsee on the road to Eslarn, the farm's north fields bordered the forest where Plewig had placed the Werewolf headquarters; also, it was uninhabited. Zollner had been the local *Ortsbauernführer* and had thought better of staying to welcome the Americans.

The farm itself could not be seen from the forest because of a row of trees. It consisted of a main building, a barn, a stable and a chicken coop arranged around an unusually spacious farmyard. Even the oozing dunghill in the center left ample space for the barbed wire enclosure being put up in one half of the yard. Some eight to ten GIs were busy turning the farmyard into a temporary PW enclosure, unloading concertina wire from a three-quarter-ton truck, setting up corner machine gun emplacements and erecting floodlight poles.

The evening was crisp and clear and the men displayed no lights, working as quickly and silently as possible. From their shoulder patches and collar insignia it was apparent that they were 97th Division military police.

Erik was satisfied. The preparations were coming along fine. And the activity could not be observed from the forest in the distance. He walked up to an MP sergeant putting up a floodlight.

"Well, Sergeant, how's it coming?"

"Okay. Should be finished in a couple of hours."

"Great. When you're through you'd better have your men turn

in. It ought to be a busy day tomorrow." He pointed to the barn.
"That barn is full of hay. You can bed down in there."

"Good deal."

Sergeant Sammy Klein glanced at the CIC agent. He was curious.
As usual his orders had been half-assed. A PW enclosure for werewolves? He knew those CIC guys were a little *meshuge,* but *werewolves?* Led by Frankenstein and Dracula, no doubt! But he was
responsible for eleven guys from his outfit. Better he should know
as much as possible about his *tsemishne* operation. Now was as
good a time as any to find out. He held the wires of the floodlight
toward Erik.

"Would you hold these?" he asked. "Out of the way? I gotta secure
this pole."

Erik took hold of the wires.

"Sure."

"Say, what are these—uh—werewolves you're out to get?"

"It's an organization of fanatics."

"Yeah?"

"They've sworn to keep their own private reign of terror going,
even after the war is over."

"They responsible for those guys in the river?"

Erik nodded. "Very likely."

Klein spat on the cobblestones.

"Helluva way to fight a war," he said with disgust.

He'd finished securing the pole to an old hand pump. He took
the wires from Erik.

"Thanks."

He began to wind them around the pole.

"Why the screwy name Werewolves?"

"It comes from a medieval superstition that certain people can
transform themselves at will into ferocious wolflike beasts."

Klein gave a short laugh.

"That's no superstition. Happens to every guy with a three-day
pass!"

Erik smiled.

"Wrong kind of wolf, Klein." He grew sober. "Anyway, those

creatures were called werewolves. They'd terrorize the countryside with, quote, fiendish acts of murder and destruction, unquote. And that's exactly what the Nazi Werewolves plan to do."

Klein nodded toward the distant forest.

"And they're supposed to be in there someplace?"

"They are. We don't know exactly where. Could be just across the fields."

Klein looked up in half-serious alarm.

"Thanks a heap! I guess I'd better post a double guard tonight. Never was much for fiendish acts of murder and destruction."

He had finished his job. He stood back to admire it.

"Well, that ought to do it."

Erik checked his watch.

"I'll have to get back to Weiden," he said. "Pick up my partner. Get my jeep and a driver, will you?"

"I'll drive you myself. Okay?"

"Can you leave here?"

"Sure. We're almost done. I'll put Simmons in charge. I want to contact Division anyway."

"Okay. We'll be back here in a couple of hours."

"Right."

Klein walked off.

Erik started for the farmhouse, when the sound of an approaching vehicle stopped him. A jeep, with only its blackout lights showing, came barreling into the courtyard and came to a screeching halt a few feet away. A major jumped smartly from the seat next to the driver and strode up to him.

"I'm Major Evans," he announced. "Where do I find the CIC agent in charge?"

"Right here, Major. Name's Larsen. Erik Larsen. Welcome to our little home away from home."

"Thank you."

The major looked Erik over.

Erik returned his attention. The first words that came to his mind were "overbearing" and "supercilious." Somehow the man's military police and rank insignia seemed oversized. Erik felt a twinge of disapproval. He cautioned himself. He had to work with this man. He'd stay away from snap judgments.

Evans had finished his inspection.

"Sorry I couldn't get here sooner—uh—Larsen," he said. "I had a couple of—uh—important matters to finish up before I could leave."

Erik smiled. It's possible his smile wouldn't have won any prizes for cordiality, but he smiled.

"We're glad you made it."

"Major Roberts of Corps G-2 has already briefed me on this—uh —escapade of yours."

Erik struggled not to react with too obvious antagonism to the man's choice of words.

"Fine," he managed. "Then you know what it's all about."

Evans looked painfully dubious.

"Ye-e-es." He sighed the sigh of a martyr. "However, I don't put much stock in the whole affair, I'm sorry to say . . ."

I bet you are, you overbearing SOB, Erik thought, his good intentions rapidly evaporating.

". . . but Colonel Streeter wanted a—uh—competent officer on the spot," Evans continued. "As an unbiased observer."

"I know."

Evans fished a pack of Luckies from his pocket.

"Smoke?"

"No, thanks."

Evans lighted a cigarette.

"I might as well tell you now—uh—"

Evans looked in vain for Erik's insignia of rank. He felt a sudden annoyance. It was a damned frustrating state of affairs that those CIC fellows were allowed to wear only officers' insignia, with no rank showing. What the devil *was* this fellow's rank? How the hell could he know how to treat him? It was enormously irritating.

"I don't think these so-called Werewolves of yours exist," he continued. "Their ridiculous radio nonsense notwithstanding."

He took a deep puff on his cigarette. He blew out the smoke with obvious self-satisfaction. These CIC prima donnas needed to be taken down a peg or two.

"The military police has never had any trouble of any kind with them," he stated.

"I'm glad to hear that," Erik said dryly. "You're lucky."

"Oh, we've had a few isolated incidents," Evans admitted expansively. "Minor ones. But there's no organized terrorist activity."

"I see," Erik said. He didn't trust himself to get into a discussion with Evans. He'd keep it brief. Evans went on.

"Still, I suppose we'll have to look into this yarn of yours, eh?" He coughed a dry laugh. "However remote the possibility may be of turning up anything concrete."

"Tomorrow will tell."

"So it will," Evans agreed. He snipped the ember from his cigarette. Meticulously he broke the paper around the butt and scattered the remaining tobacco on the ground. Then he rolled up the paper into a small ball and flipped it away. "So it will. . . . What time are you planning to get your—uh—show on the road?"

"The infantry companies will be ready to move out at 0530 hours."

"Very good."

Evans drew himself up as if to dismiss Erik.

"Well, good night—uh—"

Again he pointedly searched for Erik's rank insignia. His look of disapproval was obvious. Evans was irked. He could be talking to an enlisted man for all he knew! It was infuriating.

Sergeant Klein drove up in Erik's jeep. Erik looked at Evans.

"Good night, Major," he said. He turned on his heel and walked to his jeep.

Evans frowned after him. He was so aggravated he could taste it. He considered his situation intolerable—being forced to play nursemaid to a couple of amateur cops and their harebrained machinations. And he was not in charge of the operation. He resented that. Deeply. Especially since he didn't even know if the CIC agent outranked him! He strongly suspected he did not.

Evans—Harold J. Evans—was a former Chicago police sergeant. He'd been a good cop. Dependable. Incorruptible. But also opinonated and obstinate. Military life had not changed him.

He turned abruptly away and stalked toward his waiting jeep. . . .

The Schönsee–Weiden Road

2034 hrs

Krauss cautiously shifted his position. The dry leaves under his twisting body rustled softly.

He had selected the place with care. The woods came all the way down to the deep ditch running alongside the road; the underbrush was heavy. He estimated he was lying less than fifteen meters from the road itself. He knew he couldn't be seen.

He shifted again. It was becoming increasingly difficult to remain comfortable for any length of time the longer he had to lie under the brush waiting. He'd give it another half hour. If nothing happened by then he'd have to start back to Weiden. It was a good six kilometers. They might have to make other plans. Heinz would have to decide. Or that officer from Krueger's headquarters, who was supposed to join them with a couple of men.

The sound was hardly audible when he first noticed it. His breath became shallow as he strained to hear. The sound grew slowly louder. A vehicle. A single vehicle coming down the road from the direction of Schönsee. He pressed himself closer to the ground. It was pure instinct. He didn't have to.

The vehicle was approaching rapidly.

He squinted at the road. The night was clear and light. He should have no difficulty seeing. He'd certainly been there long enough for his eyes to get accustomed to the diffused light. His eyes searched down the road. A distant pinpoint of light grew in size and gradually split into two. The vehicle was driving with only its blackout lights on.

Krauss kept his eyes fixed on the approaching vehicle. It was a jeep. One second he could make it out; the next it was hurtling past him and disappearing down the dark road. But there'd been time enough. Krauss felt vastly self-satisfied.

There'd been two men in the jeep. A sergeant, driving. Another man beside him. The American CIC agent. The one he'd already missed once. The target.

This was the road. This was where the Ami agents would be coming through. Both of them. He'd been right.

He pushed himself back from his vantage point. He stood up. Quickly he walked to his bicycle. He brushed the leaves concealing it aside and at once started to pedal along the darkened forest path that would take him to the outskirts of Weiden—and Heinz.

They'd have to act fast. . . .

Now.

Weiden

2 0 4 7 hrs

It was close to nine o'clock when Erik and Sergeant Klein drove up before the jail in Weiden. Klein had his orders. They would all four start back for the Zollner farm at 2330 hours.

Erik entered the building. He went straight to his room. He would have two and a half hours to get some rest. He needed it. Now that it was possible to lie down he suddenly felt bone tired. He'd check with Don and flake out for a couple of hours. It might be his only chance in quite a while.

The door to the room bore the black-lettered legend UNTER-SUCHUNG & HAFT—FRAUEN: "Search & Detention—Women." Underneath Murphy had written in chalk: CIC 212—PRIVATE.

Erik pushed the door open and walked in.

He was mildly surprised to find the lights on. His eyes darted to the windows. The blackout curtains were drawn. He started toward his bed. Every time he looked at it he wondered where Murphy had scrounged it. The big, ornate brass bedstead looked utterly incongruous in the bleak and bare police detention room. Don's army cot in the opposite corner seemed to fit the situation a hell of a lot better. Still, the huge brass monster was comfortable, even if the rusty springs did creak and the old mattress was shamelessly lumpy.

He had a cozy, luxurious "at home" feeling. Crazy what you could get used to. Is there a more relative concept than comfort?

He was suddenly aware of splashing noises coming from the small alcove behind the dilapidated screen that hid the washstand with its cracked bowl and handleless pitcher.

"Hey, Don," he called. "All set on your end?"

The splashing sounds stopped abruptly. There was no answer.

"Don?" Erik frowned. He walked toward the screen. "We're taking off for the farm in a couple of hours. I want to grab some shut-eye. Shake it up, will you?" He pushed the screen aside.

He stared.

"Anneliese!"

The girl stood motionless. She watched him with wide, frightened eyes. She was clutching an OD towel in front of her in an attempt to hide her nakedness. Her dirndl blouse was hanging on a nail on the wall behind her.

Erik stared at her.

She was beautiful. Her blond hair was piled loosely on top of her head, the smooth skin on her neck was still wet where she had been washing herself. She looked wholly beautiful—and vulnerable. Her huge, apprehensive eyes never left him.

"Anneliese," he said again. His voice was gentle.

The small tip of a nervous tongue darted between her lips.

"The sergeant," she said, her voice unsteady with misgivings. "He said—he said you will both be gone tonight. He said I could stay here again. Until tomorrow. I am sorry. *Bitte,* I . . ."

Erik smiled at her.

"Take it easy. It's okay," he assured her. "We *are* going to be gone. In a short while. You can stay if you like."

The girl relaxed a little. A soft smile crept into her eyes and tugged at her lips.

"Thank you," she whispered.

She looked down at herself. She was obviously conscious of having only the towel in front of her. Holding it in place with one hand, she reached back for her blouse.

"Please?" She looked at Erik.

He smiled. He turned to leave, when suddenly the towel slipped a little from the girl's shoulder. An angry bruise marred the velvet-golden skin. Erik frowned at it.

"What happened to you?" he asked.

Anneliese stopped her move. She tensed.

"It's—it's only a bruise."

"Looks like quite a wallop to me." He looked closer at the abrasion. "The skin's broken. You'd better be careful of infection."

The girl looked up at him.

"I will be all right."

"Wait a minute. We'll fix it."

Erik opened a pouch on his belt and took out a small first aid kit.

"How'd it happen?"

"I—I fell."

He removed the packet of sulfa powder from the kit.

"You should watch your step. You—"

He suddenly stopped. Quickly he looked up at the girl before him. He found her eyes.

"It was this evening," he said quietly. "Out there. Wasn't it?"

She nodded.

He broke open the packet. Gently he began to sprinkle the powder on the bruise on Anneliese's shoulder. She stood quite still, as if afraid to move, watching him.

"Sulfa powder," he explained. "That'll take care of it."

He was suddenly conscious of the blood pounding in his ears. He felt the gradual swelling of desire, of tenderness, of need course through him.

Anneliese.

Somehow the fine yellow powder softly dusting her golden-brown skin was immensely intimate. He let the rising flood of ir-resistible excitement wash over him.

He looked into her face. Her lovely, serious, questioning face . . .

And she was in his arms. A sudden, savage embrace. Defiant. A crushing, hungry kiss . . .

The towel slipped away. Erik's urgent hands searched for and found the girl's thrusting breasts. He cupped them, he caressed them with aching longing. He coupled his mouth to one swelling nipple and drew as much of the soft, warm firmness to him as he could. His tongue played on the distending nipple. He bit down, with just enough force to make the girl moan with pleasure.

He picked her up. He carried her to the big, ugly brass bed. He had no idea how his clothing was removed.

He stared at her young, naked body. He knew he had never seen anything more perfect, more desirable, in his whole life. Nor would he ever again . . .

His eyes went down to the entrancing cusp of fine blond hair at the apex of her slender legs.

He buried his face in the downy fragrance of woman passion. . . .

He felt both completely serene and violently excited.

He moved to her. Close. Close. Never close enough . . .

Every sense he possessed was filled with her. The scent of her excitement and desire, enveloping them both in an aura of fiery sexuality, filled his nostrils; the tiny mewing moans escaping her excited him to bursting; the salty-sweet taste of her firm young breasts thrilled him; every inch of his aroused body seemed aflame with the touch of her silken-warm skin; his eyes drank in the unbearable beauty of her lovely face, moist, parted lips, eyes closed in rapture, head thrown back in eager anticipation of fulfillment, spilling blond hair in abandoned disarray. . . . Beautiful. Beautiful. Beautiful . . .

He could not get enough of her. He sought out every curve and every hidden crevice of her urgently responding body. He intoxicated himself with the smell and feel of her.

He throbbed with pleasure as her gentle hands explored him in an unending flow of discovery and caress.

Anneliese. Anneliese . . .

He moved to enter her.

She strained to receive him, a deep sob wrenched from her throat. She clung to him fiercely.

And he thrust himself into her. Again. And again. Every cell in his body, as if with a life of its own, swelled with the agony of passion. He was torn between savagery and tenderness, between the irresistible urge to ravage, to violate, to crush and the overwhelming need to caress and love. He felt himself soar until there were no further heights to reach. Then soar still higher . . .

He moved frantically, matched by the writhing of the sobbing girl.

There was no time. No world. No other life. Only *they* existed. Wholly, Absolutely . . .

And he felt himself burst, flooding into her seething being. He felt himself drained of every fluid in his body in one gigantic, everlasting moment. And he felt himself in that same instant replenished with a tide of utter fulfillment.

Anneliese . . .

From somewhere, millennia in the past, for one fraction of a second a hideous memory had stabbed its icy lance at his mind; but it had been instantly consumed in the blaze of ecstasy.

He was now not even aware that it had happened. His commitment was total. To the now . . .

They lay side by side bathed in the glow of afterlove. Anneliese moved against him luxuriously.

"Erik," she whispered. "It was never this good for me before."

He tightened his arm around her.

God, he thought. If she knew how good it was for me . . .

It had meant more to him than just physical pleasure, more than mere sexual relief. Much more. Far back in his mind he knew why. He knew that at last he'd conquered the nightmare that had haunted him for so long. He knew, but he didn't let his conscious mind dwell on it. He didn't have to. Not anymore . . .

He felt a surge of infinite tenderness toward the girl. It was because of her. He'd never forget her. Never.

The girl stirred beside him.

"Erik," she said. "Have you—have you known any other German girls? Like this?"

His mind flashed back. It was in Berlin. He'd been there for the

1936 Olympics. He'd seen her in a shop on Kurfürstendamm and instantly fallen for her. He'd followed her from shop to shop before finally getting up enough courage to talk to her. He'd never done anything like it before. Nor since. He'd spoken to her in French at first. Somehow he'd felt it would give him a cosmopolitan air. And he wanted desperately to impress her. He'd carried her parcels and insisted on getting a number where he could call her. He'd been elated when she'd given it to him, never imagining that it could be a phony. But it had been real. He'd invited her to the Tiergarten Café and had been so nervous he'd upset a full cup of chocolate all over her white dress. But they'd had an affair. A beautiful one he'd always remember. It was his first. He was eighteen. . . .

He sighed.

"No," he said.

"I'm glad," she whispered.

He stroked her naked body. She snuggled closer to him. He felt himself respond to her. He sat up. It wouldn't do. Not now. Don would come looking for him any moment. He jumped out of the big brass monster. It was really a beautiful bed!

"Come on, girl," he said briskly. "Out of my bed! You've been dillydallying long enough." He started to pull on his pants.

Anneliese laughed.

"No," she said, nestling down under the blanket. "I belong here. It is *my* bed, this big ugly thing. For tonight."

"All right," he said resolutely. He picked up her skirt, hanging over a chair. "I'll just take this along, then. To be sure you're here when I get back."

"No!"

Anneliese sat up in bed. "Give it to me, Erik. *Bitte.*"

Erik shook his head in mock exasperation. "Just like a woman," he commented. "Always changing her mind . . . Okay—here!"

He threw the skirt to her. It hit one of the brass bedposts. There was a quick, muffled *thonk*, and a small hard object flew from a little beltline pocket and fell to the floor. It rolled a short distance and lay still.

Anneliese sat frozen on the bed. Tense. Taut. The color draining from her face, her eyes intent upon Erik.

He bent to pick up the little object. He stiffened. He held it in his hand. He stared at it. He suddenly felt as if every ounce of strength in his body was being drawn from him. He felt totally, shockingly empty. His voice was harsh when he spoke to her.

"Where did you get this?"

She didn't answer, didn't move. She didn't take her wide, terrified eyes from him. She sat motionless, clutching her skirt to her as if suddenly ashamed of her nakedness.

"Answer me!"

It was a shout of anger, rage. Of anguish. Of betrayal . . . The girl sat stock still. Ashen-faced, she stared at him. His eyes were bleak as he watched her. His voice was tense, quiet—ominously quiet—as he said:

"That is an SS Deathhead ring! Now tell me, dammit! *Where did you get it?*"

Anneliese made no answer. She looked terrified. She shrank away from him, imperceptibly shaking her head.

Erik forced himself to look closer at the obscene ring. On the inside he discovered an inscription. Aloud he read:

"Standartenführer Kurt Leubuscher."

He looked up at the girl cowering before him, his eyes still bleak.

"Who is this SS colonel with your name, Anneliese? Your husband?"

His voice was bitter, cold. Anneliese whispered through bloodless lips:

"No! Please, Erik . . . No!"

He suddenly went to her. He seized her arm. It was cold. He shook her.

"Answer me! *Who?*"

She cried out:

"My father!"

He let go of her. She buried her face in her hands and sobbed in

despair. Erik watched her. He stood quietly for a moment. Some of
the anger and hurt slowly left his face. He realized that his fury was
a personal thing. He felt himself the victim of a monstrous decep-
tion. He gagged with self-disgust. But he also understood the terror
this girl must feel. He was reacting too strongly. He knew it. But
goddammit, how *else* could he be expected to act, after . . . Dammit
all to hell!

He looked darkly at the girl, torn between his feelings for her
and the inescapable duty he knew was his.

"All right, Anneliese," he said quietly. "Take it easy. Tell me
about it."

She glanced up at him. She looked immensely appealing with her
huge, tear-bright eyes. He steeled himself.

"He is a good man, my father." The girl's voice was unsteady, but
there was unexpected strength behind it. "He does not deserve to—
to—" She put her hand to her mouth to stifle a sob.

"Where is he, Anneliese?" Erik asked. "Where is he now?"

She looked up at him quickly. She made no answer.

"Come on, Anneliese. You know you'll have to tell me. Sooner or
later."

The girl looked straight at him. There was a mixture of fear and
defiance in her eyes. Suddenly the words came tumbling out.

"I know you will try to make me tell you! I know you will torture
me and try to force me to betray my father. But I tell you now—I
will not do this!" Her eyes blazed at him. "No matter what you do
to me, I will not talk!"

Erik stared at her, thunderstruck.

"*Torture* you?" he exclaimed with incredulity.

"They told us what you would do to any SS officer you caught.
And to his family. To me. They—they showed us pictures." Her
eyes filled with dread at the remembered ordeal. She flared at Erik.
"You will not do that to him! I will not let you!"

Erik was shaken. The vehemence of the girl's warped conceptions
was obviously genuine. But he didn't miss the implication of her
words. That's it, he thought. He's here!

He forced himself to take up his familiar role.

"Your father's here. In Weiden. Isn't he, Anneliese?" he asked. His voice was hard, implacable.

The girl started. She looked at him in wide-eyed fear. He returned her gaze. He could taste the bitter realization rising in his craw.

"Of course," he said, his voice icy. "That's why you couldn't seem to find a way to get to Regensburg. You were waiting until you could arrange to get *him* out, too."

He looked straight at her.

"That's why you've been making up to *me*."

He found it difficult to control his anger, his revulsion.

"And that's why you stuck your teat in my face! That's why you were so damned eager to get me into bed with you tonight!"

Anneliese lowered her head.

"No, Erik," she whispered. "No. Not tonight . . ."

"Not tonight!" he repeated. A world was shattered. His sense of loss was overwhelming. *War!* he thought with bitter acrimony. This, too, had been nothing but war. Wits against wits. Sex against sex. And, by God, sex is a powerful weapon!

Anneliese was crying softly. He looked at her for a moment but made no motion to go to her. He reached for his shirt and started to shrug into it.

"Okay. Out with it!" he said. His voice was flat, impersonal. "Where is he?"

Anneliese remained silent. Erik turned to her in sudden fury.

"What the hell *have* they told you?"

She took a deep breath. She did not look up.

"That—that you would kill my father if you caught him. Because he is SS," she said in a barely audible voice. "Or put him in a concentration camp, where he would die—slowly. That you would do anything to make me tell you where he is."

Erik stared at her.

"Shit!" he said with savage disgust. "Pure Gestapo shit!"

She winced. He frowned at her. God, he thought. They haven't missed a trick, the bastards. They've filled her full of horror stories to keep her in line. What the hell chance did she ever have? He felt a sudden surge of pity for her.

"No one's going to hurt you, Anneliese," he said quietly.

She glanced up at him.

"Then you will let me go?" She did not believe it herself.

He turned away.

"No," he said. His face was grim. "I can't do that. Not now . . ."

Anneliese seemed to sag, to collapse a little within herself. Her face was suddenly gray and drawn, empty of emotion. It was as she had thought.

"I will not talk," she whispered, her voice hoarse with hopeless desperation. "Whatever you do to me, I will not talk."

"Stop it!"

He was tired. Dead tired.

"I told you nobody's going to touch you."

Anneliese looked up at him slowly, until her eyes met his.

"And my father?" she asked. "What will you do to him?"

"I'll have to arrest him, Anneliese. He'll be interned. For a little while . . ."

She said nothing. Her silence was eloquence enough. Clutching her skirt before her, she stood up.

"I'd like to get dressed now, please."

He stood aside. He didn't know what else to do.

Anneliese walked to the alcove and disappeared behind the screen. Erik sat down on the big brass bed. He looked at it. Only a little while ago . . . he thought. He had a feeling of impotence, of complete inability to control the course of events. He hated it. He hated himself; his job; the whole damned war. . . .

But he had to try.

"Anneliese," he said. "Try to understand. I know it sounds—banal, but it *is* for your own, and your father's, good. Don't you see? If I bring him in now, if he surrenders to me, it'll be easier on both of you. I promise I'll stand by you."

He looked toward the screen. There was no sound from the little alcove. He frowned.

"I can't let him go, Anneliese. It's my job, dammit! Being an SS colonel, your father *has* to be taken in. He has to be cleared. . . ."

He paused. He listened. Anneliese made no sound.

"I promise you, if he's okay they'll let him go. No one will mistreat him. But he has to get papers. You know that. And so do you. And that's the only way to get them."

He stood up. He took a step toward the alcove. He stopped.

"Look," he said. "If I let you go now, if *I* don't arrest your father, someone else will. And without knowing the whole story. Don't you see? He can't keep running forever. Try to understand, Anneliese. Try to help. Everything'll be okay. . . ."

He stopped. He listened.

There was only silence—brutally shattered by a sudden jarring crash!

Blue-patterned chips from the washbowl sprayed out from under the seedy screen.

In two strides Erik was at the alcove. He slammed the screen aside. . . .

On the floor, sprawled among the jagged fragments of porcelain from the shattered bowl, was Anneliese. Still, white—and motionless.

Around her throat, tightly embedded in her skin, the drawstring from her blouse was knotted firmly, choking the life from her. . . .

At once Erik grabbed for the knot. Frantically he tried to undo it. Too tight. Too close. He couldn't get a grip on it. Desperately he tried to force his fingers under the string to tear it apart. It was not possible.

Feverishly he looked around, eyes haunted and wild. On the washstand he spied a razor, and he ripped the blade from it. He hacked at the cord biting into the girl's skin, forcing himself to ignore the blood oozing from the cuts he had to inflict upon her.

The drawstring snapped. . . .

He lifted her head. He called her name. Again. And again. She did not respond. Her lifeless face only stared unseeingly up at him.

He pressed his lips to hers in a desperate attempt to breathe his own life into her. . . .

But she was dead.

He sat on the floor. He cradled her head in his arms. He raged with frustration at the world.

"Anneliese," he whispered in anguish. "Anneliese . . . You didn't have to do that. You didn't have to do that. . . ."

The door burst open. Don and Pierce came running into the room. They stopped dead just inside.

"What happened?" Don's shocked voice was hushed.

Slowly Erik let the girl down on the floor among the chunks of broken porcelain. He stood up.

"She didn't believe me," he said tonelessly. He was speaking to no one. "She believed that goddamned Gestapo propaganda."

He walked to the bed. He picked up the SS Deathhead ring. For a moment he stared at it. Then he looked at the big brass bedstead. It's ugly, he thought with a sudden chill. Ugly!

Don came up to him.

"Erik—I—"

"Drop it!" Erik interrupted him. "There's nothing you can say. . . . There's nothing anyone can say."

He turned to Pierce.

"Here's a hot tip for you, Pierce." His voice was harsh. "The result of my latest interrogation."

He threw the ring to him.

"Mandatory arrestee. In hiding. Right here in Weiden."

He turned toward the still body of Anneliese. Nothing is as absolutely motionless as death, he thought. Even lifeless things can move. But not death . . .

He turned back to Pierce. His eyes were terrible to behold.

"SS Colonel Kurt Leubuscher," he said. "He's all yours!"

The Schönsee–Weiden Road

2343 hrs

Willi approved of the spot selected by Krauss for the ambush. They had a good field of fire, and the trees cast long moon shadows across the road, perfect camouflage for their special preparations. All they had to do now was wait. . . .

Even though he'd been on the go almost twenty hours straight, Willi still felt keyed up. The officer courier mission early that morning had been perfectly executed. He knew the general had been pleased, and he wondered what had been in the courier's dispatch case. He hoped it had been something of real importance. Maybe even information leading to Eisenhower's elimination! The thought excited him.

When the critical problem of Plewig and the American agents was reported to Krueger, Willi had no trouble persuading the general to let him take charge of the planned action. He'd taken only two men, one of them Steiner, who'd returned with him to Sonderkampfgruppe Karl with the captured documents after getting rid of the courier and his driver. But this time they were all armed with Schmeisser machine pistols. They needed the firepower.

He glanced toward the other men lying concealed in the darkness of the underbrush. Krauss, and Leib from the Werewolf headquarters *Sicherungsstaffel*, Steiner and he, himself, in the anchor position.

They were ready.

Suddenly he tensed. Faintly in the distance he heard vehicles approaching on the road. At least two. From the direction of Weiden . . .

He cocked his gun.

The two jeeps drove fast. Although only their blackout lights were on, the night was clear enough to see the road perfectly.

Don and Sergeant Murphy were in the lead jeep, Murphy driving. Erik and Sergeant Klein followed, Klein at the wheel. Both vehicles were combat rigged, tops down, windshields lying flat along the hood to eliminate any obstructions to possible quick fire.

Erik sat rigid next to Klein in stony silence. The sergeant had tried to strike up a conversation, but Erik had cut him short. He wasn't ready for small talk. Not yet. He was sorry. Klein was a good man. He'd apologize later.

He was suddenly conscious of the fact that his hands hurt. He looked down. With some astonishment he realized that his grip on the tommy gun lying across his knees was so tense that his fingers were beginning to cramp. With a conscious effort he relaxed them. He forced himself to think of the action ahead. He stared down the dark road. They were driving close behind Don's jeep. . . .

Suddenly, without the slightest warning, he saw it. The glint of metal in the air above the road.

An icy chill knifed down his spine. He opened his mouth to scream a warning, and at that instant the lead jeep slammed into it—a thin, strong wire, drawn tautly across the road between two trees at the exact height of a man's throat, and at a slight angle to ensure maximum cutting power.

No sound had yet come from Erik when the wire struck Murphy and Don. . . .

It was a split second of pure horror. In the eerie light it looked to Erik as if Murphy's head was instantly and completely severed—or was it his helmet flying off? Don was thrown violently from the jeep. Erik didn't see him land. In a nightmare flash he glimpsed the hunched-over, seemingly headless corpse of Murphy slumped over the wheel, as the jeep went out of control and crashed into the ditch.

Instinctively he ducked.

He would have been too late, but the impact force of the two men in front of him had snapped the taut wire with a sharp *ping*. It curled back in two furious metal whips and a chilling, high-pitched *whoosh*.

Klein had stomped on the brake, and they screeched to a crash halt up against the lead jeep, hurtling Erik across the dash.

And in the same instant several guns opened fire on them from across the road.

Erik hurled himself from the jeep. He hit the ground. Steel death stitched a deadly pattern in the dirt inches from him. He rolled behind the vehicle. He was surprised to find that he was still clutching his tommy gun. He began spraying the woods across the road with short, vicious bursts of fire. He was dimly aware of Klein also firing from cover of the ditch.

There was a sudden, earth-shaking explosion, and he jerked his head toward the other jeep. Fire from the enemy had hit the fuel tank; the vehicle was a blazing ball of flame. He had a mental flash of Murphy slumped over the wheel.

He kept on firing. . . .

He watched for the muzzle flares of firearms across the road and sent a burst ripping into the shadowy underbrush when he spotted one. He thought he saw a darker shadow thrashing briefly and fired again.

Suddenly it was over.

The shattering noise of the guns had been so all-enveloping that it seemed not to die at once but to roll away like distant thunder.

There was only silence, and the crackling of the burning jeep.

Cautiously Erik broke cover. He was aware of Klein moving from the ditch. His full attention was on the woods across the road.

But the ambushers had gone.

He ran to the blazing jeep. Murphy had been thrown clear. He was lying in the weeds nearby. Erik hurried to him. And looked.

The killer wire had done its job well.

The warm blood was still flowing quietly from Sergeant Murphy's headless neck. . . .

He heard Klein retch behind him. He fought down his own vomit. He turned away.

Don? Where was Don?

He saw him. He was lying motionless on the ground a short distance away, his head and shoulders hidden by a stump.

Hidden?

He stumbled toward him. His mind shrieked with abject horror. He could take no more . . . no more.

He fell to his knees on the ground.

Don moaned, and stirred.

Erik felt weak with relief. Carefully he lifted Don up. There was an angry red bruise across his forehead.

Klein came over. Carbine in hand, he kept watching the thicket across the road.

Don was clearing. He looked up at Erik and put his hand to his head. He saw his helmet on the ground next to him and picked it up. Across the front of it was a raw, fresh gash, cut into the very metal, where the wire had struck.

Don looked at Erik.

"Guillotine wire?"

Erik nodded.

Suddenly alarmed, Don looked around.

"Jim?"

Neither Erik nor Klein said anything. Don suddenly smashed his helmet into the dirt.

"The bastards!" he growled, his voice harsh with bitter fury. "The dirty, lousy bastards!"

Erik helped him to his feet. For a moment the two men stood looking at one another across a black abyss of horror and grief.

Erik slowly looked across the road.

"What the hell have we gotten ourselves into?" he said slowly.

He turned back to Don. His face was set in terrible resolve. He said:

"As God is my witness—we'll make tomorrow worth it!"

Part IV

30 Apr 1945

■

Schönsee

The Zollner Farm

0511 hrs

The heavy gray light of predawn lay over the Zollner farm, the fields and the forest beyond like gradually clearing sleep coating the eyes at first awakening.

In the farmyard the barbed wire PW enclosure yawned empty, waiting, the steel barrels of the guarding machine guns pointing at nothing. The presence of the dunghill was less intrusive this early in the morning; that would change as the sun began to beat down upon it later in the day. At the farmyard gate a couple of MPs stood guard. Two jeeps with MP drivers were parked just inside. In the front seat of one of them sat Major Harold J. Evans. He looked impatient.

Erik, Don and Sergeant Klein emerged from the farmhouse and walked briskly toward the two waiting jeeps.

Erik felt a twinge of annoyance when he saw Evans. Damned eager beaver! he thought. He would be in my jeep! He turned to Klein.

"Don'll be with Able Company. At the east boundary," he said. "I'll be with Baker Company at the west."

He glanced at his watch.

"Shouldn't take them more than about two hours to comb the entire forest."

Klein nodded.

"If there's anybody in there, they'll sure get 'em," he agreed.

Both Erik and Don whirled at him.

"If!"

"There'd better be!" said Don grimly.

"We'll be back here as soon as we've started the troops off," Erik said.

"Okay. We'll be ready and waiting."

Don walked to his jeep. Erik stopped at his.

"Good morning, Major," he said. His voice was cold. "Riding with me?"

Evans turned to him.

"I presume you don't mind?"

Erik didn't answer. He jumped in the back of the jeep. It occurred to him he should be damned annoyed at the high-handed way Evans had relegated him to the rear seat. But he couldn't be bothered. Evans twisted around to look at him.

"I hear you had a—a spot of trouble last night."

Erik felt it impossible to keep the bitterness out of his voice.

"Yes, Major," he said. "One of your 'minor incidents.'"

Evans shook his head gravely. "Too bad." He turned back.

"Yes. Too bad . . ." For a moment Erik stared into the gray light. His eyes were old. There was a dark void in his mind. He deliberately drove all thoughts of Anneliese, of Murphy, deep into it. Obliterated them. For now . . .

He nodded to the driver.

"Let's go," he said tonelessly.

The two jeeps started up. Klein cupped his hands and called after them:

"Good hunting!"

Evans snorted scornfully to himself. He couldn't make up his mind if he felt gratified or annoyed. True, he'd put that insufferable CIC agent in his place. Shown him that an *officer* rides up front! But he was still trapped in a ridiculous wild goose chase.

Again he gave a snort, this time aloud.

Werewolves! he thought with disdain.

Weiden

0526 hrs

    Krauss felt uneasy.

It was still early, but already the streets of Weiden were coming alive with traffic. Even in war the inhabitants of a farming community rise with the sun.

He felt uncomfortably conspicuous as he walked toward the bombed-out house, even though his conscious mind told him he was indistinguishable from the other pedestrians hurrying along. He forced himself not to look furtive as he glanced around before ducking into the cellar of the ruin.

He made his way down the debris-strewn stairs. It was dark. He slowed down.

He didn't like it. Not one bit. There were too many contacts. It was dangerous. But Heinz knew the communications apparatus. He didn't. It couldn't be helped. Not with this devil of a situation threatening the operation. He reached the cellar. For a moment he stood still, listening.

He heard nothing.

He took a box of matches from his pocket and struck one. The sudden flare of the flame seemed intolerably bright, the rasping noise deafening. He peered into the shadows beyond the circle of dim light cast by the burning match. He thought he could see a figure detach itself from the deeper darkness. The match went out.

"Heinz?" he whispered.

"*Ja.*"

He took a step forward. His eyes began to get used to the gloom. He could make out the form of his comrade.

"We only got one of them," he said, flat-voiced.

"*Verflucht!*" Heinz spat the oath.

"Steiner was wounded. We had to get him out."

"Before your mission was completed?"

Krauss felt chilled by the acid coldness in the other man's voice. He remained silent.

"Who decided?"

"The headquarters officer. Leutnant Richter." Krauss suddenly felt the need to defend the action. "We couldn't leave Steiner behind," he said. "He would have been made to talk. We had to get him out while we could."

There was a moment's icy silence.

"Your mission was vital," Heinz said coldly. "You could have killed him."

Krauss shivered.

He is right, he thought. He is right.

"What about Plewig?" Heinz demanded.

"He is at their command headquarters. We cannot get to him. Yet." Krauss was suddenly aware that he was no longer whispering. He lowered his voice. "It is too late anyway. He has obviously talked already."

"He will pay for it." There was venom in Heinz's voice. "What about the Amis? The agents?"

Krauss felt himself go cold. They might hold him responsible. But he wasn't. That young officer from Krueger's headquarters. Richter. He had been in charge. It wasn't *his* fault they'd failed to eliminate all the Americans. And yet it was he who had selected the place for the ambush. They *could* blame him. . . .

To hell with it. He wasn't going to give up now.

"They are at the Zollner farm," he said.

Heinz drew in his breath sharply.

"The Zollner farm!" he hissed. "But that's—"

He stopped short.

Krauss took a deep breath.

"I know," he said tensely. "But we may not be too late . . ."

He hesitated.

"We'll have to take the chance," he said. "We. Ourselves!"

Schönsee

The Zollner Farm

0735 hrs

GRÜSS GOTT! TRITT EIN!
BRING GLÜCK HEREIN!

Erik sat at the big wooden table in the *Bauernstube* of the Zollner farm. He was staring at the old embroidered proverb, stained with cooking-grease, stretched over a wooden frame and hanging above the door. But he didn't see it. On the table before him were several sheets of blank paper, and he had a pencil in his hand. But he was not writing. . . .

He let his eyes roam the room.

An enormous wood-burning black stove with a pile of firewood next to it; rough wooden benches and chunky chairs; uneven, crude floorboards, every crack and split caked with trampled-down dirt; walls of whitewashed stone, grimy and cracked; soiled, faded curtains in the usual Bavarian print. All of it worn and wasted with years of use.

He was suddenly acutely aware of everything. Every item. He felt utterly out of context. A total stranger.

What the hell am I doing here? he thought. All this. It has nothing to do with me. Nothing . . .

He stared at the paper in front of him. It had been a good idea. Use the time waiting to get a start on the G-2 report. But he hadn't written one word.

He was completely conscious of the tenseness gripping him. He'd watched it develop as the minutes of waiting had grown into hours. It was the suspense. Suspense has a cumulative effect, he thought. Like X-rays.

He forced himself to relax. Maybe if he got started. The date. That was it. At least he could start by writing the date. . . .

"30 Apr 1945," he wrote.

He looked at it. It was just a date. A day. Like any other day. So far. Was it going to stay that way?

He suddenly realized that he was straining to hear, listening for any sign of unusual activity outside. He was annoyed with himself. Come on, dammit! Concentrate! he thought. Concentrate on what you're supposed to be doing.

The door opened and Don came into the room. Erik looked up at him at once.

"Any sign of them?" he asked quickly.

Don shook his head.

"Not yet." He frowned. "What the hell can be keeping them? It's eight o'clock. It's been almost two and a half hours by now."

"Maybe they ran into trouble."

"I haven't heard any firing."

Erik looked worried. He stared at the paper in front of him. "30 Apr 1945" . . . "30 Apr 1945" . . .

Don was studying the embroidered sentiment over the door.

"Wonder if that goes for us, too," he mused.

Erik looked up.

"What?"

"That sign."

He translated aloud:

" 'God bless you! Step in! Bring happiness with you!' "

"Hardly. Anyway, we haven't brought them much happiness."

"Well, if we haven't it's their own damned fault. They asked for it." Don looked around the room. "Ever think of it? Right here, boy. The cradle of Nazism! Right here in Bavaria. That's where it all started. . . ."

He began to pace the floor.

"You know, I don't get it, though." He shook his head. "Most of them we talk to don't seem like such bad eggs."

"I guess most of them aren't."

"Yeah. But how the hell do you tell them apart? Without cracking them."

He kept pacing the floor, needing something to do. He began to whistle. "Lilli Marlene." Off key.

Erik stared at his paper. He frowned. He looked with irritation at the pacing, whistling Don. Dammit! he thought. How am I supposed to concentrate with that kind of shit going on?

He started to say something to Don but thought better of it. He bit his lip. . . . Did he hear something out there? No. Nothing. Not with that damned whistling. He stared at the date.

"30 Apr 1945."

Don stopped whistling.

"Ever stop to think," he said. " 'Lilli Marlene.' The only good song to come out of this fucking war. 'Lilli Marlene.' A goddamned *German* song!"

He started to pace and whistle again.

Erik looked up.

"For Christ's sake, can't you settle down somewhere?" he snapped with irritation. "And stop that infernal whistling!"

Don stopped. He glared at his partner.

"What the hell's eating you?" he growled.

"Nothing's eating me! I'm *trying* to do some writing!"

"Well, go ahead, dammit! Don't let me stop you!"

Abruptly he turned his back to Erik. The door opened and Major Evans came in. At once both Don and Erik looked at him expectantly.

Evans sauntered into the room.

"Well," he said. "Looks like the boys are out on a wild goose chase like I said, doesn't it?"

"What makes you think so?" Erik asked icily.

"You know something we don't?" Don didn't bother to conceal his antagonism.

Evans smiled. He thoroughly enjoyed being patronizing.

"Oh, come now," he said. "They've been in there a long time now. And we haven't heard any activity at all."

"Doesn't mean a thing," Don said quickly.

Evans looked from one to the other. He had the air of a condescending father addressing his wayward and slightly retarded sons.

"Look," he said with exaggerated patience. "Seventeen years in law enforcement and the military police give a man the experience, the know-how to—smell out a case." He paused significantly. He looked dramatically from one to the other. "You haven't got one!" he pronounced.

Erik fought down his anger. He got up from the table and walked over to Evans. He faced him squarely.

"We think differently, Major," he said quietly.

"Well, it's your necks. You'll be held to account. Not I."

Erik regarded the officer with ill-concealed contempt.

"I don't mind facing the music, Major," he said. "As long as I'm calling the tune. And right now I am!"

Evans flushed.

"What you CIC boys don't seem to realize is something we professionals have long ago learned the hard way. Solving a case is ninety percent dreary routine work, and ten percent luck."

Erik didn't take his eyes from the officer.

"And we CIC boys," he said, "have learned that you can *make* your own ten percent luck with a little imagination and tenacity of purpose. Ever tried that?"

Don laughed aloud. He winked broadly at Erik.

"I couldn't have put it better myself, General!" he declared.

Evans was furious. He had been bested. Bested by some—some half-assed "agent," whom he probably outranked! He fought to hold on to his dignity.

"This time your—imagination has taken you out on a limb, I'm afraid." He smiled a thin, unpleasant smile. "Werewolves? As the saying goes, 'There ain't no such animal.' "

Suddenly the door flew open and Sergeant Klein burst into the *Bauernstube*.

"They're here!" he shouted excitedly. "They're coming down the road!"

Erik and Don reached the farmyard gate together. As one they stopped short.

They stared down the road in appalled consternation.

It was a sad-looking procession that was approaching the farm. First came three bedraggled Wehrmacht soldiers, their hands clasped behind their necks. Their uniforms were dirty and torn, but somehow they all looked smugly pleased with themselves. Behind them shuffled three elderly men in civilian clothes, obviously farmers, their weathered faces showing their apprehension and puzzlement. The six prisoners were guarded by two GIs, one of them a corporal, who brought up the rear.

But for this pathetic group, as far as the eye could see, the countryside was deserted.

Erik felt a hard knot form in his guts. His throat was suddenly constricted, dry. With a conscious effort he swallowed.

It can't be, he thought wildly. This *can't* be all of them!

He started to walk rapidly toward the column. Don followed. The corporal saw them approach.

"Halt, you Krauts!" he called to his prisoners. "Hold up there!"

He went to meet the two CIC agents. He saluted leisurely, a wide grin on his face.

"Corporal Lawton reporting, sir, with these here six Werewolf prisoners."

"Is that all of them?"

"Yes, sir. That's all we could rustle up in there."

Erik stared at the pitiful group of prisoners. He didn't dare look at Don. He didn't want to see his own deep disappointment, his own concern and dejection, reflected on the face of his friend. He turned back to the corporal.

"That's *all* you could find?" he asked slowly. He didn't want to believe it. Perhaps if he asked again it would come out all right.

Lawton was obviously amused. He enjoyed the situation.

"Sure thing." He nodded. He gestured toward the three German soldiers. "You might even say them three Kraut soldiers kinda found us! They was jus' wandering around looking for somebody to surrender to—anybody a-tall—when we all came along."

He nodded toward the three old men.

"Them three old guys was chopping wood—peaceful like." He

made a show of looking dubious. "They don't look like no Were-wolves to me," he commented. "But we had orders to pick up ever'body."

"All right, Corporal!" Erik's voice was sharper than he had intended. He didn't appreciate the man's deliberate good humor. Not now. "Take your prisoners to the farm and turn them over to Sergeant Klein. Tell him to put them in the enclosure."

"The enclosure?" Lawton's eyebrows shot up in surprise. "Yes, sir! And then can we join our outfit, sir? They all went back on the line."

"Yes."

"Thank you, sir."

Lawton gave another leisurely salute and turned back to his PW column.

"All right, you all! Get a move on," he called imperiously. "*Vorwärts! Schnell . . . schnell!*"

The ragged column got under way again, trudging toward the Zollner farm. Erik and Don stood looking after them.

Erik felt drained, dismally let down. He was dimly aware that this exact moment called for a maximum effort of constructive, imaginative thinking. But his mind was dulled with discouragement. He glanced at Don.

Don turned to him. His face was grim.

"Think Joe gave us a bum steer after all?" he asked.

"No. I don't."

"Neither do I." Don sounded angry. He gestured after the departing column. "But where the hell does *that* leave us?"

"I have an answer for that."

"Yeah! And without a paddle!"

Slowly they started to walk back to the farm. For a while they were silent, each with his own bleak thoughts. Then Don spoke up:

"We can't just let it go. . . ."

"No, we can't. I value my neck too much for that." Erik frowned in concentration. "Besides, I still don't think it *is* a wild goose chase, as our friendly neighborhood MP so succinctly put it."

"Supposed to be a Werewolf chase!" Don gave a short laugh. "Tally ho!"

They walked on for a while. Their attempts at gallows humor began to pay off, neutralizing the numbing of their minds. Their thoughts once more turned to the problem—the problem which, instead of having been solved, in the last few minutes had become infinitely greater.

Erik made a concerted effort to sort out his whirling thoughts. A phrase suddenly leaped into his mind. Two lines from an old Danish hymn. He'd sung it many times with his parents in the little Danish church back in Rochester. Long ago. He'd always thought it was a great motto. *"Giv aldrig tabt, först da er du en slagen Mand!"* There sure was something to it. "Never give up, only then are you beaten!" So be it. He let events flash in review. Had he been misled? Was this whole damned thing a hoax? No. He still believed his hunch. There had to be a way, a way to break the case. Step by step . . .

It was the next step he had to find. . . .

"Okay," he said. "We've tipped our hand. If there's something going on in there, there won't be after today."

"We can forget about the Wehrmacht soldiers," Don said. "They're nothing but deserters who made it. But what about the civilians?"

"I don't know. I don't think they're part of it. More likely they were just gathering firewood, or—"

Don interrupted him.

"But they *might* have contact with the Werewolves. Know *something* about them. Remember those hundred and twenty horses."

Erik looked up with quick interest.

"You're right! It's worth a try."

"Our only chance."

There was new purpose in their minds and new energy in their steps as they walked toward the farm.

"We've got to work fast," Erik said resolutely. "No time for lengthy interrogations. We'll have to—"

"I got it!" Don exclaimed.

"What?"

"Remember the Salzman case? Remember how you got them to talk? Your star performance?"

Erik stopped short. He faced Don. He frowned.

"I remember."

"It would work with those guys, too."

"It's rough."

"Sure it's rough!" Don snapped savagely. "So is being dumped in the river with your guts blown out or your throat slit!"

He looked earnestly at Erik. "Have we any choice? What would happen if they really *were* in there and were left alone to go into action? What if they *did* get to Ike?"

Erik looked grave, thoughtful.

"We'd have to work on all three of them," he said slowly.

"Let's get started!"

They walked briskly to the farmyard gate. They were met by a sheepish-looking Klein.

"I put the prisoners in the enclosure," he said. He looked toward the compound. In one corner of the empty area huddled the three frightened old men; in another the three Wehrmacht deserters stood watching the MP guards surrounding the barbed wire PW enclosure. The machine gun positions were manned, every man at his post.

Erik had a quick thought. It's like a scene straight out of a Three Stooges comedy. . . . He said to Klein, his voice brisk:

"Sam. Take six men. Get the three civilian prisoners. Bring them outside in the field across the road."

Klein looked startled.

"Six men?"

"Get going!"

"Yes, sir!" He hurried off. Major Evans sauntered over from the PW enclosure. He looked smug and vastly self-satisfied. With a smile of pseudo sympathy he looked from Erik to Don.

"Well, you did your best, I suppose," he remarked, his patronizing manner in top form. "Too bad it turned out to be such a fiasco." He was enjoying his moment of triumph to the hilt. "But you can't say I didn't warn you!"

He glanced toward the PW enclosure, suddenly all business.

"Now. I'll take my MPs and return to Corps at once. No use wasting more time. And I'll take your—uh"—he smiled nastily— "Werewolf prisoners with me."

He nodded benevolently.

"I'll report to Colonel Streeter that I feel certain you acted in good faith." He glowed. It felt good to be magnanimous. He could afford it. He had been proved right. He smiled at Erik and Don. He felt almost kindly toward them now they had been humbled.

Erik returned his look. His face was expressionless.

"We are not sending the MPs back just yet, Major Evans," he stated quietly.

Evans was caught off guard.

"What?"

"We aren't through with them," Don explained patiently.

"But that's—that's ridiculous!" Evans found it impossible to keep his deep indignation out of his voice. What was this? Were they deliberately goading him? It was a completely unreasonable attitude to take. Their case had blown up in their faces, dammit. As he'd said it would. He felt the hot flush of anger rise from his collar.

"We need them a little longer," Erik said.

"What for?"

"We haven't given up yet, Major."

"Nonsense! Why don't you admit your blunder? Take it from me, you'll only get yourselves in deeper if you persist in this—this farce!"

"Now just a minute!" Don confronted Evans heatedly. Erik broke in:

"Major! We don't consider our job a farce. There's too much at stake here not to try everything."

Evans turned on him.

"Haven't you done enough? Two complete infantry companies

immobilized an entire morning! Looking for imaginary Were-wolves!"

The antagonism between Evans and the two CIC men was an almost tangible thing. Don spoke up.

"If you don't mind. It is our decision." His voice was cold.

"I can't agree with you."

"*Agree* with us?"

"I shall have to call this whole fool thing off," Evans stated imperiously. "I am taking my men back to Corps. Right now!"

Don started to protest. Evans cut him off.

"That's final!"

"Major Evans." Erik's voice was calm but firm. "I must remind you that you are here strictly as an observer. *I am in charge!* The MPs stay until *I* dismiss them!"

Evans glared at Erik, his face red with fury.

"You are quite sure?" There was an ominous tone to his voice. It was obvious the man controlled himself only with the greatest difficulty.

"I'm sure."

"It will be over my official protest."

"That's fine with us," Don said.

"You realize, of course, that Colonel Streeter will get a full report of this entire incident."

Erik looked at the MP officer steadily.

"That's what you're here for, Major."

"Very well! If that's the way you want it . . ."

Abruptly Evans turned on his heel and stalked off. Erik and Don looked after him. Don rubbed his neck. His gesture was most expressive.

"Boy, they're way out now," he observed ruefully.

"Let's get on with it," Erik said. He took his Colt from his shoulder holster. He inspected it.

"I sure hope this'll pay off," he said fervently.

The three old farmers huddled together apprenhensively in the middle of the field. They looked strangely ineffectual, their large, calloused hands hanging limply at their sides, their faces filled with fear and uncertainty. Ringing them stood six alert MPs, their open-holstered .45s within easy reach. The scene had the exaggerated aspect of a cartoon ridiculing "overwatch," yet there was an unmistakable air of deadly seriousness about it.

Sergeant Klein stood talking with one of the MPs. He broke off and went to meet Erik and Don as they walked rapidly from the farm.

"Okay, Sam," Erik said to him. "Stake them out!" His face was grim.

Klein turned toward the MPs guarding the farmers.

"Stake 'em out!" he called.

The MPs at once moved in on the farmers. Two men took each German by the arms and led him off a little distance. They placed the prisoners about fifteen feet apart so that they formed a triangle, all facing away from each other but within hearing distance, and each held firmly by two MPs.

Erik looked at the scene. He felt unreal, an actor about to go on in a play the end of which he didn't know. He felt an overpowering need to prepare himself for his role, to put himself "in the mood."

He looked searchingly at the three Germans. For a brief moment he deliberately opened the floodgates to the dark memories imprisoned in the deep recesses of his mind, and he let them inundate his consciousness:

. . . his first sight and smell of a concentration camp and the indescribable mass of human misery confined behind its walls. The man lying flat on his back on the filthy floor, thirty years old but looking eighty, so thin that his spine showed through his stomach; his parchment hands lying dead above his head; burning eyes sunk deep in their sockets; the victim of the inhuman "no-work-no-food" rule of the camp—hissing one word over and over and over through rotting teeth in the putrid gums of a lipless mouth: "Sugar —sugar—sugar," before he died . . .

. . . the heart-rending joy and gratitude of the liberated inmates, who used their last remaining strength to run off a little handbill of thanksgiving on the camp press: "Our Glorious American Liberators wrest us from the inhuman life of imprisonment at Untermassfeldt," it read. "The radiant sun of liberty floods our overflowing hearts with hope." He'd had to turn away when they gave it to him. . . .

. . . the mutilation of little Tania . . .

. . . the slaughtered GIs in the river . . .

. . . Anneliese . . .

. . . Murphy . . .

He took a deep breath. He walked resolutely up behind the first German.

"Name?" he demanded. There was an angry harshness in his voice.

The German started.

"Oberman," he answered nervously. "Alois."

The man started to turn to the interrogator behind him. The MPs jerked him back roughly.

"Don't turn around!" Erik ordered sharply. "Just keep looking straight ahead and answer my questions."

He spoke loudly, his voice grating with anger. There was no doubt that the two other prisoners could hear his every word.

"Do you know why you are here?" he asked curtly.

"No, Herr Offizier. I don't."

"Because you are a Werewolf!" Erik's voice was flat and hard. "A goddamn Nazi Werewolf!"

The German grew pale. He suddenly looked terrified. Again he tried to turn around to face his interrogator, and again the MPs prevented him from doing so.

"Nein! Nein, Herr Offizier," he repeated, hoarse with fear. "I am not a Werewolf!"

"No? Then what were you doing in that forest?"

"I am a forester, Herr Offizier. I was just cutting firewood." He was pleading. "Please, please . . . Let me go. I am just a forester. From Schönsee. I have a wife. Children, Herr Offizier. I am not a Werewolf. . . ."

Erik cut him off.

"Quiet! I know you *are*."

Abruptly the old man stopped talking.

"Where are the others?"

Oberman licked his dry lips. He was trembling.

"I do not know anything about Werewolves, Herr Offizier. Believe me! *Bitte, bitte*, believe me! I do not know—"

"You lie!" Erik spat the word.

"No! I swear to you! I do not know!"

Deliberately Erik drew his Colt from his shoulder holster.

"Perhaps this will jar your memory, old man!" He jabbed the gun in Oberman's back. The German started violently and grew rigid.

"You had better talk! *Now!*" Erik's voice was ominous.

"Please, Herr Offizier. I—I do not know anything! Please!" Oberman's pitiful pleading was a hoarse half whimper of terror. He fell silent.

"As you will, old man. You've made your choice!" Erik's voice was loud and harsh with disgust.

He turned on his heel and walked briskly to the second man. He stopped directly behind him. The old man began to tremble. The MPs took a firmer grip on him.

"Name?"

Erik sounded angry, cold, dangerously impatient.

"Weber, Franz."

"You, too, are a Werewolf!"

Weber was shaking with fear.

"No!" It was a cry of growing panic. "I know nothing about them! Nothing!"

Erik stood right behind the German. His mouth was inches from the back of his head. He spoke in a loud, brutal voice.

"You know why you are here, Weber? You are on trial! Right now! *My* trial! You are on trial for your life!"

Weber was mumbling to himself in abject terror.

"O-o-oh! Mein Gott in Himmel! Mein lieber Gott . . ."

Erik bore into him relentlessly.

"Answer me! Where are the Werewolves?"

"I do not know . . . I do not know . . ."

"You lie!"

"No! No!"

"Dammit, I'm sick and tired of lies! Do you hear?" Erik was working himself into a barely controlled rage. "Out with it!"

"*Bitte, bitte, bitte*—I do not lie!"

Erik raised his gun. He drove it roughly into Weber's back. The man was rigid in shock, his face distorted with dread. Erik looked drawn, tense, filled with loathing.

"Talk!" he shouted at the German. "Talk—or so help me I'll shoot you down on the spot!"

"I know nothing . . . nothing . . . nothing . . ."

Erik's face was haunted. He fought with himself. The old man might be telling the truth. He'd long since learned never to disregard the possibility that someone might *not* be lying. Such mistakes could be just as dangerous as the consequences of believing a liar. But there was no turning back now. He could not walk off the stage he'd set for himself. The play must go on. The last cruel act must be played out. . . . He rammed the gun into Weber's back.

"Talk!"

But Weber was incoherent with terror. He kept on jabbering:

"Nothing . . . nothing . . . nothing . . ."

The shot rang out like a single sudden toll of a thunderous death bell. . . .

In the same instant one of the MPs holding him clamped his hand over Weber's mouth. The German stiffened convulsively, then sagged in a dead faint in the arms of the two MPs.

The bullet had entered the ground harmlessly, inches from his feet. . . .

In a few strides Erik was behind the third prisoner. The man was petrified with horror. Stark fright dilated his pupils; he breathed in shallow sobs; he had no doubt his comrade was lying dead behind him. The SS would have killed him. Just so! He felt the icy presence of the American officer behind him. His flesh crawled cold.

"Name?"

It was an explosion in his ears.

"Gruber, Rudolf." A terrified whisper.

Erik raised his gun to the exact level of the man's neck. His eyes were riveted on the back of the prisoner's head. He seemed to be under nearly as great a strain as the German. . . .

He cocked his gun.

The click was abnormally loud.

"Well?" he asked, his voice savage.

"Ja! Ja!" Gruber nodded his head vigorously. "Wait! I talk! Do not shoot! I tell you everything! Do not shoot!"

"Start talking!"

"We worked for them, Herr Offizier. We are not Werewolves." The words came tumbling out. "We only *worked* for them. As lookouts."

"All three of you?"

"Yes! Yes. We brought them fresh food. Vegetables. And bread. And milk. They are in there. Only, I am not a Werewolf. I—"

"*Where* are they?"

"In the forest. I do not know where exactly. We had to leave the food in a sack under a big tree. They came for it after we had left. But I know the area they are in."

"You're going to show us."

Gruber fell suddenly silent.

"They will kill me," he whispered.

Erik turned from him.

"Sergeant Klein!" he called.

Klein came running over.

"Here, sir!"

There was new respect in the way he looked at Erik. He didn't seem to notice the harried, drained look on his face.

"How many men have we got?"

"Twelve, counting me."

"Get them together. Leave two men at the farm to guard the prisoners and assemble the rest here—on the double! We're going after those Werewolves!"

"Yes, sir!"

Klein took off. Erik turned to Gruber.

"And *you* will show us where to look."

The man nodded with dejected resignation. Don stepped close to him.

"When were you last in contact with them?" he asked.

Gruber turned to him.

"I saw them last night. Last night."

He stopped. His mouth fell open. He stared in thunderstruck disbelief as his two comrades, Oberman and Weber, were being led past him toward the farm. Both men glared at him with malevolent contempt.

"Last night, late, I—I saw . . ." He seemed in a daze. "I saw the general himself go into the forest. . . ."

Schönsee Forest

0909 hrs

The search detail moved cautiously down a narrow path into the forest. Don was walking point, led by a pale, fearful Gruber. After them came the MPs, nine of them, moving silently, watchfully along the path in single file, carbines at port arms. A scowling Major Evans followed, and the rear was brought up by Erik and Sergeant Klein.

Most German woodland is well tended, and Schönsee forest was no exception. Consisting largely of evergreens—pine, fir, spruce— it was laid out in a system of squares, one hundred meters on each side, and was crisscrossed by a network of trails and paths separating the squares. Cut down and replanted at the same time, the trees in any given square were all approximately the same size.

Erik and Klein were walking side by side.

"How many of them are supposed to be in there, do you know?" Klein asked.

"Somewhere between forty and sixty. Maybe more."

"Holy shit!" Klein stared at Erik incredulously. "To the twelve of us!" He swallowed. "How are they armed?"

"They're supposed to have small arms—machine guns—mortars."

Klein whistled softly. Unconsciously he took a firmer grip on his carbine. He peered intently into the trees lining the path.

"Why don't we get some troops?" he suggested hopefully.

Erik frowned.

"We had our chance, Sam," he said flatly. "Remember? They went through this very forest this morning with a fine-tooth comb. Didn't find a damned thing. We'd never get troops again. In time."

Klein grew sober.

"No, I guess not."

"We can't even be sure they're here. Whatever the old man said."

"You're kidding!" Klein looked at Erik with surprise. "You think he told you a lie? At the point of a gun?"

"I think it's possible he told us what he thought we'd like to hear," Erik said softly.

"Yeah. I see." Klein grew silent in thought.

"But *if* they're here," Erik continued, "we'll have to bluff them."

"*Bluff* them?" Klein looked up in surprise.

"Sure. Make a big show. It'd be easier for them to believe we are here in strength than that we are crazy enough to go after them with only a handful of men."

"You can say that again," Klein agreed fervently. "You sure can. . . ."

They walked on in silence.

Ahead Don and Gruber suddenly stopped. They sank to the ground. Don gave a quick hand motion to halt, and the men at once took cover off the path. Erik and Klein moved forward in a crouching run.

Don pointed to a large pine tree standing at the corner of a forest square where two trails crossed. At some time long ago the trunk had been damaged. The tree grew at an angle out over the path.

"That's it," Don whispered. "That's the supply tree."

Erik studied the terrain. The forest square directly in front of them was planted with a thick stand of spruce trees, all of them between twelve and fifteen feet tall. Shrubbery of various kinds grew between them. The spruce tree square was surrounded by squares covered with tall pines. The trails separating them were overgrown with weeds and grass. They had obviously been little used for a considerable length of time.

"That's the tree where friend Gruber and his pals used to leave the food," Don continued in a low voice. He pointed to the spruce square. "The Werewolf HQ is somewhere in there. He thinks!"

Erik frowned at the spruce area.

"We'll have to—"

He stopped. He glanced back at the handful of MPs crouched at the trail edges behind him.

"We'll have to surround the area. As best we can. Before we go ahead."

"Yeah."

Erik turned to Klein.

"Sam. Listen carefully. That area of spruce trees in front of us is a German forest square."

"Sir?"

"The square is about three hundred to three hundred fifty feet on each side. We're going to surround it."

"The twelve of us?" Klein stared at Erik incredulously.

"Yes."

Erik's voice was curt. He knew it sounded ridiculous. But what the hell else could he do? It was a real screwed up situation. He was forced to take actions he damned well knew were foolhardy. Or admit failure.

He couldn't do that. It was too important.

Was it? A flash of doubt raced through his mind. Did he refuse to give up because he was honestly convinced there was real danger? To the army? To Ike? Or did he refuse to admit failure for his own selfish reasons? To show up that bastard Evans? To keep from having to face the consequences of his own misjudgment? He

felt angry with himself for letting the thought intrude. Angry because he didn't have a decisive answer. He made himself sound
coldly efficient.

"Take all the men. There'll be ten of you. Take the path to the
right and go all around the spruce square. Position the men so they
can see each other. There'll be about one hundred feet between each
man. Take your own position last."

He pointed to the trail crossing ahead of them.

"On that corner. We'll be in the fir trees facing the spruce area.
Signal us when everyone is in position. Got it?"

"Right!"

"Okay. Take off."

Erik looked at his watch. 0927 hrs. He was aware of having looked
only seconds before. Where the hell was Klein? He stared toward
the trail crossing to his left. Nothing.

He was crouched behind the upturned root of a fallen tree. A
short distance to his right he could make out Don, and next to him
Gruber, trying to melt into the ground. Behind them Evans was
squatting close to the safe cover of the massive trunk of a tall
pine.

Erik looked at his watch again.

0928 hrs.

What the hell was keeping Klein? They couldn't have run into
trouble.

Could they?

He strained toward the trail crossing.

Nothing.

Then—suddenly—a furtive motion. Instinctively Erik's hand
moved toward his gun. His eyes were glued to the shrubbery at the
crossing, trying to penetrate it. And then he saw the hidden figure.

It was Klein.

He waved. Erik waved back. He saw Klein turn and wave to the
man next to him. He waited. He knew the men down the line would
relay the signal. He knew they'd be settling down behind their

cover, bringing their weapons into firing position, trained on the spruce area.

He waited.

He looked toward Don.

Don nodded.

Erik took his gun from its holster. He stood up. His armpits suddenly felt moist. He took a deep breath.

"Ge-ne-ral Krue-ger!" He shouted the name at the top of his voice. "General Krueger! *Ihre Stellung ist umzingelt!* Your position is surrounded! Lay down your arms and come forward!"

He waited.

He listened.

There was not a sound to be heard from the spruce area. Again he called:

"General Krueger! You are surrounded! Come forward! You have two minutes. Resistance is useless!"

Once more he listened intently. There was no answer, no movement. The silence was oppressive. The only sound audible to his straining ears was the buzz of an unconcerned insect; the only motion, a few dead leaves sent scurrying like startled crabs across a roadway by a sudden gusty breeze. He motioned to Klein to stay put, and in a crouch he ran over to Don.

"I'll try once more," he said, his voice grim. "If there is still no answer, you know what we'll have to do." He felt oddly numb.

Don nodded soberly. "Yeah. But I'm not much for it."

"Neither am I."

Erik turned once more toward the spruce area. Once more he called:

"Krueger! Come forward! We are aware of your position! We know of your organization! Come forward! *You are surrounded!*"

And once more the wait . . . and the silence.

Erik sat down beside Don. Evans came up to them. His face radiated a smug I-told-you-so.

"Well?" he asked with oily forbearance. "Are you ready to listen to reason and call it quits?"

Erik turned away from him deliberately. He did not trust himself to get into an argument with the MP officer. Not now. Both he and Don ignored the man. Evans reddened.

"You still insist on continuing this—this nonsense?"

Don turned to Erik.

"Guess it's up to us," he said matter-of-factly.

Erik nodded. Evans controlled himself with a visible effort. "Very well," he said, his voice grating venomously. "But I warn you. I'll see you busted for this! I've been in the MPs a long time. I haven't been wrong yet!"

He turned on his heel and stiffly stalked back to his place of safety.

Don stood up.

"Okay," he said. "We'd better get off our butts. Might just stumble on *something*. I never heard of anyone doing it sitting on his ass."

He beckoned to the nearest MP, who came running up. He motioned toward the cowering Gruber.

"Keep an eye on buster, here," he said. "We'll be back—I hope!" He turned to Erik. "Well?"

"After you, Alphonse!"

Erik drew his gun from its holster. It suddenly felt ridiculously small. Ineffective. He had a quick impulse to trade it for a carbine, but he at once dismissed the idea. He knew this gun. He was used to it. He knew what he could do with it.

The two CIC agents were at the edge of the trees. They glanced at one another—and entered.

From his hiding place across the trail the German forester, Gruber, stared after them, as if expecting them to blow up any second. . . .

Half an hour, dammit! In two minutes it would be half an hour since he saw the two CIC agents go into the spruce area. Klein shifted his weight. Not because of discomfort; he was getting worried. There'd been no sound from in there, no sign of life. For a moment he took his eyes off the forest square in front of him. He glanced down the trail to his left. He could make out the man

nearest to him, kneeling behind a bush. Waiting. In the pine trees
to his right he could see the old Kraut, guarded by another of his
men. And Major Evans.

The MP officer was standing up, close to a big pine tree. Klein
saw him look at his watch. He seemed impatient.

Klein had a sudden chilling thought. The major was ranking
officer now. In fact, the only officer, now the CIC agents had gone
into the spruce area. What if he should decide to take command?
Right now! There was obviously no love lost between him and the
two CIC guys. Suppose he decided to do something *narish*? Like
ordering him, Sam Klein, to round up his men and march them back
to Corps. Write off the whole damned deal as a flop. Leave the
two other guys on their own in there. What the hell would Sammy
Klein do then? He couldn't refuse a direct order, and he sure
couldn't take off just like that. *Oi schtarb!* Why couldn't he be
back at Corps making out duty rosters? Yeah, he should be so
lucky. He saw the major turn toward him.

Suddenly he tensed. His head snapped back toward the spruce
area, his eyes intent upon the trees. He'd seen it. Something. Movement.

His hands tightened on his carbine.

There! Again.

He brought his carbine up and sighted toward the surreptitious
motion. Across the sight the figure of a man appeared, coming
through the dense spruce.

It was Erik.

Klein relaxed perceptibly. He was suddenly aware of feeling
clammy all over. He brought his carbine down and waited. Erik
came up to him. He looked discouraged.

"There doesn't seem to be anything in there," he said, his voice
flat.

"That's good!" Klein grinned broadly. He looked up at Erik, and
his face grew sober. "Bad?" he asked.

"We'll have to make absolutely sure." Erik didn't seem to be
aware of the byplay. "Have your men enter the area," he said, "at

your signal. I want them to go through it and assemble in the center. Tell them to use caution, but I want every tree, every clump of brush searched!"

"Yes, sir."

"Move in"—Erik glanced at his watch—"in ten minutes."

"Right."

Klein took off at a dog trot down the path. Erik glanced at Major Evans. The MP officer came striding briskly toward him.

Without a second look Erik turned and reentered the spruce forest. . . .

Werewolf Headquarters

1023 hrs

Steiner was sweating. It annoyed him. He was aware of the sour-sharp odor rising from his armpits. The others must be, too. But nobody said anything. There was nothing he could do about it anyway, but it made him acutely uncomfortable. Besides, his damned leg hurt. The bullet had gone clean through the fleshy part of his thigh. He was lucky. It hadn't even nicked the femur. But it throbbed like hell.

He hobbled toward the radio room. Hell of a time for him to be left ranking noncom. He put his weight a little too heavily on his wounded leg and a sharp pain knifed up his side to stab at his eyeball. *Verflucht!*

Still, he was alive. . . .

When he felt the dull slam of the bullet in his leg and realized he'd been hit, his mind had flashed to the Werewolf credo. He knew in that instant he was a dead man. The others couldn't burden themselves with a casualty, and they couldn't leave him behind alive.

He'd been fully aware of it all, but it had been as if he'd been watching it happen to someone else. He'd been quite calm. The shock of the wound probably . . .

But then young Willi Richter had ordered Krauss and Leib to support him between them, and somehow they'd made it back. . . .

He thought of Willi. He owed him his life. He felt grateful to him and at the same time a little contemptuous. The young officer had taken a hell of a chance. Jeopardized the whole operation. It was only luck they hadn't all been caught. He frowned. What would *he* have done, had the tables been turned?

He reached the doorway to the radio room. He leaned heavily against the frame. The operator looked up at him.

"Take a message," Steiner ordered curtly. He wet his dry lips. "Caution all units and stations. Enemy search under way Schönsee following Plewig interrogation. No apparent danger of discovery. Maintain strict cover. Postpone all planned operations. . . ."

He stopped. He suddenly realized the enormity of the decision he had to make. Why the devil did it have to be him! He felt dizzy. He was strongly aware of the odor steaming from his armpits. Fear?

No, he couldn't take the responsibility. It wasn't his job. He just couldn't. The operation to be mounted by Unit C, it *was* a last-minute chance. It *was* imperative. Richter was already on his way. He *couldn't* stop it. Not now. Not on the off chance : . .

He looked straight at the waiting operator.

"Postpone all planned operations," he said firmly—he drew a deep breath—"headquarters area only—repeat: headquarters area only—until further orders. Acknowledge."

He waited for the operator to finish taking it down.

"Code it. Send it at once. Through the Munich relay."

"*Sofort!*"

The man began readying his equipment.

"How many of them are there this time?"

Steiner shrugged.

"Thirty. Forty. It doesn't matter."

The operator looked up at him.

"But if that's all, we could easily—"

Steiner broke in sharply.

"We are following orders. As long as they do not discover us, we leave them alone."

"And if they do?"

Steiner's eyes were cold.

"We wipe them out."

He turned to leave. The pain in his leg was becoming intolerable. He stopped.

"The general must be warned," he said heavily. "There may be plans to change."

He put his hand on the wound. Even through the bandage his leg felt hot.

"*We* can't get to him. Now." He turned to the operator. "As soon as you have sent the message, contact Weiden."

Sweat was dripping into his eyes. There was nothing more he could do. He had to lie down. . . .

Maybe—maybe it was all for nothing, all his worry. They'd never be discovered. Never.

Still, *Sicher ist die Mutter der Porzellankiste!* Mother is extra careful with her chest of china.

Schönsee Forest

1041 hrs

The thick moss on the large boulder felt soft and cool against Erik's back. He forced himself to relax, leaning against it. No good getting too damned tense and freezing up when things began to pop. If. If they did pop. He glanced at Don crouched a couple of feet away, staring intently into the trees.

It had been nearly fifteen minutes since he'd rejoined Don in the center of the spruce area and they'd heard the three shrill blasts of Klein's whistle signaling his men to start infiltrating the area.

He was acutely aware of the rock against his back. He wondered about the boulders. There were several of them, heaped together in the middle of the forest square. From the looks of them they'd been there a long time. Probably gathered there when the square was originally planted. The trees grew a little thinner here, forming a small clearing.

He searched the trees before him. He knew that Klein and his MPs were making their way through the area toward him, searching, probing, investigating. . . .

He strained to listen.

Nothing.

Where were they? How close? Would they flush anything?

He moved his back away from the boulder behind him. It was getting hard.

He glanced at his watch.

Sixteen minutes.

And then he saw the first man. Watchfully he came through the trees, moving from one clump of brush to another, his carbine held at port arms.

And another.

All around him now the MPs began to enter the little clearing, quietly, cautiously. They looked in silence at Erik and Don and stopped uncertainly.

Erik sighed.

Not a thing, he thought, with the impotent anger born of disappointment. *Not a goddamnfucking thing!*

The sudden sharp report that slammed against his ears with the force of a physical blow scattered every thought from his mind as it ricocheted from tree to tree.

A shot!

Instantly every man in the clearing hit the dirt, his weapon ready.

Klein came running through the trees into the little clearing.

Erik felt the flush of action course through him. *Here it is!*

Klein came up to the two CIC agents.

"Sorry," he said with a sheepish grin. "It was Warnecke's big feet again. Tripped over a root. Nearly drilled me a third eye!"

Erik stood up. He suddenly felt exhausted. He looked at the

men around him, watching him curiously. He knew what they were thinking.

"Listen, everybody!" he called in a loud voice. "It doesn't look as if there's anybody here."

He paused. The men were waiting.

"But I want to be absolutely sure. I want to know if anyone *has been* here! I want every clump of underbrush, every thicket searched and searched again. Work your way back out. If there's *anything* here I want it found, even if it's only a used condom! We'll assemble at the big leaning pine tree in—thirty minutes. Let's go!"

The men started to move out. Suddenly a rabbit leaped from concealment in front of one of them and bounced in a broken run across the clearing to disappear into the shrubs.

"There goes one of them now!" the man shouted.

But the laughter was strained.

Erik stood with Klein and Don watching the men make their way into the woods.

Don suddenly looked around. He turned to Klein.

"Hey, what happened to our swashbuckling MP hero?"

"Major Evans?" Klein grinned. "I guess he buckled when he should've swashed!"

It was a creditable attempt, but it fell flat.

Sudetenland, Czechoslovakia
On the Road to Unit C

1103 hrs

Willi Richter listened. He frowned. He didn't like that grating noise coming from the engine in his Volkswagen. It would be charitable to call the car they'd given him merely battered. It was shrapnel scarred; one of the front fenders was smashed flat, the frog-eye headlight ripped off; the spare tire was gone from the front hood. The top was down. Willi doubted if it was in condition ever to be put up again. He was glad it wasn't raining. He'd been on the road several hours already, and that damned noise had started twenty kilometers back. It sounded as if the whole damned motor would fall out any second.

Zum Teufel damit! he thought. To the devil with it! He had to abandon the car pretty soon anyway.

He thought back. . . .

He'd left General Krueger's headquarters at 0430 that morning, well before first light, to take advantage of the darkness to exfiltrate the area without placing the HQ in jeopardy. He'd had no trouble at all passing through the American outpost lines, crossing the border and entering Czechoslovakia.

He'd commandeered the Volkswagen from the first German unit he'd run across with the help of the general's priority orders, and he'd made his way to the nearest major command post.

It had taken the devil of a time to raise the Munich relay station and through them get confirmation regarding the transportation arrangements for the task force from Unit C, but he'd finally accomplished it. The trucks would be on the Salzburg road south of Passau at the prescribed time. From there they'd be at their destination in a couple of hours.

He felt suddenly excited. He was going to be in on the big one!

Unconsciously he stepped on the accelerator.

The Volkswagen picked up speed; the motor grated hideously. There was a sharp metallic *ping*—and the gears locked, sending the car slewing, skidding sideways down the road to an ignominious halt.

Willi got out. He glared at the vehicle.

"*Scheissdreck!*" he cursed. "Shit!"

He kicked the rear tire in disgust and set out on foot toward the Czech border and the area of Werewolf Unit C just beyond. . . .

Schönsee Forest

1114 hrs

Erik and Don sat under the big leaning pine tree. The MPs were comfortably sprawled in the grass around them. Major Evans sat off a little by himself, still wearing his I-told-you-so expression and contentedly inhaling the smoke of a cigarette. The sun stood high in the beautiful blue spring sky. Birds twittered cheerfully in the trees. Dragonflies whirred impressively in pursuit of tiny insects and a gentle wind whispered softly in the pines. The whole scene was the exact opposite of the bleak mood with which Erik and Don regarded it.

"Two hours. Two hours we tramped all over that damned piece of real estate. And not a damned thing. Not a sign of them." Don looked disgusted. "Well, like they say, if all else fails we can always give up."

"Very funny!"

"I wasn't trying to be funny."

"You succeeded."

Klein came up to them.

"The last of the men is back," he reported. "What now?" He squinted up at the sun. "It's getting on toward noon."

"We might as well go back to the farm." Don sounded dejected. "There's not a fucking thing we can do here."

He turned to Erik.

"Erik?"

"Yeah. Guess so . . ." Erik was staring into space, frowning in concentration.

"I'm going to hate having to face Streeter." Don glanced at Evans. "And I hate even worse having to look at the smug puss of that prick Evans."

Erik sat up.

"We're not out of the ball game yet," he said.

He turned to Klein, suddenly resolute.

"Sam. You and your men take the PWs at the farm back to Corps. Turn the soldiers over to the IPWs and the civilians"—he nodded toward Gruber—"including that miserable little bastard over there, to the CIC for interrogation. Don and I are going to try one more thing."

"Right." Klein stood up.

"Okay, you guys," he called. "Gather round. We're going back." He pointed at Gruber. "And bring that Kraut over here."

The MPs got up and began to gather around Klein. Evans strolled toward Erik and Don. He was carefully breaking his cigarette butt, scattering the tobacco as he walked. There was an unmistakable air of vast self-satisfaction in the way he performed the task.

Don glanced at Erik.

"I knew this was coming," he growled.

Evans came up to them.

"So you're finally coming to your senses," he said, a thin smile of derision on his lips. "I take it that now you're ready to admit I was right?"

Erik got up slowly.

"Is that how you take it?" he said pleasantly. "Well, we haven't closed the case yet, Major."

"Really?" Evans sounded deliberately incredulous. He looked toward the MPs gathered around Klein. "Well, at least you won't be wasting anyone's time anymore, except your own."

The implication that that was of little consequence was as subtle as a two-ton truck.

Don stood up.

"I don't think you have any call to refer to this case as a waste of time, Major." His voice was dangerously low.

Evans cocked a goading eyebrow at him.

"No?"

"No! You heard our evaluation confirmed with your own ears."

Evans nodded in the direction of Gruber.

"You mean that old man?"

"Exactly!"

Evans smiled condescendingly.

"I think we can discount that, don't you?"

"Why? He admitted the Werewolves were in here."

"Yes. So he did." Evans pursed his lips in exaggerated thought-fulness. He was enjoying himself immensely. It was about time those insufferable self-styled "agents" were put in their proper place. Methodically he rolled up the paper from his cigarette butt into a small ball. "But," he continued, "you seem to forget the cir-cumstances under which the old man made that admission."

Don glared at him. "Just what are you getting at?"

"Don't forget—uh—Johnson, I used to be in law enforcement back in the States, too. There are ways—and there are ways." He shook his head slowly, regretfully. "I very much doubt if anyone will seriously *believe* that—uh—confession of his after I inform them how it was obtained."

Don threw a quick glance at Erik. Erik looked grim. He said nothing. He had nothing to say. . . .

Evans went on. "After all, you had the poor fellow scared out of his wits. He would have said *anything* to save his neck."

He looked pointedly from one to the other.

"I'm afraid—uh—gentlemen, your case is a bust."

He flipped his paper ball away.

"I warned you." Evans sounded reproachful. "I told you. There's only one way to conduct a professional investigation. It takes—uh—experience to know *how*. You haven't got it."

Erik spoke with deliberate quiet.

"Nevertheless, Major, we're going on with it."

"Suit yourselves." Evans shrugged. "*I* shall have to get back to some serious work."

"Just a goddamned minute!" Don flared. "If you think you can—"

Evans whirled on him, his voice suddenly venomous.

"Don't growl, my friend, if you can't bite," he snapped. "And I'm afraid *your* bite will be highly ineffectual."

He contemplated Don for a brief moment, savoring his superiority, a nasty little gleam in his eye.

"You don't like me, do you—uh—*Agent* Johnson?" he queried.

"That's correct, *Major*." Don's voice was cold.

Evans smiled expansively.

"Well, I'm sorry if you think I'm acting like an SOB, but that's what they're paying me for."

Don looked straight into his smiling face.

"They sure are underpaying you, aren't they?" he commented.

Evans turned red with rage. Erik had trouble not laughing out loud. The MP officer eyed the two CIC agents maliciously. A note of shrillness crept into his voice.

"Okay," he said. "Okay. You've crawled way out on that limb. I shall take great personal pleasure in chopping it off."

Abruptly he turned on his heel and stalked off.

Don glared after him.

"That bastard's got a mind like concrete," he growled. "All mixed up, and permanently set!"

They started after the departing MPs.

Erik felt oddly keyed up, almost elated. He wondered briefly if it was a reaction to the slump he'd hit when the search of the Werewolf area turned out to be a flop. No, it wasn't that. He suddenly knew why. He suddenly realized that he didn't give a hoot in hell about Evans. Or what the man could do to him. He had to go on with the case because he truly believed it was important. Because he honestly felt it had to be done. And not just to save his own neck. Although he freely admitted to himself that he'd like to be proved right. Of course. But that wasn't the real motive. . . .

He turned to Don.

"Don," he said. "We won't give up. Dammit! We aren't licked until we do."

"All right," he agreed. "I'm with you. What do you have in mind?"

"Okay, here it is. Remember what Plewig said about the supplies the Werewolves are supposed to have?"

"Sure. Lots of everything. From soup to nuts. So?"

Erik spoke slowly, deliberately.

"Isn't it possible they cached some of the stuff in different places? Somewhere around their bivouac area?"

"They might have. . . ."

"Even if they weren't in that damned square where Gruber thought they were, they could still be somewhere around here. After all, he *did* point out the supply tree."

He looked earnestly at Don.

"Look. I hate to go back to Streeter looking like a couple of empty-headed—and empty-handed—idiots. Suppose we *could* find a supply dump? Or even a trace of one?"

"Yeah. We wouldn't look quite so stupid. If we could prove those damned Werewolves had been here, we'd sure blunt Evans' hatchet!"

"And there's more to it than that. If we can prove the Werewolves do exist, we can take steps—"

"Right. Beef up security—"

"Streeter said, 'Stick with it!'"

"So we stick!"

"We stick! We'll take the jeep. Cruise around the area. We'll use that square of spruce as our pivot point. Maybe—just maybe something'll turn up. . . ."

Weiden

1129 hrs

The battered bicycle leaning against the shrapnel-pitted wall of the bombed house had no tires. A heavy chain had been passed through one of the wheels and locked to the frame with a massive padlock. The debris of broken masonry had been partially cleared away from the stone steps leading to the cellar below the ruins, leaving a narrow path down into the darkness.

The two men talked in urgent whispers.

"You know what to do."

Heinz shifted his weight to his good leg. The lame one ached.

He'd been too active. It was this damned Plewig business.

"Unit B," he continued. "Five-man operational group. Emergency orders."

He felt a sudden stab of pain in his left arm. It happened. Even though the arm, severed at the shoulder, lay rotting somewhere in North Africa. It used to startle him. Now he tried to ignore it. He peered at the other man with his good eye.

"Understood?"

"It is understood."

Krauss was uneasy. He had a vague feeling that the situation was getting out of hand. All because of those two *verfluchte* American Gestapo agents. He felt like spitting on the floor, but Heinz might not understand.

"As fast as you can. Krueger *must* be warned."

"And the American agents?"

"Impossible. For now. The forest and the farm were swarming with Ami troops."

Krauss's apprehension grew.

"Then one cannot know. . . . They might—"

Heinz interrupted harshly.

"They may search as much as they wish. They will find nothing."

He paused. He put his weight on both legs and stood straight, facing Krauss.

"The rest is up to you. You will be held responsible."

Schönsee Forest

1227 hrs

It seemed to Erik that the hundred-meter forest squares were getting bigger and bigger as the jeep crawled past them along the narrow path, but he knew it was only his growing frustration deceiving him.

Don was at the wheel. The trails were heavily overgrown in some places and he'd engaged the four-wheel drive for maximum traction at the slow speed. They'd been cruising along for over half an hour, and Erik estimated they'd covered three to four miles. They'd stopped repeatedly to investigate various spots that might serve as concealment for supplies, any kind of supplies: fallen trees, boulders, mounds and depressions, heavy clumps of brush, piles of dead branches, any conceivable hiding places.

They'd found nothing.

Erik scanned the woods intently as the jeep slowly crept on. They were on the path three squares removed from the pivot point. The timber was taller and less well kept here. Erik pointed to a small pile of cut firewood stacked at the side of the path. Don stopped the jeep and Erik jumped off. He went up to the stack of wood. He looked it over carefully. He picked off a few logs and then kicked the stack apart.

Nothing.

Without a word he climbed back into the jeep and Don drove off again.

Ahead the path dipped into a short downgrade. At the bottom the trees stopped at a small clearing. Erik pointed to it; he made a "cut" motion across his throat. Don killed the jeep motor. Quietly they coasted down the slope almost to the open field below. Don stopped the vehicle and both men got out. Cautiously they crept to the edge of the clearing, taking cover in the underbrush.

Before them stretched a typical Bavarian forest pasture planted with alfalfa. An overgrown wooden fence badly in need of repair surrounded it. About fifty feet from the forest edge, where Don and Erik crouched in concealment, stood a small timbered hut. There were no windows or doors in the wall facing the trees, only the back of a crudely made stone fireplace climbing up the side of the hut and ending in a squat chimney. A pile of cut wood was stacked next to it, and a big scarred chopping block had an ax stuck in it at an angle. The area looked drowsily deserted.

For a few moments Don and Erik observed the scene in silence.

Suddenly Erik stiffened. He touched Don on the shoulder and pointed toward the hut.

Don squinted. He frowned. He turned to Erik with a puzzled look.
"The chimney!" Erik whispered. "Watch the chimney!"
Don stared.
And he saw it.
Rising from the squat chimney was the quiver of hot air. No smoke. Only the peculiar characteristic effect of rising heat, making everything seen through it shimmer like a mirage.
"Got it," Don whispered. "Hot air! Someone's in there!"
"Or was. Recently."
Don contemplated the hut.
"Could be just farmers. . . ."
"Careful not to make smoke?"
"Only one way to find out."
Erik nodded. He bit his lip. Then his face twisted into a wry grin.
"Shall we make like Dick Tracy?"
"Why not. Pruneface, here we come!"
Both men drew their guns and checked them. Don glanced at Erik. He gave a short nod.
At once the two men broke cover. Noiselessly, in a zigzag run, they sprinted from the forest across the clearing toward the hut; Erik to the left, Don to the right.
Erik ran easily. Fast. The distance to the hut suddenly seemed alarmingly greater than he'd thought. He was vaguely aware of Don reaching the opposite corner of the shack and disappearing from sight. And then he was at his end of the hut, running past a shuttered window. One part of his mind blazed with the hope that the place would be swarming with Werewolves, the other coldly realized the folly of such a hope.
He shot around the corner to the front of the hut. His pounding heart skipped a beat. Don. He was not there! And then he saw him as he came racing around the far corner.
There was another shuttered window. And a door. Closed. The two men stopped before it. They listened.
There was not a sound.

Erik took a firmer grip on his gun. He looked at Don—and nodded.

At once Don aimed a crushing kick at the wooden door. With a splintering crash it burst open. . . .

Erik was through it before the thunderous noise had died.

In a lightning flash his eyes and mind took in the scene confronting him: the hoes, spades, rakes sticking up from a big, dirty barrel leaning against the knotted wall planks in a corner of the hut; the large iron pot in the fireplace, the bright, smokeless fire; the big roughhewn table—and the five people sitting on stools around it, eating soup from plain bowls, their eyes riveted upon him in frozen shock. . . .

He was aware of Don at his side. He had a quick feeling of protection, like a cat whose back is safely snuggled against a familiar shelter. He stared at the group around the table. All of them were clad in ordinary Bavarian clothes. Three young girls in blouses and dirndl skirts. A cripple, his right arm and right leg in steel-and-leather braces. An old man in gray kneebreeches, a coarse green shirt and a gray Bavarian jacket with carved bone buttons.

Farmers . . .

Something collapsed within him, leaving a bleak void. It had been their last chance. There was nothing left to do now. Somewhere along the line they'd muffed it. He was still convinced the Werewolves existed. Just as Plewig had revealed once his cover had been broken. But now . . .

He felt drained. Deflated. He was tempted to give in to his feeling of failure, but something nagged the edges of his mind, something elusive that teased to be remembered, something he was missing. . . .

Plewig. Something Plewig said . . .

He looked searchingly at the group around the table—and suddenly he knew. Suddenly he could hear Plewig's voice: "Some of them are war wounded." *War wounded* . . .

The cripple!

And the old man?

Only seconds had gone by. The Germans were still staring at the intruders in stupefaction. Erik barked an order, his voice sharp and authoritative:

"General Krueger! You are coming with us. Get up! *Now!*"

The scrape of the wooden stool on the rough floor was like the rumble of a giant landslide as the elderly Bavarian farmer at the table automatically half rose from his seat—and stopped dead in midmotion!

For a full four seconds the strange *tableau vivant* held frozen as the two groups of figures stared at one another in mutual abysmal astonishment.

Then Krueger sat down heavily as he suddenly realized his inadvertent admission of his identity.

Erik's heart drummed wildly as if to make up a hundredfold for the single beat it lost when the old farmer stood up. He and Don had bagged the Werewolf general himself! With a bluff! He shot a quick glance at Don. Fine. Don was watching the Werewolves, a grim, set expression on his face.

Erik felt a surge of triumph. They'd done it! Dammit, *they'd done it!* They'd been proved right. Evans be damned. The Werewolves were exactly where he and Don had said they'd be! They had the general himself to prove it!

The general . . .

And suddenly he was staring cold reality in the face.

If that Bavarian farmer was indeed General Karl Krueger—if he was the Werewolf general—he would not be far from his headquarters. His Werewolves would certainly be nearby. Forty? Sixty? What did Plewig say? Crack troops. Fanatics. Armed to the teeth. They'd be all around. . . .

They were in the middle of the hidden Werewolf lair. He and Don. Alone.

Only one thing could possibly save their necks. His instinctive bluff had worked on the general. He had to keep it up. He had to turn it into one hell of a big-assed bluff!

His mouth was dry; his palms moist. Hell of a mixed-up reaction, he thought, with the detached incongruity of an uninvolved ob-

server. He had an overwhelming desire to lick his lips. He didn't.
He knew how clearly such little unconscious actions betrayed
nervousness. Uncertainty . . .

And if he'd ever needed to appear utterly confident and self-
assured, *now* was it.

"Up!" he barked. "All of you. On your feet!"

He gestured with his gun.

"Over against that wall. Hands clasped behind your neck! *Move!*"

They moved.

Krueger first, then the three young girls and finally the cripple
lined up at the wall next to the door, never taking their eyes off the
two Americans covering them with their guns. The hate seething in
their eyes was almost tangible, especially in the girls'. They might
have been pretty, Erik thought. But they were not. Their faces were
marred by the hate. Only Krueger's penetrating blue eyes seemed
without emotion as he regarded Erik and Don steadily.

"Turn around!" Erik ordered. "Lean against the wall with both
hands. Legs apart."

The five prisoners obeyed.

The crippled man had difficulties; he seemed to lose his balance,
and the girl next to him quickly took his arm to steady him, helping
him into the awkward position. Before she turned to lean against the
wall herself, she shot a withering glance of contempt at Erik and
Don.

It had been a small diversion. It had drawn the eyes of both Don
and Erik for only a couple of seconds.

But it had been enough.

As the girl standing next to Krueger and farthest away from the
cripple turned toward the wall, she quickly fumbled at the waistline
of her skirt. Deftly she extracted the tiny Lilliput automatic from a
small pocket hidden in the lining; she palmed it, unseen, in her right
hand, then placed her hand on the wall and leaned against it.

Erik covered the prisoners as Don frisked them. The girls endured
the search in venomous silence. Don joined Erik.

"They're clean," he said.

He followed as Erik walked toward the fireplace out of earshot of the prisoners, who stood off balance against the opposite wall.

"Okay," Erik said, his voice an urgent whisper. "Take off!"

"You crazy?" Don took his eyes from the Germans to cast a startled glance at Erik. "We're right in the middle of the whole damned Werewolf nest! I can't leave you here alone!"

"Two are no better than one!"

"We can take them along. . . ."

"We'd never get out alive. Go get help, dammit! Fast! I'll keep bluffing."

For a few seconds Don stared at his friend, stared at him as if he'd never seen him before. He felt trapped. He knew Erik was right. He knew they *had* to have help. And he knew *he* couldn't stay behind. His German wasn't good enough to pull off the bluff. It *had* to be Erik's game. But just leave him? . . .

Without a word he turned and walked from the hut.

Erik was alone.

He stared at his prisoners lined up at the wall. Five of them. Five backs. Five Werewolves . . . God, he never knew five were so many.

Leaning against the wall, they looked tense, coiled, ready to explode into action. Were they?

He didn't move. Neither did the prisoners. The silence was absolute. Time itself, oozing on, was quiet. As quiet as a mouse pissing on a blotter, he thought. He used to think the expression hilarious. He didn't now.

He glanced at the gun in his hand. Colt .38 special. The sum and substance of his superiority. No. Not quite. He did have an ace in the hole to back up his bluff. Knowledge. Knowledge his prisoners didn't know he had. It was about time he started to use it; he thought he could feel the Werewolves getting edgy. . . .

Suddenly the silence was destroyed by the distant sound of a jeep starting up and racing away.

Erik was genuinely shocked.

God! he thought with cold alarm. Is Don still here? He's been gone minutes and minutes already! What the hell's the matter with him?

He saw the Germans react to the unexpected sound. He knew he couldn't allow them to start thinking. He had to counteract. Now!

He forced himself to calm down. It *had* been only seconds since Don left the hut. He forced the strain from his face, the tension from his hand, gripping his gun. He knew he had to appear composed and confident.

"All right," he said easily. "You can turn around now. Just keep your hands behind your neck."

The five prisoners turned slowly to face Erik. They stood glaring at him. With a show of supreme unconcern he sat down on the edge of the stone fireplace.

"I hope you are not thinking of doing anything foolish," he said pleasantly. "The entire area is surrounded by troops, moving in on this hut."

He smiled at Krueger.

"We knew we'd find you here, General."

He watched them for a reaction. There was none. He knew they were still sizing him up, evaluating the situation. He had to keep talking. Keep showing them how much he knew about them. Make them think he knew much, much more. Keep them from thinking and appraising their position correctly.

"In fact," he continued, "we know quite a lot about you. And the whole *Unternehmung Werwolf*. You've been with the organization a long time, haven't you, General? Two years, isn't it? By the way, did you like your quarters in Poland any better than the ones in Thürenberg? In Czechoslovakia?"

He kept talking. And watching. They were listening to him. They *had* to be wondering. But they were good. They did not betray their reactions.

"Incidentally, General." Erik's voice took on a confidential tone. "Your horses, all one hundred and twenty of them, they're all being rounded up. Since they were Wehrmacht property, they are, of course, the property of the United States Army now."

One of the girls quickly glanced at Krueger; then immediately caught herself and stared straight ahead. The general's expression did not change.

"It's quite a haul, all told," Erik commented quietly. "Quite a blow to your superior officer, SS Obergruppenführer Hans-Adolf Prützmann, I'd imagine, losing Sonderkampfgruppe Karl like this." He looked straight at Krueger.

The German officer returned his gaze. His lips drew back in a tight smile. He inclined his head almost imperceptibly.

"I congratulate you," he said, his voice firm and even. "We had not expected to hold out forever, but we did not look for capture this quickly."

He looked toward the crippled man, then back to Erik.

"Will you permit my executive officer, Hauptmann Schmidt, to sit down? His leg cannot support him for long."

Erik nodded.

"Of course. Sit down, Captain."

Schmidt drew one of the stools to him and sat down, his braced leg sticking out stiffly. The others watched him. The girl next to Krueger made a small move with her hand behind her neck, her eyes fixed on Erik.

"The girls," Erik asked. "Are they administrative personnel? Or are they trained for field duties?"

Krueger made no answer. Erik nodded to the girls.

"You may take your hands down," he said. "Clasp them in front of you."

The girls glared at him defiantly.

None of them moved.

The Road to Schönsee

The jeep came hurtling down the narrow forest path, slammed around the corner onto the road without slowing and raced toward the little town of Schönsee.

Don was tensed over the wheel. As he sped past, he hardly noticed the small group of men walking on the road shoulder in the direction from which he had came. They were carrying farming implements. One of them, who wore a dirty leather cap, was pushing a bicycle, an old rucksack strapped to the handlebars. The bike had no tires.

The jeep negotiated a sharp curve. Ahead the road was straight. In the far distance a column of vehicles could be seen approaching.

Don rammed the gas pedal to the floorboard. The jeep literally flew down the road. . . .

He didn't see the little group of men with the bike turn down the forest path into Schönsee forest. . . .

The Hut

Erik smiled pleasantly at the young Werewolf girls.

"Suit yourselves." He shrugged. "I only wanted you to be a little more comfortable."

With deliberate contempt one of the girls spat on the floor. It was a melodramatic, childish display, and yet a chilling gesture of insolence and defiance.

Krueger smiled a thin smile.

"I am afraid my secretarial staff does not think very highly of American officers," he said.

"In that case their taste is not as good as yours, General. I understand you are very fond of roses."

Krueger regarded his adversary attentively. A look of speculation crept into his eyes.

Erik recognized it. It was the how-much-does-this-man-know look. He racked his brain to dredge up every scrap of information he'd wrung from Plewig. What else? If only he'd let the guy ramble on. . . .

"And, of course, Armagnac," he said with nonchalance. "Now there I agree with you. It's great. Too bad it looks like you'll have to go without it for a while."

Krueger watched him with a faint smile.

"You seem well informed on my personal tastes," he observed. Almost imperceptibly he moved his head.

Erik didn't miss it. He's listening, he thought. He's beginning to

wonder why we stand here bullshitting. I can't lose him now!
Aloud he said:

"Of little importance, General. I agree."

He made himself comfortable on the edge of the fireplace.

"Frosting on the cake. Of course, the more significant details *are* more interesting. I had quite a fascinating talk with a certain gentleman recently. I believe you know him. Reichsamtsleiter Manfred von Eckdorf?"

For the first time Krueger couldn't hide the flicker of surprise in his eyes.

"Von Eckdorf?"

"Yes. Just before he died."

The Road to Schönsee

Don skidded his jeep to a halt diagonally across the road, blocking it, forcing the oncoming column to stop. He saw with satisfaction that it was an I & R platoon convoy. Armored cars. Top firepower. A jeep came racketing to the front of the column and screeched to a stop. A first lieutenant jumped from it before it was fully halted and strode toward Don. Two GIs covered him with their tommy guns.

"What the hell do you think you're doing?" the lieutenant shouted angrily. "Get that fucking jeep out of here!"

Don faced him urgently.

"Lieutenant! I'm a special agent. CIC—Counter Intelligence. I've got a buddy back there in real hot water. I need your men. Follow me. Immediately!"

The lieutenant stared at him. Then he grinned.

"CIC, huh? The 'Christ I'm confused' boys! Real true to form, aren't you?"

"Cut the clowning! Just get moving!"

The lieutenant didn't budge.

"Not so fast! First we'll find out *who* can order *whom* to do *what!*"

His manner suddenly turned sharp. "Let me see your credentials!"
He held out his hand.

Don could taste the bile of frustration. He cursed under his breath, but he knew the officer was right.

He dug for his ID. . . .

The Hut

The five Werewolf prisoners stood staring at Erik.

It had become a growing effort for him to sustain his air of confident composure. How long had it been? It seemed like forever. He could feel the moisture of anxiety ooze in his armpits and trickle down his sides. He knew that little traitor sweat beads would be forming on his forehead, but he wouldn't dare wipe them off. He could only pray that the prisoners would not see them. He fought to keep his voice conversational.

"The Reichsamtsleiter was most informative," he said. "At this very moment, General, our troops are moving in on your operational units. It's the end of the Werewolves."

Krueger's steady eyes watched him pensively.

"Perhaps," he said. He turned his head to one side to listen. This time he didn't bother to cloak his action. "Perhaps not . . ."

Erik looked at the prisoners closely. There had been a subtle change. He was acutely aware of it. Familiarity breeds contempt, he thought. That's what's happening to them. They're getting used to the whole goddamned situation. The shock is wearing off. They'll start to do some serious thinking now. . . .

One of the girls slowly took her hands from the back of her neck and clasped them in front of her. She glared at Erik with open challenge. He debated if he should call her on it. He decided to ignore her. But he knew the rules of the game were beginning to change.

Where the hell was Don?

Krueger turned to him.

"Your comrade has been gone a long time, has he not?" he asked quietly.

To Erik it was the most chilling, the most ominous question he'd ever heard.

He felt control slipping through his hands. . . .

His bluff was about to be called.

The Road to Schönsee

Lieutenant Larry James examined the CIC credentials in his hand. Seem okay. He handed them back to Don. What a snafu operation, he thought with annoyance.

Don turned toward his jeep.

"Let's go!"

"Hey, look. This is an I & R platoon. We got a hornets' nest of stiffened SS resistance to deal with. We—"

Don whirled on him.

"Do you question my identification?" he snapped sharply. "My authority?"

"Hell, no. Don't get your balls in an uproar. But there's a whole damned panzer division up there, headed for the mountains. We can't just up and follow you. I've got my orders."

"I'm countermanding those orders! Right now!"

"Look here—uh—what *is* your rank?"

"My rank is confidential. But I can assure you, *Lieutenant,* that I'm not outranked now! Let's go! *That's an order!*"

He turned on his heel and strode quickly to his jeep.

"Okay—it's your funeral."

Don called over his shoulder.

"And contact Major Evans, Harold J., on your radio. Corps MPs. Tell him where we're headed."

He gunned his jeep and barreled off down the road toward Schönsee forest. . . .

The Hut

The very atmosphere in the little hut was charged with suspense. Krueger's penetrating eyes had narrowed. There was a calculating look on his face as he studied Erik.

"Exactly *what* are we waiting for?" he asked, a new edge to his voice.

"My partner is talking with one of your men, General. Plewig. Josef Plewig. Your personal orderly," Erik informed him. He had to get them to listen to him again. He *had* to! "We want nothing overlooked once we leave here."

At the mention of Plewig's name, Krueger's face darkened. The others started. They glanced quickly at one another. Krueger softly exclaimed:

"Plewig . . ."

"*Verräter!*" Schmidt spat the word. "Traitor!"

"Don't be too hard on him, Captain," Erik said. "He merely saw the utter futility of your whole operation. . . ."

Suddenly Krueger interrupted him, his voice sharp with a new ring of authority.

"Schmidt. Have you heard any sounds of activity outside the last few minutes?"

Erik stood up, at once alert. His gun was pointed straight at Krueger. It did not waver.

"No talking between you!" he ordered curtly.

"*Nein,* Herr General." Schmidt ignored him.

"I thought not."

Erik cocked his gun. The click was abnormally loud to his ears. He was committed. All the way. He was past the point of no return. . . .

"I warn you," he said, startled at the harshness in his voice. "Don't make a move!"

The Werewolf prisoners tensed. Five pairs of hate-filled eyes bore into Erik. The girl next to Krueger looked flushed. The general glanced at the gun in Erik's hand.

"How many rounds does a Colt revolver hold?" he asked pointedly. "Six? Could you kill us all? Before—"

"You'll be the first!"

Krueger shrugged.

"No matter."

With a chill of awe, Erik knew he meant it.

Slowly Krueger began to let his arms sink down from their position behind his neck. The others followed suit, never taking their eyes off Erik.

Erik moved his gun until it was pointed squarely at Krueger. Now that the chips were down he felt deadly calm, wholly alert. He was no longer bluffing. Now it was a matter of survival.

Suddenly the Werewolf girl with the hidden gun exploded into a blur of action.

With a hoarse animal cry she whipped her hands down, aimed her tiny weapon at Erik and fired.

But in the same instant, during the split second it took for the girl to get a firing grip on the small gun, Erik dropped to one knee, his own gun never wavering from Krueger. With his left hand he reached for a low wooden milking stool standing near the fireplace, and with the same uninterrupted motion hurled it straight at the girl's legs. The single bullet fired by her shrieked past Erik's temple, slammed into the fireplace, gouging stone chips, ricocheted off with a piercing whine to embed itself in the wall behind him at the exact moment the heavy stool crashed into the girl's shins. With a groan of pain she went down, her second shot boring into the floor before her.

So startlingly fast had the action been that the other Werewolves were just beginning to react when Erik, his gun and eyes inexorably fixed on Krueger, called out:

"Hold it!"

His voice was deadly with icy control.

"Your general *dies!*" His eyes for an instant flicked to the girl huddled on the floor, her eyes bright with pain, her gun still clutched in her hand. "And *you* will kill him, if you don't drop that toy pistol! *Sofort!* Right now!"

The girl shot a glance at Krueger, then she turned her eyes back to Erik; eyes that were terrible to behold.

For an eternal second the group of Werewolves remained tensely motionless. If they rush me, I've had it, Erik thought with curious detachment. Then, with a half-whispered oath of frustration and impotent rage, the girl dropped the Lilliput gun on the floor. The sound was thunder.

She struggled to her feet.

"Kick it over here," Erik ordered. "Careful!"

The girl obeyed. The little gun skittered across the rough floor, followed by everyone's eyes except Erik's.

He stood up.

The five Werewolf prisoners glared at him. They were like taut, malevolent coils. Waiting. Waiting for the moment of unspoken decision in which to rush him, the moment that *had* to come. It was just a matter of time. Damned little time. And time was the only thing he couldn't control with a gun.

"Put your hands back on your heads," he ordered sharply. "All of you! Face the wall!"

They did not move.

Erik's gun was aimed steadily at Krueger. He brought up his other hand. Carefully he gripped the gun with both hands, extended it slightly and sighted straight down the barrel, pointed exactly at Krueger's forehead.

"*Now!*"

There was not a sound. No movement—and then the prisoners slowly began to move away from one another, their eyes riveted on Erik, steadily widening the area he had to command.

He was losing the last tenuous shreds of control. . . .

He was suddenly aware of something else. A distant dull roar of many motor vehicles, shaking the quiet of the forest, growing louder and louder. The noise of cars grinding to a halt; the clanging of half-tracks, the rumbling of trucks mingled with shouted orders and the sounds of many men.

It was the most beautiful symphony of sounds Erik had ever heard.

His gun began to shake in his hands; he brought it down to rest against his abdomen; it was still aimed straight at Krueger.

The general suddenly seemed to collapse a little within himself. His arms fell uselessly, forgotten at his sides, and he bowed his head in bitter resignation.

Suddenly the door to the hut crashed open. Don and Lieutenant James came rushing in. Don was at once at Erik's side.

"Erik!"

Erik managed a crooked grin.

"Talk about the marines!" he said.

He replaced his gun in his shoulder holster. He knew his hands were shaking. He didn't try to hide it. His throat felt constricted and tight as if he were about to cry; his eyes suddenly smarted. He didn't trust himself to carry the whole thing off with the show of nonchalance he'd like. He barely managed:

"Just—give me a minute. . . ."

And he left the hut.

Alone.

He had endured a lifetime. A lifetime that was all of nine minutes long. . . .

Outside the hut he leaned against the wall. He closed his eyes for a moment. He took a few deep breaths and felt the tenseness gradually leave him. At least he wasn't shaking anymore. . . .

All around him the men of the I & R platoon were deploying, ring·ng the pasture. Erik watched. The quite forest clearing had suddenly become the scene of mercurial activity. U.S. Army vehicles converged on the pasture in a cacophony of noise: jeeps, half-tracks, armored cars, weapons carriers. GIs were fanning out on the double, rifles at port arms. At regular intervals they dropped to the ground, facing the forest, guns ready. Others surrounded the hut. The whole operation took place at top speed with the maximum organization and efficiency of a crack combat outfit.

Erik saw it all. But he didn't see a little incident that happened on one of the several trails leading from the clearing. . . .

A small group of farmers came hurrying down the path away from the pasture, so suddenly swarming with GIs.

One of them, pushing a tireless bicycle loaded with an old rucksack, wore a dirty leather cap.

Krauss.

The expression on his face was one of urgency and alarm as he pushed the old bike rapidly along the narrow trail.

Suddenly, around a bend in the path, two U.S. Army vehicles came tearing down the trail headed straight for the group of farmers. The lead vehicle was a jeep, an officer sitting next to the driver; the other vehicle was a weapons carrier packed with MPs.

The farmers scrambled off the narrow path out of the way of the oncoming vehicles. The old bicycle slipped from Krauss's grasp and rolled under the wheels of the jeep. Metal clanged against metal, and both the bike wheels spewed out behind the jeep, twisted out of shape. The jeep and the weapons carrier screeched to a halt. Krauss dashed to the mangled bike and the old rucksack lying next to it. He reached it at the same time as the officer from the jeep. Both men stood staring at the rucksack. It had split wide open. From the torn canvas spilled a handful of ammunition and two Luger pistols. . . .

Erik did not see this. If he had, it would have meant nothing to him.

Don came from the hut and walked up to Erik.

"Am I glad to see you!" He felt like touching his friend. But he didn't.

"Not half as glad as I was to see you!" There was no doubt that Erik meant it.

"How the hell did you do it? What happened?"

"One more minute . . . I tell you, one more minute and I'd have had it."

Don shook his head in mock wonder.

"And you're the guy who never wins at poker!"

He grew sober.

"What now?" he asked. "We got the old man, but we still don't know where the rest of the Werewolves are. I wouldn't know where to begin to look."

"I think I know how to find out." Erik looked thoughtful. "This whole case has been one damned bluff from the start. Why stop now? I'll get Krueger to show us."

"You nuts? That old bastard wouldn't show you right from left!"

"I'm sure he wouldn't. Not if he knew he was doing it." He started for the door, then stopped short. He stared toward the far end of the clearing.

"Well, I'll be damned!" he exclaimed. "Look who's here."

From a forest path a jeep emerged, followed by a weapons carrier crowded with MPs. The jeep had a mangled bicycle slung over the rear seat. Standing up next to the driver like a conquering Caesar was Major Evans, herding a small group of men before him, hands on heads.

"Oh, him," said Don. "I invited him."

"How nice of him to come. And bringing his own farmers!"

Erik entered the hut, followed by Don. Lieutenant James and a couple of his men were guarding the prisoners. Erik walked up to the I & R officer. His manner was one of assured command, his voice loud enough for all to hear.

"Okay, Lieutenant," he announced briskly, "we're ready to round up the rest of them. Have your men fall in and follow us." He turned toward the Werewolves. "Detail four men to take the prisoners back to Corps." He looked directly at Krueger. "Except you, General Krueger. You are coming with us."

He drew his gun and motioned with it toward the door.

"Let's go!"

For a brief moment Krueger stared at him, then he turned and walked to the door. His bearing was surprisingly military and dignified despite the simple farmer's clothes he wore. Erik stopped him.

"Remember, General," he cautioned pointedly. "No tricks. We are right behind you!"

Without a word Krueger walked on. He didn't turn around to see
if the Americans were following him. If he had, he would have
seen the broad wink Erik gave Don. But he marched straight from
the hut and headed across the pasture.

Erik and Don were right behind him. . . .

Grafenheim
The Area of Werewolf Unit C

1309 hrs

The black-and-white paint of the diagonal stripes running
down the signpost was peeling badly. The sign itself, cut in a crude
arrow shape, read: GRAFENHEIM 4 KM.

This was it.

Willi stood on the trail at the forest edge. The hill sloped down
in front of him to a small valley, a cove of cultivated fields cutting
its lighter greens into the darker colors of the evergreen woods covering the foothills. The trail that had taken him across the Czech
border forked at this point. The signpost pointed west, to the left.
In the distance, at the mouth of the valley, Willi could make out the
village of Grafenheim. The dale itself was little more than one
kilometer across. Somewhere, in the woods on the other side, was
the area of Werewolf Unit C.

It had been a long trip. Krueger's HQ at Schönsee was located
some 100 or 150 kilometers to the northwest, but Willi thought he
must have covered at least twice that distance to avoid enemy held
territory, before that damned Volkswagen gave out.

It had been absurdly easy to reach this spot, he thought. No
risky infiltration, more like taking a pleasant stroll in this beautiful
Bohemian forest. He'd stayed off the roads, of course, and he'd seen
no enemy troops at all. The situation must be fluid as hell. He was
grateful. It made things a lot easier. Both now and later. But he was
also appalled at the signs of collapse he'd seen among the German
troops milling about in Czechoslovakia, in the narrowing strip of

territory between the advancing American and Russian forces. Time was running out.

Instinctively he touched his breast pocket and felt the slight crinkle of paper. Orders for the commanding officer of Unit C. General Krueger's last-minute instructions.

He felt a surge of excitement and pride. In a few hours, he thought with the dramatic exaggeration of youth, the course of history will be changed!

He returned his attention to the signpost. He tested it. Yes. It was loose. As advertised . . .

Grabbing it tightly, he turned the sign a full 180 degrees to point directly east.

He glanced across the valley. He knew he was being observed.

He sat down and leaned against the inverted signpost. He waited. Someone would come for him.

Schönsee Forest

1317 hrs

Generalmajor Karl Krueger marched steadily along the forest path. He had only a few minutes in which to analyze the situation, evaluate it, make his decision and act upon it. Without a single, thought-consuming "if" or "if only," he accepted the fact that he had been captured. He was puzzled by the manner of the enemy intelligence operation. It made him uneasy. The Americans appeared to have a great deal of information, but their conduct seemed unduly haphazard. He dismissed that thought as being nonessential at the moment. Besides, with Americans one could never know. The paramount issue was how to proceed *now*, in order to minimize the setback and safeguard the primary mission.

Fact: He, personally, was removed from direct action. However, he could still influence the progress and the scope of the enemy operation. Fact: His HQ unit was immobilized. Regrettable. But there were competent officers with the other units. And Richter carried detailed orders. No reason. No reason at all the mission should not be carried out successfully. It was imperative. There was still a vast number of troops ready to occupy the Redoubt. Time. Time was what was needed. Even hours would count. He made his decision. He would cooperate with the enemy intelligence officers. He would seem to accept defeat. He would retain their interest and attention, limit their sphere of operation to his own area as long as possible. *That* was already lost. The key mission was still to be mounted.

He came to a trail crossing. Resolutely he turned left. He knew what he had to do. . . .

Erik and Don walked directly behind the German officer. Following them came Lieutenant James, his men deployed in a tight skirmish line behind him. On one flank Major Evans and his MPs were making their way through the woods.

Leaving the forest clearing, Krueger had taken the same path by which Erik and Don had arrived at the hut. Now, with growing realization, Erik looked around. The area seemed disturbingly familiar. There, there at the side of the path was the stack of wood he'd kicked apart less than an hour ago. He glanced at Don. Krueger appeared to be headed for the same part of the forest they'd already searched, tramped all over for hours—and found nothing. He was certain of it. He had a sudden chilling thought.

Was Krueger wise to them? Wise to the trick of letting *him* lead them? Did he realize they had no idea where the Werewolves were? Was he deliberately leading them by the nose, taking them to a place he knew was safe? Giving his men a chance to escape?

In his sudden apprehension Erik's eyes darted around. It *was* the same area. There, on the corner down to the right, stood the big leaning pine tree. The supply tree. And ahead was the forest square planted with the thick stand of spruce trees, all of them between twelve and fifteen feet tall! It was the same damned forest combed by two infantry companies earlier in the day; the same damned spot searched by Evans' MPs and pored over tree by lousy tree by himself and Don!

Krueger had led them to the only spot in the whole goddamned forest they knew was clean!

He had bluffed the bluffers.

Erik's mind raced. He had to play the game to the end. There was nothing else he could do. Absolutely nothing.

He turned to look back. Wordlessly he motioned for Lieutenant James to have his men surround the spruce square.

Oh, God—again!

He saw the men fan out. He deliberately kept his eyes averted from Major Evans'. With Don he entered the stand of spruce trees, following closely behind General Krueger. . . .

The boulders in the little clearing in the center of the square looked exactly as they did less than three hours ago. Erik could even see where the thick moss had been flattened on the boulder he'd been leaning against. The mark stood out like a garish billboard.

Krueger stopped. For a moment he stood in silence, staring into space.

"Well?" Erik's tight voice betrayed his tenseness.

Krueger sighed. "We are here," he said quietly.

"Don't give us that!" Don sounded angry. "We're been here before. There's not a damned thing here!"

Krueger's shoulders stiffened. Slowly he turned to face the two CIC agents. He stared at them with icy eyes. Grim-faced, they returned his stare.

"You never did know!" he whispered with shocked incredulity. His face grew dark. He sagged imperceptibly. "You—never—knew."

Erik spoke harshly.

"What are you giving us?"

Krueger looked searchingly at him, his penetrating eyes cold and distant. He glanced around the clearing. Through the woods Lieutenant James, Major Evans and several of the GIs could be seen converging on the area. Krueger nodded slowly as to a secret thought. Then he faced Erik squarely. When he spoke his voice was once more controlled and calm.

"Feldwebel Steiner!" he called. "Feldwebel Steiner! *Antreten!*"

He stood still. Waiting.

There was not a sound to be heard. All the men were motionless, staring at the German standing erect, aloof in the clearing. Waiting . . .

Erik watched him. He strained to listen. He heard nothing, but the hackles on the back of his neck prickled the chill of an instinctive warning.

Krueger frowned. Once more he called:

"Steiner!" His voice was sharp with authority. *"Antreten! Sofort!"*

Erik and Don exchanged grim looks.

Nothing . . .

Erik felt bitterly cheated. Only moments ago they'd had it made, and now . . . The old man was giving them the runaround. The game was far from over; it was *his* move. And dammit, he had not the slightest idea what to do. He glared at the German. He could smell the stink of anger and frustration in his nostrils.

Suddenly every muscle in his body grew rigid. Not six feet from where he stood the ground began to move.

Slowly a square piece of turf raised itself a few inches. Sliding away to one side, it revealed a hole in the ground no more than two feet square.

A man came climbing up from below. He wore the uniform of a German Wehrmacht Feldwebel. He took a few steps toward Krueger. He limped, but he clicked his heels, came to attention and saluted smartly.

"Zu Befehl, Herr General!"

Dumbfounded, Don stared from the hole in the ground to the man standing at attention before Krueger and back to the hole from which he had appeared.

"Underground!" he said, unable to keep the awe out of his voice. "The whole goddamned installation must be underground!" He turned to Steiner. Curtly he motioned with his gun.

"Get your hands up! On your head! Move!"

Steiner looked questioningly at his commanding officer. His right hand subtly stole toward his belt buckle. Krueger stood stock still.

Silent. His eyes averted from the sergeant. The man scowled. Slowly he placed his hands on top of his head. He was fighting for every second, but he had to be careful not to overdo it; not to make the Americans suspicious. He'd delayed obeying the general's surrender as long as he dared. Long enough to give hurried instructions to the radio operator. Berlin *had* to be informed. That had top priority. Then the Munich relay station. The other units had to be alerted; new chains of command activated. The Unit C mission safeguarded. He had to keep the Americans out of the dugout long enough for the transmissions to be completed. He *had* to. He glared coldly at the enemy officer who approached him. . . .

Erik frisked the German noncom thoroughly while Don covered him. The man was unarmed, but in the breast pocket of his uniform tunic he found a few folded papers. He took them over to Don. Unfolding one of them, he whistled softly.

"Hey, I hit the jackpot!" He showed the document to Don. "Look at this. A complete roster of the unit!" He read: "*Sonderkampfguppe Karl. Gliederung des Führungsstabes.*" He turned to Steiner.

"Is this your unit?"

Steiner quickly glanced at Krueger for guidance, but the general remained silent.

"Well?" Erik demanded.

Steiner gave no reply. Erik stepped up to him.

"Answer me!"

Steiner did not look at Erik. He stared straight ahead.

"I cannot know, Herr Offizier," he said. There was a trace of mockery in his voice. "I do not know what document the Herr Offizier is looking at."

Erik shoved the paper in front of his face.

"All right, look!" he snapped. "And talk!"

Steiner glanced at the document.

"Yes, Herr Offizier," he said. "That is the roster of the headquarters unit."

Don joined them.

"Terrific!" he said. "All we have to do is call the roster and we'll know if we've got 'em all! How can we miss?"

Erik walked over to Krueger. Soberly he regarded the German Werewolf general.

"General Krueger," he said quietly. "Order your men to come out and offer no resistance. I want to avoid unnecessary bloodshed. I'm sure you do as well."

Krueger stood stiffly erect. He made no reply. It was as if he had not even heard Erik. Erik continued:

"It should be obvious to you that they have no chance of escaping."

Krueger was clearly fighting a battle within himself. His eyes were bleak. He shook his head slowly, heavily.

"I—I cannot do this," he said. His voice was firm, although a near whisper.

Erik's first impulse was to give the man a direct order—or else! But he looked at the German officer. He saw the struggle raging within him. And he understood.

He glanced speculatively at Steiner.

The German sergeant glared back at him. *Er kann mich am Arsch lecken!* he thought venomously. He can kiss my ass, if he thinks I'll do it!

Erik dismissed the German noncom from his thoughts. It was his job. He looked about him. All around the clearing GIs stood ready. He raised his voice:

"*Achtung! Achtung! Kampfgruppe Karl!*" he shouted. "Your position is taken! You are surrounded!" He had a sudden crazy flash of *déjà vu;* it all seemed to have happened once before. . . . "Your commanding general is our prisoner," he continued. "Lay down your arms and come forward!"

For a long moment all was silent and motionless, as if the entire forest square itself were holding its breath.

Then, cautiously, apprehensively, two men climbed up out of the dugout hole from which Steiner had appeared. One of them, the second man up, was the radio operator. He glanced at Steiner and imperceptibly nodded his head.

Steiner's stiff shoulders relaxed. His glowering expression turned smug. Automatically he glanced toward the command dugout entrance shaft as if expecting to see someone else emerge.

But the dark hole gaped empty.

He frowned slightly, then suddenly looked away with obvious disinterest.

It was a poor performance, a transparent attempt not to call attention to the dugout. It would have fooled no one.

But Erik and Don were scanning the forest clearing. Neither of them had been watching Steiner.

And then, all through the area, little squares of turf began to move, some of them literally under the feet of the startled GIs. A strange spectacle began to unfold itself. One by one, square holes opened up, and from them emerged a band of sullen, grim Werewolves, clad in a weird conglomeration of mixed uniforms and civilian clothes.

Slowly, grudgingly, unwholesomely they rose from the ground. Like bubbles from a tar pit, Erik thought.

Some of the GIs began to round up the reluctant Germans and collect them in the center of the clearing; others, on orders from Lieutenant James, held their positions, ringing the area. . . .

Pfc Warnecke stood at the edge of the clearing, his back to a clump of spruce trees. He was tense. He hadn't been allowed to forget the last time he was here. His MP buddies were still ribbing him for tripping and firing his weapon at nothing. Shit! But not this time. If he fired his gun this time, somebody would damn well know he'd been shot at!

He stared with grim determination at the scene before him, ready for anything. . . .

A few feet behind him the ground began to move. . . .

A square of turf stealthily, silently lifted up and began to slide away from a hidden dugout shaft.

Warnecke was unaware of it.

Warily a man's head appeared in the dark hole, then his shoulders as he started to climb out. In his hand he held a bayonet, honed to razor sharpness. Noiselessly he emerged from the dugout, his eyes riveted on Warnecke's back. . . .

Warnecke was absorbed in the drama being played out in the

middle of the clearing. The I & R platoon officer—what was his name? James, Lieutenant James—was herding a couple of Were-wolves toward the growing group of prisoners. Warnecke saw him turn and look in his direction—and suddenly whip up his gun to aim straight at him!

He felt the lightning chill of astonished shock knife through him, and at the instant James fired he hit the dirt!

He felt a heavy weight crash down across his back—and inches from his face a gleaming bayonct blade buried itself a full half foot into the ground.

For a brief moment he lay in uncomprehending shock. Then he felt warm moisture spreading across his hand and arm. He yanked it free and stared at it.

Blood . . .

And he suddenly knew.

With gagging revulsion he rolled from under the dead Werewolf. He stared at the body in horrified amazement. He shuddered. Then he turned toward James.

"Thanks, Lieutenant!" He wanted in the worst way to follow up with some sort of clever wisecrack. He couldn't think of any. And he knew he couldn't trust his voice.

"Just watch your step, soldier!" James raised his voice. "That goes for all of you! Watch yourselves! These guys are tricky. Don't give 'em a chance. Team up! Back to back. Team up!"

At once the GIs moved to seek out partners. Erik turned to Steiner.

"You! How many more dugout entrances are there?"

Steiner looked at him coldly. He shrugged.

"I cannot tell you."

"Can't? Or won't?" Erik snapped angrily.

"I do not know more than one other." Steiner pointed to an already exposed shaft opening. "No man knows more than his own and one other. It is for security."

Erik studied the man briefly, then he turned away from him. He raised his voice:

"*Achtung! Achtung!*" he called. "In ten minutes the roster of

Kampfgruppe Karl will be called. Any man found hiding after the roster has been called will be shot! I repeat: Any man found hiding after the roster has been called will be shot!"

From a dugout shaft close to Don a man climbed out. He looked around, placed his hands on his head and stared at Don.

Don looked him over. The man wore a wide grin. The bastard thinks it's all fun and games, does he? Don thought. He felt annoyed.

"What the hell's with you?" he growled.

The man's grin widened. He answered in heavily accented English, obviously proud of his accomplishment.

"It is you," he stated.

Don scowled at him.

"Who'd you expect? Adolf Schicklgruber?" His voice was acid.

"You are lucky to be alive!"

"Can't argue with that, in general. But why in particular?"

The man looked fleetingly uncertain.

"I do not know what you mean," he said. "But it is you I saw. Here. This morning." Don listened with interest. "We saw you. You and your men," the German continued. "It is only because we have orders to not shoot unless we are discovered that we did not kill all of you. You are lucky that you did not find us. If you had—"

Don interrupted him.

" 'If' is a tricky little word in the English language, Buster," he said dryly. "No telling *what* it predicts. Look around you!"

The clearing was crowding with Werewolf captives. And still they crawled from the underground shelters. A couple of GIs were hauling a man from a shaft by his collar. Curiously they peered down into the hole.

"Hey, lookit!" one of them called. "They got themselves a motorbike down there! Hot damn!"

Erik had been looking over the papers he'd found on Steiner. He walked up to Don.

"This is dynamite," he said, unable to keep the excitement out of his voice. "Pure dynamite! There are references here to the three other units. The operational units. A, B and C. And there's a list of outside agents and their areas of operation. Their SOP security setup. Everything!"

"We better get that stuff back to Corps right away."

Erik nodded.

"We'll take the general along. Evans and James can handle things here."

"Anyway, James can!" They walked over to Krueger.

"Please come with us, General," Erik said. "We are leaving here."

Krueger looked at him.

"I have one request." He spoke with quiet dignity.

"What is it?"

"My uniform is in the executive dugout." He glanced down at his Bavarian farmer's clothes with faint distaste. "I request permission to change."

Don pulled Erik aside. He spoke urgently.

"Watch it, Erik. He was caught in civvies. You know the rules."

"I know."

"He's tricky!"

"Look. The guy'd probably feel a lot better if he could face our brass in uniform and not dressed like some cruddy farmer. What's the difference? The record'll show he was taken in civvies. Besides, if we grant him his request now we can put him a little in our debt. Might make him more apt to cooperate later on."

Don was not convinced. He shrugged reluctantly.

"Okay, it's your neck." He grinned. "Guess you're so used to having it stuck out you can't stop!"

Erik smiled. "I'll go down there with him. I want to take a look around before we take off anyway."

He called:

"Warnecke! Over here!"

The MP came trotting up. Major Evans joined the group. Erik turned to Warnecke.

"You come with me," he said. "We're going down into the general's dugout."

He started for the entrance to the executive dugout. Evans stopped him.

"If you're going down there," he said, "I want to go along. I want to see this Werewolf layout."

Both Erik and Don turned to him.

"Major!" Don exclaimed with mock surprise. "I thought you didn't believe in Werewolves!"

Evans reddened. But he kept his silence. Erik motioned to Krueger.

"Okay, General. Let's go."

Krueger nodded. Briskly he started toward the shaft.

Erik's attention never left Krueger as he followed the Werewolf general down into the command dugout, yet he was able to get a good picture of the ingenious installation.

In the square "planter tray" forming the "lid" to the entrance shaft grew the same grasses and weeds as on the surrounding forest floor. When in place, resting on the four massive corner posts of the shaft, exactly level with the ground, it was virtually impossible to detect. Erik could attest to that.

The shaft itself had a permanent ladder built onto one side. It was some ten feet deep and shored up with rough planks.

Erik joined Krueger at the bottom of the ladder. The dugout itself was lighted by several naked bulbs strung along the wooden ceiling, seven feet high. He looked around.

He was in a room he estimated to be about eight by six feet. The shaft entrance was located in one corner. Immediately to the left was a crude double-decker bunk. Weapons crates, ammo and grenade boxes lined the walls, which were made of unfinished lumber. Like being inside a giant packing crate, he thought.

Two open doorways reaching all the way to the ceiling led to other chambers. Krueger headed for the one at the far left of the shaft chamber. Erik followed. He was aware of Evans and Warnecke coming down the ladder from above.

He glanced into the room on his right as he passed the open doorway. It was about the same size as the first chamber. It, too, had a double-decker bunk, and along the far wall a competent-looking radio receiver-transmitter setup was installed. Here crates and boxes were also piled in every possible place, and along one entire wall rows of stacked batteries loomed heavily. Power, Erik realized, for the radio and for the sparse dugout illumination.

Krueger entered the third room. It was the size of the two other chambers combined and quite obviously his own quarters and those of his immediate staff.

Two double-decker bunks formed an angle in the near right corner. One of them, standing against the right wall, had a curtain which could be drawn across it. Erik briefly wondered if it was Krueger or his female staff members who required the privacy.

Facing the open doorway was a table strewn with papers and books. Behind it and on the left wall large area maps had been tacked up. Even here crates and boxes took up all available space. Several automatic weapons were stacked against one of the bunks.

Krueger walked to an open clothes rack standing against the far wall. His boot steps sounded hollow on the wooden planks.

Drainage system below the flooring, Erik's mind registered. Probably leading to a sump pit.

He looked up. In the ceiling where the open doorway joined the two areas he saw an air vent fan. It was not working. He couldn't help being impressed. The air vents from this dugout and from the others as well had to run up through the trunks of the trees growing on the dirt roofs. Only way they could remain undetected.

Krueger turned toward Erik. He waited.

Erik went to sit on the corner of the table. Evans entered the room. He looked around, trying just a little too hard to seem unimpressed. He went over to inspect one of the wall maps, as Warnecke took up position in the doorway, leaning against the jamb, cradling his carbine in his arms.

"Go ahead, General," Erik said pleasantly. "Sorry I can't give you more privacy." He indicated the stacked weapons. "I wouldn't want you to succumb to temptation."

Krueger smiled a small, wry smile. He inclined his head slightly.
"Of course."

He turned to the clothes rack, selected a uniform and laid it on
the bunk. He began to shrug out of his Bavarian jacket.

Erik watched him. He felt good. The operation was paying off
after all. Everything was going his way. Idly he began to riffle
through the papers on Krueger's desk. He'd gather them all together. Take them back to Corps. You never knew what you might
find.

Krueger was unbuttoning his vest. Erik let his eyes roam the
chamber.

"Tell me, General, the other units—are they underground, too?"

Erik's manner was disarmingly informal. He gave the impression
of simply making small talk.

Krueger seemed not to hear him, but he stiffened slightly.

"Oh, come on, General," Erik bantered. "We *have* all your
records!"

Krueger was removing his coarse peasant shirt. He sat down on
the bunk and began to take off his boots. He glanced up at Erik
with his special little smile.

"Yes. They are," he said matter-of-factly.

"So your outside agents fed you information. You'd pick the
targets and send your orders to the operational unit nearest to it.
They'd mount a force of Werewolves, make the strike, and disappear back into their cozy little homes away from home in the
ground."

"That was the plan."

Krueger was pulling off his heavy woolen socks.

"And Ike?" It was a casual question.

The German officer faltered imperceptibly. Then he quickly
continued to undress.

"Ike?" His tone of voice had the exact inflection of polite curiosity. No more.

"The Supreme Allied Commander. General Dwight D. Eisenhower to you."

"I do not know what you mean." Krueger sounded distant. There was an unmistakable tone of dismissal in his voice.

Erik smiled. He was amused.

"Oh, come now, General," he said good-naturedly. "You know exactly what I'm talking about."

He looked at Krueger.

"The assassination," he supplied helpfully. "Did you really think you could get to him?"

Krueger said nothing. He stood up and turned his back to the Americans. Erik waited. He'd give the man a little time to think. To realize how completely his entire operation had failed. He looked at the German officer. He was amused to see that the Were-wolf general wore long underwear. But then it must get cold in that damp, unheated dugout. He didn't blame the man for wanting a bowl of hot soup in front of a nice warm fire. He let his mind dwell on the scene in the hut. Krueger must have felt quite safe when the first search of the forest by the infantry failed to discover the Werewolf installation. Safe enough to leave the dugout and go to the hut. Erik grinned to himself. He sure owed a lot to a bowl of soup!

Krueger had almost finished getting into his uniform. Erik began to gather together the papers from the general's table. He glanced only perfunctorily at them as he picked them up.

Krueger was buttoning his uniform tunic. He turned back toward the others. Above the right breast pocket of his field-gray tunic gleamed the silver *Hoheitsabzeichen,* the German eagle clutching a swastika; above the left was an impressive row of ribbons representing both military and Nazi decorations. The second button-hole down boasted the red, white and black ribbon of the Iron Cross. The transformation from Bavarian peasant to Wehrmacht general was startling.

He looked up at Erik—and froze. Despite his instant effort to conceal his sudden concern, his face twitched in silent alarm. For a moment he stood immobile, staring at the American and the papers in his hand, the uniform buttons forgotten.

Erik glanced at him, and Krueger at once averted his eyes and continued to button his tunic.

Erik just caught the last flicker of Krueger's look of alarm. It was enough. At once he felt the surge of alertness whip through him. Something just happened. Something he missed!

He contemplated the German thoughtfully. Did the man seem more tense? Or, rather, more deliberately relaxed?

He tried to catch Krueger's eyes, but the general avoided his. Did he make a point of doing so?

Erik was puzzled. Uneasy. Something was going on. Something he'd better figure out. And fast! His mind raced. He stared at the German. Standing erect, Krueger looked straight at Erik.

"I am ready," he said calmly.

Erik stood up. He returned Krueger's direct gaze. He suddenly felt himself in a duel, a duel of emotional control, of unspoken action and reaction, and he realized with dismay that he didn't even know the stakes! He only knew it was a duel he had to win.

He was abruptly aware that he was crumpling the papers in his hand. He glanced at them—and barely managed not to betray the thought that lanced into his mind.

He flexed his shoulders in a gesture of relaxation.

"Okay, let's go."

He threw the papers on the table with a show of indifference. As he did, he shot a glance at the Werewolf general.

And he caught it!

Krueger's eyes flicked momentarily toward the papers on the table, then returned at once to stare blandly at Erik. It was barely perceptible, but the man's face had lost some of its tenseness. Krueger looked relieved.

It *was* the documents that concerned him!

Erik whirled back to the table. He grabbed the papers and held them out to Krueger.

"What's in these documents, General?" he demanded, his voice suddenly hard as flint.

He watched for Krueger's reaction. He almost missed it. A

slight widening of the eyes; an almost undiscernible drain of color; the sardonic smile gone. But the German's voice was steady, unhurried when he spoke.

"Take them along. Read them." He shrugged with unconcern. "They are reports. Daily reports . . . Routine."

He dismissed the subject and started toward the door.

"Hold it!" Erik snapped. "Stay right where you are!"

Krueger froze. Erik began to study the papers in his hand.

"I'm suddenly curious to see what kind of *routine* a Werewolf follows. I think I'd better find out. And not later . . . Now!"

He began to examine the documents, one by one. He read fast. But he let nothing slip by. He was certain he'd find something.

Krueger glared at him. Beneath his bushy brows, his cold eyes glittered with icy fire. The muscles in his lean jaw corded as he unconsciously bit down hard. All of a sudden his taut body seemed charged with barely bridled violence. His eyes darted from Erik to Evans standing at the wall map. The MP officer was watching him warily. He quickly glanced toward Warnecke. The man stood in the open doorway. His gun was in his hand, ready to use.

Suddenly Krueger's eyes widened. At once he shifted his gaze back to Erik. With a show of bored irritation he turned, took a couple of steps toward the bunk and leaned against a corner post. Warnecke followed his move closely, his attention wholly focused on the Werewolf general.

He was completely unaware of the soundless, furtive movement in back of him. . . .

On the far wall of the entrance chamber behind him, a small section of the shoring planks, its outline undetectable among the natural cracks and joints of the rough boards, was slowly, silently being pushed out and cautiously placed on the floor below.

Moving with molasses motion, a man, crouched in the exposed opening, noiselessly lowered himself into the room. From his belt he drew the black steel of a .08 Luger and took careful aim at Warnecke's back. . . .

The seconds seemed eternal. Krueger could contain himself no longer. He permitted his eyes to flick toward the dim entry chamber behind Warnecke. He froze. His mind raced wildly.

Damn the man! He'll kill any possible chance we have of using the escape tunnel if he fires that gun! he thought in desperation. I *must* stop him!

He forced himself to look at Erik. He forced himself to make his voice sound casual.

"Your friends up there," he said quickly, glancing up at the ceiling. "Will they not get impatient if you stay down here reading all those reports? They are, as I told you, of no consequence."

Erik did not answer. He had a sinking feeling as he read on. The papers were routine. Duty rosters. Schedules. Regulations. They *were* of no consequence. But dammit, *he'd* decide when to stop reading, not some goddamned German! With angry annoyance he put the paper he'd been reading aside and doggedly started on the next one.

And suddenly his every nerve end chilled. Here it was! What he'd been so certain would be there! His eyes devoured the words on the document in his hand. . . .

The Werewolf crouched behind the unsuspecting Warnecke instantly understood the general's warning. Quickly he put the gun away. He reached up to the visor of his Wehrmacht field cap. He yanked sharply at the rim. It gave way, and from the visor he pulled a four-inch-long curved knife blade. It was razor sharp. . . .

Erik looked up in excitement from the document in his hand.

In that instant the Werewolf made his move. He leaped upon Warnecke from the back, and with one swift slicing motion he cut his throat.

Warnecke's death cry died aborning in a hideous gargling groan, the convulsive expulsion of air spewing bright red droplets of blood from the gaping wound as he collapsed.

The instant Warnecke went down Evans whirled on the assailant, gun in hand. But the Werewolf had anticipated just that. With a well-aimed kick he sent the gun spinning on the floor. . . .

In the same instant that the man had leaped to attack Warnecke,

Krueger hurled himself upon Erik, taking him completely by surprise. With the incredible strength of desperation he held him in a viselike, painful judo grip, preventing him from drawing his gun and coming to the aid of Evans, who, weaponless, confronted the Werewolf assassin inexorably advancing on him.

Erik struggled desperately in Krueger's grip. He felt the bone in his arm beginning to snap.

"*Erledigen! Schnell!* Finish him!" Krueger spat out the words.

Evans backed against the table. He shot a quick glance behind him, searching for a weapon.

And he found it.

He grabbed a pencil lying half hidden among the papers and, grasping it like a knife pointed away from him, made a vicious stab toward the stomach of the advancing Werewolf. The man instantly drew up. He pulled his stomach back. In so doing he leaned slightly forward. . . .

Evans' stab had been a feint. Without a break in his fluid, powerful motion, he jabbed the sharply pointed pencil deep into the man's exposed jugular vein.

For a split second an incredulous look of surprise and mortification winked in the man's glazing eyes; he *knew* in that instant that he had been tricked, but he had been powerless to repress his own reflex action.

The force behind Evans' jab was so great that the pencil snapped off in the flesh of the Werewolf. Already-dead fingers plucked at the blood stained stub and the man tried to shriek his agony as his life spurted from him.

Before he hit the floor Evans had retrieved his gun. He whirled on Krueger.

"Enough!" he called sharply. His eyes flicked briefly toward the body of Warnecke. "I'd love to have to use this, you bastard!"

Krueger at once released Erik.

Erik stared at the dead Werewolf. He was deeply shaken. He could feel the bitter bile rise in his throat. He fought it down. It left his gullet burning and raw. He turned to Evans.

"Thanks!" he said. "And thank God you knew that good old OSS standby!"

Evans glanced sourly at the broken pencil on the floor.

"The pencil?" He shrugged. "We do have *some* basic training in the MPs," he said sarcastically.

Erik took a deep breath.

"Well, thanks anyway."

Evans gave him a cold look.

"No thanks necessary—uh—Larsen. I was protecting my own skin."

Erik knelt by Warnecke. But he knew he was dead. He gathered the documents from the table. Then he looked at Krueger.

The Werewolf general stood stiffly erect. The faint, wry smile was back on his lips and in his eyes. He returned Erik's angry stare calmly.

Erik nodded at the doorway.

"Get going!"

Krueger made a slight bow. The perfect Prussian Junker officer. He walked toward the ladder.

Erik's bleak eyes followed him.

A game, he thought bitterly. He acts just as if it were a god-damned game. He made his move and lost. No one can blame him for that, can they? No, sir. He'll try again, of course. Isn't that what it's all about? One great, glorious game played out by gentlemen officers? Shit!

He kept his eyes averted from the two dead men on the floor as he followed Krueger and Evans to the ladder.

Topside Don came up to him.

"We've got forty-eight enlisted men and seven officers," he announced happily. "I think it's the lot."

He gestured expansively around the clearing. A large group of Werewolves, some in uniform, some not, stood facing an officer. The man was calling off the names from a roster in his hand. Grimly the Germans were responding. Don turned to Erik. He looked closely at his friend. He suddenly grew sober.

"Hey, what happened down there?"

"Never mind that now," Erik countered urgently. He was watching Evans reenter the command dugout with a couple of men. Tearing his attention away, he showed one of the documents from Krueger's table to Don.

"Take a look at this."

"What is it?"

Don took the paper.

"The Werewolves have a mission. Unit C. A big one. Laid on for tonight!"

"What's the target?

Erik looked at him, his eyes grave.

"The jackpot, Don. The priority mission."

"*Ike!*"

Don stared at the document in his hand.

"How?"

His eyes flew over the words on the paper.

"Save it. There are no details." Erik went on rapidly. "The task force will be mounted from Unit C. The location of the unit is given. About seventy-five miles from here, still in Corps area. In the woods east of Grafenheim. But not *where* in the goddamned woods! They mention a rendezvous, but not where it's to be. Transportation. They refer to a previous order, but it's not here either." He looked solemnly at Don.

"Don. They sound so damned positive they can pull it off!"

"We've got to get this back to Corps! But right now!"

"Let Evans do it."

"Evans?"

"He and his MPs. They can take Krueger and the other prisoners back, too." He went on with quiet urgency. "We don't have the time, Don. We don't have the time to persuade the brass that we need another two companies. We don't have the time to set up an operation through Corps. And we can't even warn anyone. We don't know against what! No; you and I are going with Lieutenant James and his platoon. To Grafenheim. It says here that's their jump-off point."

Grimly Don surveyed the area before them.

"We thought this was it," he said. "We thought we'd put the lid on this damned case."

He looked soberly at Erik.

"It's just been blown wide open!"

Grafenheim
Werewolf Unit C

1519 hrs

Never in his life had Willi been so keyed up.

It was wild!

It would work!

And *he* would be part of it. He, Untersturmführer Wilhelm Richter, would have a hand in changing history!

The briefing, just finished, had been perfect. Absolutely perfect. Clear, concise, straight to the point. He was vastly impressed with the leadership of the mission. And the men. Krueger had known exactly what he was doing when he selected the special para-commandos from Unit C for the mission. It wasn't only because it was the unit nearest the jump-off point. It was the men. A couple of them were even veterans from Colonel Skorzeny's fantastic rescue of Mussolini from that Alpine mountaintop. The best!

With a glow of pride and confidence he remembered how he and all his comrades had felt the day they learned about Skorzeny's fabulous exploit. . . .

It had been impossible. They'd told Skorzeny it couldn't be done. But he'd done it anyway, despite their predictions of disaster. He'd crash-landed gliders on a postage-stamp shelf sloping from the top of Gran Sasso mountain, snatched the Duce from the Italian garrison with a handful of men, and escaped with him by literally pushing a small plane, a Storch it was, off the cliff into a ravine, diving until the plane became airborne!

It had been a gallant, an inspiring feat. He remembered the

elation, the tremendous lift he'd felt; he, every soldier—all of Germany! It had put new heart into the whole war effort.

It had been big. Real big.

This time it would be bigger. . . .

Everything was going like clockwork. The CO of Unit C had not been in contact with the Führer's representative, that pompous little ass from Berlin, Reichsamtsleiter von Eckdorf, for the last couple of days. No last-minute orders or changes had been received from Krueger via the Munich radio relay station.

The mission was on.

The mission that would change the course of the war. The mission that would rally the defenders of the *Alpenfestung*, the invincible Alpine Fortress: the Werewolves, the Hitler Youth, the SS troops—all of them!

He savored the brilliant operational plans as he would a great wine, letting it wash over his awareness. . . .

H Hour was after dark. The commandos, a small, hard-hitting force of trained *Fallschirmjäger*, paratroopers, would exfiltrate the unit area and make their way to German-held territory only a few kilometers away. From personal experience he knew how simple that would be. On the Salzburg road just south of Passau they would rendezvous with the waiting trucks.

Password: *Feuerkampf!* Countersign: *Siegreich!*

From there it was a two-hour ride to the underground airfield at the edge of the Redoubt area just north of Salzburg.

Three airplanes would be waiting for them. Three U.S. transports. C-47s. Reconstructed from planes shot down, repaired with cannibalized parts from other crashes. Simple. Ingenious.

Then takeoff.

It would be the darkest time of night when they'd be over the drop zone and their target. . . .

He took his Luger from its holster. For the tenth time in the last hour he inspected it. He cleaned off an imaginary speck of dust.

Topside the shadows would be lengthening.

Soon . . .

They'd make it.

Skorzeny made it.

It would be the same kind of action. In reverse.

For *rescue* substitute *assassination!*

Munich

1603 hrs

Oberrechtsrat Dr. Meister of the Munich *Städtischen Ernäh-rungs und Wirtschaftsamt* stood on the steps of the Town Hall on Marienplatz, waiting.

To him had fallen the burden of surrendering this historic town, the capital of Bavaria, to the invading American troops.

Munich had already suffered severe damage from repeated air raids, and the streets were all but deserted.

Since early morning of this Monday, April 30, the ominous thunder of heavy guns had rolled across the inner city from the suburbs, which were undergoing terrifying artillery barrages.

Now all was quiet.

Several vehicles from the U.S. Seventh Army wheeled into the square and came to a halt in front of the Town Hall. A major stepped from one of them and approached Dr. Meister.

The German glanced up at the tower clock. It was exactly five minutes past four o'clock in the afternoon.

Munich surrendered.

Fighting had been unusually heavy right up to the city outskirts. SS units had been massed before the city in an all-out effort to stay the advance of the American troops. In the city itself executions of civilian and military leaders who advocated nonresistance had been summarily carried out by firing squads. Destruction was to be seen everywhere, on every road leading to the town, much of it the result of field artillery fire.

On the shoulder of the road from Heidendorf, at the edge of a crater-pitted field, lay the shattered remains of a wagon still hitched to the mangled corpses of two horses.

The passing troops gave it a wide berth. The stench was over-powering. The wagon had been a liquid manure tank. No one had the slightest desire to investigate what—or who—might be lying in the wetly glistening, stinking mess. The strange torn and twisted bits of metal and glass that mingled with the splintered wood had been undisturbed since the wagon took a direct hit at exactly twenty-eight minutes past one o'clock that afternoon. . . .

Grafenheim

1952 hrs

The night was clear. Darkness had drawn its shroud over the countryside so gradually that he hardly had been aware of it. He found that his night vision was astoundingly good. It was important. They were counting on just that.

He glanced at his watch. Almost eight. Where the hell were they? Had he figured it wrong? He didn't like the incertitude nagging his mind.

Again he studied the terrain before him, so damned familiar to him by now. The fork in the dirt road leading from the forest lay clearly exposed, one branch leading to the village of Grafenheim, the other bypassing it to the north; the open fields on either side of the road, the little copse of trees off the north branch, the broken farm wagon in the ditch just before the road forked . . . And the men? He knew they were all there, though he couldn't see any but Don and Lieutenant James, lying next to him on the ground. Both men were staring silently at the quiet, empty road.

He looked at his watch again. He was surprised to see it was still a few minutes before eight. What if they were in the wrong place?

They had arrived at Grafenheim just as the sun was dipping down behind the low mountains of the Bayrischer Wald to the west, gilding their crowns of evergreen with crimson. They had studied the terrain and picked the spot for the ambush carefully. It was the only action they could take. It would have been hopeless folly to try to ferret out the Werewolves from their unit installation somewhere in the forest beyond. Especially in the dark. He knew that only too well. They would have to wait for *them* to make their move.

The road before him was the only one coming from the forest area where the map showed the unit to be located. They would have to come that way. Unless . . .

Again he glanced at his watch. Eight—not quite. They'd been in position, waiting for close to two hours.

The plan was sound. It was simple. It would work.

If the Werewolves showed up.

They *had* to, dammit! Their alternative would be to cross into Czechoslovakia. That wouldn't make sense. Not with the jump-off point shown as Grafenheim. But *if* they did? . . .

Corps had been ordered not to cross the Czech border in strength and run the risk of barging headlong into the Russian forces pressing on from the east. With Germany cut in two by the Americans, several German armies intended to garrison the Alpine Fortress were bottled up in the Bohemian bastion. They had little choice but to stay there, unless something happened to uncork the bottle.

He looked at his watch. He knew what he would see. He couldn't help it. Eight.

Come on, dammit!

He felt Don tense beside him. Quickly he looked up.

From the woods two shadowy figures had emerged. They walked on the dirt road partway to the fork. They stopped. For a while they stood still. Listening. Watching . . .

Erik hardly breathed. He prayed that no one would make a move. He knew how far and how clearly sound carries at night.

One of the men, carrying what appeared to be a rifle, turned toward the forest. Then he lifted the rifle above his head pointing straight up at the starry night sky.

Erik let out his breath. The man had made the signal: Area free of enemy.

And from the forest behind him they came. Two along the road. Two more. Dark, shadowy figures moving silently, cautiously. From the woods into the fields paralleling the road they came. Erik automatically began to count them. Ten. Fourteen . . .

A couple of the men were pushing bicycles along the dirt road, loaded with bundles. Or packs. Eighteen. Twenty-one . . .

Some of them looked oddly humpbacked. Rucksacks. All of them seemed to carry farm implements. Or weapons. Thirty-two. Four . . .

They could have been farmers. But their walk was different. Sure. Alert. Somehow feline. It gave them away.

Like night-marauding predators, Erik thought. Like a pack of— wolves.

Forty . . .

He stopped counting. He looked grim. The Werewolves were mounting their mission in force.

He was aware of Lieutenant James slowly raising his gun, aiming it toward the oncoming Werewolves. A few more seconds . . .

Suddenly a shot rang out!

Goddammit! Erik thought in a flare of anger. *Too soon!*

Even as the echo of the shot billowed across the fields the lights flashed on. Six. Ten. A dozen vehicles placed in a semicircle before the advancing Werewolves all at once poured the dazzling light from their headlights over the men. Blazing, blinding, the light bathed the nightscape in glaring white. In the split second before he clamped his eyes shut Erik saw the Werewolves, caught in the searing light like accursed pillars of gleaming salt stand frozen, then hit the ground. They had them! Eyes screwed tightly shut, he turned his head aside. As he had been told to do. It was his protection. His carefully built up night vision had to be preserved. It was the ace in the hole that would give them the upper hand.

For a few confused seconds the thunderstruck Werewolves were assailed by the eye-scorching light beams. There was sporadic shooting; scattered bursts of automatic fire. Then Erik heard an authoritative voice shout:

"*Licht ausschiessen!* Shoot out the lights!"

Immediately he heard a volley of shots, the sharp tinkle of shattering glass, and then he felt the lights turn off on all the vehicles.

He opened his eyes.

His night vision was still intact. He could see.

Not so the Werewolves.

Blinded by the sudden, dazzling light, they now found themselves isolated in the darkness enveloping them, unable to discern anything but the most exposed muzzle flashes from the guns of the ambushers. They hugged the ground. A few of them sprang to their feet and ran for the protection of the forest. They were plainly seen by the GIs who had protected their eyes from the light. They were cut down.

Erik was dimly aware of a single streak of light cutting across the field on his far right. The headlights on the flanking vehicle were still on. That is, one of them was. He knew the position was held by Lieutenant James's jeep, manned by his driver. Part of his mind realized that the driver must have been hit before he could extinguish his light.

The shooting had become heavier. The GIs had made their flanking moves to cut off the Werewolves from retreating into the woods. They were pocketed.

Suddenly Erik froze. He snapped his head toward the jeep with its glaring cyclops eye.

A figure came hurtling from the shadowy cover of the broken farm wagon straight toward the jeep. For a split second the man froze in a crouch, a black silhouette against the blazing headlamp. He fired a single shot, then he leaped for the vehicle. A formless shape tumbled from the jeep. Erik heard the motor roar to life, and he saw the jeep spurt dirt as it slewed around and shot down the road toward the village.

Erik was on his feet.

"Don!" he shouted. "Get our jeep!"

He whirled toward Lieutenant James.

"We'll go after him. Get the rest. All of them! I want two men. With us."

James did not take time to answer. He at once motioned to his two nearest men.

Don came skidding to a halt on the road. Erik and the two GIs jumped in, and the jeep took off, wheeling around the road fork in pursuit of the stolen vehicle which was just entering the dark village ahead, its single headlight sweeping wildly across the squat farm buildings.

Don pushed the gas pedal to the floor. The jeep raced along the dirt road. They had to catch the fleeing Werewolf. They could not let anyone get away. Not a single man.

Ahead the one headlight on the stolen jeep was suddenly turned off. . . .

Willi's jeep jolted along the cobblestoned pavement of the deserted village street. He drove as fast as he dared without lights. It was a calculated risk. He was hoping his pursuers would not know in which direction he traveled when he left Grafenheim. He might be able to throw them off.

He *had* to make it!

Unit C had been betrayed. How? By whom? Unimportant now. But the mission could still be mounted. Still be successful. It was of the utmost importance. To his fatherland. To his Führer . . .

He must reach the rendezvous point. He had been thoroughly briefed. He could activate an emergency plan. Get substitute troops from the Redoubt garrison. He could still pull it off!

He reached the turnoff to Passau, almost missing it in the dark. He stopped. He drove a few yards down the wrong road and stopped again. In the distance he could hear the pursuing jeep roaring toward him.

He stomped with all his might on the brake and gunned the engine. The wheels spun, churning the ground, raising clouds of dust.

Quickly he backed up and drove down the Passau road, picking up speed as he raced away. He hoped the headlights of his pursuers would pick up the settling dust, and that they would take the wrong turn.

The hand grenade hanging from his belt interfered with his driving. He unclipped it and placed it on the floor.

He was suddenly acutely aware of being wet. He was puzzled. Had he pissed in his pants? Then suddenly it hit him. He gagged.

It was the seat. The driver's seat of the jeep. It was saturated with blood. It was soaking through his pants. The American must have bled extravagantly, might have been dead before he shot him. He was sickened by the slimy, moist feel of a dead man's blood on his skin. His whole body cringed in revulsion, straining to get away from the loathsome spot.

But he stayed.

He forced himself to dismiss it from his mind. Damn it! He wasn't a squeamish bitch!

He glanced back over his shoulder.

The headlights of the pursuing jeep were still there.

They were gaining. . . .

He wasn't going to make it.

He compelled himself to look at the situation in the cold, uncompromising light of reality. No wishful thinking.

He still had a sizable lead. The Americans were gaining on him, but slowly. However, he would have to abandon the jeep before he reached the front lines. No matter how fluid the situation was, he was bound to be stopped if he came barreling along like this. Especially with another jeep in pursuit. He would have to make it across on foot, but he wouldn't have the time. Not with that *verfluchte* jeep steadily closing on him.

So. He couldn't make it. Not alone. He needed help.

But where could he go?

Where?

He hurtled past a road junction. He caught a flash of a signpost: WALDGRUBE.

Suddenly he knew where.

The mine!

Only a few kilometers. He knew exactly how to get there. He'd passed the place on the way back from the gold delivery to Rattendorf. With that SS major. Kratzer. More than two weeks ago. They were just finishing construction then. They'd be ready.

It was one of the hidden Redoubt approach fortifications. Built into an abandoned graphite mine in the mountains. He could get help there. The Americans would follow him, that was certain.

It would be the last damned thing they would ever do!

He turned on his single headlight.

Now it was only a matter of speed. . . .

The heavy wire fence topped by a forbidding barrier of angled barbed wire looked rusty and run-down in the glare from Willi's single headlight. The big wire gates on massive iron frames hung open, one of them askew, the huge top hinge broken.

There was no sign of life. The old mine area had the desolate look of a long abandoned site.

Willi slowed down only a little. He followed the black-gray dirt road toward the drift mine entrance blasted into the rocky side of the mountain.

His headlight swept across a scene of disuse and decay. A few shacks, their rusty corrugated iron sheets sprung and buckled; a wooden shed, the weathered boards broken and rotted on one side; a paint-peeling barracks, its doors and windows missing. At the mine entrance the weird shapes of a conglomerate collection of abandoned mining equipment seemed to take on a baleful life of their own as the black shadows cast by the probing headlight moved and meshed grotesquely. Crushers, drillers, pumps, Willi guessed. A good touch.

He brought the jeep to a halt close to the entrance and jumped out. The two huge iron doors to the tunnel gaped open. Silent. Dark.

Willi was tense. Everything depended upon how he handled himself.

He was impressed by the camouflage of the fortification. He had seen no sign of recent improvements. It was exactly as it should be. They had been careful. . . .

Quickly he started for the entrance. He looked down to avoid tripping over the ore-cart rails running into the mine. He cursed.

Careful, but not careful enough. In the dirt he saw the unmistakable tire tracks of heavy German military trucks. Looked like Büssings. And a few footprints made by hobnailed boots. Recently made. It was an inexcusable oversight. He felt outraged. He would have to have it cleaned up.

He was suddenly conscious of the grinding roar of the pursuing jeep. It sounded close. The Americans would be just about to enter the mine area.

He ran the last few feet to the tunnel mouth. He was not concerned that he was not challenged. The defenders of the fortification must have the same orders as the Werewolves: Don't give yourself away until discovery is certain.

He stopped in the gaping hole that led into the mine interior. He took a deep breath.

"Hier Sonderkampfgruppe Karl!" he shouted into the waiting darkness. His voice sounded abnormally shrill to his own ears. He suddenly wished it had more timbre. *"Die Amis sind hinter mir her!* The Americans are behind me! I am alone! I am coming in!"

At once he started to run into the dark tunnel. He was aware of his heart beating heavily. A chilling feeling of anticipation crawled over his whole body.

Would they believe him? . . . Would they shoot? . . .

There was no shot.

He was safe.

Erik motioned for Don to stop the jeep at the broken wire gate to the mine area and to kill the motor.

The black letters on the peeling white paint of the sign hanging crookedly on the fence next to the gate spelled out:

ZUTRITT VERBOTEN!

KREIS PASSAU GRAPHIT A/G

Grubekennkarte Vorzeigen

"What's the sign say?" asked one of the GIs.

"It's a graphite mine," Erik answered him. "It says: 'Entry forbidden. Mine pass must be shown.'"

"Boy, that's real Kraut," the GI cracked. "With them everything's either forbidden or compulsory."

For a moment they sat in silence, listening. The night forest was quiet. There was no sound of the fleeing jeep ahead of them. It had stopped.

The old graphite mine had been the destination of the escaping Werewolf.

Why?

Erik studied the deserted installation lying starkly revealed before him in the cold glare from the jeep headlights.

The place looked utterly forsaken, crumbling away with disuse. The picture of abandonment.

But there was something wrong with the picture. Some little thing that made him uneasy. What was it? He had the uncanny feeling he was looking right at it but didn't see it.

He scanned the scene before him. Neglect. Disintegration. Decay. Weeds growing all through the debris and around the ruined structures. Everywhere, except—

He stared. He suddenly felt a surge of excitement. Except on the dirt road itself.

If the area *were* abandoned, if it were not used at all, wouldn't the road as well be overgrown with weeds? Or was it the hard-packed graphite-and-dirt compound that prevented it?

He gave a brief order. The two GIs climbed from the jeep and quickly took up positions on either side of the road, weapons at port arms. Erik drew his own gun. He turned to Don. He nodded.

Slowly they all began to advance along the empty road, the headlights knifing ahead of them into the darkness. . . .

The stolen jeep looked oddly out of place standing near the gaping black tunnel mouth, its cyclops eye dead and dark.

Don pulled up before the entrance. The twin headlight beams stabbed into the gloom of the mine, revealing only a long, wide, empty tunnel drilled into the mountain bedrock itself. In the distant shadows it appeared to make a bend.

Erik looked around quickly. He at once noticed the truck tire tracks. He studied the broken pieces of mining equipment left outside the tunnel, and the ore-cart rails leading into the mine, disappearing in the distant darkness, running along wooden ties laid on top of the hard ground. The ties were badly cracked and split, but a few of them, although discolored and scarred, looked new.

The two men stared soberly at one another. They spoke in taut, hushed voices.

"What do you think? Is he in there?"

"Got to be."

"I don't like it."

"Neither do I." Erik nodded toward the rails. "This damned place isn't as innocent as it looks."

"Well? What do we do? Go get help?"

Erik looked earnestly at his friend.

"Who stays behind?" he asked quietly. "You? Me? Both of us? I'll tell you something, Don. I for one have had my belly full of waiting for one day." He gestured toward the mine. "And what about that guy in there? We've got to get him."

"I suppose so. But—"

"Don. Have you ever heard of a major operation that didn't have an alternative plan?"

"You got a point."

"I figure that guy is all set to pull something. He's sure proved himself to be a resourceful bastard. Can we be sure there isn't another way out of here? Can we be sure he doesn't take off while we sit around on our collective fat ass, waiting? He can't be too damned far ahead of us. Not with that jeep sitting over there. Can we afford to wait?" Erik paused for a moment. Then he said firmly, "I say we find out what we're up against before we holler help."

Don made a wry face.

"So we stick our necks out again, right? This time on a different block." He shrugged, "Okay. I'm with you."

"You stay here. Cover our rear. We'll go on in. See what we can find."

Don climbed out of the jeep. Erik slid over behind the wheel. Don looked at him, his eyes grim.

"Hey! If you do run into something, old buddy, don't be a fucking hero, okay?"

"Okay, old buddy."

They moved out.

Within seconds they were swallowed in the murky gloom of the mine. . . .

Erik drove slowly down the middle of the tunnel, following the rails. He had engaged the four-wheel drive for maximum traction. In the shadows on either side of the jeep he could make out the ghostly figures of the two GIs. The wide horizontal bore of the drift mine ahead of him, clearly revealed in the beams from the jeep's headlights, was empty. Affixed to the rough, drill-scarred ceiling he could see a heavy electric cable running the length of the tunnel. Evenly spaced light bulbs hung from it. They were dark. The black-gray walls of the mine tunnel absorbed an amazing amount of the reflected light; his headlight beams were like twin lances of white brilliance spearing the gloom ahead of him. In the distance the drift made a bend to the right.

Erik felt intolerably exposed. Every nerve end, every sense was at peak intentness, alert to the faintest sound of danger, the slightest movement in the darkness ahead.

There was nothing. . . .

Don crouched just inside the tunnel. He had a clear view of the area outside. His eyes never left it. Gun in hand, he listened tensely to the receding sound of Erik's jeep going deeper into the mine.

He wished *he* could be the one in there. For once. But, dammit, it had to be Erik. He knew it. They both knew it. When a personal confrontation was probable, Erik's knowledge of German had to be the deciding factor. He never questioned it. Neither of them did. Shit!

He strained to listen for that first sign of trouble—that first shot —hoping he would not hear it, yet knowing he would, anxious for it to happen so the unbearable forebodings would end.

Like waiting for that goddamned other shoe to fall, he thought.

But the muffled drone of the jeep continued undisturbed, growing ever fainter. . . .

Erik reached the bend. Cautiously he guided the jeep around it, hugging the rails. His world was filled with the grinding rumble of the jeep in low gear, with tenseness and with tormenting anticipation as his eyes followed the twin circles of brilliance cast by his headlights slowly moving across the tunnel wall before reaching into the blackness around the turn. . . .

Suddenly, over the laboring motor noise, he heard the sharp clang of metal striking metal in the gloom ahead.

At once he switched off the headlights and drowned in darkness. He killed the motor. He stopped breathing. He listened.

He could hear the fast surging of his own blood in his ears; the small noises of the jeep engine quieting; the heavy breathing of one of the GIs. Nothing else. The metallic clang was not repeated.

For a moment he sat in blackness, a blackness as absolute as nonexistence. He was loath to turn on the lights again and offer himself as a target impossible to miss. There was nothing he could do about it. Or was there?

He again started up the jeep. He switched on the headbeams. The light was suddenly blinding. He slid over to the passenger side and put his left foot on the gas pedal. Steering with his left hand, gripping his gun in the right, he slowly continued around the tunnel bend. Anyone in the darkness before him would not be able to see him because of the dazzling headlights; they would assume he sat behind the wheel. This way he might cut down the chance of being hit in the first blast. . . .

He was almost through. He suddenly gave a hard pull on the wheel. The jeep spun around the last few feet and poured its light over the scene before him.

In a flash the entire unbelievable sight etched itself on Erik's mind.

The vast mine cavern lost in distant darkness, stacked, piled, heaped with an incredible array of stuff.

Mounds of rusty old ore carts and mining equipment pushed against the rock walls to make room for neat stacks of crates and cases, stenciled legends specifying shop machinery and a profusion of military stores and supplies, all unopened . . .

Rows of gun racks—empty. Stacks of lumber, logs and beams, and military barracks bunks—unassembled. A row of freshly painted signs leaning against boxes and chests piled next to the black mouth of a side stope, reading: LAZARETT—Hospital . . . LAGER—Storeroom . . . RÜSTKAMMER—Armory . . . and Communications, Motor Pool, Mess Hall . . .

Piles of wooden chairs and stools; boxes of tools, hardware and electrical equipment—all still sealed . . . Everything necessary to equip a military installation completely . . .

All of it untouched.

His mind raced to understand the sight that assailed his eyes. He saw all of it at once.

All of it—and the lone figure of a man crouched dangerously at the center rails, imprisoned in the bright headlight beams. . . .

Willi was shocked into a moment of immobility as the blackness was ripped away and he could see.

His conscious mind refused to accept the evidence of his senses. He half expected the enemy jeep to be blasted out of existence by his hidden comrades. But the thought died instantly in the stark glare of reality.

The redoubt stronghold was uncompleted. Unoccupied. Dead.

He was alone.

He had denied the doubts that had begun to gnaw at the edges of his faith as he groped his way along the tunnel rails into the darkness of the mine, inexorably pursued by the deep-throated grinding sound of the enemy jeep. But now?

He stared at the vacant bastion.

Useless. Impotent.

He shivered as the full weight of his doubts struck him.

The *Alpenfestung?*

With a small cry of disillusion and rage he dropped to one knee, facing the hated, blinding enemy.

He fired.

His first shot crashed through the windshield on the driver's side, shattering it. The second one shot out one of the glaring headlights.

At once the GIs returned the fire.

Willi felt a tap on the outside of his arm. He instantly appraised the situation. There were too many of them. He hurled his gun away.

"*Kamerad!*" he shouted. "*Kamerad! Nicht schiessen!* Don't shoot!"

He stood up. He raised his hands over his head. He was surprised at the sudden twinge of pain in one of them. Had he been hit? He dismissed it. His mind whirled. The next few moments were crucial.

Intently he watched the three men walking up to him, silhouetted against the headlight. He took their measure. Two of them were Ami infantry. Enlisted men only. The third? An officer perhaps. Three of them . . .

He thought fast. He'd made a mistake coming here. But he wasn't through yet. Not yet. He'd have to reach the jeep at the tunnel entrance. He'd left the hand grenade in it. On the floor. He could blow up the pursuers when they came after him out of the tunnel. With a little luck he could still reach German-held territory. . . .

He stretched his arms toward the black tunnel ceiling.

"*Kamerad,*" he said. He smiled.

Erik watched him closely.

"Cover me," he said to the two GIs.

The men took up positions on either side of the Werewolf. Erik stepped in front of him.

The two young men stood staring at one another.

Suddenly Willi grimaced in pain. He looked up at his wounded arm. Blood was oozing through his sleeve.

The two GIs instinctively followed his glance. For an instant their attention was diverted, and in that instant Willi acted. He yanked down his hands, grabbed the nearest man and hurled him savagely into Erik. Stepping back, trying to keep his footing, Erik tripped over the rail behind him. Both he and the GI went down.

Willi was already racing away. If he could only get out of the light into the shadows . . .

The GI still on his feet quickly recovered from his shock. At once he raised his carbine.

Erik shouted, "Don't shoot!"

The GI fired.

"He's not going anywhere!" Erik's words skidded on even as the shot rang out, reverberating through the cavern, filling it with the thunder of violent death.

Willi stumbled. He took a couple of faltering steps. He collapsed.

Erik ran to him. He was angry. Disgusted. With himself. He hadn't wanted this man to die, dammit! He should have known better. This was a Werewolf. A fanatic. He should have known he'd try something.

He was at the fallen man's side. Still alive. Erik turned him over. The shot had penetrated his lung. The exit wound in his chest gaped gory, ragged. He was choking on his blood. His breath bubbled with pink froth.

Erik raised him up. He took off his jacket and put it under the young Werewolf's head. He knelt by him.

Don came running out of the darkness. He looked at Erik.

Erik shook his head.

"He's had it."

Willi fought the red waves of pain that pummeled at his consciousness. *The mission,* he thought in desperation. *I must save the mission—the mission. . . .*

He felt his strength draining from him. He suddenly smelled fresh pine trees. He smiled. He had felt strength drain from him before. With Gerti . . . *"In Ordnung!"* But now . . .

He had to stay strong. For his son. For his and Gerti's son. To make a great and glorious Germany for his son to live in . . . For —the mission!

His thoughts ebbed and flowed. His misty eyes slid over the harshly lighted mine cavern. It glitters, he thought. It glitters with Jew gold. The silence is raucous with the cries of outraged crows. . . .

He suddenly heard the Werewolf motto boom in his mind. "*Es gibt keine Kameraden!* There is no such thing as a friend! If your mission is at stake, attack him. If need be, kill him!" He had to save the mission. Now. The enemy must not . . . must not . . .

He was suddenly frantic with despair. Panic-stricken. He must make certain they did not destroy the mission. It was up to him. He must give them another target. An important target. *There is no such thing as a friend! Kill him! Kill him! Kill!*

He grabbed at Erik.

"I—" he whispered in his agony. "I am a Werewolf! I am—from Werewolf headquarters." Urgently he tugged at Erik. "I am from —General Krueger!"

He suddenly felt calm. He knew exactly what he had to do. Krueger was a friend . . . a father. . . . There is no such thing as a friend. . . .

"I—will take you there," he breathed. "I will give you—General Krueger. . . ."

He stared with burning eyes up into the face of Erik.

"Now," he said. "Now! We must go there—now!"

The black, red, blinding, dark billows washed over him. He felt himself sinking down into a sea of nothingness—then bob to the surface of lucidity.

He glanced around the mine tunnel. Impotent! He felt his whole world crumble. . . .

All of a sudden he desperately needed affirmation. He tried to sit up—but his body would not obey. He looked up into the face of the enemy looming over him. He whispered:

"It—could have worked? . . ."

His eyes pleaded. This was the most important question of his life. His very reason for being. For having been . . .

"It could have worked," he said once more, sudden strength in his voice. "It was all set. *It could have worked.* . . ."

But the eyes that stared into the shadows of the futile redoubt stronghold no longer saw the shattered dream.

Erik looked down at the young Werewolf.

"It could have worked," he said quietly.

Berlin

2017 hrs

The destruction was infernal. The city, in flames under heavy artillery bombardment by the Russian forces, was being blown asunder. Far to the northwest an ever-changing crisscross lattice-work of searching lights reached into the red-black night sky. From time to time, ground-shaking explosions blotted out the constant cacophony of roaring fires, crashing masonry and the distant wails of ambulance and fire engine horns. The death cries of a city.

Through the nearly impassable street outside the Chancellery ruins a small figure scurried through the rubble, skirting the shell craters, cringing in fear at every thunderous blast. It was a Wehrmacht soldier.

He ran across the street. His greatcoat was much too large for him, hanging loose at the shoulders, the sleeves falling over his hands, the skirts flapping at his heels. He was a message runner. Two days before he had turned fourteen.

A shell crashed into the already dead and empty ruins of a building nearby. The boy soldier threw himself behind some broken masonry. He peered toward the Chancellery. His youthful face was grimy and streaked with sweat, or tears. He looked mortally frightened but determined. He clutched the dispatch case slung over his shoulder and ducked down, as another artillery shell burst a little farther away.

He got up and raced for the Chancellery buildings, disappearing into the dark, tortured stone bowels. . . .

The Chancellery garden was a desolate scene of ruin.

The massive steel door of the blockhouse entrance to the Führer Bunker gaped wide open. Next to the abandoned cement mixer squatting just outside, a shallow trench had been dug in the ground. A ravenous fire was burning fiercely in it; greedy flames, devouring a formless mass, spewed greasy black smoke into the fiery sky. Empty gasoline cans lay strewn about in the rubble; a shovel, its handle broken, protruded grotesquely from a shell crater.

In the shadows of the shattered wall Colonel Hans Heinrich Stauffer, his set face grim and hard, stood staring at the fire pit. The stench of burning bacon had lessened considerably, he thought. It was at least bearable.

Three SS officers stood rigidly huddled together at the bunker entrance. He knew them all. Günsche, the Führer's bodyguard; Kempka, his driver; and Linge, his personal valet.

Stauffer stared at the hellish scene with a cynical twist to his mouth.

Was this the glory of a great leader's death? he thought. To be watched by a bodyguard, a chauffeur and a valet?

A shell crashed into the crumbling garden wall. The three officers disappeared into the safety of the bunker.

Stauffer remained.

It still didn't seem real.

None of it . . .

Until only hours ago he had been convinced that Hitler had every intention of going to Berchtesgaden to lead the continued battle from the *Alpenfestung* personally. After all, the Führer had sent most of his household staff down there earlier in the month to prepare for his arrival. And when his own personal pilot, Hanna Reitsch, had flown into the beleaguered city only a few days ago, he'd been certain she'd come to fly the Führer out. Stauffer knew she'd been trying to persuade him to leave at once, but he'd kept on delaying his departure, almost as if he'd been waiting for something to happen. A last-minute reprieve?

And then, only this morning, she left. Without him.

Stauffer wondered what had been going on at the last situation conference held in the bunker at noon. The last conference Hitler would ever attend, he thought. Stauffer hadn't been present. He knew a courier had brought a dispatch to the bunker immediately afterward, and he knew that after that Kempka, who was in charge of the Chancellery garage, had received orders from the Führer himself to round up two hundred liters of gasoline. Two hundred liters!

He looked toward the blazing fire trench. The leaping flames reflected their obscene feast on his pale, bleak face. He didn't know he was shivering. He didn't hear the constant roar of the Russian artillery bombardment. Only the single fateful shot that took the Führer's life rang out and echoed endlessly through his mind.

He was suddenly aware of a small figure darting into the garden from the Chancellery ruins. A dispatch runner.

"Soldier! Over here!" he called.

The courier, breathless from his run, came smartly to attention before him. His hand shot out.

"Heil Hitler!"

Stauffer stared at him. Hardly more than a child, he thought. A deep, sorrow-filled compassion flooded through him. Compassion for this little boy soldier, for himself, for his ravaged country . . .

"What is it?" he demanded.

"A dispatch, Herr Oberst!" The boy drew himself up proudly. "For the Führer's eyes only!"

For a moment Stauffer stared at the eager boy, his eyes strange and remote. Then he slowly turned to look toward the hellish fire pit.

"You are too late, my boy," he said, his voice distant.

The young courier stared at the raging fire. The twisting, tortuous flames washed his horrified face with red. He looked back at Stauffer, questioning, unbelieving. . . .

The officer held out his hand.

"Give it to me," he said quietly.

As if in a trance of horror, the boy opened his pouch and handed the dispatch to Stauffer. The fire pit irresistibly drew his terrified eyes.

Suddenly a shell crashed into the battered wall close by. The boy started violently. But he stayed.

Stauffer nodded toward the blockhouse.

"Get down into the bunker," he ordered. "Go on!"

The boy soldier ran for the protection of the stronghold.

Stauffer stared at the dispatch in his hand. Slowly he walked up to the fire pit. He looked out over the fire-ravaged city. His city. The holocaust before him was all-consuming. The funeral pyre of a dying era . . .

He glanced at the dispatch in his hand. He was about to tear it open. He stopped.

Did it matter? he thought bitterly. What difference, whether it reports an imagined victory or the failure of a last desperate effort?

His face was stony, rigid—devoid of motion but for the flames reflected in his bleak eyes. Slowly he crumpled the paper in his hand and flung it into the pit.

It flared up in a brief bright blaze and died in the hell-born fire.

Epilogue

The Schönsee Werewolf Headquarters Unit, *Sonderkampfgruppe Paul*, commanded by Gen. Paul Krüger, was discovered and wiped out on 30 April 1945, its operations terminated. Begun at 0600 hours, the operation was over by early afternoon. Late that same day Adolf Hitler committed suicide in his bunker in Berlin.

Three days later, on 3 May 1945, the XII Corps Secret G-2 Periodic Report # 262 contained an annex which described in detail the action and the capture of the Werewolves. It is here reproduced:

```
                         S E C R E T

 SECRET
 AUTH: CC XII CORPS    G-2 PERIODIC REPORT    From: 022000B
 DATE: 3 May 1945                             To : 032000B
 INIT: J H C

                                              HQ XII CORPS
                                              In the Field
                                                  032200B

 NUMBER 262
 MAPS: GSGS — 4416, 1/100,000

 Annex No. 1 to G—2 Periodic Report No. 262, Hq XII Corps.

    On 28 April 1945, ZINGEL, Josef, a German soldier in civil-
 ian clothes, surrendered in WEIDEN, Germany to Special Agents
 WILLIAM G. HOCK, CIC Detachment, XII Corps, and IB J. MELCHIOR,
 MII Team 425-G, XII Corps. ZINGEL was given a preliminary
 interrogation during which he stated that he was a member of
```

a Werewolf organization hidden in the wooded area N of SCHONSEE
(P4812), having deserted on 24 April 1945. The unit to which
he was assigned was commanded by a Col. KRUGER and numbered approximately 250 personnel armed with mortars, machine guns, and small arms and with hidden supplies sufficient
to last them for more than four months. The organization was
originally a school for partisans and guerillas, but its present
mission was to operate as Werewolf bands behind the American lines. All installations were underground and extremely well
camouflaged. ZINGEL offered to lead US troops to the location
of the Command Company and to assist in the capture of the
entire organization.

The report of this interrogation was submitted to the AC of
S, G-2, XII Corps, who directed that action be taken immediately. Accordingly, ZINGEL was taken to the 97th Infantry Division Headquarters where further interrogation was conducted
and plans were made to conduct a search. On 30 April 1945,
two infantry companies from the 97th Inf Div were assigned
the task of screening the wooded area in which the Werewolf
headquarters was supposed to be located. This screening resulted
in the capture of one officer and six enlisted men, three of
whom were wearing civilian clothes and posing as foresters.
No military installations of any kind were observed. Interrogation of the prisoners was conducted and it was learned that
the Werewolf headquarters was still occupying the area as of
0900 hours that morning. One PW was directed to lead the searching
party to the exact spot where the headquarters had been bivouaced
that morning. A search was made on an area approximately
one hundred yards square by twelve men for a period of an
hour and a half with negative results.

The searching party was then disbanded, but HOCK and MEL-
CHIOR decided to continue the investigation. The original informant, ZINGEL, was directed to lead the group to some of
the hidden supplies of the organization and he took them to a
small shack concealed in the forest. The shack was entered and
two men and three women were found inside, all dressed in
civilian clothes. ZINGEL immediately identified one of the men
as Col KRUGER, commanding officer of the Werewolf organization. The other man was a 1st Lt and the women were
Wehrmachtshelferinnen (German WAC's), all members of KRUGER's
staff. KRUGER was informed that the existence of his organization was known to US troops and he agreed to surrender his
entire staff. KRUGER was then taken to the 97th Inf Div CP
where another searching party was formed and KRUGER was
directed to lead the party to his headquarters. KRUGER then
took the searching party to exactly the same area that had been
searched twice previously. On an order from KRUGER, German

soldiers in uniform began appearing from concealed dugouts throughout the area. The final count of prisoners taken was six officers and 25 enlisted personnel. All records of the organization, including sketches showing the location of buried food and arms, maps of future operations, one civilian automobile, one motorcycle, and two small radio sets were also captured at the headquarters.

The above incident is the first known capture of an entire Werewolf headquarters. The following information concerning this particular Werewolf organization was obtained from interrogations of Col KRUGER and ZINGEL, and from the personal experiences and observations of Agents HOCK and MELCHIOR, and should be helpful in locating and destroying other similar enemy organizations.

HISTORY:

On 16 Sep 44, Col KRUGER was commandant of a German Army school at THURENBERG, CZECHOSLOVAKIA which taught various courses including guerilla tactics. In February, 1945, the school received an order from HIMMLER to add a course in "Werewolf" activities. On 1 April 1945, the school was closed and the training staff, numbering between 200-300 men under command of Col. KRUGER, moved to SCHONSEE, Germany (P4812). It was contemplated that a school would be set up at SCHONSEE but this was not done because of destroyed transit facilities and the approach of US troops.

MISSION:

In the early part of April the training staff received the following orders from OKH (German High Command):

"To stay behind, evade capture, and then harass and destroy supplies of US troops in the rear. Special emphasis was put on gasoline and oil supplies."

ORGANIZATION:

Upon receiving the above order, Col KRUGER divided the group into four units - "A", "B", "C", and FUHRUNGSSTAB (headquarters). Units "A", "B", and "C" numbered between 60—100 men each with approximately 40—50 in the headquarters unit. Units "A", "B", and "C" were located in a triangle around the headquarters unit and each operational unit had radio communication with the headquarters. Col KRUGER'S immediate staff consisted of a Captain and three 1st Lts, and all of them held high ranks in the Nazi party and were determined to fight to the last.

TACTICS:

Operations were to begin three or four weeks after being overrun by US troops. The plan was for each unit to receive designated targets from the headquarters. Bands of from 10 to 20 men were then to be sent out to destroy the target and to return immediately to their unit. No targets were to be located nearer than fifteen kilometers to the unit. Secrecy and camouflage were relied upon for security and all personnel had strict orders to conceal themselves if US troops came into their area and under no circumstances to open fire in the bivouac area. No routes of escape had been planned. Members of the unit usually wore the Wehrmacht uniform, but a few members disguised themselves as foresters and were used as outposts to report any approaching danger.

EQUIPMENT AND SUPPLY:

This unit was equipped with regular Wehrmacht uniforms, camouflage suits, fur jackets, and other items of winter issue. Some members were dressed in civilian clothes for reasons stated above.

Their ordnance supplies consisted of mortars, machine guns, sub-machine guns, rifles, and various types of side arms. Each man was issued a very small pistol which could be very easily concealed on the person. The ammunition supply for each type weapon was ample for four months of ordinary operations. The unit had one civilian type sedan and one Wehrmacht motorcycle which were well hidden in the woods, and 120 horses which were dispersed on farms throughout the vicinity. Food consisting of canned meat, bisquits, crackers, chocolate, and canned vegetables was sufficient for over four months. Additional food supplies such as bread, potatoes, fresh vegetables, and smoked sausages were obtained from local sources. The unit was supplied with water by a brook passing through the area.

CONCEALMENT AND CAMOUFLAGE:

The headquarters and billets of the captured Werewolf unit were concealed underground. The dugouts were constructed in such a manner as not to destroy the live trees around them. The dugouts were located on the slope of a hill which was densely covered with fir trees of the Christmas tree variety. The entrance to the dugout was usually located in the midst of a clump of trees.

The entrance to the dugout was a hole approximately 24 inches in diameter and four to five feet deep. Approximately two feet down, this hole extended horizontally to a length of eight to ten feet. The dugout has a capacity of three men and has a wooden floor and a drainage ditch. Walls and roof are reinforced with lumber. The entrance is covered with a strong lid on which turf is growing and which blends perfectly with the surrounding ground. (see sketch attached).

The area was camouflaged solely with live vegetation. Great care was taken not to form any paths in the area. The dugouts were dispersed without pattern over a large territory. To give an example of the perfection of the camouflage of the dugout entrance, the following instance is mentioned. During the course of the second search of the area, an accidental shot was fired by a member of the searching party. Several members of the searching party threw themselves on the ground less than five feet from some of the dugout entrances without noticing their presence. The German soldiers in the dugout could see the members of the searching party and later remarked on this incident.

An automobile was concealed in a very dense section of the woods by carrying it on logs into a clump of trees. The larger trees were bent low enough to permit the passage of the car over them and it was carried by the men over the bent trees and placed in the selected spot. The trees were then released and the car was camouflaged with additional branches.

In future searches of suspected Werewolf biouvac areas, the following factors should be considered in determining the most probable location of the unit:

1.   A very densely wooded area with small trees and shrubbery.
2.   Presence of a stream as a source of water supply.
3.   Signs of persons having recently inhabited the area (although the German soldiers were extremely careful to destroy such evidence).
4.   Signs of German Military boot prints in the area.

In case any of the above factors prevail, a minute inspection should be made of areas where the shrubbery is most dense. It is recommended that in the inspections the same method be used as in probing for mines. In as much as each dugout contains metal weapons, it might be practicable to employ mine detectors over the area.

MISCELLANEOUS

The organization used members posing as forest workers to obtain and prepare certain food supplies for distribution at night to the personnel hiding in the woods. These members possessed recent discharge papers signed by the unit commander, Col KRUGER.

These persons also were the outposts and sentinels of the organization and upon capture were able to point out the exact location of the area but not the individual dugouts.

Local civilians were required to furnish bread and fresh foods for the organization and likewise to furnish food and shelter for the 120 horses in the organization's possession.

One important factor was the use of crippled officer personnel as key members. These officers were to be used as observation personnel to reconnoiter and to locate targets for the tactical bands to destroy. The executive officer, a captain, had one crippled leg in a heavy cast and one 1st Lt had a crippled leg and arm. They both possessed recent discharge papers signed by Col KRUGER.

Some of the members of the unit spoke English.

Claybrook
by R.S.R.

CLAYBROOK, G–2

During the period following the discovery and annihilation of the "Kampfgruppe Paul" Werewolves, XII Corps G-2 reported: "Evidence of bona fide Werewolf activities was conspicuously absent during XII Corp's period of occupation . . . things were remarkably quiet. . . . There were, it seemed, no more Werewolves."

This G-2 Periodic Report, written in the customary terse military language, detailing the capture of the Werewolf headquarters unit near Schonsee, was drafted by corps personnel who had not been part of the action, and consequently some minor inaccuracies and omissions occur. Although the case on the whole is well presented, some detail of necessity has been left out.

The command dugout, for example, was considerably larger than the individual dugouts described in the report; it could hold six to seven men, and it contained a periscope device that ran up through a tree trunk. This was how some of the Werewolf personnel had been able to see our futile search, as mentioned in the report.

Papers found in the command dugout indicated that Col. Paul Krüger actually had been promoted to general, but the

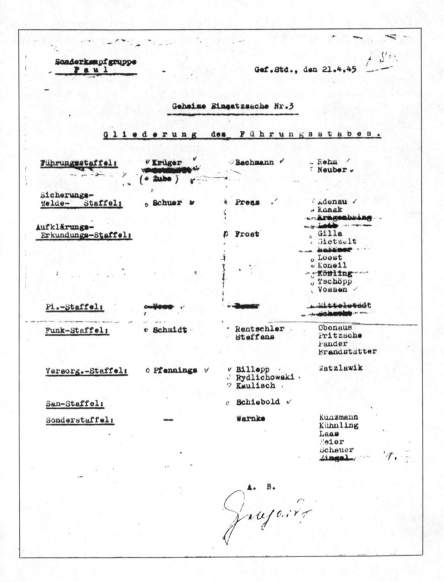

```
Sonderkampfgruppe                          Gef.Std., den 21.4.45
   P a u l

                    Geheime Einsatzsache Nr.3

            G l i e d e r u n g   des   F ü h r u n g s s t a b e s.


Führungsstaffel:        Krüger          Bachmann        Rehm
                                                        Neuber
                        ( Zube )

Sicherungs-
Melde-  Staffel:        Schuer          Press           Adenau
                                                        Knaak
                                                        Kragenbring
Aufklärungs-                                            Lotz
  Erkundungs-Staffel:                   Frost           Gilla
                                                        Gietzelt
                                                        Kaiser
                                                        Loest
                                                        Koneil
                                                        Kößling
                                                        Tschöpp
                                                        Vossen

Pi.-Staffel:            Voss            Bauer           Mittelstedt
                                                        Schmidt

Funk-Staffel:           Schmidt         Rentschler      Obonaus
                                        Steffens        Pritzsche
                                                        Pander
                                                        Brandstatter

Versorg.-Staffel:       Pfennings       Billepp         Watzlawik
                                        Rydlichowski
                                        Kaulisch

San-Staffel:                            Schiebold

Sonderstaffel:          —               Warnke          Kunzmann
                                                        Kühnling
                                                        Laas
                                                        Meier
                                                        Schauer
                                                        Zingel


                              A.  B.
```

A copy of the actual Werewolf roster found on Captain Gebhardt.

official orders had not yet reached him. The ingenious belt buckle gun described in the text was developed especially for the Werewolves.

Finally, it was decided by G-2 that it would serve no purpose to include in the periodic report the standing orders to kill General Eisenhower, as well as other high-ranking officers. The matter was considered sensitive and classified, and only years later was it routinely declassified.

Ib Melchior

Editor's Note

For his action against the Werewolf organization, which at the time was reported in the world press, Ib J. Melchior was decorated by the U.S. Army in a ceremony presided over by the commanding general of XII Corps, Maj. Gen. S. LeRoy Irwin. His citation accompanying the medal reads in part:

"Melchior acted as chief interrogator in the search for this organization, accompanying the troops who made the search. . . . Melchior's enthusiasm, sound judgement, initiative and devotion to duty were largely responsible for the successful completion of the mission and the destruction of an organization which was equipped and prepared to cause serious damage to our communications and supply lines."

Bibliography

The following books and publications are amongst those that, besides the author's own observations, investigations and documentation, have furnished authentication and facts for *Order of Battle* in regard to the conditions and events in the Führer Bunker in Berlin during the last few days before Hitler's death; the existence and activities of the Werewolves and the National Redoubt; the attempts to assassinate the Supreme Commander; events of the war itself; and details of Hitler's death as well as other factual material:

Allen, Col. Robert S. *Lucky Forward: The History of Gen. George Patton's Third Army*. New York: Vanguard Press.

Bullock, Alan. *Hitler: A Study in Tyranny*. London: Odhams Press. 1952.

Carlova, John. "General Eisenhower's Narrow Escape." *The Reader's Digest*.

Delarue, Jacques. *The History of the Gestapo*. London: Macdonald. 1964.

Dulles, Allen. *The Secret Surrender*. Weidenfeld & Nicolson. 1967.

Dyer, George. *XII Corps—Spearhead of Patton's Third Army*. The XII Corps History Association.

Eisenhower, Dwight D. *Crusade in Europe*. London: William Heinemann. 1948.

Foley, Charles. *Commando Extraordinary*. London: Longmans, Green & Co. 1954.

Hauser, Richard. "The Most Dangerous Man in Europe." *True Magazine*.

Havas, Laslo. *Hitler's Plot to Kill the Big Three*. London: Neville Spearman. 1967.

Havas, Laslo. *The Long Jump*. London: Neville Spearman. 1967.

Hunter, Jack D. *The Expendable Spy*. London: Muller. 1966.

Johnson, Thomas H. "The Most Dangerous Man in Europe." *Argosy Magazine.*

Linge, Heinz. "The Private Life of Adolf Hitler." The Philadelphia *Bulletin,* 1955.

Mecklin, John M. "Nazi Underground." *PM,* May 28, 1945.

Military Intelligence Services. *Order of Battle of the German Army.* (Restricted.)

Morenz, Dr. Ludwig. *München im Jahre 1945.* Münchener Stadtanzeiger Nr. 40/41.

Musmanno, Michael A. *Ten Days to Die.* London: Peter Davies. 1951.

National Archives, Monographs, U.S. Army Historical Division.

National Archives. Records: "International Military Tribunal—Trial of Major War Criminals."

Ryan, Cornelius. *The Last Battle.* London: Collins. 1966.

Shirer, William L. *The Rise and Fall of the Third Reich.* London: Secker & Warburg. 1960.

Skorzeny, Otto. *War Memories of the Most Dangerous Man in Europe.* New York: E. P. Dutton & Co., Inc.

Sondern, Frederic, Jr. "Adolf Hitler's Last Days." *The Readers Digest.*

Speer, Albert. *Inside the Third Reich: Memoirs.* Weidenfeld & Nicolson. 1970.

Taylor, Geoff. *Court of Honour.* London: Peter Davies. 1966.

Toland, John. *The Last 100 Days.* London: Arthur Barker. 1966.

Trevor-Roper, H. R. *The Last Days of Hitler.* London: Macmillan & Co. 1947.

Tully, Andrew. *Berlin: Story of a Battle.* New York: Simon & Schuster, Inc.

Whiting, Charles. *Gehlen: Germany's Master Spy.* New York: Ballantine Books.

Wiesenthal, Simon. *The Murderers Among Us.* London: Heinemann. 1967.

In addition, numerous news items and articles in the world press during May 1945 about the author's capture of the Werewolf leaders and of the resulting destruction of organized Werewolf activities.

About the Author

IB MELCHIOR was born and educated in Denmark. After graduating from the University of Copenhagen, where he majored in literature and languages, he joined a British theatrical company, the English Players, as an actor and toured Europe with this troupe, becoming its stage manager and codirector. Just prior to the outbreak of World War II in Europe he came to the United States with this company to do a Broadway show.

Then followed a stint in the stage managing departments of Radio City Music Hall and the Center Theatre Ice Shows in New York. When Pearl Harbor was attacked he volunteered his services to the U.S. Armed Forces. He served with the U.S. Military Intelligence Service, spending two years in the European Theater of war as a military intelligence investigator attached to the Counter Intelligence Corps. He was personally involved in the action upon which the story is based and was decorated by the U.S. Army as well as by the King of Denmark, and was subsequently awarded the Knight Commander Cross of the Militant Order of St. Brigitte of Sweden.

After the war Mr. Melchior became active in television and also began his writing career. He has directed some five hundred television shows and has also functioned as director or in a production capacity on eight motion picture features. He has won several national awards for television and documentary film shorts that he wrote and directed, and has written scripts for various TV series. Among the feature motion pictures he has written are *Robinson Crusoe on Mars* and *Ambush Bay*.

In addition, Mr. Melchior has published novelettes, stories, and articles in many national magazines, as well as in several European periodicals; some of these have been anthologized. He has also written for the stage. *Order of Battle* is his first full-length novel.

Ib Melchior lives in Hollywood with his wife, the designer Cleo Baldon, and their two sons. He is an avid collector of military miniatures and historical documents. His father is the Wagnerian tenor Lauritz Melchior.